HOW TO SUMMON A FAIRY GODMOTHER

FAIRIES AND FAMILIARS: BOOK 1

LAURA J. MAYO

orbitbooks.net
orbitworks.net

Cover design by Alexia E. Pereira
Cover illustration by Zoë van Dijk
Cover copyright © 2024 by Hachette Book Group, Inc.
Author photograph by Anna Solo Photography

Orbit
Hachette Book Group
1290 Avenue of the Americas
New York, NY 10104
orbitbooks.net
orbitworks.net

First published as an ebook and as a print on demand: October 2024

Orbit is an imprint of Hachette Book Group.
The Orbit name and logo are registered trademarks of Little, Brown Book Group Limited.

The publisher is not responsible for websites (or their content) that are not owned by the publisher.

The Hachette Speakers Bureau provides a wide range of authors for speaking events. To find out more, go to hachettespeakersbureau.com or email HachetteSpeakers@hbgusa.com.

Library of Congress Cataloging-in-Publication Data
Names: Mayo, Laura J., author.
Title: How to summon a fairy godmother / Laura J. Mayo.
Description: New York, NY : Orbit, 2024. | Series: Fairies and Familiars; book 1
Identifiers: LCCN 2024022908 | ISBN 9780316581158 (trade paperback) |
    ISBN 9780316580717 (ebook)
Subjects: LCGFT: Fantasy fiction. | Novels.
Classification: LCC PS3613.A96298 H69 2024 | DDC 813/.6—dc23/
    eng/20240528
LC record available at https://lccn.loc.gov/2024022908

ISBNs: 9780316580717 (ebook), 9780316581158 (print on demand)

To Will, Isla, and Malcolm. I love you so much.

Chapter 1
Where Glass Slippers Are Not Exclusively Used for Footwear

Theodosia Balfour's ball gown was made of fine white silk, and that's where the compliments ended. The bodice was fitted, but it reached all the way up to her throat. Her mother always found it necessary to say that a lady needed to leave some things to the imagination when dressing, but Theo had seen nuns with less restrictive necklines. The sleeves found their inspiration from marshmallows, excelling in both fluff and volume. Not to be outdone, the skirt took up the poofiness challenge and asserted dominance. In the unlikely event of anyone at the ball wanting to dance with her, they'd have to do it from the next room, just to make space for its circumference. And yet, none of those horrifying qualities could compare to the fabric pattern. Twisting down and around the entire ensemble were stripes of green and red, making Theo look like a giant walking peppermint candy. If she was to get noticed, it would only be for looking like she had lost a fight to a confectioner with a vendetta.

"Theodosia, if you're waiting for me to tell you that you look beautiful, you'll be here awhile," her mother, Lady Balfour, said when Theo expressed her apparently outlandish desire to not want to feel hideous. "I did not select that gown because I thought it would help you be attractive. I selected it because you will need to stand out if you want the prince to pay any attention to you. Which, I'm sure I do not have to remind you, is not a talent you possess on your own."

Theo's sister, Florentia, wore a mint-green dress with a tight fit of boning in the waist, the skirt flaring out around her in an explosion of matching bows and ribbons. When Flo came downstairs after putting it on, she twirled around the drawing room, caressing the fabric as she envisioned herself dancing with the prince. All Theo saw was a spinning green cake topper.

However, Theo knew it didn't matter what they wore. The odds of Prince Duncan noticing the Balfour sisters were slimmer than their mother's own corseted waistline. If he were forced at gunpoint to pick Flo or Theo from a line of three women, the kingdom would need a new prince. He'd met them before at various royal functions over the years, but if he'd bothered to spare more than a brief nod at their curtsies, Theo couldn't remember it.

But that pesky detail was not going to spoil Flo's excitement. Ever since their stepsister, Beatrice, stopped attending events and stealing the spotlight, Flo could finally shine, and she was determined to capture Prince Duncan's attention this time. Even though it had been years since Flo and her stepsister were at an event together, competing with Beatrice had left its mark, carving a brutal gouge of jealousy through her already thorny nature. She would have young men admiring her, asking her to dance, bringing her drinks, only to be dropped like a corn husk doll the instant that porcelain beauty, Beatrice, showed up.

If Flo and Beatrice were dolls, Theo was a rock some child had drawn a face on, such was the romantic interest she inspired in potential suitors. But while she didn't have the same level of enthusiasm for the ball as her sister, it was hard not to get sucked up into Flo's excitement. Theo, even in her silly dress, was hoping that maybe this ball would be the one to buck tradition. She was a titled lady just like her sister. Why couldn't she also fantasize? Maybe not about becoming a princess, but there were going to be plenty of other available men there. With any luck, one of them might be interested in her.

With those fantasies dancing handsomely around their heads, they went to the ball.

———————————— • ————————————

It was going just as well as every other ball before. The kingdom's royalty had turned out in full, each level of nobility presenting their eligible daughters to a very unimpressed Prince Duncan. With every passing minute, he was becoming dangerously close to slumping right off his chair and onto the floor.

The invite-only ball's sole purpose was an attempt by the king to find his son a bride. The previous few galas had not resulted in any love matches at all, though that did not deter His Highness, who kept throwing more and more lavish parties in the hopes that maybe his son just needed to see the same eligible ladies more than once to decide that one of them might be good enough. But this ball was set to be the last one. The prince had had enough. The king had finally had enough. If Duncan didn't find his bride this time, then they would have to take the search elsewhere.

On the guest list was, of course, the royal house of the Earl-dom of Merrifall, headed by the twice-widowed countess, Lady Martha Balfour.

Her first marriage had been to a wealthy merchant, with whom she had two daughters. It lasted for just a short while until his untimely death, a sickness of his lungs coming to claim him.

Because of her first husband's affluence, she had been a part of a number of high-society circles, which is where she met the widowed Earl of Merrifall. It was another sign of good fortune that their daughters were so close in age, Florentia being ten when they were married, Beatrice, nine, and Theodosia, eight. But only five years later, Lady Balfour was left with two husbands pushing daisies and three daughters to look after.

And while technically all three girls were of society age, only two were ever allowed to attend any royal function: Florentia and Theodosia. The reasoning was simple: Lady Balfour didn't want Beatrice stealing the eye of Prince Duncan away from her own children. And since this was the last chance for Florentia and Theodosia to make a good impression, she would ensure her little blond stepbrat stayed far away from the palace.

Unfortunately for the Balfours, the order of presentation was not alphabetical, so before either of the sisters had the opportunity to curtsy to the prince, *she* arrived.

When the herald standing at the door asked for her name so she could be announced, she didn't give one, choosing instead to make an understated entrance. But in no way was she able to fade into the background. She glowed with light, like a star that had fallen to earth. From her sunshine blond hair, to her resplendent dress, to her magnificent if not impractical glass shoes that tinkled like icicles when she walked, there would be no blending in for Lady Beatrice Balfour, daughter of the late Earl of Merrifall.

It was as if Prince Duncan's heart stopped the moment he saw her. The party, the people, and the palace all melted away as he walked toward the shimmering newcomer. And when he finally reached her, the entire ball came to a standstill. Even the music stopped, the string ensemble too mesmerized to remember that they were supposed to play their instruments. So every person in the grand ballroom saw him take her hand and heard him ask if this was a dream, such was her ethereal beauty.

Whispers of *"Who is she?"* whipped through the grand hall, everyone speculating as to the identity of this woman. Some were even saying she was a visiting foreign princess. How humble she must have been to not want to be heralded into the ball.

Of course they had all forgotten her true identity. Due to the fickleness of noble attention spans, she had completely fallen out of their collective memory the second she stopped showing up to events. Beatrice had not been seen in public since her father died four years prior.

But that didn't matter to anyone at the moment. Not when this gorgeous enigma and the prince danced the night away, falling more in love with every step.

The three other Balfours did not recognize her at first. After all, it couldn't possibly be Beatrice—she was locked in her room, still in her dirty clothes, ashes under her fingernails, with no way to even get to the ball.

But somehow, it was Beatrice.

And when that realization danced past them on glass slippers, their hatred for their already detested stepsister and stepdaughter swelled like a river in a storm.

Taking his cues in manners from Beatrice, Prince Duncan waltzed her right out of his own party, leaving everyone else behind with the now-slimy cheese platter and room temperature punch.

Flo, jealousy eating her alive, was close to losing any semblance of ladylike behavior. She was only just able to stop herself from shrieking, and instead was emitting a high-pitched squeal like a possessed teakettle.

If the king could weaponize the look of pure malice on Lady Balfour's face, he would no longer need a standing army. Theo could almost feel the heat pouring off her as she twitched in anger. If Theo hadn't been so shocked at the situation, she might have grabbed an extra glass of water, just in case she needed to splash it on her mother before her head popped off and lava spewed out.

But before Lady Balfour had a chance to fully ignite, a guard approached.

"Excuse me, Lady Balfour?"

Her mother took a deep breath, nostrils flaring, straining to regain composure. "Yes?"

"Follow me." He walked off without waiting to see if she was behind him.

The three Balfours were led to a small courtyard. Little seating areas dotted the walking paths that wove like a maze between flower bushes. It was a perfect, private garden for a romantic walk. Which was probably why Beatrice was there. However, instead of being on an intimate interlude with Prince Duncan, she was standing between two guards.

Beatrice's eyes widened when she saw who was approaching, but Theo could not read her expression. For a moment, she almost looked relieved.

The guard who had escorted them to the garden cleared his throat and once again asked, "You are Lady Balfour, Countess of Merrifall, is that correct?"

"Yes."

"This young woman claims to be Lady Beatrice Balfour, daughter of the Earl of Merrifall." He gestured to Beatrice, whose hands were clutched to her chest, her head moving in an almost imperceptible nod.

Lady Balfour's confusion warped into a cruel smile. "Lady

Beatrice Balfour? Why, that would be impossible. Lady Beatrice is at the manor in her room, right where I left her."

Beatrice was vibrating with shock and anguish. "No. *No!* Tell them the truth! Tell them who I am! Theo, Flo, tell them!"

Lady Balfour glared at her daughters, that earlier madness shimmering in her eyes, silencing them without a word.

"Well, that settles that. Let's go." One of the guards took Beatrice's arm.

She shrugged out of his grasp. "Wait. Just wait. Duncan will be back any moment. He will tell you who I am. Please, just wait for him."

Lady Balfour gasped dramatically, her hand on her chest. "How *dare* you! First you impersonate a member of an esteemed royal household and then show such disrespect! That is *His Highness, Prince Duncan*, to you! Guards, take this impostor away at once!"

Theo watched as Beatrice took a small step backward. She looked like a trapped rabbit as her eyes, wide and frantic, darted between the guards as they closed in. And curiously, she halted, shrinking by a few inches as she did so. Suddenly, Beatrice dropped to the ground. At first, Theo thought she had fallen, but as quick as she had gone down, she popped up. And in each hand was a glass slipper.

She did not have size on her side, but what she did have was the element of surprise and the guards' underestimation of just how desperate she had become. Because, like a cornered prey animal when fleeing was no longer an option, Beatrice chose to fight. Faster than blinking, she threw a shoe at the guard in front of her. Her aim was perfect, the glass resounding with a *ping!* as it bounced off the guard's head. He fell to the ground, clutching his face and repeatedly shouting, *"My eye!"*

But Beatrice hadn't watched the trajectory of that shoe. She was too busy using the other one to club the second guard next to her. With a little yelp of a battle cry, the tiny warrior swung, striking him in the throat. It was a sloppy attack, Beatrice not known for her fighting skills, but it was effective. He coughed and sputtered, backing up until his legs hit a bench and he toppled headfirst into a rosebush. Still gripping one shoe but leaving the other where it landed in the garden path, Beatrice ran straight for Lady Balfour.

Stunned into inaction by the crazed and flailing Beatrice, she was completely unprepared when Beatrice rammed in between her and Flo. Lady Balfour crashed into the remaining guard with such force it was all he could do to remain standing. Flo was thrown into Theo and they both went tumbling down onto the pebbled path. It was the first and only time Theo was thankful for her ridiculous dress, the sleeves preventing her head from directly hitting the hard ground. However, it made her hate Flo's dress even more, as she was now buried in mint fabric and getting elbowed in the gut repeatedly by her sister, who was trying to stand.

By the time Flo had found her way out of her own skirts and Theo was saved from a tragic death by fabric asphyxiation, Beatrice had sprinted out of the garden.

The guard who hadn't been accosted by ladies' footwear sprinted after her.

"She's getting away!" Lady Balfour was screaming and gesturing at the two injured guards.

The first guard tried to give chase, but his progress was severely hindered by his new lack of depth perception, a chair proving to be a formidable obstacle as he ran full speed into it. In a dazzling display of acrobatics, the chair and the guard both somersaulted into the hedge. The other had managed to extract himself from the guard-eating shrubbery, but that could only be considered a small victory. Still wheezing and coughing, he was now covered in dozens of bloody, thorny scratches. He, too, tried to run after Beatrice, but breathing being essential to running, his progress was slower than it might have otherwise been had he not been sucker punched with a glass shoe.

Lady Balfour picked up her skirts and joined the chase, her daughters finally upright and hot on her heels. When they reached the front courtyard, some guards were already on horseback racing down the drive, presumably chasing after a pumpkin-shaped carriage.

After waking their old driver by smacking him with his whip, Lady Balfour shoved her daughters into their carriage. "Home! Now!"

Theo and Flo sat quietly in their seats, hands in their laps with the hope that if they stayed still enough, their mother might forget they were there. Because with every mile, Lady Balfour seemed to be coming more and more unglued from her normally well-regulated, near-emotionless composure. Every few minutes, her eyes would widen and a vein on her forehead would twitch as a fresh wave of anger rolled over her. Then she would huff and sputter, talking to herself in a muddled mess of language usually reserved for sailors.

When they reached Merrifall hours later, Theo suspected Beatrice might not have returned at all. They had been only a few minutes behind her, and there was only one driveway leading to the manor, but there was no trace of Beatrice's carriage turned getaway vehicle.

However, when Theo looked up at the otherwise-dark manor, there in the west wing was a faint, flickering glow coming from Beatrice's window.

Lady Balfour must have spotted it, too, given the fervor at which she vaulted from their carriage and sprinted inside. By the time Theo and Flo had made it through the door, their mother was already at the top of the staircase. But instead of heading straight for Beatrice's room, Lady Balfour went the opposite way toward her own suite.

Theo thought she and Flo were also moving at quite a clip, but their mother was putting both them and prize-winning racehorses to shame. Before they had even made it halfway up the stairs, Lady Balfour bolted past the landing and to the west wing. Not knowing what else to do, the sisters scurried after her.

They halted at Beatrice's room. Beatrice, no longer in her fancy dress, was backing into the hallway with her hands in the air, tears streaming down her face. Lady Balfour stepped out after, arm outstretched, pointing a flintlock pistol at Beatrice.

Flo grabbed on to Theo's arm with a vice grip.

Theo slammed her hand over her mouth to stifle the shriek that was threatening to burst out, the terror of seeing the earl's gun pointed at anyone again almost more than she could bear.

"Mother?" Flo dared to ask, her voice no louder than a scampering mouse.

"*Quiet*," Lady Balfour whispered. With her eyes nearly bulging out of her head and her lips pursed so tight they had lost all color, she motioned for Beatrice to keep walking. "*I am fixing this. She will not ruin us.*"

Beatrice continued walking backward, her hands still raised, leading the strange procession to the tower. From the bottom of the tower stairs, Theo and Flo watched as Beatrice climbed the wrought iron steps and went into the room. Lady Balfour slammed the door shut after her, fished a key out of her pocket, and locked the door.

With the key in one hand and the pistol in the other, she closed her eyes, took a deep breath, and sighed to the ceiling in relief, as though a great weight had been lifted. Then, without even a glance at her daughters, she went to her rooms.

Without knowing what else to do, Theo and Flo went to their rooms as well.

Unfortunately, their lady's maid had gone home for the night. Having no other way to get herself out of the silk monstrosity, Theo grabbed the fabric at her shoulders and pulled forward with all her strength until the buttons on the back popped free and she could shimmy out of it. She looked at it sitting on the floor like a plop of cake frosting and thought about destroying it further, but that would take energy she just did not have. She left it in a pile instead, making it the maid's problem.

Theo crawled into her bed, wishing the whole evening had not happened.

————————————— • —————————————

When Prince Duncan showed up the next day to whisk Beatrice away, turning her into a princess, Theo *really* wished the whole evening had not happened.

Almost as soon as the royal carriage left the estate, Beatrice's fantastical story exploded throughout the kingdom: Wanting to go to the ball but having no means to do so, poor, angelic Beatrice sat alone covered in soot next to the fireplace she was forced to clean and cried. To her surprise, *poof*, out of nowhere her fairy godmother appeared, asking if she would like to attend the ball. Of course Beatrice said yes. But, alas, she had no dress, and no way to get there. Not a problem for her benevolent patroness—the fairy said she would gladly help Beatrice, because Beatrice was pure of heart and deserved to go.

First, the fairy godmother solved the problem of transportation by finding a pumpkin and converting it into a carriage. Then, spying two mice running through the grass, she turned them into horses. A dog was transformed into a liveried footman. Last but not least, the fairy godmother turned her attention to Beatrice, dressing her in a gown so splendid it was said to have been made of spun silver.

However, Beatrice was not given free rein to party the night away. Most certainly not. Like many proper ladies before her, she was given a curfew, and it came with consequences for not adhering to it. Unlike everyone else, though, her repercussions for a lapse in responsibility and time management were magical. She only had until midnight to have a grand time at the ball. For once the clock struck twelve, her dress would vanish, and every other part of her enchanted facade would revert back to what it had been (except the shoes, naturally). But since she was the pinnacle of trustworthiness, she made it home just in time. It would have wrecked the whole evening if the grand finale was Beatrice sitting on a pumpkin in nothing but her underwear and fancy glass slippers surrounded by rodents and a stray farm dog in the royal courtyard.

Prince Duncan, dismayed that his mysterious true love had fled the palace, immediately set out to find her. He'd been dancing with her for hours, so of course there had been no time to ask even the most basic of conversation starters such as *What is your name?* or *Where are you from?* And certainly no time for more in-depth questions like *Is that your natural hair color—so if I'm asked to describe you later I can say "blond" with confidence?*

His only clue as to her identity was one glass shoe left behind in her haste. But, women's shoe sizes being as individual as fingerprints, he had all he needed to positively identify her. So he scoured the countryside searching for his bride, shoe in hand, hoping to find the foot to whom it belonged, and thus, the perfect woman attached to that foot. When he found her, locked in a high tower by her horrible, awful, evil, despicable, poorly dressed, and mirror-shatteringly ugly stepmother and stepsisters, he whisked her off to his palace, where they instantly became engaged to be married, to the delight of the kingdom.

A magical fairy tale for the ages.

A cartload of horseshit was what it was.

Chapter 2
Where Good Things Finally Start Happening

Eighteen Months Later

"Where is Evans?" came a familiar shriek from the next suite.

Quick padding of feet on the hall carpet followed closely after, heading straight to Theo's room. Flo threw open the door and stood like a ghoul in the doorframe, her hair unbound and in tangles from her ears to her waist, her white nightgown still swaying at her knees from her angry march.

"Is she in here?" Flo's eyes were darting around the room, looking for their lady's maid like a sight dog on the hunt.

"No," Theo said.

"Do I seriously have to dress myself?" Flo grumbled, huffing back to her rooms.

Flo might have been willing to surrender, but Theo was going to stay put until Evans came to work.

Forty-five minutes later and Theo was still in her undergarments, crankier than ever. Fine. If Evans thought Theo was prickly before, then she'd better hang on to her dull bonnet because Theo was about to go full hedgehog.

She grabbed the first dress she could find and shimmied into it, but found with no small amount of annoyance that she couldn't do the buttons up the back by herself. Her indignation did not allow for rehanging the garment, and instead she hooked it on her foot and kicked it in the general direction of the closet for Evans to pick up.

After finding a dress that she could get into without assistance, she sat at her vanity to pin her hair away from her face. Her mother called Flo's hair the color of warm black tea and it shone in graceful, thick curls down her back. She called Theo's the color of a murky puddle, with sighing non-assurances that they could somehow work with it. It usually involved plenty of hair accessories to *distract from the hue*, as her mother would say. Instead of luscious curls that cascaded down her back like Flo's, Theo's waist-long hair sat on her head as if it heard every insult and acted out of spite, some sections curling, others lying straight, the rest trying to reach a compromise by just being wavy.

She entered the dining room in time to watch Flo hack at her tart and then stab it like she was hoping she could make it cry.

Her mother set down her teacup on its saucer. "Theodosia, you are a *lady*, not a donkey. I could hear you clomping from all the way upstairs."

Lady Balfour's hair was in its usual high, tight bun, the

grays glittering like tinsel—the only style her mother's aging lady's maid could manage with her arthritic fingers. Unfortunately, it had the effect of elongating her neck, which on someone else might be a boon, but for a woman whose neck was already stretched to its limit, it made her look like a marionette.

"Where is Evans?" Theo demanded.

"She quit," Flo snapped, not looking up from her plate.

"What?"

Their mother sighed. "Yes, unfortunately—or should I say fortunately since we won't have to deal with her lack of work ethic and bad attitude any longer—she has left us. No matter. I will post an ad soon for her replacement."

Well, good riddance to that lazy woman. It wasn't like she did a good job on the best of days. There were thousands of lady's maids out there who could style hair and button buttons better than that nitwit. More's the pity to Evans's next family.

But Theo knew there would be no replacement. They couldn't afford one.

The crown had saved Merrifall from complete collapse after Beatrice became princess. But paying outstanding debts did little to help Lady Balfour's continued mismanagement of the estate—arguably her biggest failure as a countess. Theo knew her mother hadn't purposefully run the estate into the ground. She just did not possess the knowledge or wherewithal to run a royal household by herself.

Her first husband had handled all their money, giving her an exorbitant allowance each month for her parties, dresses, and other necessary items to keep her in good standing among her friends and enemies. She happily spent her money and let her husband deal with the rest. In the few years after he had passed, Lady Balfour and her daughters lived off the sale of his business, the house servants and lawyers handling the funds.

And it was the same story with her next husband. The earl's manor and grounds were well-known throughout the kingdom as being one of the finest for his title. She reaped the benefits of her royal station, while he dealt with everything else. But once he died, she was stuck with a royal estate that she had no idea how to manage.

Soon, the renters on the earl's estate began to dwindle as the bills began to grow. Without tenants to farm the land, a good number of fields on and around the estate became waist-high with weeds, rendering them unusable for crops or livestock. And without agriculture, their estate had no true means of support. Loans given on her title alone were the only source of income, and those had become rare of late, likely due to a certain story making its way to the creditors.

Since there was still no money coming in, she couldn't afford the staff required to keep a manor of this size operational. Without the proper amount of grounds and house staff, Merrifall had been slowly falling into disrepair.

The current skeleton crew of servants was getting most of the work done, but where her mother found the money to pay them, Theo had no idea. The lone scullery maid had taken over Beatrice's chores, so at least the family's most frequented rooms were usable. Their mother still had her lady's maid, and up until this morning, the sisters did, too. Their carriage driver was now their stable hand as well, but he was certainly not long for this world. A stiff breeze would easily send the old man tumbling, if he could even stand up in the wind long enough. But he could lift a pitchfork so he stayed.

Theo stalked to the sideboard to get something to eat.

Flo had woven her hair into a braid draped down her back and somehow managed to get into a dress, but Theo barely hid her smile when Flo's braid shifted, revealing that the buttons had not been matched correctly up the back.

"You look lovely this morning, Flo," Theo said, smirking as she filled her plate.

Flo scowled at her. "I'd remind you, Theodosia, that I am to be called *Florentia* exclusively. A proper lady does not go by childish names."

Theo scoffed and, like her sister, began assaulting her breakfast as much as she was eating it. Flo gave her a pointed look, implying that scoffing was not proper lady behavior.

Now that Flo was engaged to her beloved, Ambrose, she had no shortage of helpful advice for what a "proper lady" did and did not do, delighting in making it quite clear that Theo was lacking. Newest to the list of unladylike behavior was calling each other by their childhood nicknames.

Theo finished her breakfast and made her way to the music room upstairs, leaving her sister and mother to discuss Flo's upcoming nuptials. Theo had met Ambrose a few times at various balls and gatherings over the years, and while she didn't find anything special about his pinched features and constantly annoyed countenance, Flo was enamored. All Theo remembered of his personality was his perpetual distaste in everything, whether it was the food, the sounds, the

19

company, and in one instance, the floral centerpieces. So Flo and her betrothed were well suited for each other.

Theo still despised Beatrice and was loath to give her any compliments, but she was smug knowing that no matter how much planning went into Flo's wedding, it would never be near as fanciful as her stepsister's had been. With all the posturing Flo was doing, one would think she, too, was marrying a prince instead of the second son of Lord Maxwell, the Earl of Avenshire.

Avenshire wasn't nearly as large or grand as Merrifall, but it was fully staffed, so Flo was counting down the days until she'd walk down the aisle back to a life with some semblance of luxury. Theo also couldn't wait until her sister got married—then their mother could focus on finding a husband for her.

———————————●———————————

Alone in the music room, Theo took her seat next to the harp. She had admired it from the first day they had moved to Merrifall, when Bea had excitedly given her and Flo the grand tour, spending quite a bit of time showing off the music room and her late mother's prized possession.

It was a magnificent instrument. The light maple wood pillar and neck were carved with trees, vines, and leaves, but when she looked closely, hidden within were woodland creatures darting through the forest scenes. As a child, Theo had sworn she'd seen them move out of the corner of her eye. Bea had told her she saw that sometimes, too, and when she had asked her mother, she was told it was a fairy harp. Theo believed her.

Bea was just learning to play, she'd said, but maybe the girls would like to learn as well. She assured them her mother would have loved for them to take an interest in her harp. The girls all had to take music lessons to prepare for their future marriages anyway, but Flo didn't take to the instrument, saying she could never get it to sound right, and was content to sing instead.

But Theo loved the harp. She and Bea continued their lessons up until the earl's death, when Bea no longer had time to practice, what with all her chores and such. So the harp became Theo's. She'd often catch Bea in the music room touching the strings when she was supposed to be working, but Theo would chase her off, not wanting her to get the instrument dirty and ruin the strings with cinder-covered hands.

Notes filled the room and swirled around the ceiling as Theo played a simple piece. Her music teacher had long since left, and having no funds to hire a new tutor, Theo practiced on her own, challenging herself with new pieces when she got bored. Beatrice's mother had a substantial sheet music collection, and Theo had yet to run out of any new music to play.

In fatter times, Theo would have had the servants bring tea to the music room, but as there was no staff to do it now, her grumbling stomach sent her out of practice and toward the dining room where, with any luck, her sister wouldn't be.

Theo had just reached the main staircase when her mother appeared in the foyer, her lips in a tight upward arch. She was tapping a tri-folded letter impatiently against the finial.

"What is it, Mother?"

"Wonderful news."

"Oooh, what news?" Flo was making her way down the stairs, eager to hear.

"Theodosia finally has a marriage proposal!"

Theo gripped the banister. "I do? Who?"

"Oh, Theodosia, you'll never believe it. I still don't quite know how I managed it. A duke!"

Theo let out a squeal that would have been the envy of every schoolgirl in the kingdom. "Who? Please tell me who!"

"The Duke of Snowbell."

Another high-pitched squeal.

"What?" Flo was glowering at both her mother and Theo.

Theo had only ever heard of Snowbell in passing, one of the smaller dukedoms, sitting snug against the mountains in the north of the kingdom. The duke himself was a bit of a mystery, not coming to the palace for very many events, so Theo had never actually seen him in person before.

But none of that mattered in the slightest.

"I'm marrying a duke! I'm going to be a duchess!" By this point Theo was twirling around the foyer, reveling in both her good fortune and the look on Flo's face. "Who's the proper lady now, Florentia?"

"Girls, girls, please," her mother said, smiling. "We will be going to his estate in a week's time so he may meet you and celebrate your engagement. We have much to do to prepare, girls! Much to do!" She flourished the letter and strode off.

"Why do *you* get to marry a duke?" Flo asked, jealousy dripping off her like water after a bath.

"What, *Lady Florentia*? No longer content with the second son of an earl? I promise, dear sister, I will deign to invite you to my many balls and fabulous parties that I have between all my other duties as a duchess." She smiled at her sister, teeth gleaming with spite, then threw her nose into the air in a move that would have made her mother proud, had she been there to witness it.

Leaving her sister to sulk, Theo walked back up the stairs to her rooms, already planning what fabulous dresses she would pack for her visit to her future husband.

Theo had combed through her closet for dresses appropriate for meeting a duke and came up with far less than she had hoped. Flo was barely speaking to her and was made even more mad when their mother gave Theo permission to raid her wardrobe. But even her sister's options weren't grand enough for the duchess Theo wanted to fashion herself into. And the suitable dresses she did find needed to be laundered.

She made a pile of the dresses she was going to take with her and set off to find her mother's lady's maid. It wouldn't be too difficult. That crooked servant wasn't able to do anything quietly anymore, what with her swollen ankles and waning hearing. Theo found the woman by sound alone, hobbling down the hall away from her mother's rooms with the empty afternoon tea tray.

"Morris!"

The woman did not turn.

"*Morris!*" Theo tried again, louder. But the woman continued on. Theo sped up and stepped in front of her. Morris jumped, the silverware spilling from the tray, the tea service thankfully managing to stay on. Her mother would have been very annoyed if Morris broke yet another teapot.

"Stars above, you nearly gave me a heart attack, girl!"

"Morris, I laid out some dresses for my upcoming trip to the duke. I need them sent out to the laundress."

"You need what?" Morris squinted and turned her ear toward Theo.

"There are dresses in my room that need to be sent to the laundress!" Theo shouted.

"We are no longer sending laundry out. Well, not dresses. Just your underclothes now. If you need any of them washed, leave them by your door."

"What do you mean we're not sending dresses out? How am I supposed to get the dresses cleaned?"

"Wash them yourself."

Theo balked at the ridiculous suggestion. "Wash them myself? Have you finally lost your mind? I'm about to be a duchess, Morris. A *duchess*. I will not be laundering my own clothes. It would wreck my hands and I cannot have that before I meet my duke."

"Well, good luck finding someone around here to do that for you."

"I already have. I'm talking to her right now."

"I don't know when you think I'll have the time to do that."

"I guess we'll have to see what Mother has to say about it, won't we?"

Morris narrowed her eyes. "Well, Theodosia, until then, it's still your problem. Now, for the love of all things good, please do one nice thing today and pick up those spoons so I don't have to bend over."

"No."

Instead, Theo marched back down the hall to her mother's suite to let her know just what her lethargic lady's maid had said to her. It seemed to Theo that Morris was not taking her engagement to the duke as seriously as she should. But her mother wasn't as big of a help as she'd hoped, saying instead that she'd have the scullery maid wash the dresses.

———————————————•———————————————

Theo was pacing her closet for the fifteenth time, still not happy with her wardrobe when an idea struck her. They couldn't purchase new dresses, but she did know of a place in the manor with some dresses and shoes that might very well work. Frankly, she couldn't believe she hadn't thought of it sooner. Beatrice wasn't coming back for them, so as far as Theo was concerned, Beatrice's mother's old dresses were fair game.

After Beatrice's initial attempt at sneaking away to the ball had been discovered and destroyed, her mother removed all the other dresses and shoes that Beatrice had hoarded, putting them in her own closet for extra insurance that her stepdaughter couldn't try to pull that stunt again. Theo had asked her mother why she didn't take any of these exquisite, expensive clothes for herself, but Lady Balfour said that it was gauche to wear the dead wife's dresses and she could more than afford her own. So Morris had put them back in Beatrice's room the day after she was swept away to the castle.

There they stayed, all but forgotten until Theo's brilliant brain wave.

And she would absolutely not share her prize with her sister. This was Theo's time to shine and Flo was not going to steal her spotlight or be the center of attention again. Making sure Flo was otherwise occupied, Theo sneaked into the west wing. Theo was the only one who still came into this part of the manor with any frequency, as it contained the music room, but she had not ventured beyond that in ages. Turning the corner after passing the music room, she came to the old family suites. Cobwebs hung in the corners and the thick carpet was muted from a layer of dust.

She expected Beatrice's door to groan on rusty hinges, but it opened without so much as a squeak. When Beatrice left, her room had been closed off. Any furniture that could go other places did, and the rest was covered in sheets. Theo slipped inside unheard, and wove between the squat little ghosts to the dressing room.

And there, hanging at the back of the closet, Theo was greeted by at least forty dresses in every color of the rainbow.

She spent an hour holding up dresses to herself, delighted to find they would fit her quite well, swaying and sashaying in the mirror while imagining conversations she was going to have with her duke. Eventually she narrowed her choices to ten dresses that she would take for the three-day stay.

Now for the shoes and accessories. The slippers had been returned to the closet in a giant heap, but with a bit of searching and organizing, Theo found enough pairs to match the selected dresses.

Theo didn't remember Beatrice ever wearing jewelry, nor could she find any displayed in the dressing room, but that didn't mean she had none. If this was Beatrice's mother's dress collection, her mother's jewelry collection must have been one to rival it.

Hoping that her mother hadn't already found and sold the jewelry, Theo began to rifle through the large chest of drawers against the wall. The small top drawers yielded some necklaces, two silver coins, a few rings, and some hairpins, but nothing exquisite. Even so, Theo set some of the finer pieces aside to take with her. The middle drawer housed Beatrice's underclothes. Theo dug through those anyway, just to make sure Beatrice hadn't been sneaky by hiding the good stuff. But no, just underclothes.

The bottom drawer seem to contain only a few small quilts and silk kerchiefs, nothing Theo had any interest in pillaging. She had almost shut the drawer when something glinted from the back. She pulled out the quilts, throwing them into a heap behind her until she revealed a small wooden box with gold-accented corners, the source of the glinting. Theo grinned. She knew Beatrice had been holding out on her. If that devious princess only knew she'd been outwitted. There was luckily no lock on the box, and Theo eagerly flung it open, but to her annoyance the only thing she found was a stack of letters. She glanced over them as she shuffled through, checking for anything of value; finally something caught her eye—what looked like a bundle of fabric wrapped around a few loose papers. She could feel something weighty inside. But when she unwrapped it, Theo gasped at the face she hadn't seen in years. Hidden within the fabric was a small portrait of a beautiful woman with bright blue eyes, blond hair tumbling down her back in soft waves. She had a gentle smile on her face, like someone had told her a joke while she posed for her portrait and she was trying not to laugh. Beatrice's mother.

This was the last remaining portrait. A survivor of a time Theo had seen her mother go too far.

There used to be quite a few portraits of Beatrice's mother hanging up throughout the manor. Some of just her, like this one. Others of her and the earl, and some that included baby Bea as well. As soon as she married the earl and moved in, Lady Balfour wanted them all taken down. She said she didn't like having the eyes of the dead wife watching her at all times, wherever she went. The earl obliged and took down most, but not all. He kept the portrait of her that hung in their bedroom. Theo knew it had bothered her mother to no end. Always in competition with a dead woman. Of course she'd never actually admit that, but Theo saw that she would go out of her way to not look at them.

When the earl passed, Lady Balfour did not wait long before she went around the manor taking the rest of the portraits off the walls. She put them into some unused room where they sat for years.

Until the day Beatrice had done something to upset Lady Balfour. For the life of her, Theo couldn't remember what it was. But while Beatrice was finishing her chores, Lady Balfour was moving all the portraits outside.

Theo had never forgotten the sound of Beatrice's screams or Lady Balfour's vindictive smile as all the portraits went up in flames like a giant funeral pyre. Theo and Flo had stood there watching them burn, frightened in the face of their mother's cruelty.

Just holding this portrait was making the conflicting feelings of that day come rushing back to sit on her chest. Not wanting to be reminded any longer, Theo wrapped the portrait back up in its shroud and put it back where it had been hiding.

With Beatrice's mother tucked away, Theo turned her attention to the other find. Even before reading them, Theo could tell these papers were different from the letters that had been in the box. She grabbed the crumpled papers and spread them out in front of her. Indeed, these weren't letters but very old parchment, faded and worn around the edges. One side of each sheet was jagged, as if they'd been torn from a larger book. And the subject matter...

Theo read it with wide eyes.

The heading on the top page read *On Summoning a Fairy*.

She had only made it a few sentences down the first page before she heard Flo's high-pitched whine echoing down the hall. If there weren't words involved, Theo would have assumed some injured animal had gotten caught in the house. Unfortunately, the sounds were getting closer and she heard her name mingled with the complaints.

As fast as she could, she replaced the papers and the box. After shoving the quilts over them and shutting the drawer, she hurried from the room and out of the west wing.

Chapter 3

Where Fantasies
Cannot Compare to
Her Fiancé, the Duke

The rest of the week went by in a blur with Theo, Flo, and their mother gathering everything they would need for four days of travel and three days with the duke. The dresses did end up being laundered by the scullery maid, who also helped the girls pack. The papers that Theo had pushed to the back of Beatrice's drawer were also pushed to the back of her mind amid all the excitement.

Theo kept Beatrice's mother's dresses a close secret, only bringing them out to the carriage the moment before they were to leave, the trunk that contained them being the very last piece of luggage strapped to the back.

The journey to the duke's estate took them two full days of uncomfortable carriage travel, Theo's anticipation making it feel much longer. Dangling her good fortune over her sister's head did help pass some of the time, though.

They finally arrived in late afternoon on the third day. Even though Flo had been sulking for the entire journey, she, too, gasped as the duke's estate came into view.

The duke did not live in a manor, he resided in a castle. A castle that easily rivaled the king's for spectacular beauty. Sprawling green gardens sculpted to perfection surrounded the expansive bone-white stone walls. As they approached, Theo had to turn her head in either direction to see the ends. A great many turrets speared the sky like a crown, their silver roofs sparkling in the warm spring sun like diamonds. Rows of dogwood trees on either side of the drive dropped blooms like flower girls, lining the path to Theo's duke. She could almost hear the wedding bells chiming as they came to the grand courtyard.

A line of servants was waiting at the entrance as their carriage came to a stop. Theo was hoping to be greeted by the duke, if only to see her sister's face as her betrothed made a grand, romantic welcome to her new wifely paradise. But a butler stood at the top of the stairs to greet them instead.

"On behalf of the Duke of Snowbell, I'd like to welcome you to his home, Wainwright Castle. The duke gives his apologies for not meeting you himself but has asked me to greet you and show you to your rooms. If you'll please follow me, your luggage will be joining you promptly."

This was all just as well, as their mother used the walk to their rooms to make excuses for traveling without staff and ask if there were any lady's maids who may be able to attend to them.

Morris might have been old but was perfectly capable of travel. Their mother decided, and Theo agreed, that the woman didn't fit into the image they were crafting, so she stayed behind. Theo had asked before they left their manor how they would explain their lack of servants, but her mother simply said she'd handle it and to keep quiet when the time came.

They were shown to their rooms with an invitation to dinner at seven and assurances that lady's maids would be sent to assist before then.

Theo's room was pastel-colored luxury, almost three times the size of her room at home. It would have felt almost too large if not for the huge, ornately carved bed covered in heaps of fluffy blankets. Theo went to the open window, the crisp mountain air rippling the curtains. When she looked out at the view, she saw a patchwork quilt of farmland and forests leading to the tree-covered foothills at the base of the snow-capped mountain range in the distance.

And this room was for *guests*. She couldn't wait to see what the rooms for the duchess looked like. She wondered if she'd get a tour while she was here or get to be surprised after the wedding.

———————————————— • ————————————————

A few hours before dinner, a middle-aged lady's maid named Sampson came to Theo's room to help her dress and do her hair. Theo had picked out a perfect navy-blue dress with a long, flowing skirt from the selection she had brought. But when Sampson looked at it, she frowned.

"The duke isn't going to like it," Sampson said.

"Why not?"

"It's . . . well, it's not his style."

"But it's beautiful. I thought it would be a great dress to meet him in."

"He won't like it."

"Well then, what am I supposed to wear?"

Theo held out a few more dresses to Sampson, who shook her head at every single one. Then she disappeared for a moment, leaving Theo standing in her underclothes, returning with a gown made of thick velvet in a dusty-rose color, emphasis on dusty.

"I can't wear that. That is hideous."

Sampson didn't try to deny it, but she was already hanging it up, preparing to help Theo into it.

"No, really. I can't wear that. That color does not suit me *at all.*"

"It is what the duke would want you to wear." Sampson's tone made it quite clear the conversation was over. Theo relented and put on the dress, then Sampson went to work on her hair.

Her hair was a disaster. After Sampson had finished, Theo demanded that she take it out to redo it. Fashioned in a style that was popular one hundred years ago, her hair was slicked to the sides of her head with a bathtub's worth of pomade and pulled into an explosion of tight curls in the back of her head, leaving loose some more ringlets at the front. There was so much grease holding her hair down that she should probably stay away from any open flames as she now posed a significant fire risk.

Sampson refused to change it no matter how bitterly Theo whined. But before she could really lay into her, the maid waltzed out.

Theo looked in the gilded mirror at the finished product, sneering at herself. She had always assumed her forehead was of average size, but with the atrocity that was her hair, it was now a strangely prominent feature.

And the dress was worse. The bodice had support in all the wrong places and while Theo didn't want her cleavage to be on full display, she also didn't want to look like she was smuggling pancakes down the front of her dress. Since the waist was cut too high, her proportions looked drastically off, like a paper doll that had been cut up and glued back together without its torso. Most unfortunate, however, was the color. Initially, she had been worried it would wash out her complexion, but this color went far beyond that, giving her the appearance of being quite unwell. How could *this* be the look the duke wanted to see?

Right. The duke. Her betrothed. If this was the duke's idea of his dream duchess, then she would wear it. Her mother and Flo were still getting ready, so with her greasy head held high and nothing better to do, she decided to walk around a bit and explore her new home.

She wandered through the exquisite halls until, by chance, she came across a large sitting room with windows overlooking the gardens. Paintings of previous dukes and their families going back hundreds of years lined the walls. And soon her likeness would join them. How long after her wedding would she get her portrait done? She'd like the artist to capture her as a young duchess if her face was to adorn these walls for the next five hundred years.

It was only after she made it to the more recent portraits that she noticed something odd. Every woman in the paintings from the last eighty years all had the exact same hairstyle—the one Theo was currently sporting. Interesting. But if this was the castle style, maybe Sampson did her a favor, after all. At least Theo looked like she fit in here.

While looking at yet another painting of a woman with the strange updo, movement outside caught her eye. Strolling along a gravel path was a young gentleman. As she watched, a butler approached him, then, after a brief exchange, bowed to the gentleman and walked off again.

The duke!

And he was *gorgeous*. He had given the butler a crooked yet dashing smile, showing off dimples that Theo could see all the way from her vantage point. His short caramel hair was debonairly windswept, a quick flick of his head moving it out of his eyes. He wore a tailcoat and breeches, seemingly having just come from the stables, a black top hat tucked under one arm. Theo cataloged horseback riding as another possible romantic activity they could do together, in addition to moonlit walks and rowboats built for two.

All of a sudden it didn't matter if he found ludicrous hairstyles attractive. Theo would wear her hair this way every day for the rest of her life for that man. And right now, he was alone.

She rushed down the stairs and to the garden, fantasizing the whole way about the tale of their romantic first meeting:

The duke was strolling alone through the garden when he spied a woman walking among the flowers. Even from a distance, he could see her hair was divine. Unable to help himself, he walked closer to the mystery woman, his pulse racing faster with every step. Such was her breathtaking beauty that when he finally approached, he found himself stumbling over his words, nervous in her presence. She looked at him, her smile like an arrow straight to his heart, and as she curtsied said, "You must be the duke. I am Lady Theodosia, your betrothed. How wonderful it is to finally meet." And just like out of a fairy tale, he took her hand. Overwhelmed with happiness, they danced together in the light of the setting sun to the music of their hearts.

He was still in the garden when she had finally found her way outside. She tried to calm her breathing, whether from excitement or the exertion of speed walking she didn't know. Trying her best to be demure and acting as though she hadn't seen him, she made for the part of the garden where their paths would intersect.

And sure enough he stopped in his tracks, his sharp blue eyes staring straight at her, a grin blooming on his face. "Well, hello. You must be the fiancée."

"How—how did you know?" She returned the smile. It was all happening!

"The hair." He motioned to his own head, miming curls.

"Do you like it?" She wanted to make sure to leave him an opening so he could compliment her. Maybe something along the lines of *I had heard rumors of your beauty, but all the poets in the kingdom do not have words enough to describe how radiant you truly are.*

But instead: "Good gracious, no. You look like my grandmother. But I'm sure the duke will like it fine."

Wait, what?

"You're not the duke?"

An unpleasant laugh burst out of him. "No. No, I'm his grandson."

What?

Gravel crunched behind her and the not-duke smiled in adoration at the person approaching.

"My darling."

Stunning could hardly begin to describe the woman who breezed past Theo to clasp the not-duke's outstretched hands. Her dark brown skin glowed, complemented further by the robin's-egg-blue lace dress styled in the latest court fashion. The setting sun shone gold against thick, tight black curls that cascaded down to her shoulder blades looking like she had been crowned with thousands of tiger's-eye gemstones. And made all the more resplendent next to Theo's stiff yet oily ringlets. In fact, next to this woman, Theo looked beyond silly—she looked unhinged.

The not-duke brought both her hands to his lips, kissing them as she giggled.

The woman turned to look at Theo, her lover's smile turning to a mischievous grin. Where the not-duke's eyes were sky blue, hers were the nighttime opposite. A brown so deep and dark it was almost black. And while his eyes might have been piercing, hers could sever limbs. Theo could tell they missed nothing as those eyes scanned over her from head to toe, sizing up prey.

"Ah, the fiancée has arrived. What a pleasure." Her face indicated to Theo it was anything but. "I wonder," she continued, "after the wedding, can I call you my step-grandmother? It would be such fun since you and I are the same age. Wait, how old are you?"

"I am about to turn nineteen."

The woman tipped her face to the sky, her laugh like the trill of a songbird. "You're younger than we are! How truly wonderful."

Theo could feel the traitorous blood in her cheeks giving away just how mortified she was as both of them continued smiling at her. Any irreverent remarks that Theo could have fired back had been pushed out by her brain trying to parse the information from the insults. And the confusion of the situation left her rooted to the garden path like she had sprouted there, unable to excuse herself from the couple delighting in her embarrassment.

The duke's grandson.

Was her age.

Actually slightly older than her.

Did her mother know about this? She must.

Theo had never thought to ask about the duke's age. Flo's fiancé was only two years older than her. Theo just assumed it was the same with hers.

In a cold but somewhat merciful dismissal, the woman said, "We will see you at dinner." She took the not-duke's arm, and then the two lovebirds turned and walked deeper into the garden. Theo could hear their laughter as she pushed her legs to walk as fast as she could back to the castle while still looking like a lady who had all her dignity intact. Maybe faster, the curls on the sides of her head bouncing like springs off her ears.

She had yet to meet the duke.

So he's older. That's fine! After all, he's still a duke.

———————————— • ————————————

The questions and reassurances played badminton in her head all the way to the dining room that she found with a few pauses in direction and finger-pointing from the servants. She hoped that her red cheeks looked like a lovely sweeping of blush since her embarrassment had yet to fade. And it didn't seem like it ever would, because every servant who saw her smirked at her hair and dress. Strangely, only a few bothered to hide it.

She knew she'd arrived at the dining room when she found Flo and her mother making polite conversation with a few others who had gathered. And in their midst was an older gentleman. That must be the duke, then.

Yes, he was roughly the age of her mother, and yes, his hair was tipping more toward salt than pepper, but his chiseled jaw and striking blue eyes that he had passed down the line to the not-duke grandson made him rather handsome. He wasn't old. He was *distinguished*. And he was a duke.

As Theo made her way toward the group, congratulating herself on her excellent future, she put on a refined smile, stood a little taller, and brushed those infernal curls out of her face. Her mother and the duke stopped their conversation at her arrival, so she used the opportunity to curtsy and address him.

"Good evening, Your Grace. I am Lady Theodosia. It is an honor to finally meet you face-to-face."

The duke bunched his eyebrows in confusion. And since he wasn't saying anything, Theo's eyebrows started doing the same until her mother spoke up.

"Theodosia, this is not the duke," her mother said in a firm voice, letting Theo know she was being an astounding embarrassment.. "This is his son, the earl, Lord Victor Harrington the Fourth." As her mother spoke, a woman came up beside him. "And his wife, Countess Amelia Harrington."

Oh. Oh no.

"Forgive me. My mistake. Lovely to meet you both."

Theo stiffened at the snort and chuckle that came from behind her and stepped aside, knowing exactly who she would find. Smiling in a way that let her know they'd heard everything were the not-duke and the gorgeous woman from the garden.

"Ah, here they are." The earl smiled at the newcomers. "My son, Lord Victor Harrington the Fifth, and his charming fiancée, Lady Isadora Chesterfield."

They both nodded at the assembled group, Lady Isadora's bright, saccharine smile lingering on Theo.

"My father is technically the host, but he won't mind if we go into the dining room and take our seats." The earl gestured for the seven of them to enter, lending his arm to seat Theo.

"Lady Theodosia, you're to sit here next to the duke." He escorted her to the chair next to the head of the table. After she was pushed in, the rest of the group took their seats while they waited for dinner to start.

Even though it was *her* engagement dinner, no one asked her any questions or attempted to make any conversation with her at all. Instead, she focused on trying to diffuse her awkward silence by looking at least somewhat pleasant as Lady Isadora prattled on about her upcoming wedding while desperate-to-be-included Flo tried to interject with her own wedding planning tribulations. Time seemed to lose all meaning as the conversation turned into an indecipherable drone punctuated by flower names or fabric types.

A clunk-and-shuffle noise started from outside the room, growing ever closer until the dining room door was opened by the butler to finally reveal the duke. Everyone stood as he entered, his wooden cane slamming to the floor, his scuffing shoes following until he reached the head of the table next to Theo.

Oh, no, no, no.

No wonder the duke favored Theo's current hairstyle—he had been alive when it was first made popular.

The man was ancient. Not distinguished, not seasoned. Just so very, *very* old. Theo thought she might have family heirlooms younger than him.

The duke stood only slightly taller than her, but his skin was so wrinkly and saggy it looked like he had borrowed it from a much larger man. And his unfortunate body type was that of an egg that someone had put into trousers.

Save for some wisps of white hair bravely hanging on to the top of his head, he was almost completely bald, the last cobwebs refusing to wave the flag of surrender. But given the amount of hair oil he used in styling those poor remaining strands, he may have thought he still had a full head of thick locks. Indeed, the top of his head was so shiny that a strong light reflected off of it could be used to signal ships. The Harrington blue eyes were there, but where his son's and grandson's eyes were like daggers, the duke's were the cheese knife equivalent. And they were currently assessing Theo like she was a mare at auction.

Sure enough, after pausing his roving eyes at her chest, he said, "I was told you'd be prettier, but you'll do," and then sank down into his chair, hooking his cane onto the arm. It was all she could do not to scowl. She knew no one was spreading rumors about how pretty she was. But it was a slap to the face knowing the duke didn't think she had even lived up to the likely mild description of her being "somewhat nice to look at."

Once he was seated, the rest of the table sat back down and the first course was brought. Wine was poured into his glass to the brim. Theo was too stunned to say anything at all to him, but he didn't seem to care one bit as he chugged half the glass like it was about to be taken away from him. He needn't have worried, as it was filled back to the top the second he set it down.

The whole dinner was beige and bland: every food in every course so devoid of flavor, as if seasonings were a personal offense. The first course was a cream of indistinguishable vegetable soup, followed by a fillet of breaded whitefish. Even the salad course wasn't spared, the chef using only the white bottoms of the iceberg lettuce.

Theo was cutting minuscule bites of her boiled chicken breast main course when Lady Isadora tried to engage the duke in conversation.

"Your Grace, will you be attending?" Isadora asked.

"Attending what?"

"The prince and princess are hosting a party for the unveiling of the princess's expanded botanical garden. Will you be attending?"

Beatrice and her inane botanical garden. Before she was married, she had commissioned almost every gardener in the kingdom to plant flowers around the entirety of the castle walls. And not just decorative flowers, either. Beatrice also had rings and rings of medicinal flowers like lavender, echinacea, and Saint-John's-wort spiraling around "for her people to use at will."

She made sure to show them off at her wedding as well. There had been such an obscene amount of flowers in the royal chapel that butterflies and bumblebees were flitting through the aisles and landing on ladies' hats, much to everyone's amusement. And after the ceremony, the carriages proceeded from the chapel to the palace in a single line like a colorful, winding snake, each carriage having been decorated with swaths of petite yellow flowers while the guests were watching the wedding.

The floral theme continued even into the palace. Theo thought the chapel held the top prize for sheer volume of flowers, but the grand ballroom made that look like a conservative smattering. More flowers than she had ever seen in one place bedecked every surface, including petals scattered around the floor. It was as if the ballroom had been turned into an outdoor garden.

And in the year since, the garden grew along with her garden party.

The duke grunted. "Of course not! Way too far to travel. You can give them my best wishes when you see them."

As he talked, bits of food were flying from his mouth and landing on the floral centerpieces like little shooting stars of spittle, meat, and bread.

A sly smile appeared on Isadora's face. "Understandable, Your Grace. Lady Theodosia, will you be attending?" The way she said it made Theo stiffen. Did Isadora know Prince Duncan had barred her family from visiting the palace and that there was no way she was invited? Her tilted head and twinkling eyes were leading Theo to believe that she did.

"Possibly" was all Theo could manage.

Isadora's smile widened. "If you do attend, it very well may be the last event you travel to. I do so hope you don't enjoy attending balls or any functions off the grounds. His Grace is not one for leaving the estate."

To which the duke answered, "Quite right!"

Theo plastered on a syrupy-sweet smile. "Oh, that's all right. I'm sure I can host some wonderful balls and parties here. I'll be sure to invite you."

It didn't land the way Theo had intended, as Isadora's smile only got bigger. The duke, shaking his head after gulping his wine, said, "We haven't thrown a ball here in thirty years. Don't like them. I barely like this dinner. Too many people. No. No balls, no parties, no yapping women taking over my drawing room with pointless get-togethers."

The dinner continued on in a one-man horror show of bad manners, more terrible food, and drunkenly slurring words. It was hard to know exactly how much the duke had been drinking, because after every slurp his glass would just be filled to the top once more by a waiting butler assigned to do only that, the empty bottles whisked away as if to conceal the evidence.

When dinner came to an end, the group moved to the drawing room where tea, more wine, and cookies that looked like tan charcoal briquettes and tasted like paper were laid out. The duke plopped down in the center of the sofa while, once again, the conversation went on around him. Not that he appeared to care in any capacity. He had his friend the wine-glass to keep him company.

"Theodosia, your mother tells us you are musically inclined?" Countess Amelia turned to Theo in an effort to free herself from talking with Theo's mother, who had not left the countess's ear alone all evening. It was actually sur-prising that Countess Amelia was still being civil and main-taining a polite facade. She had been sitting next to Theo's mother at dinner and more than once looked like she'd rather spear her own eye with a fork than continue talking to her—an effect Theo's mother had on a very high number of people. Her current composure was quite laudable, really.

"Yes. I play the harp."

"Ah, well, there's no harp here at the moment, but maybe after the wedding we can have yours brought here." Theo was surprised that while she didn't seem to like Theo, she seemed genuine in what she was saying.

Theo was about to tell her how nice that would be when the duke spoke up.

"I don't want a harp here. Dreadful noise. Can't you play the piano or, better yet, sing?"

It was a test of wills to fight her face muscles from contorting from neutral to shocked disbelief. She'd never met anyone who didn't like harp music, much less declare the instrument barred from their premises. The harp was about as inoffensive as an instrument could be.

"No, Your Grace. I don't play piano or sing."

Theo's mother wasn't shooting daggers with the look she was leveling at her daughter. She had brought out the trebuchet. If she squeezed her jaw together any tighter she was liable to crack teeth. But Lady Balfour was not about to let Theo's rejection of the duke's musical preferences embarrass her or sink the conversation.

"Oh, but Theodosia is gifted at playing any music and would have no trouble learning the piano; isn't that right, dear? Also, she has a lovely singing voice, Your Grace."

"How delightful!" Isadora's voice rang out. "Well, I, for one, would love to hear you sing." She was looking at Theo like a cat who cornered a mouse.

"I can sing, Your Grace," Flo shouted. Theo knew it was only so her sister could steal the attention for herself that she spoke up, but for once Theo was grateful for Flo's perpetual jealousy.

The duke gestured for her to stand in the center of the room, and the others took their seats. Theo tried to find a chair far away from the duke, but her mother managed to force her down onto the sofa. Back muscles straining, she worked to maintain her rigid posture so as not to touch him.

"I'll need accompaniment, if someone would be so kind." Flo gestured to the piano in the corner.

The grandson grinned at Isadora like they were in the midst of a fun game, though Theo supposed they were having great fun at her expense. He sat at the piano and Flo named a song. Flo warbled a tune as he played along, much to the amusement of the duke, while everyone else smiled with closed lips and tried to figure out a polite way to cover their ears.

Theo always imagined the notes of the harp like dandelion fluff dancing in a warm summer breeze. Flo's voice, on the other hand, reminded her of the sound made when throwing pebbles at the greenhouse windows—plinking and squeaking and leaving the listener wondering with dread if the glass would crack.

Everything else might be going terribly, but at least Theo had the small pleasure of watching her sister murder a melody with her off-key singing voice.

A smatter of polite clapping followed the last blaring note. Before Isadora could request an encore, the duke banged his cane on the floor a few times and declared the evening over. Defying physics, he got to his feet and hobbled out of the room without so much as a backward glance at the others, the *thump, thump, thump* of his cane following him through the foyer and up the stairs.

"Hope you like early bedtimes," Isadora said, laughing at Theo as she and her fiancé left the room arm in arm. The earl and countess also bid their good nights and left Theo, Flo, and their mother to find their own way back to their rooms.

Chapter 4
Where Theo Gets
an Accurate Look
at Her Future

"Did you know about this?" Theo hissed at her mother the moment the door to Lady Balfour's room shut behind them.

"About what, Theodosia?"

"Him! The duke!"

"What are you talking about?"

"He's...he's...Mother, he's ancient. Why didn't you tell me he's been alive since last century?"

"He's a duke, Theodosia."

"Mother, I am younger than his grandson!"

"He is a *duke!*" Her mother turned to her mirror, shutting down any remaining conversation.

Theo stomped back to her room to take out her ridiculous hair, which proved just as obnoxious and problematic as putting it in. The pomade had settled in and solidified so thoroughly that by the end of the night she looked like she was wearing a helmet, and removing the pins that had held the hairstyle together did absolutely nothing to dismantle it. A bar of gentle castile soap had been left in her bathroom, but it might as well have been more pomade for all the good it was doing in product removal. She only managed to get her hair clean after finding a bar of soap so caustic it probably would have stripped the finish off the furniture. And even then it took her four washings while scrubbing so vigorously she was surprised she still had fingerprints.

But the next morning Sampson returned, tub of pomade at the ready. Staring at her once-again normal-size forehead in the mirror while the lady's maid unscrewed the lid, Theo grimaced.

"Can you not put it into that ghastly style today?"

"It is what the duke wants."

"But it's not what *I* want, and it's *my* head. I look old."

"It doesn't matter what you want. This is the duke's castle and you're the duke's fiancée and what he says goes."

"Don't do the preposterous hair!"

"I don't work for you, girl. I work for the duke."

"You're going to be the first one I fire when I say 'I do.'" Theo crossed her arms and glared at Sampson in the mirror.

"They weren't wrong about you. You're a real nasty piece of work."

"I'm glad I'm living up to your expectations."

But what did the staff know of her? Who was "they," anyway?

All Theo could do was pout while Sampson shellacked her

hair flat against her scalp on either side of a brutal middle part and primped the ringlets on her temples until they stayed in her peripheral vision like horse blinders.

Once again, Sampson insisted she put on a gown that would be better suited for upholstering a couch. Theo only won the fight when she threatened to go to breakfast in her nightgown and Sampson realized Theo wasn't bluffing. Even so, Sampson still almost didn't help her into the delicate chiffon dress in a hue that reminded Theo of violets in spring. At least this particular dress fit her correctly and brought out the "not actually sick" of her complexion. Maybe it would elicit a compliment from the duke better than *You'll do.*

The duke took his breakfast and lunch in his rooms so he was not present while she had a quick and quiet meal, but she did receive word from one of the butlers that she was to be taking tea in the garden with him that afternoon.

———————————————— • ————————————————

For her tea with the duke, the staff had set up a table under a white tent at the edge of a veranda overlooking a vast formal garden. The main gravel walkway led to a large two-tiered fountain, the only curved line that Theo could find. The rest of the garden was a geometric marvel of straight lines and right angles. Each hedge was trimmed into precise squares, smaller paths intersecting plots containing low-lying shrubbery with nary a leaf out of place. It was only around the outer edges that any flowers were growing, but even those were restricted to their designated positions and blooming exactly where they were told.

The duke was already sitting down drinking his tea when she reached the tent. His only acknowledgment of her arrival and curtsy was a nod in between bites of a shortbread biscuit that was crumbling so badly he was wearing most of it, a small pile resting on top of his protruding gut.

Following soon after was her mother and Florentia, who also each curtsied before taking their seats.

"Good afternoon, Your Grace. Such lovely weather today. I suppose we have you to thank for the idea to have tea outside," her mother said while a butler poured them all tea.

The butler then produced a flask from the inside of his jacket and added a dark liquid to the duke's cup. It blended into the black walnut color of the tea so well, if Theo hadn't seen him do it, she'd have been none the wiser that the duke was quite the lush.

"If I had my way, I'd be eating inside, but my physician says I am to get some fresh air, so here we are." He gulped his spiked tea and then gave Theo a long look, appraising her in the same manner as the night before, this time adding a frown.

"Didn't your lady's maid tell you I detest that color? You're going to be a duchess, not some thespian. She should have helped you dress. She knows what I like."

Theo looked down at the dress, wondering how purple was somehow associated with actresses or that it could even be considered something negative. Her eyes went back to the duke, but before she could respond, he continued with his assessment.

"What's wrong with your eyes? Is that some sort of sickness?"

Theo looked down at the table. She hated anyone pointing out her eyes, especially in front of her mother. Flo had chestnut-brown eyes, just like their mother and father. Theo's eyes, however, were a striking green hazel with speckles of a brown so dark they were nearly black, like the opposite of stars, sprinkled in. When Theo was a little girl, she liked them for being unique. But when strangers saw them, for some reason most found them to be quite disconcerting, staring hard at her for a moment before trying not to look her in the eye again.

Lady Balfour's fears about Theo's unusual feature realized, she launched into practiced damage control. "Oh, no, Your Grace. Just an unfortunate quirk! But not to worry, no one else in the family has those eyes, so we are confident it is not hereditary."

The duke was again frowning at her. "You don't talk much, do you?"

Theo tried to keep her chin low so she could hide her eyes behind her lashes and think of something to say to refute his claim, but he carried on anyway.

"Suppose that's not a bad thing. No incessant chatter." He took the flask from the butler who was refilling his teacup and dumped the remaining contents into it until it overflowed onto the saucer.

Theo's mother forced a laugh a bit too high and loud. "Yes, Your Grace. You won't have to worry about your new wife talking your ear off with nonsense."

And at least Theo wouldn't have to worry about socializing with the old drunk and she could live out her misery in peace and quiet.

But just as she discovered the smallest of silver linings in her storm cloud of eternal woe, the shouts of children broke through her mother's attempt to salvage the conversation. A boy and a girl, both under the age of ten if Theo had to venture a guess, ran up to the table and straight to the duke.

He smiled at them while they each gave him a kiss on the cheek. *They must be the earl and Countess Amelia's other children.* Amelia seemed to be a bit old to have children this young, but Theo didn't know much about babies to know for certain. But if they were Amelia's children, then at least they'd live somewhere else and could easily be avoided.

"Is she here, Father? Is she here? Can we meet her?" the two little voices asked while jumping in place.

Father? Oh, god no.

The duke laughed. "Yes, children. Here she is, your new stepmother, Lady Theodosia." He pointed to Theo, and the two children bounded to her chair.

"Our new mother! Our new mother!" They each grabbed one of Theo's hands.

"I'm sorry, who are you?" Theo asked, eyes wide as she removed her hands from their clammy grips.

The girl was jumping up and down again, her little brown curls that had been tied in ribbons bouncing along to her enthusiasm. "I'm Lady Margot. I'm eight. And this is my brother, Little Lord Nathan. He's five. And you're our new mother!"

As if remembering some lesson she was supposed to know, she backed up a step and brought her brother to her side. Standing together in front of Theo, Margot curtsied and

Nathan bowed. In the most dignified voice the little girl could muster, she said, "We are honored to meet you."

She smiled at someone behind Theo. When Theo turned, she saw a woman in her midtwenties on the path twenty feet away. The woman nodded her encouragement, pleased at the children's behavior.

No matter how hard Theo tried, the cringe that had plastered itself to her face would not budge. She had been completely unaware of any little brats being part of her life.

"Children," the duke said. "Why don't you take your new mother on a walk through the garden so you can get to know her?"

"What? Why?" Theo gripped the arms of the chair as if she was about to be forcibly removed from it. Which she was.

Her mother somehow managed to reach a hand under the table to pinch Theo in the side, causing her to jump up with a squeak. Once Theo was standing, Margot and Nathan each grabbed a hand and led her away from the tent. Theo glanced back only to see the duke chugging the remains of his tea and her mother attempting a beguiling smile, still trying anything to keep the conversation going.

After a few paces, the children let go of her and ran on ahead, the woman taking a place beside Theo.

"Hello, Lady Theodosia. I am Miss James, the children's governess. It's lovely to finally meet you. I'm sure we will be seeing a lot of each other, so I'm glad I'm getting this chance to talk with you."

Theo wondered if the woman wearing a simple black dress with her hair in a tight bun could ever be anything other than a governess. So on point was her whole display that if there were a governess-making machine, Miss James would be the product that stepped out. She seemed to be the type of person who had a perpetual smile on her face. The type of governess Theo found only in books, with soft eyes and rosy cheeks who would sing songs and heap on praise for the littlest of successes. The type of governess Bea grew up with. A far cry from the governess Theo grew up with, even though they happened to be the same person.

"I didn't know the duke had young children," Theo said.

"Yes, their mother was the duke's second wife. She passed away a few years ago when Nathan was only a year old and Margot was four. They don't really have memories of her, so they are very excited to have their father remarry. The children have seen portraits of their mother and were quite delighted to find that you wear your hair the same way."

"This hairstyle is not delightful; it's hideous and was done against my will," Theo said. "Did she off herself?"

"What? No. Why would you ask that?"

Theo gave the woman a dubious look. With all the ridiculousness she'd seen here so far, why wouldn't she ask that? Good thing to know if that was how the last wife went.

"Well, what did she die of?"

"Influenza. She was a very kind woman and her absence was felt all throughout the estate. Even the servants stayed in mourning for much longer than was expected." Miss James sighed, watching Margot and Nathan dart between the hedges.

"How long have you been the governess?"

"I've been with the family since Margot was born, originally hired as the nanny. But after their mother died, the duke didn't want to cause any further distress by hiring someone new to take care of the children, so I stepped in as governess in addition."

"You're still the nanny, too, right?"

She laughed. "I honestly don't know if there is a distinction anymore. I take care of the children and have begun their education. I'm assuming, though, that once you are married and move here, you'll take on some of the more motherly duties. They're looking forward to that."

"Looking forward to it? No. No, they shouldn't be. I do not want that at all." Theo shook her head, her curls whacking her in the face.

Miss James gave her a reassuring smile. "Oh, it's normal to be nervous about stepping into that role, but I assure you, the children are thrilled to have you be a part of their lives. I'm sure you'll do fine. They really are dear."

"I'm not nervous. I don't like children."

Miss James halted on the path, stopping Theo with a touch on the elbow. "How can you not like children?"

"I just don't. They're loud, much too energetic, they cry over nothing, they're often sticky. You can keep doing what you're doing and leave me out of it."

As if on cue, Nathan picked up a toad, holding it up to Margot's face. She screamed and burst into tears, the two of them sprinting through the garden as Nathan laughed and Margot carried on shrieking.

Theo didn't bother hiding her look of disgust. It was best

that they all saw how she truly felt about the situation. She could save everyone quite a bit of time and effort by not pretending.

Miss James scowled at Theo, her eyes glistening. "They are so excited. So very excited to have a mother, and you... you are going to break their little hearts. I...I..." Miss James shook her head and either wouldn't or couldn't continue as she wiped away a tear.

Theo scoffed at the scene and turned back toward the castle, leaving Miss James to do her job. She could hear her soothing the children, convincing Nathan to put down the toad and assuring Margot that toads did not bite and she was in no danger.

"Where is she going?" Margot asked.

"She, um, she wasn't feeling well so she is going to lie down," Miss James said. "She said to tell you she enjoyed meeting you and is looking forward to seeing you soon."

The table and tent were deserted when Theo got back to the veranda, so she continued into the castle to go back to her room and put as much distance between herself and the screeching terror-tots as possible.

———————————•———————————

The final morning, Sampson once again came to do her hair and put her into an unfortunate dress. Theo tried to refuse again, but after yesterday's embarrassment, Lady Balfour made sure to get her daughter into a dress the duke would approve of.

But Theo was done with the hair.

She sat at the vanity, letting Sampson brush it. But when she reached for the pomade—

"I got in the dress. You're not doing the hair."

"It's what the duke wants."

Theo could have argued further, but she knew it would not accomplish anything. Instead, she rose from the chair, took the jar of pomade, and walked to the window. Then, after throwing open the sash, she chucked it as hard as she could. It sailed in glinting, glorious flight toward the sun like a felled warrior guided by a Valkyrie to hair care Valhalla. The funeral hymn of shattering glass echoed off the castle walls.

"This is important, Sampson, so listen up. The level of misery we inflict upon each other is entirely up to you."

But words had abandoned Sampson, and she gaped in horror at Theo as though she'd said she liked to drown kittens in her spare time. Fine.

Theo sat at the vanity again and pulled her hair away from her face with two combs. "Dismissed."

———————————•———————————

The duke did not come down for breakfast, which Theo was glad of, but Lady Balfour would not let her escape the castle until the three of them bid him farewell. They found him in his suite finishing his breakfast and reading the morning newspaper.

"Your Grace," their mother said after they'd curtsied, "we wanted to thank you for hosting us at your beautiful home and are looking forward to the wedding."

He barely looked up before waving a hand to dismiss them. The ladies curtsied again and turned to the door.

"You two can go. She can stay for a moment." He pointed a stubby finger at Theo. Her mother gave her a stern look to signal that she'd better not do anything to embarrass herself or the family and then walked out with Flo, the butler shutting the door behind them.

Theo stayed where she was, not wanting to venture any closer for fear she would be in range of bits of food being spat across the table as he spoke. But he didn't invite her to join him before he started talking.

"I will be blunt," he said around a mouthful of eggs that seemed poised to leap out of his face should he enunciate too many words involving *sh* sounds. As if he hadn't been blunt this entire time. "Your beauty and charm were overstated. Your mother and sister are pleasant enough, so we will just have to pray those looks are what get passed on when we have children because you are rather dull in both appearance and conversation. You need some more meat on your bones, and from looking at you, I'm not sure you have the hips for child-bearing. You'll just have to hope they are wide enough when you give me more heirs because I don't want to have to find a fourth wife. That is all."

If he had bothered to look at his fiancée, he would have seen the revulsion smeared across her face the way bacon grease was smeared across his. But instead, he took a massive bite of his toast and dismissed her with another wave of his hand.

She curtsied and hurried out the door, the butler not bothering to hide his smirk.

Spurred on by a sudden, urgent need to get to her carriage and away from the castle, she was speeding through the halls, grace and decorum the least of her problems. She had turned down a hallway, just about to reach the foyer, when Isadora rounded the corner. Theo paused, debating if she should just accept the embarrassment of finding a different way out of the castle before Isadora could spit any barbs her way.

But that small moment of hesitation cost her. Isadora flashed a sadistic smile, approaching as if knowing Theo would escape if she waited too long to catch her quarry.

She stopped only a few feet from Theo, looking her up and down. "Lady Theodosia. You look...mature? Classic? Elderly?"

"Why, thank you, Lady Isadora. You as well. In the words of the duke, your dress is worthy of the finest thespian."

Isadora's eyes narrowed. Good. Theo's arrow landed. Hoping that was the end of it, she made to walk past Isadora, but it seemed Isadora was ready to vie for the last word.

"I saw your carriage being loaded out front. Were you not going to say goodbye before you left? It has been such a delight meeting you, your not-at-all-insufferable mother, and that vision of poise you call your sister. Tell me, does she constantly smell something foul or is her face just stuck like that?"

Theo tried to inventory every ball she'd ever been to, every event large or small, to determine if she'd had any interactions with Isadora before but came up empty. She could not figure out any reason why Isadora would hold such a grudge against someone she'd never met.

"Did I do something to you, Isadora?"

"To me? No." She tipped her head forward, her smile turning conspiratorial. "But I'll let you in on a little secret. My fiancé is a close childhood friend of Prince Duncan's. They talk, you see. The prince had a great many things to say about you, your nasty sister, and your horrible, horrible mother. I know you're not allowed anywhere near the prince or princess, that you've been banished from the palace, and that you're prohibited from using her name or title for your own benefit anymore.

"Also, given that Victor and I visit them quite often, I have the honor and pleasure of counting myself among the princess's friends. How she managed to stay so kind, *so good*, after living with you is a mystery to me and a testament to what a truly wonderful person she is."

What a wonderful person Beatrice is?

Once again, Beatrice was ruining everything. She wasn't even a part of Theo's life anymore and was still finding ways to make Theo miserable, this time sending others to torment her. The real mystery was how that scheming princess managed to con everyone into believing she was so great. The only one she hadn't fooled was Theo.

And if Isadora thought she could talk to the future Duchess of Snowbell like that, she'd better think again. Theo was more than happy to remind her of exactly who she was dealing with.

"You do realize that when I'm married I'm going to outrank you." *And then I'll make you sorry you ever treated me this way. You'll wish you had shut your mouth when you had the chance.*

"Oh, I do know. And I don't care. Who do you think you

are, Lady Theodosia? Do you honestly think you're some grand prize? Why do you think he chose to get engaged to an eighteen-year-old youngest stepdaughter of a dead earl? Because no one else was accepting the position and your mother is desperate. You're just a pathetic social parasite with options so limited you have to be the third wife of an ancient duke who nobody else would marry. You might outrank me for a precious few years, but then what? If you're thinking you can just run out the clock until you're a widow and then have your 'happy ever after,' think again. The next duke may allow you to live in the dower house when your husband dies, but one day *I'll* be duchess, and if you're still there, I'll have it knocked down and have you removed from the estate.

"In fact, if I were you, I'd already be trying to figure out where you're going to go when your marriage ends as part of your wedding planning. You can't go running back home. Your mother's estate is bankrupt. Oh, that look on your face. We know. We all know you're only a few weeks away from selling the silverware to pay for your dinner.

"So feel free to threaten me with rank all you want. It's laughable that you think anyone here—including the servants—would listen to whatever *Her Grace, Duchess Theodosia*, has to say about anything."

Theo scowled at the mention of servants. "Do I have you to thank for the servants being rude? You must be the reason they've been nasty to me." Probably on the orders of Beatrice.

"No, Lady Theodosia. *You're* the reason they've been nasty to you. There were rumors about you and your heinous family long before I opened my mouth. Servants talk. You just confirmed what they'd already been saying—no one is surprised. The only ones I feel sorry for in all this are poor little Margot and Nathan, since once their father dies they'll be legally strapped to you. Do you know Miss James was trying to shut down all the negativity? Naive as it may be, she wants to see the best in everyone. She heard what the servants were saying about you and made them stop whenever she was around because, one, she didn't want the children to hear anything negative about their father's new wife, and two, she wanted to believe everything that was being said about you was false. Not only does everyone respect Miss James, but those children are the darlings of the castle, so they listened to her and watched their mouths. But we all saw her after you met the children in the garden. She was in tears. *In tears* after spending five minutes with you. If the servants didn't hate you already, making the nicest woman here cry sure did.

"So go ahead and scoff, stick your nose in the air, threaten, and be as horrid as you want. It means nothing to me. No, that's not quite true. It makes me smile knowing that you'll be left to wonder if anyone spit in your unflavored food every day. Your marriage and your life here will be unpleasant at best. And it will be everything you deserve."

Isadora lifted her chin and walked off, victory trailing her like a cape. But when she reached the end of the hall, she paused.

"Silly me. There is one more thing I forgot to say. Congratulations on your engagement." She departed with a smile so cold and vicious, Theo expected the windows to frost.

Theo had been wrong about Isadora. She was not simply

a whetted blade of casual cruelty. She was a battle-ax. Each word out of her mouth had hacked away at Theo, and in her triumph, Isadora took the bloody shards with her as spoils of war.

Theo only realized she had been walking again when she saw her carriage in the courtyard framed by the open front doors, a few servants tying the last pieces of luggage to the back. Flo and her mother were already being helped inside.

She didn't notice Margot and Nathan until she nearly crashed into them. The two children stood together smiling up at her, tiny bouquets of flowers in their hands.

"Lady Theodosia," Margot said, beaming. "We wanted to say goodbye before you left. It was so nice to meet you and we are so happy you are going to be our mother." They both extended their little arms, holding out the flowers.

"Stop calling me that," she growled. "I am *not* your mother."

"But Father said when he marries you, you will be our mother," Margot said in a small, confused voice.

"I am no one's mother. Especially not yours." She snarled down into their little, wide-eyed faces, Margot flinching when she stared into Theo's eyes. The all-too-familiar look of unease made Theo that much more incensed at the girl.

"And let me tell you something that I would have thought by now to be perfectly clear. You do not want me as your mother. I have learned stepparenting from the best and I do not mean that as a compliment. I do not want children. I do not like children. And we will all be happier if we stay far, far away from each other. Even better—you pretend I don't exist and I'll pretend you don't exist. Goodbye."

A gasp came from beside her. Theo looked over to see a horrified Miss James, her hand covering her mouth.

"You dreadful, *wicked* woman," the governess said.

Theo shrugged at the teary Miss James, half in agreement and half in challenge. Then she stormed out to the waiting carriage, Margot's sobs chasing her until the door was shut.

Chapter 5
Where Theo Should Probably Think of Something Before She Ends Up Married

Theo had a two-and-a-half-day carriage ride to brood over the events of the previous days. There had to be some way to salvage the situation. But the idea that this marriage was a positive turn was getting smaller and smaller the closer she got to her home.

She was going to marry a duke.

She was going to be a duchess.

It was everything she had desired since she was little.

Her fiancé, the duke.

Old, crass, disgusting, insulting.

Finally leave her broken-down manor.

Live in a beautiful castle.

Stuck in his castle.

Alone.

Not alone. Among an entire staff predisposed to hate her. Theo grew up with that. She didn't need it to follow her to her marriage as well.

Wear archaic, unflattering dresses just so he can call her ugly.

Never to play the harp again.

Never to leave.

Be responsible for his annoying little brats.

Worse, be expected to produce children of her own with him.

The thought of her wedding made her shudder. The thought of her wedding night made her want to throw up.

Theo was loath to admit it, but Isadora was right. If she married the duke, her life would be hell. And that was not how things were supposed to go.

They arrived home in the late afternoon on the third day. Flo and Lady Balfour retired early, worn and weary from traveling. While tired, Theo was too restless to turn in. Even after using the entire journey to think, she still had not come to any sort of decision on what she should do, on how she could make this situation work.

So instead, Theo went to the music room and sat down at her harp. At first she played a well-worn piece, familiar under her fingers. Not showy enough to be boastful, but not simple enough to be lazy. The song she played for the duke in her previous fantasies.

Her hands moved through the song like they were on an oft-treaded path, the beautiful harp her stalwart companion.

The duke would take this away from her. Separate her from one of the few things in her life that brought her any happiness—maybe the only thing that brought her happiness.

The jolly tune bounced around the room as she plucked.

The duke did not deserve this song. As she thought about him, her hands moved swifter, her fingers more vindictive.

She played for him a new song. There was no pageantry here, no delight. The notes lashed out like a cornered animal, striking out not to hit but to intimidate, to let the aggressor know there was violence lurking if pushed. The explosive melody was a spitting, hissing snake that would not go down without a fight.

She was left breathless as the last notes resonated on the strings. She didn't place her hands on them to still the noise, instead letting the harp finish what it needed to say, what she needed to say. And as the clash of sound slowly faded, the tangled knots in her head that she had been picking at smoothed into a straight line.

She was not going to marry the duke.

She would talk to her mother. Plead her case. And while it may be a fool's hope, maybe her mother might listen and they could find a way to back out of the engagement. It was true that Lady Balfour was a social climber turned pariah and she was banking on this marriage to put her back into society's good graces, but even she couldn't want this future for Theo. Theo would just have to make her mother see that she was setting her daughter up for a lifetime of misery but that they could fix this together.

———————————— • ————————————

"He is a duke, Theodosia. A *duke*."

Not wanting to ambush her mother at breakfast, as well as giving herself time to form a compelling argument, Theo waited until afternoon tea the following day to convince Lady Balfour to halt the engagement. "But, Mother, I'd be miserable. Trapped with no friends."

"You don't have friends. And you don't need friends when you're a duchess."

"He's old. He thinks I'm ugly."

"If you're waiting for someone who thinks you're pretty to marry you, then I've got some bad news."

"No, that's not it. He's a—"

"A *duke*, Theodosia! A DUKE!"

"That can't be your answer to everything!"

"It is my answer to everything! I have secured you a marriage to a duke. My daughter will be a duchess and is still complaining."

"But—"

"Once again, Theodosia, the effort I have put into this for you is going completely unappreciated. Do you think I am hiding a list of other offers? That I've had to barricade the door to prevent all your other suitors from breaking in and demanding your hand in marriage? You had no options. But because I love you, I persevered. I reached higher than I thought possible and my hard work paid off."

"No, if you'd just listen—"

"Aiming even higher, Theodosia? Have your sights set on

becoming a princess? Found a fairy godmother to assist you with that since your own mother's efforts aren't good enough for you?" The snark and sarcasm was thick enough to scoop with a spoon.

"No! I just—"

"You are a spoiled, entitled brat. Do you know how good you have it?"

"*How good I have it?* Nothing about this situation is good! I'm about to sacrifice my whole life!"

"Sacrifice? *Sacrifice?* You wouldn't know sacrifice if it walked up and slapped you in the face. Becoming a duchess is not sacrificing anything!"

"Anything would be better. Anyone else."

"You have no dowry, Theodosia! And the duke has still agreed to marry you!"

"I don't have a dowry?"

Theo was incensed. She knew Flo had a dowry. Not a large one, but at least one that would allow her to marry into an earl's family. Theo just assumed she had one, too. But evidently that had been lost along with the rest of their fortune.

"If you think he's so wonderful, why don't you marry him? Then you can be the duchess." Theo hadn't said it to be serious, but the look on her mother's face said she had struck a nerve. She gasped. "You tried, didn't you? You tried to marry him first. But he decided he'd rather have your eighteen-year-old daughter than you. If he thinks I'm unattractive, what does that say about you, Mother?"

With the swiftness of an asp, Lady Balfour shot to her feet

and slapped Theo across the cheek, the impact sounding like a firecracker. Theo recoiled, almost falling out of her seat, her eyes burning from the sting. But when she looked up at her mother still towering over her, there was no remorse. Only frozen fury as she beheld her daughter's shock and heartbreak.

An angry red handprint was already forming on Theo's face. Proof that both women had hit their marks.

At first, Lady Balfour just continued to stand over her daughter, hands clenched at her sides. But after a moment, with a terrifyingly soft voice, she said, "You are marrying the duke or I am disowning you."

Theo ran from the room, holding her cheek but leaving her pride behind. She only just managed to shut her bedroom door and fling herself onto the bed before dissolving into tears.

Disowned. If that was to happen she wouldn't have anything, not even the "Lady" in front of her name. No title, no right to any inheritance, no money. Nothing. A beggar on the street.

She knew this was no bluff.

If only she did have a fairy godmother.

Theo didn't believe for one second that an actual fairy popped into the estate and fixed Beatrice's ruined dress and life, but with all hope lost, it really was a nice fantasy to think there was still some escape hatch, still someone who would help her.

Beatrice was always reticent about where she got her ball gown, how she found the carriage and horses, and where those absurd but beautiful shoes came from, never actually confirming or denying the magical story she had everyone believing. Theo was convinced she had stolen everything, but no one in the kingdom reported a gilded carriage pulled by two sparkling palominos missing.

But where did that ball gown come from? It would have been impossible for her to have kept the gown a secret. Theo had seen every other dress Beatrice's mother had owned and none looked like what had shown up at the royal ball. It had to have come from somewhere outside the manor.

Theo thought of those dresses again. The ones she had spent so much time selecting, daydreaming about, and fawning over. That day in the closet when she was so excited about getting married.

That day in the closet.

When she found those papers.

On how to summon a fairy.

The memory stopped her crying in an instant, curiosity winning out over sulking and sobbing.

She got out of her tear-soaked bed and poked her head out the door, listening for anyone who might be around and hearing no one. As quiet as a mouse who didn't want to get married, she sneaked down the hall, past the music room, and back into Beatrice's room, this time locking the door behind her.

———————•———————

She knelt down in front of the chest of drawers, removing the quilts and the box, then took out the papers stuffed in the back. She laid them out again, this time with a bit more care and caution as she reread the pages.

The text was indeed quite old, not done by a printing press and instead written out in very delicate and precise script, the letters at the top ornate and embellished. But this was not simply a handwritten note, it was the work of a master. And even though the pages themselves were faded and worn, the ink was still black as night, every word clearly legible.

She only admired the craftsmanship for a moment, as it was the contents of the pages that she found much more interesting. Written as more of an instruction manual, the page in her hands read:

On Summoning a Fairy in a Time of Need

First and foremost, summoning a fairy can proceed poorly, should one not be considerate of the risks. Should one summon a fairy without proper preparations and cautions, problems can outweigh any advantages that may be gained through such invitations to the mortal realm.

If you wish to proceed, remember to always be polite, respectful, and formal. Not abiding by appropriate manners and protocols can lead to upsetting the fairy you wish to summon, ending in mischief at best, death at worst.

As Theo turned to the next page, a smaller piece of cream-colored paper slipped out. On it was a small illustration of flowers in white, pink, and yellow, the yellow flower circled twice in ink. The printed caption underneath the illustration read EVENING PRIMROSE. Next to the caption someone had written *pear tree sheep meadow*.

Theo set the small page aside and read the second page:

Spell to Summon a Fairy in a Time of Need:
Ingredients and Supplies

- *A summoning object—something small and shiny (a silver coin, jewelry, gemstone, etc.). Must not be made of or contain any traces of iron, as this will repel the fairy and void the summoning spell.*

The words *silver coin* had been circled twice in the same ink as the flowers.

- *1 drop of fresh blood from the person conducting the summoning*
- *10 evening primrose flowers collected during a B'tween Time, preferably between night and dawn's first light, or during the sun's last ray before the end of the day. Must not confuse evening primrose flowers with Saint-John's-wort flowers, as the latter is toxic to the fairy and will void the spell.*
- *1 full glass of wine made of either honey or stone fruit, poured from a previously unopened bottle, uncorked by the person conducting the summoning*

A note under this simply said *plum.*

The spell must be conducted near a body of water.

The note next to this said *frog fountain.*

The spell should commence at the midnight hour.

Then she read the third page.

To Begin the Summoning

Arrange the offerings of the flowers and wine in close proximity to the body of water. When the summoner is ready to commence the spell, the summoner will put the drop of fresh blood onto the summoning object, then cast it into the body of water.

If a fairy has deigned to respond to the summoning, one will appear within the midnight hour.

Should the fairy appear, the summoner is to welcome the fairy and present the offerings. The summoner should be clear and concise when providing the following welcome:

"I welcome you, fairy, and am honored and humbled by your presence and acceptance of my invitation. I have requested an audience with you to beseech you for your assistance."

Only after the fairy accepts the offerings and hears the summoner's request should payment or bargains be discussed.

Use the following guide for discussing payments or bargains.

Theo turned it over but found nothing written on the back, and a more thorough search of the drawer yielded no additional pages or the book where the spell was torn from.

She read and reread the pages.

Up until now, fairies were stories told to children to make them behave. But what if... what if Beatrice actually had summoned a fairy to help her?

Foolish. Foolish and childish and ridiculous.

She looked again at the written notes on the spell page and illustration. She knew where the "pear tree sheep meadow" was. Beatrice and Theo used to go there when they were children to climb into the pear tree, eat so much of the fruit they'd feel sick, and watch the spring lambs play. Then they would each take turns picking out their favorites and naming them.

She also knew where the "frog fountain" was.

As for the wine, plum wine was in abundance in their wine cellar.

And the circles around *silver coin* spurred another memory, this time much more recent. Theo jumped up and pulled open the top drawer. Sitting exactly where she'd left them between some necklaces and rings she hadn't taken were the two silver coins. An easy item to toss into the water and not sacrifice any jewelry. Maybe Beatrice originally had three coins.

But while Theo could easily connect the dots back to Beatrice as the note writer, it could also be chalked up to coincidence. None of the notes were revealing any secrets that only Beatrice would have known. Theo supposed it was entirely possible that Beatrice didn't know this was even in here, tucked away behind her quilts and letters.

Her letters.

Theo rummaged through the box until she found what she was looking for: a letter written by Beatrice. It was a simple note, just a benign back-and-forth correspondence, but her writing was there. When Theo held the letter next to the writing on the spell, it was clear as day. The extended swoop of the *f*'s, the curly *e*'s, the long dip of the *p*'s—the handwriting on the spell belonged to Beatrice.

So Beatrice really did attempt to summon a fairy.

Of course, if anyone would have found a way to summon a magical being and keep it a secret exclusively for her own selfish benefit, it would have been Beatrice.

What if…?

If the fairy godmother magically got Beatrice married to a prince, maybe she could magically get Theo out of a marriage to a duke.

But the whole idea was ludicrous. Fairies couldn't be summoned because fairies didn't exist.

Unless…

She folded the pages, stuffed them down the front of her dress with the two coins, and brought them back to her room.

Chapter 6
Where If the Worst Idea Is the Only Idea, It Is Now the Best Idea

She put the pages and illustration into her top drawer, finally convincing herself the whole thing was ludicrous. For all she knew, Beatrice had just used the "spell" as inspiration to craft her over-the-top origin story about the ball. That was probably it.

It had been a nice fantasy while it lasted, dreaming that she, too, might be rescued from her terrible fate by benevolent magic.

Her mother greeted her at breakfast as though their argument yesterday did not happen and like Theo's face wasn't still just a bit puffy from her bout of crying. Which was unsurprising. Her mother not only believed she was justified, but the day she apologized for the maltreatment of her children would be the day she backflipped her way to the king's palace wearing nothing but a hat.

The rest of the day went by as usual. A stroll through the front garden—the only one still being maintained, though just barely—afternoon tea in the drawing room followed by listening to Flo make the same noise as a squealing piglet while hitting the high notes of her new song, practicing her harp, then dinner.

It was there that her mother sprang the news. This time she wasn't brandishing the letter, and instead had tucked it into some fold of her dress, rightly assuming that if Theo saw the duke's seal on a piece of paper, she was just as likely to run for the hills as to stand and listen to the contents.

"Theodosia, I've received word from the duke today. He must have sent this letter right after we left. Which is excellent, since it means your behavior didn't completely revolt him. In fact, he's requested that you move to his estate immediately. You'd live in the guest wing, far away from his rooms to maintain your propriety. But it will be much easier to plan the wedding from there since that's where it will be held, and he'd like a very quick engagement."

"*What?* How immediate is 'immediately'?"

"Well, we will need to pack you up, but we are leaving in two days."

The conversation not being about her, Flo spoke up. "But what about my wedding, Mother?"

"Oh, Florentia, not to worry. I will escort Theodosia and help her settle in, then return here for those last-minute details in plenty of time. Then, after your wedding, which

Theodosia has already received special permission from the duke to attend, you'll be a married woman and won't need your doting mother anymore, so I'll return to the duke's estate to help plan her wedding."

Flo smiled. Her mother could soothe any of Flo's moods by telling her she'd *be a married woman* soon—the apex of all her wants and wishes since she was small. It had been Theo's as well up until very, very recently.

Her eldest daughter now calmed, Lady Balfour turned the full force of her attention back to her youngest, looking at her as though daring her to say something negative. But Theo's mind was blank.

"Is that enough time?" *To figure out how to get out of this? To formulate a new plan? To come up with a more convincing argument?*

As usual, her mother misunderstood. "We will have to be quite diligent about packing, but I'm sure we can gather all your belongings in that time. You're correct, though. It will be a tight deadline so we cannot delay!"

She was out of time now. There was nothing left she could do. That lucky, lucky Beatrice. She got swept off to the palace while Theo was about to be carted to a pretty prison.

But what if it worked? What if her fairy godmother was real?

Ridiculous though it was, the intrusive thought gave her a sudden burst of hope.

Tomorrow. She would try. It wasn't like she had anything left to lose.

The next day Theo found empty trunks stacked outside her room with instructions to fill them quickly with all her things so they would be ready for the carriage. As she packed, as slowly as she could get away with, she planned as well. If magic *was* real and Beatrice had summoned a fairy for help, this might be the only shot Theo had at getting out of this mess, and she couldn't waste it.

By early afternoon, her room was empty save for some hair accessories and her outfit for the carriage ride, everything else having been stuffed into the trunks. The good thing about her traveling clothes was that they also made excellent expedition clothes, suitable for both a chilly carriage ride to her doom and slinking around the estate after dark on a cool spring night.

Flo and her mother were in their regular spots in the drawing room as Theo sneaked off to gather the supplies, so the odds of her being noticed were slim. First, she went to the kitchens to find a large wineglass, which she wrapped in a linen napkin. She grabbed a spare satchel from a peg near the door that the cook used for collecting fruits and vegetables from the gardens, then went to the wine cellar.

The door opened with a whine and it was one of the rare moments that Theo was thankful for the lack of staff. The cook hadn't yet returned from whatever errand her mother had sent her on and the scullery maid was off in another part of the manor doing her household chores. Even still, Theo lit a candle and closed the door behind her so as not to arouse any suspicion.

She had to keep reminding herself, though, who cared if

she aroused suspicion? She wasn't a little child at the mercy of the earl's staff anymore. This was her manor, too, and she was an adult. An engaged adult woman—almost as adult as it got. If she wanted to go into the wine cellar, she could go into the wine cellar and tell the cook and maid to mind their business and station should they question her. Beatrice wasn't here anymore to convince her to take treats from the earl's mean old cook. If she wanted to take cookies from the cookie jar now, there was no one there to slap her hand, call her a foul creature who was corrupting dear, sweet Bea, and tell the earl.

But those moments had turned into muscle memory and she still crept around the kitchens and cellar as though the earl's horrid servants were lurking about, ready to punish her.

The cellar was just one brick-lined corridor with a dirt floor and empty wooden shelves lining either side of the cool, damp space. She walked until she reached the shelves where the plum wine was kept. It wasn't hard to find, since they were the only bottles that remained down here.

The plum trees in the orchards used to give fruit in such abundance the estate couldn't even sell all of it. So much that when they were ripe, plums found their way into almost every dish on the menu, sweet or savory. In addition, the harvest was made into wine. While it seemed that everyone loved to eat plums, no one enjoyed the wine, so it sat untouched in the cellar, the collection of bottles growing until the estate winemakers stopped producing it. Her mother may have been discreetly selling off the finer bottles in their wine collection, but the plum wine was worth nothing, so a bounty remained on the shelves.

Theo selected one of the less-dusty ones and put it into

her satchel. As she walked back up the stairs, her candlelight reflected against something metallic hanging on the wall. Looking closer, she realized it was an assortment of corkscrews. Praising her own foresight, she packed one into her bag as well.

She returned to her room, adding the coins and the spell instructions to the satchel, making sure she was all prepared for later. Dinner was shortly thereafter, Theo joining her mother and Flo for a boring, typical meal filled with Flo's musings on her wedding, her mother chiming in with helpful tidbits about flowers, dresses, and snarky comments about the weight of Flo's future mother-in-law.

When they went to the drawing room, Theo excused herself, feigning a stomachache and saying she was going to lie down early. After reconfirming that Theo had packed up all her things, her mother told her it was a good idea to get plenty of rest so she wouldn't look as haggard as she did now when she saw her betrothed again in a few days' time.

Once back in her rooms, Theo changed into her traveling clothes, slung the satchel across her body, then took the servants' stairs to the kitchens. She hadn't bothered to stuff pillows under her covers to make it look like she was there. No one was going to check on her anyway.

The cook and maid had both gone home for the evening, leaving the way clear for Theo to sneak out the back door.

———————————•———————————

It was an easy walk to the old pear tree, familiar even though she hadn't visited it in years. It had already been an old tree when she was a girl, and the time since had aged it further. The branches, crooked from years of weather, now looked like a giant hand had snapped the limbs then put them back as though forcing the wrong puzzle pieces to fit together. And while they were thick, the branches were fragile, no longer able to hold the weight of two little girls having grand adventures.

Theo looked to the very top of the tree for her hair ribbon, half expecting to see one of her greatest childhood achievements still flying in victory, but it had long since disappeared, from time, wind, or both.

The shiny pink ribbon also marked the last day she had ever been to the tree. Young Theo had had the idea to see how high she could climb. When she made it to the top, she tied her hair ribbon to the highest branch as proof of her daring and climbing prowess. When Bea tried she slipped, tumbling out of the tree and spraining her wrist. The two girls raced back to the manor to get help, Theo practically carrying the sobbing Bea. Bea had her arm wrapped and was given extra sweets. Theo was spanked and scolded by the earl for tricking Bea into harm's way with her dangerous and mean-spirited idea. Bea never bothered to correct her father and Theo never returned to the tree.

She couldn't bring herself to get any closer this evening, either. It was difficult to look at the tree and not be able to disentangle the good and bad memories. They had wrapped themselves around each other until they were inextricably bonded. The exhilaration of the climb, the sweetness of a juicy, ripe pear, the thud of Bea hitting the ground, the ache on her own bottom from a brutal punishment, joy of a new-found sisterhood, the bitter taste of betrayal.

She turned away from the tree. She had things to do besides.

Like find the evening primrose flowers before the B'tween Time of the sun's last ray at the end of the day. She left the pear tree for its neighbor, the sheep pasture, completely over-grown from the lack of happy little lamb hooves playing and grazing on it, to hunt for the flowers. A hunt that was fin-ished in record time, her quarry not exactly elusive. The field was covered in yellow evening primrose buds, the flowers also waiting for the B'tween Time to bloom.

She should have been toe-tappingly impatient while she waited at the edge of the neglected meadow, especially since the reason for being out here in the first place was a deadline hovering overhead like an anvil being held aloft by a fray-ing rope. But instead she felt a strange sense of peace, a relief from the earlier memories. Being out here again, facing the meadow and not the tree, she was greeted by the childhood state of careless freedom, adding a little lightness to her heart. Not as an embrace of a familiar friend—more like an old acquaintance who tipped his hat in passing recognition.

But, as was the case for Theo, little girls running amok and believing in magic grow up to become young ladies who have no time for such frivolity. Not when there are marriages to prepare for. Remembering that marriage, she squashed down the feeling. Because in the likely event of this ploy not work-ing, this would be the last time she'd ever feel it anyway.

At the crescendo of the evening's cricket and spring peeper calls, the last rays of the sun tinged the yellow tips of the primrose buds orange, glowing like little flames scattered throughout the field.

Now that the B'tween Time was nigh, the buds began to open. And just as the sun sank behind the trees and the glow faded from the flowers, she picked the still-warm blossoms and added them to her satchel. She took one last look at the meadow, the apricot and lilac colors of the sunset darkening into twilight before she made her way to the sprawling garden behind the manor.

While the farmland had been serenely reclaimed by the wilderness around it, the garden had revolted. It was as though the garden had resented its confinement and spent the last years at war with structure and design, as if seeing the other forgotten spaces of the estate meant this garden was now unbound from the rigidity of grandeur.

Statues were being choked and smothered by moss and ivy, the once-smooth stone now fluffy and green. Topiaries, left like abandoned children, had rebelled in the absence of discipline, with neither nature nor nurture providing guidance on how to grow. Instead they chose anarchy, some crawling out of their plots and pots across the garden, others reaching new heights with formations of their own design. Creeping thyme had turned the straight paved walkways into winding, wending paths like deer trails through a forest. The flowers here also took inspiration from the meadows, realizing they needn't be so strict in where they bloomed, freely letting their seeds roam where they pleased.

There had been many fountains in the gardens of the estate, some large and grand centerpieces, shooting water high into the air, and other small, intimate pieces of art tucked away in hard-to-find places. When she came out to the garden when she was little, if she wasn't paying attention, she'd miss the path or take the wrong one and end up at a completely different hidden alcove. But Theo loved that. It made the garden seem magical, like it was playing with her, moving the paths when she wasn't looking.

Maybe it was due to the memories of the meadow or the absurdity of what she was going to do, but in the faint light of the moon, the fireflies twinkling ahead of her in the path, she felt that magical feeling again, like when she would pretend to be a fairy princess with wands made of sticks and wrapped in flowers. Because now the garden looked like it had in her childhood imagination—wild and undiscovered. It was hard to tamp down the feeling that arose in Theo, when she realized she liked this garden much better than the duke's. But tamp she did, reminding herself to grow up, even if it wasn't as easy this time.

It took her much longer than expected to reach the frog fountain. The peaceful little sitting area had always been one of the more difficult places to find, and now the search had become almost impossible. Doubling back on her trail more than she cared to admit, she finally found the path that would bring her there. It was overgrown with grass and vines, the paved stones underneath almost invisible.

Stepping over hedges and pushing aside branches, she came to the small circular courtyard. The area being too wide to colonize, even for the most opportunistic plants, meant the spiraling stonework of the courtyard was still intact. At equal intervals around the perimeter were three wooden benches, their white paint chipped, revealing weathered gray wood underneath.

At the center, standing only slightly taller than Theo, was the fountain. The three-tiered pedestal's spouts were carved to look like leaves but were otherwise unadorned. At the very top sat the little stone frog. Once upon a time he had gurgled water, but since the fountain was no longer operational, the pudgy fellow now just looked like he was shouting to the sky.

The pool itself was wide, the basin walls reaching just under waist height. It was still filled with water, but the surface was covered by a layer of duckweed so thick it could be mistaken for solid ground.

Even though she had plenty of time before midnight, she set to work preparing the spell—it was either that or sit in silence while her mind oscillated between how silly she felt being out here and how nauseous she got thinking about the duke's estate. She counted out ten flowers and arranged them neatly on the edge. Next, she unwrapped the wineglass from the cloth and added the wine bottle but left it corked. Lastly, she set down the silver coin and checked her pocket watch, counting down the last hour.

At two minutes to midnight she uncorked the plum wine and filled the glass. At one minute she panicked, realizing as she held the silver coin that she had no way of drawing blood. She scanned the courtyard, finding nothing and wondering how hard she'd have to bite herself to bleed, when she spied a single rose peeking out at her from behind a hedge. The white bloom was so bright in the moonlight it was a wonder how she had first missed it.

She plucked off a thorn and rushed back to the fountain. Trying not to spend much time thinking about it, she stabbed the point into the pad of her forefinger until it pierced her skin, clamping down a squeak of pain behind pursed lips. A small dot grew as she squeezed her finger over the coin until it dropped onto the surface, her blood shining like a garnet against the silver.

As both hands of the pocket watch lined up, she tossed the coin into the fountain.

Chapter 7
Where Theo
Strikes a Bargain

The duckweed swallowed up the coin without so much as a ripple, the tiny plants refilling the hole as though nothing had disturbed the surface. Theo stepped back, not sure what she was supposed to be doing now. The spell just said that a fairy may show up within the hour.

As Theo resigned herself to a sizable wait time, a light breeze stirred the leaves around Theo's feet and she watched as they drifted toward the other side of the fountain. When she looked at the bench on the far side, a woman reclined across it.

Sitting on the ground near her was a red fox, the end of his tail twitching as if impatient. A mockingbird was perched on the back of the bench, its head cocked but still as a statue.

Theo jumped in surprise, the yelp that escaped her sounding more like a rusty door than a young lady. Her fight-or-flight response hadn't bothered to show up, leaving Theo stuck wide-eyed and gaping.

The woman sat up and draped an arm over the back of the bench. "Well, hello there." Her voice was like a cup of hot chocolate—dark, rich, and smooth.

Did the spell actually work?

Theo's heart was pounding. "Are...are you a fairy? Beatrice's fairy godmother?"

Now sounding like a bored cup of hot chocolate, the woman chuckled. "I am, indeed, a fairy. Are you asking if I'm the one who did the dress, shoes, and magic pumpkin ride to the palace?"

"Yes?"

"Then yes! 'Tis I! In the flesh. Look upon me and weep. Weep, mere mortal!" The woman did an overdone, rather sarcastic sweep of her arm that wasn't still slung over the back of the bench.

"Do people do that?"

The woman shrugged. "Some do. Let's be honest, my beauty is unparalleled."

Theo had to agree. She was arguably the most beautiful woman Theo had ever seen. And yet... Theo wasn't entirely sure what she had been expecting, but it wasn't this. If anything, she had pictured a kind, older-aunt type—plump, rosy, cheery, and peering down at Theo behind spectacled eyes with a well-practiced look of matronly concern. But none of these words could be used to describe the woman who had just appeared.

Her pitch-black hair that hadn't absorbed all the light

around it was shining silver in the moonlight. It was pulled away from her face in a low sweeping chignon, pieces of hair loose and swaying in the light breeze, showing off her delicate, pointed ears. Her pale skin glowed like mother-of-pearl and she wore a long yellow silk dress with straps that were as thin as a spider's thread and a plunging neckline that sunk to just between her breasts, reminding Theo more of a nightgown than an evening gown.

And she was a real fairy! It worked!

In one graceful movement, the woman stood up and walked toward Theo, her dress flowing like water around her statuesque frame as she moved to the fountain.

She examined the offerings with her hands on her hips as though she was an appraiser, then picked up the flowers and sniffed them. She raised her eyebrows, nodding to herself in approval.

Theo cleared her throat, trying to remember the words the spell had said to use. She had read the spell over and over, but now that a fairy—a real-life fairy!—was in front of her, the pages in her mind went hazy.

Finally, she managed to speak.

"I welcome you, fairy, and am honored and humbled by your presence and acceptance of my invitation. I have requested an—"

The woman held up a finger at Theo's face and shushed, still looking over the offerings. Thankfully for Theo, the woman wasn't looking at her, or else she would have seen the indignation flash across Theo's face before smoothing out to the expressionless mask she'd honed under her mother's strict training.

No, this...*fairy*...was absolutely not what Theo had been expecting.

Out of thin air, a long ivory-colored pipe appeared in the woman's hand, the sleek stem dipping low to a bowl carved to look like a tulip. She put it between her teeth as she picked up the evening primrose flowers, pulled the buds off the stems, then stuffed them into the bowl. Striking a long match on the stone of the fountain, she lit the flowers in her pipe, puffing on the mouthpiece until they caught and burned. Satisfied, she tossed the match into the water where it sizzled on top of the duckweed before sinking.

She took a long drag, the delicate flowers that had glowed in the sunset now actually aflame. After holding it in her lungs for a moment, she tilted her head back and blew out a long breath of smoke. Both Theo and the fairy woman watched it coil upward until it vanished into the dark sky.

With a loud sigh, she turned to Theo. "Right, what do you want?"

Theo cleared her throat again. "I have requested an audience with you to beseech you for your assistance."

The woman puffed on her pipe, shorter this time, and motioned with her hand for Theo to continue, as though she had somewhere more important to be and this was taking way too long. Theo understood she was being rushed so she decided to cut to the chase, hoping efficiency would appease the strange, impatient fairy over formality.

"I need to get out of an arranged marriage to the Duke of Snowbell."

"Huh. And why do you think I can do that?" The fairy

woman set the still-smoldering pipe on the fountain and moved on to the wine. She picked up the glass and held it up to the moonlight, swirling the dark purple contents.

"Well, you got Beatrice into a marriage. I'm hoping you can get me out of one."

The fairy woman took a long gulp, swallowing audibly, then cocked her hip, placing a hand on it. She looked Theo up and down, studying her with a mix of contemplation and consideration, using the same discerning eye she'd trained at the offerings.

Theo was struck by the sudden realization that she had no idea what to do with her arms, or her whole body for that matter. There was no emulating this fairy's poise, so she held her fumbling hands behind her back instead, hoping that her rigid posture would disguise just how uncomfortable and unsure she was.

The fox had moved to sit on the fountain edge and the bird had taken up a spot on the top of the frog's dry nose. Now all three were watching her intently. She tried not to look at any of them for longer than necessary.

After taking another long drink the woman spoke again, a smile growing on her full lips, her cheeks pushing out the boredom that had sat there moments before, eyes alight with amusement. "Wait a minute. Aren't you one of the wicked stepsisters?"

"Wicked?"

"Oh, you know, you know," the fairy said, waving her hand. "You made Beatrice's life so miserable she needed a fairy, some rodents, and a squash to get her out. Had a fun little nickname for her, if I'm not mistaken. So that's you, right?"

"I guess?"

"Which one?"

"What?"

"Which sister are you? There are two of you, if memory serves. Older one or younger one?"

"Younger."

"And now it's your turn to come crying to me."

"I'm not crying—"

"Why should I help you?"

Theo's mind went blank again. The spell did not cover argumentative fairies who seemed rather disinclined to offer aid.

"Because I summoned you with offerings and asked nicely?"

"Were you *not* going to ask nicely? I'm supposed to help you because you did the bare minimum of manners? Look, the wine is fine, but I've had better. Nice job on the flowers, though. But that does not a partnership make. That's where you've capped out on persuasive arguments?"

This was not going well at all. Even though she was losing control of the situation and the book said to remain formal and polite, she was not above begging. "Please. Please, I'll do anything. I can't marry the duke."

The woman tsked. "Dangerous thing to say to a fairy. You must be desperate. It's a big ask, you know, getting you out of a marriage."

"How is that big? You got Beatrice married to a prince. I don't want a prince. I just don't want to get married to the duke!"

"No, no, wicked stepsister. Beatrice did not ask me to help her marry a prince. She asked me to get her to the royal ball. And, if you were there, and I'm assuming you were, you saw the caliber of my work. Some of my finest. But again, I just made sure she got to the ball in style. She did the rest. So yes, you do have the bigger request."

"So you won't help me?" Typical.

"I didn't say that. I didn't say I would, either, though, but we are still chatting, sassy lassie, so maybe hold the temper a bit longer."

The fairy woman sat down on the edge of the fountain, crossed her legs, and took another drag of her pipe. "Holding out for a love match?"

"No. I'm not quaint or idealistic. But I cannot marry him. He's old and disgusting."

"Rumor has it he's quite wealthy, though. You'd be comfortable all the rest of your days. Oh, and I've heard his castle is *gorgeous*."

"Yes, it will be a lovely view on my way down when I throw myself from the highest tower after the wedding, before the wedding night," Theo mumbled.

The fairy laughed. "You could marry him and then I could kill him," she suggested, as if offering a menu substitution.

Theo thought of Margot and Nathan. As Isadora so helpfully pointed out, she'd be saddled with them the instant their father died. And also, as much as she didn't want anything to do with those two snot-nosed cretins and would be more than happy to ship them off to the farthest boarding school, she did know what it was like to have a father die and then be stuck with a replacement parent who didn't particularly like her. Everyone would be much better off if she spared them from that fate.

"No. No, I don't want that."

The fairy shrugged and puffed on her pipe. "So, here's the thing, wicked one. Wait. What's your name?"

"I am Lady Theodosia Balfour."

"Fancy. Do I have to say all that every time or do you have something shorter? What do your friends call you?"

"I don't have friends."

"The evil stepsister doesn't have a close group of gal pals? Well, push me over with a feather, I am *shocked*."

Theo answered with a sneer and an eye roll, politeness be damned.

"So everyone calls you Lady Theodosia Balfour at all times? That's a real mouthful. I certainly have time, but you don't and we could save heaps of it if I don't have to call you Lady Theodosia Balfour every time I address you."

"Theo, for short."

"Perfect," she said, eyes glittering. "Well then, hello, dear Theo. I'm Cecily of the Ash Fairies. You may call me Cecily. There's no shortening of that, but you can go longer, should you want to. Add any honorifics as you see fit. What was the one you used the other day, Phineas?" She turned to the bird who said nothing but tilted his head. "Oh yes, 'Her Deliciousness Cecily of the Ash Fairies, Most Benevolent Mistress with the Resplendent Tits.'" She looked back at Theo. "Feel free to use that one."

Theo nodded, eyebrows creeping up her forehead in disbelief. "Sure."

"Right, so where were we? Oh yes. As I was about to say, my unscrupulous Theo, Beatrice was kind. Clever—very clever, don't get me started—but convinced me she was ultimately a good person with a sad, sad story. Which is why I agreed to help her. And you... well, no minstrels will be singing songs about your compassionate works, I'm sure. But there is a kernel of goodness in you since you don't want me to slaughter the duke on your wedding night in order to take his fortune and keep your undergarments firmly in place."

"I didn't realize that was a test," Theo said with a snort.

"Of course it was a test, dear. But since you passed, I'll make a deal with you."

"You will? You'll get me out of the marriage? I—"

"Wait, wait, my spiny new friend. I'm not just going to do it right away. You'll have to do a bit of up-front work before we get started. Because again"—she held up two fingers, wiggling them with her next words—"a much bigger ask and a much meaner disposition. So let me lay it out for you. Prove to me that inside that nasty exterior is a good person just waiting to come out and I'll help you."

Oh, of course. Up until now, Theo was so overwhelmed by the magical being in front of her she forgot who she was talking to. This was *the* fairy godmother. The one who "rescued" Beatrice, believing all her lies with seemingly no hesitation. And, like everyone else in Theo's life to date, this fairy also didn't bother to question any of it or find out the truth for herself.

Fine, then.

If this was what Theo needed to do in order to get her own *happy ever after*, then so be it.

"How am I supposed to do that?"

Cecily drank the last of the wine, holding the glass high as the final drops slid down into her mouth, and then set down the glass on the fountain again.

"Tasks. Three tasks, to be specific. Do them and demonstrate you are capable of goodness, of mending your wicked ways, and I'll agree to get you out of that marriage. What do you say?"

"What are the tasks?"

"You'll find out when you do them. But each task will be to help someone other than yourself. You will reap no reward aside from knowing someone else has benefited from your actions."

"So I complete these three tasks and then you'll stop the marriage?"

"Careful of the wording, dear. You're dealing with a fairy. You, my nefarious Theo, will be in my service for the completion of three tasks of my choosing to prove yourself to be worthy and good. Whilst in my service, you shall have all the privileges that come with working for a fairy. Simplified, you can enter the fairy realm, won't age, will be quicker to heal, et cetera. Upon completion of the three tasks, I, Her Deliciousness Cecily of the Ash Fairies, Most Benevolent Mistress with the Resplendent Tits, agree to halt and otherwise prevent your betrothal and marriage to His Grace and Glorious Spitter of Dinner, the Duke of Snowbell."

"What if I don't complete the tasks?"

"Then hopefully I'll get invited to the wedding, my blushing bride. So, are we agreed?"

Theo nodded. She could do this. Whatever it took.

"Then say the magic words!" Cecily flourished her arm as though casting a dramatic spell. Then in a loud stage whisper added, "*It's a deal.*"

"It's a deal."

A slow smile spread across Cecily's face. "Wonderful."

"So, what's my first task?"

"You'll find out soon enough, but I'm loving the enthusiasm. Highly motivated. Keep it up. For now, go home, get some sleep. Crochet, or torment the staff, find a puppy to poke with a stick, or do whatever it is you do for fun. I'll let you know when I need you."

"Well, it's just that I'm supposed to be moving to the duke's castle tomorrow." *And I don't want to go.*

"Tomorrow? The wedding is tomorrow? Cutting it real close, meeting with me now. No wonder you're so excited for your tasks."

"No, not tomorrow. He just wants me to move in so I'm close for the very short engagement he wants."

"Phew! Not to worry, then. You know I don't live at this charming fountain, right? I can travel to you there. It's not a problem."

But the look on Theo's face showing that it was, in fact, a problem was not lost on Cecily.

"Ah. I see." She tapped an elegant finger on her chin while looking over Theo again. "I'll tell you what. As a show of my commitment to our bargain, I'll make sure you'll stick around here for a little while longer."

Cecily rose from the fountain and tapped the contents of

her now-spent pipe onto the duckweed. With a quick snap of her fingers, the pipe vanished. As she wiped her hands together, she spotted the fox and bird who were still watching them both.

"Oh, my apologies for the lack of introductions. That's Phineas," she said, pointing to the bird. Then, pointing to the fox, she added, "And that's Kasra. They're your colleagues, of a sort. You'll see them soon, too. Goodbye!"

She gave a brief wave to Theo and in a blink they were gone, leaving Theo alone at the fountain.

Theo looked down at herself, sure that she would have felt something after making a deal with a fairy, but she felt the same as she usually did. If it hadn't been for the empty glass, she wasn't sure she'd believe anything happened at all.

———————————●———————————

Theo almost fell out of bed, having been woken by someone shaking her. She opened her eyes to the sight of her mother standing over her bed, hands on her hips, scowl fixed in place.

"Theodosia! Get up! The carriage is being loaded and it is near time to go! Honestly." She stalked out the door muttering to herself about lazy, ungrateful daughters.

Theo waited until her mother shut her door, then sat on the edge of her bed.

After staggering out of the dark garden and through the back door, she had been too tired to do anything other than flop onto her bed and burrow into the sheets. Looking down at herself, sure enough, she was still in her expedition dress, brambles and dried grass clinging to the fabric in spots. Her finger had healed, though, and all that remained was a tiny red dot from where she had pricked herself. She went to where she had dropped her satchel and, checking the contents, found that the wine bottle, now only two-thirds full, and the glass were inside.

So, that part happened, then.

She walked to her window and could see her mother pointing at pieces of luggage that the old driver was trying to squeeze onto the carriage. She couldn't hear what her mother was saying, but it was obvious she was doing her customary routine of telling everyone else how to do their jobs, including loading trunks.

She had thought Cecily would have kept her word and prevented Theo from leaving. Silly and senseless of her to believe in magic.

Everything last night felt so real. But maybe it wasn't. Maybe she hallucinated the fairy. Or, right after pricking her finger she fainted, then stumbled home and dreamed up Cecily.

Because she was leaving today. By the looks of it, she was leaving within the hour. She wished she had woken earlier to play the harp one last time. Instead, like a fool, she ran around the property until the early hours of morning hoping magic would save her. What she should have done was remind herself of what her mother, her sister, and everyone else in her life made sure she knew—she was Theodosia Balfour. Good things did not happen to her.

Wanting to make sure she didn't start getting sentimental, she walked toward the front door ready to just get on with it, only to find Flo waiting.

"Well, I suppose we should say goodbye," Flo said. "The next time you see me I'll be walking down the aisle."

"I suppose so."

"But, Theodosia, I want to make sure you know that the duke won't be at my wedding, so don't think you'll steal the spotlight from me with any talk about you being a duchess. It is *my* day. *Mine.* Save that showboating for your own wedding. Do you understand?" Flo was speaking to her the way a governess might talk down to an impulsive child. Not an unfamiliar tone to Theo, but annoying nonetheless.

"That's your goodbye?"

Flo just crossed her arms.

Theo did her best mischievous smile. "I honestly hadn't thought about it. But since I know now it means that much to you, Florentia, I *promise* I will do my *best* to blend into the scenery on your *most special of special days.* I wouldn't *dream* of talking about my upcoming wedding to my betrothed, His Grace, the Duke of Snowbell."

Flo's eyes flashed, now worried her warning had given her sister ideas and ammunition. Good. Let her stew over whether Theo was being sarcastic.

"Goodbye, Flo. See you soon."

With nothing left to say, Theo joined her mother waiting beside the carriage, Flo following to see them off.

Just as Theo's boot touched the carriage step, a shout cut through the crisp spring morning.

"Wait! Lady Balfour, wait!"

The driver, Lady Balfour, Theo, and Flo all stopped and stared at the boy, no more than twelve, hurtling up the drive, waving a piece of paper over his head.

When he made it to the carriage he doubled over, hands on

his knees and gulping air like he'd just been held underwater. Theo thought he might very well throw up from exertion. But remembering he had an important task, he took a huge breath and tried to speak, holding out the paper.

"Lady—*gasp*—Balfour. I have—*gasp*—an urgent le—*gasp*—letter from—*gasp*—from the Duke of—*gasp*—Snowbell."

Lady Balfour leaped at the poor boy, snatching the letter from his outstretched hand. His delivery complete, he took an awkward bow and walked, exhausted, back the way he came.

Theo rushed to her mother's side as she tore open the seal and scanned the page.

Lady Balfour gasped. "We aren't going to the duke's castle!"

"Really?" Theo tried not to sound too excited, but her mother glanced at her, eyes narrowed.

"It seems there has been a fire in the wing with the guest rooms. The duke says that as much as he was looking forward to having you at the castle, at present you'd be much more comfortable staying here while they repaired your suite." Her mother flipped the paper over, searching for more writing. "It doesn't say when they'll have it ready. I'll have to write immediately to see when we should reschedule. It's a castle. They don't have any other suites?" She looked for the delivery boy, but by that time he had made it almost to the gates.

"Well," Lady Balfour snapped at the driver, who looked like he might cry, "you'd better get to unloading these." With Flo right behind her, she disappeared back inside. Theo followed, glad she was at their backs so they couldn't see her smiling.

She took great pleasure in unpacking her things.

Chapter 8
Where Theo Gets
Instructions from
a Cranky Fox

It was well into the third week since the duke's fire and the days were once again bleeding together.

They had received no further news about when the castle would be repaired enough for Theo to make the journey. As it turned out, there had been a pretty intense blaze destroying the suite she was supposed to occupy, and the smoke damage to the surrounding rooms was so significant that the entire guest wing was uninhabitable. Oddly, a letter reiterating the news and instructions came a few days later.

There also had been no sign of Cecily, no indication that she had been anything other than a dream, so it was easy to chalk up the fire to coincidence and not a fairy bargain. Setting a castle wing ablaze didn't seem like the work of a fairy godmother anyway. And the longer she went without any trace of magic, the easier it was to believe she had invented the whole thing.

While she might have been given a reprieve from moving to the duke's castle, the engagement was still on. So she did not return to the field or the garden like maybe she would have if she knew she was staying. It seemed a shame that she hadn't gone out there more as an adult, since the only one scolding her for getting her clothing dirty would have been Morris, and it wasn't like she was going to take away dessert. But it would be a pointless undertaking to find something else she enjoyed only for the duke to keep her from it.

Unlike walking around the grounds, though, she threw herself into playing the harp, deciding that if this was to be all the time she had left, she would make it count. Also, if she wasn't playing music she was listening to Flo and her mother, the topic of her wedding now so obnoxious it almost made her want to go to the duke's. Almost.

One morning, during a particularly dull breakfast and conversational assault on her patience with Flo, she excused herself and went to the music room. She selected a few warm-up pieces from the sheet music shelves and then went to Beatrice's mother's music collection. Hers were so unlike the other music Theo played. The tunes never went where she expected them, the tempos, either. But in that was the fun. It felt like the music she would have played to accompany the orchestra of crickets in the meadow.

She sat down and let her fingers loosen up and feel the music. Once she had worked out any stiffness, she began to play in earnest. The notes of the song wound their way through the strings like vines, bursting and blooming with unexpected twists and turns. She plucked and strummed, closing her eyes and imagining what it would be like to twirl around to the song, wild and free.

After she finished, she silenced the strings and sighed in contentment. When she opened her eyes, she let out a sharp chirp of surprise at the red fox sitting in the chair by the bay window. She would have thought him to be a fuzzy figurine had it not been for his tail that was wrapped around his black legs, the white tip twitching.

The fox made no move to get off the chair, so for a few moments they did nothing but stare at each other. How did a fox even get into her music room? Either the housekeeping had gotten so poor that animals were now moving in, or the fox arrived magically. Theo didn't know how she felt about both of those being viable options.

Hazarding a guess, even though she felt a bit silly talking to an animal, she asked, "You're the fox that was with the fair— Cecily...Kasra?"

In a flash of light, where the fox had been now sat a man. Theo shrieked, falling backward. Her skirts caught on the stool and her feet hit the music stand, taking it toppling down with her as she crashed to the floor, legs tangled, sheet music covering her like she was the cast-off pile for yesterday's newspapers.

She kicked her way free, sitting up against the wall, eyes wide at the man in the chair.

"Well, aren't you just the picture of grace and poise," the man drawled, one ankle crossed over a knee.

"You're a ... you're a person!"

"And so perceptive!"

She glared, still gasping in shock, her hand over her pounding heart. Once again, neither of them spoke as they watched each other. He appeared to be a young man, only slightly older than Theo herself, and strikingly handsome. His face, framed by thick, wavy, shoulder-length black hair, was almost unreasonably angular, as if a sculptor carved him and forgot to smooth the edges. And his dark eyes were still taking her in, this time with an expression of annoyance that a fox face could never convey.

His clothes were of good make and quality, but he didn't wear them with any sort of affinity for style. The top two buttons of his plain white shirt were unbuttoned, collar hanging open, as though he had started at the bottom and when he got toward the top thought, *Eh, good enough.* Very unlike the other young men Theo was used to seeing—the fussy, stuffy men at court and the fancy balls, with meticulous hair and clothes so starched they could stand up by themselves, saving their former wearer a spot in the drink line.

"Are you going to stay in a pile this whole time, or do you think you should brush off the papers, reset the stool, and get up?" He asked this as though he had a million better places to be and could get to them if Theo would just get up off the floor.

She scowled, trying to remove the stool from her dress but failing, the stool now acting like it enjoyed its new home in her underskirts and did not want to leave. Once she had righted it and stacked the sheet music back on the stand, she sat down next to her harp, not wanting to sit any closer to him.

He kept his expression the same, adding an impatient tapping of his fingers on the arms of the chair, then sighed when she was settled.

"Finally." He was about to say more, but Theo had had enough, that angry part of her not caring whether he was magical or not.

"You can cut the attitude, you know. I'm not sure scaring someone half to death by showing up as a fox and then turning into a person warrants being annoyed at that someone's perfectly reasonable reaction."

He snorted. "You're scared of a fox?"

"It's the middle of the day! My first thought wasn't *Oooh look, a magical forest creature who works with a fairy and can turn into a cranky fellow!* It was *There's a fox in my house in the middle of the day and it's probably rabid!* And then, *poof*, you're a strange, slovenly man insisting I'm the one who's odd here. Sorry I didn't have the reaction of *This is perfectly acceptable.*"

He rolled his eyes. "Aren't you ladies supposed to be, you know, ladylike? Polite, quiet, respectful, demure?"

"Wicked stepsister, remember?" Theo intoned. "And also, you're a fox, not a gentleman. What would you know about it?"

"Wait, you think I'm a fox who turns into a man?"

Theo raised her eyebrows and crossed her arms as though her answer was obvious.

"Other way around, you daft girl. I am a man who turns into a fox."

"Well, rumor has it that Beatrice's fairy godmother turned a dog into a footman. Are you saying that was the other way around as well?"

"No, that was actually a dog. That was different. All the dog had to do as a person was sit and stay."

"Oh, excuse me," she drawled. "You see where I'm getting lost here, then. My tutelage in magical animals failed to cover the finer points of fairy shape-shifting. I was going to tell you I was impressed that a fox had the ability to dress himself as well as you did. But now"—she made a show of looking him up and down—"I still say you look as though a woodland critter who eats rats and runs around screaming after dark decided to dress you."

"And you look just as smug and conceited as your reputation would suggest."

"Better than no reputation at all. For all her stories about the fated ball, Beatrice didn't mention anything about you. Guess you weren't as important as the dog. Oh, and if you're trying to insult me, you should try for something I haven't heard a thousand times over already."

"You're gracious and generous and everyone wants to be your friend."

"What? Is that your insult?"

"I thought you told me to tell you something you've never heard about yourself before. Bet no one's honestly told you that."

Her jaw dropped. "I haven't met many fairies, but you have the honor of being the rudest." That would have to do by way of a cutting comeback, the place in her brain that called up clever retorts now just a chalkboard that had a bucket of water splashed on it.

"I'm not a fairy."

"Then what are you?"

"Just a man."

"You're a man who works with a fairy?"

"Works *for* a fairy."

"Did you also make a bargain with her?"

"Long story. Not something I'll be sharing with the likes of you."

"Did you come here just to show off your little magic trick and try to outdo me in nastiness, then?"

"No. I came here to tell you it's time for your first task."

Theo straightened at that, eliciting a small, satisfied smile of victory from Kasra.

"Cecily wants you to meet her at the frog fountain tomorrow at noon."

"Is that where the task is? Do I need to bring anything? What should I wear?"

"No, it's not where the task is. Don't bring anything. Wear whatever you want."

"That's it?"

He shrugged. "I was sent to tell you that. Watching you overreact off a stool was a nice bonus. Brace yourself."

In another quick burst of light, a fox sat where Kasra had been. He jumped off the chair and trotted out the open music room door.

———————————— • ————————————

While Kasra said it didn't matter what she wore, all she could think when she was staring into her closet the next morning was *What does one wear to an unknowable fairy task?* She had nothing that even closely resembled Cecily's outfit. Even Theo's skimpiest nightgown was more modest.

Should she wear a ball gown even though the meeting was at noon? Her sensible expedition ensemble in case she had to do more walking or manual labor?

Theo decided to split the difference and chose a ruffly blush day dress that her mother said made her look "sweet" and "inoffensive," which Theo supposed she should aim for appearance-wise to prove to Cecily on her first task that she could be both of those things. She put her hair in a simple braid, kept jewelry to a minimum, and selected shoes comfortable enough for walking, just in case. She looked in her mirror one last time before leaving, satisfied that her outfit was, on the one hand, quite lovely, but on the other, appropriate for a noon appointment. Something a *good person* would wear.

Getting out of the house proved, once again, extremely easy. Flo and her mother had made a trip to the village, and since they would be eating there, the cook had left Theo a few prepared meals and went home for the day. Theo simply walked out the back door to the garden.

Chapter 9
Where Theo Goes to the Court of the Woodland Elves

When she arrived at the fountain, Kasra was sitting on one of the benches. His legs were stretched out in front of him, and he was wearing a similar ensemble as yesterday with the same lack of attention to detail. His hair was again loose and windswept in a way that suggested he didn't too much care what it was doing up there, as long as it stayed out of his way. The stubble on his face, a dark shadow against his golden-olive skin, continued the sentiment. Theo wouldn't have been surprised to learn a mirror didn't factor into his day at all.

To his right sat a tiny mockingbird, the same one Theo recalled perching on the fountainhead when Cecily was summoned.

She nodded to the fox man. "Good afternoon, Kasra. You look well."

He smiled at the obvious jab. "Good afternoon, Lady Theodosia. As do you. My eardrums are glad you're not screaming today."

"Really? I'd wager that women screaming at the sight of you is something you're used to hearing quite frequently."

He gave her a lazy grin.

There was a flash of light, and where the mockingbird had been was now another man. He seemed to be around the same age as Kasra, but otherwise sat in contrast to him. His blond hair was pulled back neatly as though he had combed it for a while until it sat just right. He wore a navy-blue jacket, every gold button buttoned, over a crisp white shirt. While Kasra's boots were dull with wear and use, this other man's shone even in the muted shade. His face was round with bright pink cheeks, like a little cherub who had been allowed to grow up. And his sparkling eyes watched Theo with endless amusement. "What, no hysterics for me?"

"If that's what you were aiming for, then sorry to disappoint. That trick could only be used once. After yesterday, I'm just going to assume that every animal looking at me for longer than two seconds could turn into a person at any moment. And also, not that I have any desire to compliment him, but a fox is a tad more frightening than a mockingbird."

"We'll see about that. Maybe I'll visit your window in the dead of night and knock like a character straight out of a penny dreadful."

"It worries me slightly that the two of you are taking such an interest in making me scream."

The blond man laughed. "Not to worry. Though I am sure

Kaz would much rather hear that than the quiet sobs of disappointment he normally gets from the ladies."

Kaz, as he was called instead, rolled his eyes as Theo stifled a laugh.

The man jumped up and bowed, as if presenting himself to a queen on her throne and not a young lady next to a weedy fountain.

"I am Phineas, human familiar to Her Excellency, Cecily of the Ash Fairies. Delighted to meet you. I'm sure we are going to have a wonderful time together, especially if you keep getting under our dear Kaz's skin."

Theo gave him a small curtsy. "Lovely to make your avian acquaintance."

Kaz scoffed at the two of them. Phineas winked at Theo with a devious smile.

"So, what do we do now?" Theo asked.

"We wait for Cecily. She'll be here in just a moment." Phineas had returned to the bench and sat back down.

"Actually, right now, my dearest Phineas." Cecily glided over to the bench from wherever she had materialized from. Phineas offered her his seat, which she accepted. While still just as beautiful in the daylight in her periwinkle chiffon dress, Cecily appeared to have a hint of dark circles under her eyes. Theo wondered if fairies could also suffer from a lack of sleep.

Cecily slung her arm over the back of the bench and watched Theo, who once again felt as though she were onstage and told to perform without warning. Not knowing what else to do with her body, she curtsied at the fairy, a tad lower than she had for Phineas, hoping Cecily would see it as a sign of respect for her elevated station.

"Hello, my foul friend. Love the punctuality. Ready to start your journey of betterment?"

Theo nodded.

"Excellent! On to your first task, then. Currently wallowing in the Court of the Woodland Elves Prison is a garden gnome by the name of Dwyn. Before we continue, yes, he has committed the crime of which he is accused. However, should you fail today he will be imprisoned for much, much longer than I believe is necessary and only because of who he has committed the crime against.

"So your duty today is to restore justice to the justice system and release the gnome. Remember, this task has zero benefit for you, your reward being the satisfaction of knowing you've made a difference in the life of our downtrodden friend, Dwyn. Since you've never been to Elf Court and I only wish for you to be successful in your endeavor, Kaz and Phineas will be escorting you and helping where they can, understood?"

Theo hoped Cecily saw her standing with a blank expression as a moment of quiet contemplation, when really it was her brain working very hard to not explode. Many things about working for a fairy had been unexpected, and now on that list was the discovery that not only did a great many magical beings exist, but she'd be working in close proximity to them. Among them, garden gnomes who ran afoul of the law. But she couldn't very well deny the existence of one magical creature while speaking directly to another.

So instead of demanding that Cecily name every other fairy-tale being she was aware of until her mind sorted through it, Theo did a surface-level run-through of the facts she was just presented, focusing on the bits she could make sense of.

"Yes, but...if he is a gnome, why is he in the Court of the Woodland Elves?"

"Excellent and observant question, Theo! I am quite pleased with your astute attention to detail! Because his accuser and the one Dwyn perpetrated the crime against is a fairy. When there is a crime committed against different magical courts, an impartial court takes the complaint. In this case, it is the Court of the Woodland Elves. With me so far?"

"I think so."

"Wonderful! So if there are no further questions, let's get you ready. As darling as you look in that adorable getup, we will need to do a bit better if you are to be taken seriously as Dwyn's representative at the Court of the Woodland Elves."

Cecily looked over Theo, brows scrunched, finger on her chin. "Got it!"

Theo felt a sensation like thousands of flower petals brushing against her skin, and when she looked down at herself, her dress had transformed. Theo's plain day dress was now a flowing deep green chiffon gown, the color of a midsummer field. The straps over Theo's shoulders were made of a gold chain that looked like leaves, their thin links the only thing preventing the dress from falling off her otherwise naked top, her back left bare.

With a snap of her fingers, Cecily conjured a mirror.

Theo gasped at the stranger staring back at her. Her hair was left loose but now in gentle curls down her back, a gold leaf circlet studded with peridots around her head and across her brow. Many thin gold bracelets and rings adorned her wrists and fingers. Her speckled hazel eyes had been rimmed in smoky black kohl, her cheeks swept with bronze shimmer.

"Thoughts?" Cecily asked.

"I can't wear this!" While the dress was beautiful, Theo was not a fairy. She was an engaged *lady*. Everything about this ensemble screamed *Scandal!* Being taught from puberty that showing this much skin would have her accepting blame for men's eyes popping out of their sockets and ruining their souls, the thought of this as her *good person* outfit was giving her heart palpitations.

"Of course you can. You're wearing it now."

"But…but my arms!" She rubbed her bare arms for emphasis. "Won't there be men there?"

"Yes. But a dress that you'd wear at a human court to blend in would have no one taking you seriously at Elf Court, or any court for that matter. Since you are representing me, I'd prefer you look the part of someone who is supposed to be there, rather than an uptight human who lost a fight with the bed linens. Wear something like that if you want—it's your body and I won't stop you, but it seems to me you'd only be doing it to please someone else, in this case someone human who won't be there anyway. Make sense?"

Theo stared at her reflection, considering whether she should change. Cecily had a point. No one was going to know who Theo was, so she could get away with wearing this dress and looking this nice.

When the silence stretched on, Cecily added, "You look beautiful, my dear; doesn't she, gentlemen?"

Phineas put a hand to his heart. "You are a vision of beauty. The fairest maiden of justice and valor."

"Sure," Kaz said, hardly looking her way and picking at his cuticles.

"There you have it. Glowing approval from your colleagues. Don't worry; they're not going like that, either. Well, Phineas is because he is always dressed for the occasion." She smiled and winked at him like they shared a secret—a look that he returned.

"But Kaz..." The clothes he was wearing shimmered like sun on water as they transformed into an outfit similar to Phineas's except with black pants and a deep rust jacket with gold buttons. His hair was tied back, highlighting his impressive bone structure, but he kept his day-old stubble, the effect making him look rugged, roguish, and slightly mysterious.

Playing into Theo's theory, Kaz pretended the mirror didn't exist and made no effort to look at himself.

Cecily clapped her hands together, the apparent signal for Phineas and Kaz to stand next to Theo.

"Perfect. Everyone ready to restore justice and freedom to our friend? Remember, Theo, he needs to be released at any cost. Great! Journey to goodness! Good luck!"

"Wait. At any cost?" Theo asked, but her question was lost to the breeze that was swirling around the three of them. Leaves blocked out the view of the fountain, but she felt no wind, her dress unmoving amid the gusts. When it subsided, Theo knew she was far, far away from the frog fountain.

———————— • ————————

The trio was standing in a forest surrounded by trees triple the size of any she'd ever seen before. The bases and trunks were so large, entire houses could fit within their circumferences. The forest floor was dark, as if the sun had set. But looking to the canopy, she could see that it was still daytime; the leaves were just so thick the light could not reach this far down.

Phineas and Kaz, probably having seen this all before, were already moving.

Kaz realized she wasn't following and motioned her onward. "Come on, we still have a bit of a walk."

Up ahead was what looked like a green river winding through the trees, glowing luminaries lighting the way. When she reached it, she found the river was actually a path made of moss. And there were others traveling on it. There were other fairies like Cecily, ears tapered to a point, their movements fluid and languid. But also small, stocky beings whose skin took on a slight gray hue. Whether that was their actual color or the light playing tricks, she didn't know. A few sprites flew by at eye level, talking animatedly in a language Theo had never heard before.

A group she assumed must have been Woodland Elves went past. While looking similar to fairies, everything about them was slightly different, slightly exaggerated. Their faces were longer, narrower. Cheekbones sat just a bit higher. Brows more arched. They looked very much like they were not from the woods, but of the woods. Like the stories of magical creatures growing from seeds or sprouting from underneath mushrooms.

It was as if every fairy tale she had ever read had come to life before her, and it was only when Phineas took her arm in his and escorted her down the path that she began to move again.

"Quite a sight, isn't it? You get used to it. Important, though, no matter who you're dealing with, be respectful. As much as I enjoy watching you dig at Kaz, each and every one of these creatures would have no problem turning you into a rodent, an enchanted flower, or a doll just for looking at them the wrong way. Here, humans are at the bottom of the pecking order. Something to keep in mind during your dealings today." Phineas patted her arm.

After a brief walk, the path widened and they were standing in front of a palace that seemed as though it had grown from the forest itself, as natural as any other tree surrounding it. Massive gates blocked the entrance, and looking at the intricate details that curled and swirled throughout, Theo couldn't tell whether they had been carved or magically grew that way.

The gates opened, and along with the other travelers, Theo, Phineas, and Kaz walked through. They received dark glares from the sentries as they did, but were let into the grand hall just the same. Unlike the forest, the grand hall was well lit by thousands of lanterns hanging from the branches that made up the roof. Phineas, still holding tight to her arm, steered her to a banquet table along the far wall that was laden with piles of fruits, vegetables, meats, and cheeses. Others were filling plates and mingling, and it seemed Phineas wanted to do the same. He released Theo when they got to the table, and both he and Kaz partook. Too anxious to eat, Theo stood off to the side so as not to be in the way.

As she took in the sights before her, she realized Cecily was right. Theo was blending in here, others having similar dress styles to hers. And to her immense relief, no one was spending any time looking at her at all. A nice departure from the stares of mild revulsion she received when standing next to Flo or Beatrice at events.

But the feeling was short-lived when she caught the eye of someone leaning against the wall.

He wore a dark tunic over black leather pants, made to look even darker against his moon-white skin. The sides of his head were shaved, displaying his clearly pointed ears, leaving a mop of black hair on top that was slicked back, the ends tinged an emerald green the exact color of his eyes.

He kept those eyes on her, a knavish half smile playing on his face that made her feel like he had been waiting for her to notice him. Before she could turn, he was moving toward her. She put her back to him and faced the grand hall, expecting he would get the body-language message that she was not interested in talking.

No such luck. He walked in front of her, closer than would have been proper in any human context.

"Hello." His voice was thick, syrupy, and strangely inviting. Typical of someone who traded in charm and flattery but with an undercurrent of mischief.

Theo tried a polite smile and nod, then looked back at the food table, hoping to find Kaz and Phineas, who had somehow disappeared. She couldn't figure out why a fairy male would be so entertained by speaking with her, but it instantly made her wary. No one else had looked twice at her, yet he had come right up.

"I don't think I have seen you here before," he said.

She sighed. "No, I can't imagine you would have. I've never been here before."

"Well, that explains it, then. A woman as lovely as you would certainly not go unnoticed."

Great, now he was insulting her looks. Turns out magical gatherings had something in common with human ones, after all. She clenched her jaw, temper sparking to life.

"So where are you from?" he asked, the corners of his smile growing wider.

"Far, far away." In truth she had no idea where she was. She certainly felt far from home.

"So, how is it that a beautiful mortal came to the Court of the Woodland Elves?"

"Floated in on a light breeze."

"Of course. And what are you doing here?" He was still making that infuriating smile, enjoying taunting her while acting like she was flirting right back. Like she was supposed to be so grateful he was talking to her that she'd take any insult just to keep him there.

Same fruit punch, different cup.

If he wanted to be snarky, then fine. He packed a picnic basket of snark. She had a wagon, and the driver was experienced.

"Right now, at this very moment? Speaking with someone who is indulging me in such banal conversation I'm considering confessing to a crime I didn't commit just for an excuse to be physically removed from it, since any hint more polite than that seems to fly past him like a pixie with an urgent appointment." She tried to steel her tone, letting him know the conversation was over.

He burst out laughing. "Clever. What's your name, gorgeous?"

Relief washed over her when Phineas and Kaz returned to her side so she could excuse herself with more finality. But the fairy's grin turned wolfish when he saw who had approached.

"Oh, I see. You must be Cecily's new pet. Theo, is it?" He looked her over again with no shortage of humor.

Before she could take umbrage at being called a pet and figure out something devastating to say in return, Kaz chimed in. "That's *Lady Theodosia* to you, Locklan. Only her friends call her Theo and she has none of those."

So much for a sweltering comeback. She closed her eyes and let out a sharp breath.

Locklan laughed again. "Hello, Kasra, Phineas. Glad to have this sharp-tongued, striking beauty as a member of your cohort now? Certainly better to look at than each other." He gave Theo a wink as though she was in on the joke.

"Well, they are certainly better than present company in their creativity in mocking me. *Charmed* to meet you, Locklan. Even more charmed to leave you. Excuse us, we have important matters to deal with."

Locklan tilted his head but then smiled and bowed to her. "Yes, I'm sure you do. The pleasure of making your acquaintance was all mine, Lady Theodosia. I am looking forward to seeing you again."

She conjured her most ferocious smirk and curtsied in return, turning on her heel and striding off as confidently as she could.

Chapter 10
Where Theo Vows to Help a Garden Gnome Find Justice

Where she was confidently striding to she didn't know, hoping Phineas or Kaz would give her a direction before she confidently ran into a wall.

Neither one held her arm, but Kaz moved to walk just ahead of her, guiding her toward the front of the hall and to a series of stone archways that she had failed to notice on the first pass.

"Who was that?" she asked when she was pretty sure they were out of earshot of the fairy.

"That was Locklan," Kaz said.

"Yes," she said flatly. "But who is he? Why does he know you? Why does he know me, for that matter?"

"He runs in similar circles to Cecily," Phineas chimed in.

"He's pretty high up in fairy society. And not to mention a tall drink of eye candy. He knows how to wear leather pants, that's for sure. You'll just have to wait for next time to see him walk away." Phineas looked behind them. "Though, by the looks of it, I'd say he is thinking the same about you."

Theo snarled at the thought of Locklan's gaze still on her.

"Remember what Phineas said before we got here about being nice and polite?" Kaz asked. "Catch flies with honey and all that? Try that so Phineas and I won't have to stop eating to save you from saying something foul that we'd all regret."

"First of all, he approached *me*." She was about to add that she had already said some of those foul things to Locklan and was ready to give an earful to Kaz, but the trio had stopped. In front of them was an armed and armored sentry standing guard at one of the arches wearing a highly decorated metal helmet, the nose and cheek guards protecting their namesakes but leaving the rest of his face visible.

Phineas made a slight but respectful bow. "Good afternoon. We are here to see a prisoner. May we pass?"

The sentry looked them over, unmoved both physically and metaphorically.

Phineas started to speak again but was interrupted by the sentry. "You three are not going down there."

Kaz spoke up. "We are here on the orders of—"

"I don't care, you filthy human."

Kaz tensed, narrowing his eyes at the guard. "You must let us pass."

Oh, so he could be curt, but she couldn't? Where was this honey he spoke of?

The guard raised himself up to his full height, his hand moving to rest on the sword at his belt. "I don't have to do anything for you. Go away before I send you down there to your very own cells."

She stepped between the two men. If Kaz wanted a nice and polite Theo then he'd better get ready for the show. She cleared her throat, preparing to employ the tried-and-true Lady Martha Balfour method for getting what she wanted: throw someone else under the cart and do it with a smile.

"Excuse us for the misunderstanding, sir, and for the way he spoke to you. Quite the typical human, Kasra tends to forget his place. I do hope you will forgive the poor, misguided brute. Our mistress keeps him around for his beauty, obviously not his brains. In fact, if brains were measured in horsepower, his cart's being pulled by a three-legged goat." She turned to Kaz. "I'm happy to explain that joke to you. It would give the goat a break and I'm sure he needs it." She turned back to the guard. "Honestly, if I had a gold coin for every time I needed to help Kasra find his way out of a room with only one door, well, I wouldn't need to work for a fairy, would I?" She gave him a conspiratorial smile and he returned it with a grin of his own.

But then her smile widened. "Speaking of fairies, human though we may be, we are here on fairy business. We were sent to speak to one of your prisoners directly, and as you know, it would be quite problematic should we not be able to complete our task. And it would be *such* a shame to have to report back that we were halted and otherwise prevented from carrying out a direct order. But, should you need further clarification on the matter, I can summon her and you can explain face-to-face what exactly you are taking issue with. I'll be sure to let her know your opinions on our cleanliness." She lifted her brows, daring him to call her bluff. Which she was desperately hoping he didn't do, since she had no idea if any of what she said was at all the threat it sounded like.

Theo could see his jaw tensing beneath his helmet. Through clenched teeth, he asked, "Which fairy?"

"Our most splendid and benevolent mistress, Cecily of the Ash Fairies." Again, she had no idea what she was saying, but was that a flash of surprise under that helmet? The sentry glared at the three of them, Kaz scowling, Phineas looking confused, and Theo trying her best to look self-assured. He lingered the longest on Theo.

"You, and only you, may go down to the cells. These two must stay here."

Kaz immediately started to argue.

"Just. Her."

"I'm so pleased we could come to an amicable solution," Theo said with a reassuring dip of her chin.

She was just about to step past the guard when Kaz grabbed her arm.

"What do you think you're doing?" he hissed, dragging her away from the sentry. "You can't go down there by yourself! You don't know what you're doing! Phineas, tell her!"

"She might as well." Phineas shrugged. "We aren't getting down there. I think it's our best option."

Kaz sputtered in disbelief. "Phineas, you can't be serious. She could easily muck this up."

"Thank you for your firm belief in my abilities, Kaz. You're the one who nearly sabotaged us, not me. I'll remind you, this is my task and I'm going to do it."

"You don't know who else or what else might be down there."

"Oh, don't act for one minute like you would care if I got eaten by some mythical beast they've got guarding the place. I'd expect you to offer me up on a silver platter."

"According to you, I wouldn't have the brainpower to coordinate it. Thanks for that, by the way. Not what I meant when I said 'catch flies with honey.'"

"You wanted polite, I gave him polite. But keep your honey, Kaz. I'd rather catch my flies with the corpses of human familiars who spout nonsense platitudes. Now, remove yourself."

She made a show of straightening her dress after he released her. "Oh, and you're welcome." She dared anyone to find candies sweeter than the smile she gave him. It only grew when batting her lashes caused his jaw to twitch.

She walked back to the sentry, who moved aside so she could pass.

Halfway down the hall, she turned and gave Kaz and Phineas a resolute wave, hoping they didn't see how nervous she was with each step farther into the corridor.

She wasn't given directions, but in an effort to look like she knew exactly what she was doing, Theo employed the same tactic she had used with Locklan and just kept walking.

At the end of the corridor, she came to a staircase. As she went down the stone steps, the lanterns became fewer and fewer, the air cooler and cooler as she realized she was probably underground.

The stairs emptied her out in another corridor, this one much shorter. The only lanterns lighting her way now were at the end, framing a wooden door. It was so dark she could hardly see the walls next to her, the air so thick and stagnant she felt as if at any moment the floor would drop out and she'd have to swim.

She quickened her pace until she was standing at the carved door, this one further reinforced with metal in the form of leaves and vines.

She knocked. A little window slid open and a pair of eyes looked out.

"I'm here to speak with one of your prisoners, a gnome by the name of Dwyn." As the pause grew longer, the eyes still not moving, she added, "On the orders of Cecily of the Ash Fairies," since that seemed to do the trick last time. The small window slid shut again and Theo heard the grinding sound of metal on metal as a lock was turned and the door swung open.

She stepped through, the guard closing and locking it behind her. She followed him down the long dungeon hallway, barred cells lining either side. The guard never turned his head, accustomed to the walk past the prisoners, but Theo couldn't help stealing glances at the occupants. She'd never been in a prison before, much less one that was host to a bevy of magical creatures. Some were sitting right at the bars, reaching their arms out and calling, others were on their cots sleeping. Not everyone appreciated her gawking like they were zoo animals, though, and while she didn't understand the languages, the gestures were universal.

When they were almost at the end of the hallway, the

guard stopped in front of a cell, pointed, then walked back to his post, leaving Theo standing alone. She looked into the dim alcove. Sitting on a cot was a very small man wearing a pointed red wool hat, with pants to match and a blue shirt. His eyes were cast down watching a spot on the floor, swinging his little brown work boots off the edge like a child in a time-out chair.

"Excuse me, sir?"

He didn't turn or make any indication that he had heard her. She had the realization that maybe he didn't understand her, which would be quite the problem, as she had no experience speaking any other languages, magical or not.

She tried again anyway.

"Excuse me. Are you the gnome Dwyn?"

The man's head slowly turned toward her.

"Is that you? Are you Dwyn?"

He nodded.

"Hello. My name is Lady Theodosia Balfour. You may call me Theo. I was sent here to help you with your trial. Can you speak with me for a bit?"

He looked at her with angry disbelief. "Why would you help me?"

"From what I was told, your punishment is unjust and I want to help free you. Can you tell me what happened?"

He hopped off his cot and came to stand at the bars. Only when he was up close did she see how tiny he was, his head only reaching her waist. So he wasn't forced to either crane his neck or speak directly to her crotch, she sank to her knees so she was eye to eye with the sad old man. Normally, she would have cared about what the dirty floor was doing to her dress, but she figured a *good person* wouldn't mind, so she wouldn't, either.

He removed his hat in the presence of a lady, the white hair on his head lying flat in a perfect imprint, and was nervously wringing it between his hands.

Prison had taken its toll on the gnome. His eyes were fierce but the circles underneath so purple it looked like he had crushed pansies to use as war paint. The exploded ball of twine that was his beard was long past the point of saving, even if he had access to pounds of grooming oil and a comb made of steel. She'd seen mice with more organized nests than what was on his poor face.

And oh, his poor face. It took a lot for Theo to feel sorry for anyone, but the little tear tracks that carved through the grime on his cheeks cut straight to her heart.

"It is unfair, Lady Theo. Horribly unfair."

She nodded her encouragement for him to continue.

"They only arrested me because it was a fairy who complained. They didn't even want to hear my side! Just threw me down here to rot!"

"But what happened? What did you do?"

He was twisting his hat so hard she was surprised it wasn't tearing.

"You can tell me. I was told that you did do what they say you did, but the punishment that they are laying on you is grossly exaggerated."

He nodded fervently, his blob of a beard a half step behind. "I turned a vineyard barren so no grapes can grow anymore."

"I see. Why'd you do it?"

"The fairy...he...he tore down my tree! My home!" The little fellow began to sob, pressing his face into his now-creased hat.

"He tore down your house? Why would someone do such a thing?"

"My home was on the edge of the vineyard and he said it was creating too much shade. He knew it was my home. I told him so. But he ripped it out of the ground anyway! He destroyed my house for some grapes! And now...now they're going to imprison me for three hundred years and bar me from my ancestral homeland!"

"When was this?"

"Fifteen years ago."

"You've been here for *fifteen years*? And they want to keep you here for three hundred more?"

Dwyn nodded again, his wet eyes threatening to overflow.

Theo was shocked. How dare they pick on this gnome! If someone had torn down her home, she'd have done far worse than corrupt some grapes.

"This is an outrage! I will not let that happen. I'll speak at your trial and make them see what a perversion of justice this is."

"You'd do that? Why?"

"Because, Dwyn, I know how it feels to be punished unfairly."

A few tears slipped out, treading the familiar trails, but he looked hopeful. She gave him her best smile in return.

"I have to go back up. I'll see you at the trial and we will fix this."

"Thank you, Lady Theo."

"Thank me when you're a free gnome again."

She left the dungeon the way she came in and cruised into the grand hall with new purpose. Kaz and Phineas found her right away and she told them what she'd learned about Dwyn. The two familiars didn't look quite as determined as she felt, but they helped Theo formulate her defense, nonetheless. As they talked and worked on her script, her confidence grew. She could do this—she could bring some actual fairness to the world.

"Whoever that fairy is, I'm going to make him regret the day he messed with Dwyn," Theo finished with conviction.

Chapter 11
Where It Becomes Quite Clear Theo Was Never Trained as a Lawyer

Theo, Kaz, and Phineas milled around, even more attendees having come in since Theo had been in the dungeon. She saw Locklan through the crowd once more, but he didn't approach again, too deep in conversation to notice Theo staring.

A hush came over the hall as three figures entered, slicing through the assembled crowd like sharks in a school of fish. As they reached the dais at the front, Theo gasped. The Woodland Elves whom she had seen earlier, with their ethereal beauty and grace, were magical. These elves were mystical, radiating otherworldly power. They were cloaked in white, the material swaying around them like they were underwater. Gold crowns sat atop their heads.

They looked like they had been stripped of all identifying

characteristics. Their skin was so devoid of color it was translucent, the veins showing through giving them a blue tint. And all three had eyes that looked like they were made of crystal. They were almost mirror images of one another, differences only marked by small tells.

Kaz noticed her gawking and elbowed her in the ribs.

"Ow! What?"

"Close your mouth and get that look off your face. You look like someone hit you over the head."

He wasn't far off. Everything she'd seen today was confusing and just kept getting more so as the day wore on.

"Who are they?" She was doing her best to put her face back to neutral, but while she had managed to close her mouth, her eyes were still as round as saucers.

Phineas, at least, understood what she meant.

"A great pride of the Court of the Woodland Elves is their impartiality. The High Justices are neither male nor female so as not to let it cloud their judgment. When they become justices, they give up that piece of themselves. Just as they give up their looks."

"And their eyes?" Theo stared into the unseeing gemstone eyes of the center High Justice.

"They are rendered blind at the start of the trials, gaining their eyesight back once they have finished. Should there be any visual evidence, a court assistant watches, then shows them only the parts they need to see." Phineas pointed subtly to an elf in a silver robe standing to the side of the dais wearing a crown of a much smaller caliber.

"I'm supposed to speak in front of them." She wasn't sure if that was a statement, question, or maybe a plea to get her out of here.

Kaz chimed in again. "When you speak, you address them as a unit, no matter who asks a question. Refer to them as High Justices, or Your Graces. Nothing else. Again, just be polite and respectful."

She nodded only a little, afraid that any larger movement would make her throw up from nerves.

Court started in earnest not too long after. Prisoners were brought up from the dungeon, some having another speaking on their behalf, others defending themselves. The cases ran the gamut from petty theft all the way to a stabbing, which was declared by the High Justices to be an act of passion instead of a premeditated case of cold-blooded murder. But the perpetrator, a broonie who stood no taller than Theo's knee, was still sentenced to five thousand years in prison.

While intimidated, she had to admit the High Justices were unbiased and impartial. Surely the justices would see truth and reason for Dwyn and his case. As the day wore on, turning into early evening, Theo's assuredness grew.

Just as Theo was beating down the desire to demand her case be heard, she saw Dwyn being led in front of the thrones, shackles on his ankles and wrists. He was looking around the crowd. Looking for her, she realized. When they locked eyes, his face lit up and she did her best to look confident and encouraging.

She didn't let him see, but anger rippled through her. What did they have against this old gnome? Even that murdering broonie wasn't shackled.

She just had to hope that the same fairness that had been granted to the others was granted to Dwyn.

No, she wouldn't hope. She would *make* them give him a fair trial.

The center High Justice's voice rang out across the hall. Theo had heard the resilient sound echoing over the heads of everyone all afternoon, but now it felt like it pierced straight into her stomach, coiling around it and squeezing. As much as she was incensed about Dwyn's treatment, she was nervous. How she wished she had found a bathroom before now.

"Dwyn, Garden Gnome of Shady Hollow, you are accused of rendering the grounds of a sacred fairy vineyard barren and infertile with a blight."

Sacred?

"Does anyone wish to speak for the accused?"

Theo didn't move until Kaz nudged her.

"I do." Theo tried to sound sure of herself as her voice resonated over the heads of the assembly and across the hall. Phineas patted her on the back as she walked toward the front to stand next to Dwyn.

"Will the accuser please come forward."

She heard heavy footsteps behind her, and her righteous anger flared again. She might be a lowly human to everyone else, but the High Justices were blind and hadn't asked who or what she was. She could defend Dwyn against this overbearing fairy who sought to harass a homeless gnome. Dwyn stiffened beside her as the fairy stopped in front of the justices.

Theo turned to look at the accuser and destroyer of homes and saw Locklan.

Smiling at her.

She whirled to Dwyn. "*That's* whose vineyard you destroyed?"

He nodded sadly.

"The accused may speak first."

It took Theo a moment to realize the High Justices were talking to her. Showtime. She could do this. She could fight for the side of justice. She could free Dwyn and show Cecily she could make a difference and be a good person. In fact, in this moment for the sorrowful gnome counting on her, she wanted to be.

She cleared her throat, hoping her voice wouldn't shake too much.

"Thank you, High Justices," Theo began. "The gnome Dwyn has not denied that he has committed that which he is accused of. He could have pretended that he didn't do it, but he has come before you wanting the truth to be heard. I am certain you will feel as I do about this case after hearing his motive.

"You see, Your Graces, Dwyn's tree—his ancestral home—sat on the edge of the vineyard. It was shading the vineyard, which I would like to remind the High Justices is what trees do, not something Dwyn can control. The accuser threatened to tear down the tree, and even after Dwyn explained it was his home, the accuser did it anyway. He destroyed Dwyn's home for some grapes. In his anguish and despair, Dwyn rendered the ground barren. So no other gnome in the neighboring trees would have to suffer the same fate. In his actions, he has saved countless other homes."

Was lying in court considered the mark of a good person?

Maybe, if it was lying to help Dwyn. No, not quite a lie. So she embellished a bit. Maybe it was true? Who was to say that Locklan wouldn't have torn down the entire forest?

The High Justices nodded, the center elf then inviting Locklan to speak.

The corners of his mouth were quirked up. Not a good sign.

"That was quite an impassioned defense, but I'm afraid Lady Theodosia has left out a bit of important information. The vineyard that we are discussing has been one of the producers of our ceremonial wine for half a millennium. The tree in question was eighty years old. While Lady Theodosia is correct that I tore down the tree, that conversation first began when Dwyn planted the tree on the edge of the vineyard."

"You planted the tree?" Theo hissed at Dwyn.

Locklan continued. "I had tried to explain that while the land on which the tree was planted is not under my stewardship, law dictates I do have the authority to protect the vineyard from that which would harm it, in this case, a fast-growing tree that would block the sun for the entire day. In my attempt to explain this to Dwyn, he, in more colorful and less polite terms, told me to go away."

So what? Theo thought, her indignation rising. *What is with their insistence on civility? Is no one ever allowed to be unkind to a fairy without having their house ripped down?*

"Excuse me, High Justices, but how is that relevant to the issue? Is he on trial for being rude? Is he not allowed to speak freely to you, Locklan, or is that another charge I was unaware of?"

"She is correct," the left High Justice said, hands folded in their lap. "We will disregard that statement."

Locklan raised his eyebrows at her as she smirked. Got him. Dwyn smiled up at her.

"Please continue," the middle High Justice said, waving an elegant hand toward Locklan.

"As the tree grew I compromised, trimming it back at my own expense to encourage cooperation. Then the tree started dying. When I tried to explain to Dwyn that if the tree collapsed it would destroy his home and wreck the vines I've been trying to save, he ignored my warnings. The only solution I saw was to remove the tree. I offered to help him find new accommodations in his ancestral homeland of Shady Hollow, but he refused."

Huh?

She looked at Dwyn. "I thought you already lived in Shady Hollow?"

"No, I said my ancestral home was Shady Hollow. The tree wasn't there. The tree was at the vineyard." Dwyn said it like she was some sort of dolt for not knowing where Shady Hollow was.

But no matter. This was salvageable. His home was still destroyed, regardless of location.

Locklan hadn't stopped. "Which I thought was highly unusual, so I did some investigating. Turns out the reason he wanted to live next to the vineyard was so he could make wine. I discovered he had been stealing the grapes—our *sacred* grapes—and using them to make wine in his basement, and then selling it illegally."

A few in the assembled crowd gasped.

"*You did what?!* That is an important tidbit of information, *don't you think*?!" Theo ground out. Dwyn at least had the good sense to look slightly ashamed.

Theo spoke up again. "High Justices, he is not on trial for making and selling wine, so I don't see how that information is relevant."

Locklan was smiling at her like this was all a game. "I am not the one who brought up motives, Lady Theodosia. I'm simply responding to your allegation that he did so purely as revenge for me tearing down the tree, which I am saying is not quite the full story."

Theo scowled. This was not going the way she had planned. For all that preparation, Theo, Phineas, and Kaz had not prepared for Dwyn being a giant liar.

"The accuser is correct. We will take it into consideration. Please continue."

"I confronted him with the evidence and he once again gave me colorful directions as to where to put my head."

"Again, not a crime!" Theo belted out a bit more desperate and high-pitched than she had intended.

"Apologies. After our delightful conversation, I had to make the decision to remove the tree to prevent further damage to the vineyard, as well as put a stop to the illegal activity. Dwyn retaliated, destroying the vineyard by putting a blight on the grapes so they would no longer produce. We have not been able to use that vineyard for wine production since."

Theo's stomach was somewhere in a puddle around her feet. She was supposed to be standing up for what was good and right. And now she was trying—and failing spectacularly—at defending a vengeful, shortsighted, foul-mouthed gnome moonlighting as a black marketeer.

"I am asking that Dwyn remove the blight and serve three hundred years, as well as banishment from Shady Hollow," Locklan finished.

"I will not remove the blight! I will never remove the blight!" Dwyn started screaming and rattling his manacles, making Theo swear in surprise.

"High Justices," Theo said after collecting herself. "Setting aside motives for a moment, the punishment of three hundred years seems rather excessive. Additionally, a banishment seems to go past the point of justice into retribution and vindictiveness. This is someone's life being compared to grapes."

Locklan held up a finger. "Three hundred years would be the standard length of incarceration for this sort of thing, Lady Theodosia. And the banishment was not my idea. I was specifically requested by the Gnome Governor of Shady Hollow to have Dwyn permanently removed from the settlement."

"What? Well, doesn't three hundred years seem excessive to anyone else? He's already served fifteen years for the crime and he's sorry." She was trying her best to sound impassioned, but it was coming out more as a frustrated whine. Flo would be proud.

"Not sorry enough to remove the blight," Locklan said.

"I will not!" Dwyn added helpfully.

"Shut up, Dwyn!" Theo begged the belligerent gnome.

The middle High Justice spoke. "The years he has spent at the Court of the Woodland Elves Prison are unrelated to the

143

charge here. He has served fifteen years for assaulting a guard when he was initially arrested. It was fortunate that healers were able to reattach the guard's nose."

The High Justice had been quite stern, but Theo could see Locklan holding in a laugh.

Theo rounded on Dwyn, barely able to keep her voice down. "*Are you kidding me?* You took off someone's *nose*? What is *wrong* with you?!"

No wonder Dwyn was shackled. He was arguably the most violent criminal they had brought in so far, homicidal broonie be damned.

"Do you have anything else to add to Dwyn's defense before the High Justices render their verdict?" the middle High Justice asked.

"I...I..." *Shit.* She failed on her first task. She and Dwyn would both be sent to their respective prisons. Maybe they could trade places. Slap a dress on Dwyn, and the duke probably wouldn't notice. He might even find the gnome more attractive. He'd surely enjoy Dwyn's fighting spirit.

But before the High Justices could say anything further, Locklan spoke. "High Justices, if it pleases you, I would like to invoke a parley. May we take a recess so I may speak to Lady Theodosia in private and we might come to some sort of agreement?"

The High Justices considered, then nodded. "Parley is granted. This case will take a recess and recommence when the parties have returned."

Locklan turned to Theo, inclined his head toward a door, and started walking, a court attendant leading him out an archway. Kaz and Phineas took up places beside her, leaving Dwyn behind in the grand hall. They followed Locklan to a small room with a long table and chairs in the center.

"No, no. I do not wish to speak to the forest critters. Just the beautiful Lady Theodosia, thank you." Locklan ushered Theo inside and shut the door in the faces of Kaz and Phineas.

"Please have a seat," he said, gesturing to a chair. He sat down opposite her, his forearms resting on the table. "Hello again, gorgeous." He gave her a flirty half grin. "I didn't realize Dwyn was such a hero to the other gnomes with his honorable blight. Did he leave out some crucial details when he was sobbing to you in the dungeons or were you just taking some wild liberties?"

A little bit of both, but Theo was not about to say so. Instead, she scowled and made a noise somewhere between a sigh and a snort. Did he really need to start the meeting with an insult to her looks and a dig at her failings?

"What do you want, Locklan?"

"Are you familiar with what a parley is?"

"First you belittle my appearance and now my common sense?" She gave him a hateful little smile. "I'm sure you must think yourself very original, but you're walking a well-worn path."

A look of confusion flickered on his face. "Belittle you?"

"If you're asking if I know what talking is, then yes, Locklan, I'm familiar." She put a hand to her chest with a look of mock innocence. "Oh, pardon me, was that tone rude? Should we call for the jailer to take me away and lock me up due to your delicate sensibilities?"

He tipped his head back and laughed. "Each time we talk, I like you more and more."

"If only I felt the same. Did you call a parley just to lob insults? I hope so. Like Dwyn, I, too, can think of many fanciful ways to tell you where I think your head should go." She crossed her arms and placed them on the table, matching his posture.

"Insults? When did I insult you?"

She waved a hand. "Did you call me in here just to gloat, then?"

"Oh, no, I was having way too much fun out there to want it to stop. But I figured I should put you out of your misery."

"Why? You won. If you hadn't stopped it, you'd have gotten everything you wanted."

"Not quite everything."

"Then let's get on with this, Locklan. Stop being coy and parley what you need to parley."

"I need the blight gone."

"You heard the tiny terror. He said 'never' and aside from asking nicely, which I don't think he's going to go for, I have no way of making him do that. You'll have to have the High Justices force him to remove it."

"They actually *can't* force him to. But you might be able to. You still have a bit of currency I don't think you're aware of."

"Oh? And what is that?"

"You are a mortal."

"Astute. A few helpful guards made it quite clear earlier that was a glaring shortcoming."

"Not in this instance, Lady Theodosia. To take him at his

word, no matter how long he goes to prison for, he won't remove the blight that he put on my vineyard."

"What does that have to do with me being mortal?"

"There is an old law, a loophole, if you will, that says mortals can take on the debt of an immortal."

"So?"

"So, he could be released from prison today. You can take on the debt for Dwyn, then you'd settle the debt with the court, and he would owe you instead. Since you are in the employ of Cecily, he would owe her."

This loophole seemed rather cruel.

"You want me to go to prison for three hundred years instead of Dwyn? As you pointed out, I'm mortal. I'd die before a third of the sentence was served. I will not be doing that."

"I don't want you to go to prison for three hundred years, and since I'm the accuser, I can request what I wish your debt to me will be."

"I'd owe a debt directly to you," she said, enough suspicion coating her voice to paint the room.

"Yes." Locklan smiled innocently.

"What would you want, then?" What sort of horrible punishment would make up for three hundred years in an Elf Prison? She'd read plenty of fairy tales. Dance until she died? A toad attached to her face? Bugs spilling out of her mouth whenever she spoke? He did seem pretty irritated about his sacred vineyard, and it would surely have to be horrid to replace three hundred years of incarceration.

"Are you musically inclined?"

"What?"

"Do you play an instrument?"

"I play the harp."

"Perfect. I am in need of someone to play music."

"Play music?"

"For a party I'm having."

"You want me to play the harp at a party?"

"Yes."

"Until I die?"

"What? No."

"Not for three hundred years, though."

"You seem very hung up on that number."

"I don't trust an immortal to have any understanding of my by-comparison tiny lifespan."

"Just one night."

"That's it? You're going to pretend this whole vineyard debacle didn't happen if I play music at a party you're having? Forgive me for being a wee bit skeptical."

Locklan laughed. "No. Dwyn also has to remove the blight before he is released."

"But you don't even know if I can play all that well."

"I'm sure you'll do fine."

"How do you know Dwyn will remove the blight if I take on his debt? He seemed quite adamant."

"I'm sure he will if it means walking out of here today."

"But—"

"Look, I know I'm immortal and have nothing but time, but this is getting tedious. Are you willing to accept my offer? You take on the gnome's debt, owing it to me and playing the harp at my party. Dwyn removes the blight and leaves a free gnome, owing the debt to you, and in turn, Cecily."

"What about the banishment?"

"Honestly, that's between him and the governor of Shady Hollow. I don't even know what kind of torment he unleashed upon them if he's not wanted there. But I am curious." His eyes lit up. "How about this? If you can find out and tell me at the party, I'll take an hour off of your time owed to me."

Theo watched him for a moment. There must be a catch here. But she couldn't seem to find it. Was this a good deal? He purposely left Kaz and Phineas out of the room. Was it so he could trick her? Would Cecily be upset that she made another bargain with another fairy? Or would she be more upset that Theo turned it down and didn't get Dwyn released? She did say at all costs. "Fine. It's a deal."

"As much as I love hearing those words as a fairy, it isn't until we get it approved by the High Justices, so let's go do that and I can get home and you can get our delightful friend Dwyn his freedom."

Chapter 12

Where a Garden Trowel Is Either a Great or a Terrible Weapon Depending on Whether You're on the Wielding or Receiving End

Kaz and Phineas were standing outside the door when Locklan opened it to escort Theo back to the great hall, his arm out for her to hold. She dismissed him with a look of disdain. He winked and walked off.

"So, how'd it go?" Phineas asked when Locklan was a fair bit ahead of them.

"You know, I have no idea. I just made another fairy bargain, though. Make of that what you wish."

"You did what? What did you bargain away?" Kaz asked.

"I'm playing harp at a party?"

"For three hundred years?"

"That's what I asked! But no. One night. And Dwyn has to remove the blight. I don't know. Seemed like a good deal at the time, but feel free to do your usual, Kaz, and tell me how foolish I am."

Kaz shrugged. "No, actually that seems pretty good. Just playing the harp, right? There were no other words that he sneaked in?"

"Not as far as I could tell. So now all there is to do is get it approved by the High Justices."

When they returned to the grand hall, Locklan was already letting a court attendant know they had finished their meeting. As soon as the High Justices concluded the case in front of them, they called Locklan and Theo back.

Dwyn was returned to the hall and took his spot next to Theo.

"I believe I negotiated a pretty good deal for you, Dwyn. Surprising, but your outbursts about not ever removing the blight gave you a tiny advantage."

"And I stand by that! Never will I remove the rot that has infested the land!"

"You will if you'd like to walk out of here right now. That's what he wanted."

Dwyn narrowed his eyes, giving her a suspicious look. "What about the banishment?"

"He said he'd leave that to the governor."

"Ha! Which means I'll never be banished! That coward! There's a reason that little slug had to ask a big fairy to do his dirty work."

Theo was just about to ask him what he did that was so bad, but court had started.

Instead, they smiled at each other.

The whole time they were talking to each other, Locklan had been laying out the terms of the bargain. The High Justices turned their attention to Dwyn.

"And you, Dwyn of Shady Hollow, agree to remove the blight fully and completely, resolving your debt to this court and the accuser?"

"Yes!" Then added, "Your Graces!" when Theo whispered it to him.

"And, Lady Theodosia Balfour, as a mortal you agree to take on the debt owed to the accuser by the terms already agreed to, thus the debt owed of Dwyn be transferred to your favor?"

"Yes, High Justices."

"The High Justices will agree to your terms to see this matter settled. Dwyn, upon release you will immediately end the blight, the transfer of your debt to Lady Theodosia Balfour complete. Should you not remove the blight, the debt owed to Lady Theodosia Balfour will be void and you will be remanded to the Prison of the Woodland Elves for the duration of three hundred years."

The three High Justices each raised a hand, palms facing the crowd. Lights glowed in their hands for a brief moment, sealing the agreement with magic. As soon as the light dimmed, the guards were leading Dwyn away. Theo followed, wanting to see for herself that Dwyn was released, Kaz and Phineas a step behind her.

Kaz was reaching into his jacket's inside pocket as Phineas gave her a small nudge. "You did it!"

"Did you have doubts?"

"Me? Never! Kaz might have taken one look at you and declared this task an abject failure, but not me."

"I said no such thing." Kaz shook his head and sighed, Theo chuckling at his response. He held out his hand, offering Theo a coin.

"What's this?" She picked up the little gold coin and examined it. Cecily's profile was on one side, a leaf embossed on the other.

"A coin for Dwyn. Sort of a symbol of the debt he owes her. The bargain is sealed in magic already from the court to you. This passes on the debt to Cecily. Final piece of your task."

She smiled at the coin in her hand, high off her success, and then again when she looked at Dwyn, who was speaking with Locklan. Dwyn made a series of complicated movements with his hands and then bowed. Locklan nodded to Dwyn, then to the guards who began to unshackle Dwyn and return his tools.

He buckled a baldric on himself like he was a warrior. But instead of weapons, he had garden trowels of varying sizes, forks, a handheld scythe, scissors, and strapped to his back like a sword, a garden spade. The handles were smooth from what must have been hundreds of years of work, the wood darkened where his hands touched, mottling them like turtle shells. But the fine metal from which the business ends were crafted gleamed like jewelry under the lantern lights, the impressive points glinting like they had been freshly sharpened. It was clear he had done a masterful job caring for them, and their time apart did not seem to do them much harm.

All she had left to do was give Dwyn the coin and her first task was done. She felt a small swell of pride in herself. But more than that, looking at Dwyn, his chest puffed out, head held high, she felt happy. While she knew it was the entire point of the task, she did feel like a better person for helping Dwyn without any reward for herself.

When he had finished he turned to Theo, looking for all the world like he was going to battle a garden.

"Well, Lady Theo, I can't thank you enough for all you did for me. When I first saw you, I thought there was no way an insignificant mortal was going to help me at all. But you did. You are much smarter than you look." The gnome was beaming as though he was heaping on the highest praise.

"Uh, thank you, Dwyn. And thank you for letting me help you. Just don't do anything that puts you back in jail. I don't want to have to make any more bargains for you again." She winked as he chuckled.

"Then I guess this is goodbye!"

"No," Theo said. "Just a 'see you later.'"

She held out her hand with the coin for Dwyn to take. But much to Theo's surprise, he took one look at the coin and balked.

"Wait, what is that?"

Theo could see the wheels of comprehension spin and sputter in his head like a confused mule at a cider press.

"A coin for the debt you owe," Theo said, stopping him before his brain could grind to a full halt.

"To you?"

"That's how I secured your release. I took your debt."

"I thought that meant you'd just pay the debt! What are you going to make me do?"

"You thought I would just take your debt and you'd do nothing? Not how this works, Dwyn. Plus, I can't make you do anything since I am working for a fairy, so you'll owe her. She told me to give you this."

"A fairy?" Dwyn gasped and took a step backward, looking in horror at the coin in her still-outstretched hand like it would come alive and eat him. But then his eyes turned ferocious as he glared at Theo. "You...you...you lying traitor! You deceitful squash beetle! Get that away from me! Get away from me!"

"Excuse me?, I just set you free!"

"No, no, you horrible cabbage worm, you betrayed me!"

"I did no such thing. Now take the coin and we can leave."

"Get away! Help! Mortals are attacking me! Get away, you spider mite!"

"No one is attacking you! Take the coin!"

"NO!"

Before Theo could take his hand and drop the coin in, Dwyn spun around and took off running down the corridor.

Without thinking, she sprinted after him, catching up in a few short strides, and grabbed his shoulder. Dwyn yelled out as he turned, one of his sparkling tools in his hand.

"Now wait just one minute—" she said.

But a quick pressure and a sharp pain cut her off. Both Theo and Dwyn stared at each other, shocked. Dwyn broke first, looking back down at her stomach. She followed his eyeline and saw, sticking out of her dress, one of his well-worn handles that he had strapped to himself. Which was weird because what could that be doing there?

Dwyn yelped and fled again, but Theo wasn't paying much attention. She was still fixated on the garden tool just beneath and a little to the left of her belly button. The sudden explosion of pain burst through her confusion and was radiating outward from the implanted trowel.

Kaz caught up first and took in her look of shock.

"I've . . . I've been stabbed!"

"What?"

Theo's response wasn't to explain the situation further. Rather, she started screaming.

"It's fine, Theo. It's fine." He was talking fast, hands up in front of him like she was a startled horse he was going to catch before she ran off.

"It is not fine, Kaz! I've been stabbed with a garden trowel!"

"Easy, easy. You'll heal quickly. It's all right." His tone seemed to suggest he knew she wasn't so much about to fall to pieces as ready to leap.

"That gnome stabbed me, Kaz!"

He guided her toward the wall. She put her hands on either side of the trowel, not daring to touch it. The pain was becoming even more intense as the adrenaline started to recede, her side throbbing around the metal intrusion.

"Theo, I'm going to pull this out. It is going to hurt."

"It hurts already!"

Phineas had just caught up and froze when he saw Kaz and Theo.

"You've been stabbed!" The pink of his cheeks started to drain, taking all his other color with it, leaving him looking almost gray. "Oh, no. No, no. I have to go. I can't. No, no, no." His hand went to his mouth like he was going to vomit and he tore down the hall the same way Dwyn had run.

"Ignore him," Kaz said, Theo noting that someone sprinting away in horror while retching was a bad sign. "Are you ready?"

Before she could even nod, he grabbed the handle and yanked, the trowel coming out with a stream of blood. She shrieked and swore, doubling over until Kaz pushed her upright again, pressing her against the wall. He threw the trowel to the floor behind him as he knelt in front of her, gathering the bottom of her skirts and using the extra material to press on the open wound.

She looked at the trowel on the ground, red viscous liquid now coating the blade, reflecting the lantern light—her blood. Kaz's hands were also coated crimson, the wound having seeped through a layer of fabric already. Theo would be the first to admit she wasn't a doctor, but she was relatively confident that too much of it was now on the outside of her body.

Her breath was coming in short gasps, the air not quite reaching to the bottom of her lungs. But no matter how fast she inhaled, she still felt like it wasn't enough, like all the air had been sucked out of the room.

"It really hurts," she cried out, her voice sounding like it belonged to someone else far away.

It was overwhelming, every sensation in her body funneling down to her sliced-open abdomen and turning to agony, and she was getting woozier by the second.

"Kaz...Kaz...I don't feel good."

"You just have to hold on until the wound closes. Theo?"

He had been working with cool determination, trying to stymie the bleeding, but looking at her, he stopped.

"Sit down," he commanded, helping her slide down the wall.

But her heart was pounding. Pounding so hard she could feel it in her head. It was too fast. If it was this fast, that meant it was pumping blood out of her at this speed. And at this speed, she would surely bleed out.

"I'm going to die. I'm going to die. I'm dying, I'm dying, I'm dying." She hadn't put much thought into how she would go, but gutted with a trowel by a garden gnome in a corridor of an elf palace that up until this morning was make-believe had definitely not made the list.

"No! Look at me!" He was shouting at her. Because that's what she needed in this moment, she thought. Someone yelling at her.

She closed her eyes and wrapped her arms around herself as a sob burst free from between gasps.

She felt warm hands on the sides of her face pulling her head away from the wall.

"Theo, look at me." This time his voice was gentle, and it was so surprising, she opened her eyes. Kaz was only inches from her face, staring straight into her eyes.

"There, good. Keep looking at me. Keep your eyes on me."

She'd never stared at anyone in their eyes before, certainly not from this close a distance. The feeling was so jarring it shook her from her panic and pain. She was hit by the instinctual urge to look away first before he could be upset and stop helping. She knew he wasn't particularly fond of her, but in this moment, she needed his kindness, and needed him to not be disgusted by her. Needed him to not leave her alone. She couldn't go through this alone.

Not again.

"Just keep looking at me. Breathe. I'll do it with you, just follow me. Watch me and breathe."

She returned her eyes to his, Kaz never wavering, never looking away. Just staring and staring at her, sharing deep, mirrored breaths as the pain began to retreat.

His eyes were beautiful. She didn't know if it was the lack of blood or something else entirely, but she was falling into their beautiful depths. She wondered if he knew there were streaks of amber in them, like someone had mixed molasses and honey together.

She kept breathing with him as the pain lessened. A tingling feeling like ice had been pressed onto her—the gash was closing. Kaz never let her go, never stopped breathing slow and steady.

After a moment, he must have realized she was no longer panicking.

"Are you all right now?"

"I...I think so?" Her breath was steady, her body felt like all its pieces were in the right place and whole. "I can't believe I got stabbed by a gnome."

Kaz laughed, his shoulders dropping with a release of tension, his eyes crinkling at the corners. She wondered if she'd ever have noticed if he wasn't still so close. It was the first time she'd seen him genuinely amused, and she didn't know how, but it made him even more attractive.

Realizing she was no longer in great pain, in another intimate gesture, he wiped away her remaining tears and stood.

"How does your stomach feel? You think you can walk now?" He extended his hand.

She nodded. "It feels like I was punched in the stomach really hard."

He smiled. "Better than feeling like you've been stabbed, that's for sure. You might be sore for a few days, but it should go away soon."

He pulled her to her feet, giving her hand a squeeze.

Once standing, she gingerly touched the spot where the trowel came in and went out. There was only a bit of tenderness and an angry red slash beneath the hole in her torn and bloody dress.

"Surprisingly, you get used to it," Kaz said as she inspected herself. "Lucky he only got you in the side. Bigger injuries take a bit longer to heal."

"Have you been stabbed before?"

"Oh yeah." He laughed. "Been shot, too. Hurts every time. It's scary the first few times it happens, though. They say you'll heal fast, but it's hard to believe when your blood is pouring out of you."

"Yes, exactly." Then she added, "Thank you."

"Don't mention it." He shrugged.

She put a hand on his arm, bringing him to a stop. "No, I want to mention it. You could have left me by myself or ignored me, but you didn't. It wouldn't have been the first time. And I appreciate it."

He watched her, his expression unreadable. "I would have never let you experience that alone."

She smiled in gratitude laced with a tinge of sadness, knowing Kaz had no idea just how much his words meant to her in that moment.

"So what do we do now?" Theo asked, picking up the coin from the floor.

"Well, we find Dwyn and give him that coin. He couldn't have gotten far. Want me to do it and you can stay here?"

"No. No, I'm coming." That gnome hadn't seen the last of her.

They made their way down the corridor to the sentry standing at the entrance to the grand hall.

"Excuse me, sir? Did you see a gnome running by here a few minutes ago?" Kaz asked.

The guard nodded and pointed to the moss road.

They picked up their pace to a jog, the path now a dark pine green in a sea of black, the luminaries only offering small circles of light.

Theo looked around. "Where's Phineas?"

"He'll catch up."

But then they heard a rustling noise in the woods up ahead.

"Kaz! Theo! I got him!"

They reached Phineas just as he was coming onto the path, hauling a struggling Dwyn by the shirt collar, his baldric no longer on him. Phineas looked as though he'd been in quite a scrap. His ponytail was tangled with twigs and leaves, and even in the dim light, Theo could see a black eye forming. Dwyn had one to match.

Theo marched over to Dwyn and stuck a finger in his chest. "Listen here, you landscaping pocket demon! I stood up for you! I believed in you! I trusted you! I got you released from Elf Prison! You lied to me the entire time and then stabbed me with a garden trowel! That really hurts! You are lucky that your weapons are missing because I am murderously curious to see if you'd survive a stabbing like the one you gave me! Here is the coin." He was flailing and kicking, but this time she went for his shirt pocket, dropping it in with a smirk. "Bye now, Dwyn."

Phineas released his hold and Dwyn fell to the ground like a sack of sand. He got to his feet and pointed a finger at Theo. At first she was afraid he might be getting ready to curse her but instead he shouted, "I hate you, you *thrip*!"

"The feeling is mutual!" she shouted back as he ran into the forest.

The three of them stared at him until he was swallowed up by the darkness. Theo turned to Phineas. "Are you all right?"

Phineas rubbed his swollen jaw. "You wouldn't think he is very quick, but he's got lightning fists, that one. I only just missed your fate by yanking the baldric off him and throwing it as hard as I could behind me."

Theo turned to the snorting noise coming from Kaz. He was looking at the ground, biting a knuckle, his mouth twitching. She couldn't help the giggle that escaped her, the sound releasing whatever hold Kaz had over himself. Phineas joined in and soon the trio was doubled over laughing.

Someone cleared their throat close behind them.

"Seems like I missed some fun." Locklan smiled, but it changed into a look of horror when he took in Theo. "Are you all right?"

"I'm well, thank you. Dwyn decided to show his thanks by stabbing me with a garden trowel. I appreciate your concern." Theo curtsied, holding out her skirts that were still wet and painted in blood. Locklan swore, causing the trio to burst into laughter again.

"I'm glad it didn't dull your sparkle, Lady Theodosia."

"What can I do for you, Locklan?" Theo asked when their bout of laughter subsided.

"I am just reminding you of the debt you owe me."

"Short lifespan, not short memory."

He smiled. "It's in two nights. At nine, sit at your harp and start to play."

"That's all?"

"That's all. I'll get you from there. See you soon, gorgeous." He winked, then vanished into nothing.

She snorted. "He's a real piece of work, that one."

"Are you ready, then, Theo?" Phineas asked, ignoring her remark.

"To do what?"

"To go home."

Before she could respond, a wind whipped around them, clouding the forest from view. She had expected to see the frog fountain again, but when the wind cleared she was standing on the steps of a very large manor.

———————————●———————————

With zero fanfare, Phineas ushered the other two through the front doors into a cavernous foyer. A massive crystal chandelier high above them was casting a warm light on the white marble below, rich gray veins making the floor look like giant sheets of a cracking glacier. Two staircases wound up from either side to the second level, the black wood banisters and railings carved to look like slithering snakes.

On both sides of the foyer and beyond were doorways leading to places Theo couldn't see from her vantage point. Only one had light coming from it.

"So, gentlemen, this isn't my home," Theo said.

Phineas laughed. "Ah, right, sorry. We went to our home. Cecily's house. Where Kaz and I live."

"You live here?"

"Sure do!"

Before any of them could move, Cecily's voice rang out from one of the side rooms.

"Are those my dearest familiars I hear?"

"It is! Your faithful, humble, undeniably attractive servants have returned. Kaz is here, too," Phineas called to the other room. Kaz rolled his eyes as Phineas grinned in a way that Theo had noticed was reserved for whatever inside joke he and Cecily shared.

Theo followed the two familiars into a drawing room just as ornate as the foyer. Cecily was sprawled out on a plush chaise longue still looking as elegant as ever, but stretching like the three of them had just interrupted her nap. She pushed herself up to sitting as Phineas planted a kiss on her cheek. He sank down in the chair next to her while Kaz fell into another one.

Cecily took in Theo, still standing.

"Oh, where are my manners? Welcome to my home, my

sanguinary Theo. Have a seat. By the look of you, you have quite a story to tell. Wine?" As she said the word, a glass of wine appeared in the hands of Phineas and Kaz, as well as Cecily.

"Uh, sure. I mean, yes please."

A glass of dandelion wine appeared in her hand, its golden hue glowing like a sunrise. She took a small sip—tart and delicious, it was like spring had exploded on her tongue.

"So," Cecily began, eyes dark with mischief. "Since none of you are on your knees begging forgiveness, I'm assuming it went well and Dwyn now has a coin of mine in his possession?"

Kaz snorted. Theo was let in on the joke by Phineas. "She's never actually made us do that."

"Hey, don't give away all my secrets. She just got here."

"My apologies, my fairy queen and mistress," Phineas said with a grin.

"Anyway, who wants to start with why Theo is covered in blood?"

"She was stabbed," Kaz said matter-of-factly.

Theo didn't know what she thought Cecily's reaction would be, but it certainly wasn't the one she got.

Cecily put a hand to her heart and looked at Theo with a proud smile. "Stabbed? On your first-ever fairy task?" She said it like Theo was a five-year-old child who had just learned to tie her shoes. But Theo was smiling right back. Now that she was healed, the whole thing felt like a distant memory.

"By a gnome," Phineas said, drumming up suspense.

Cecily's eyebrows raised in anticipation, knowing by Phineas's tone he had one more morsel up his sleeve.

"With a garden trowel to the gut."

Cecily roared with laughter. She wiped her eyes as she looked at Theo, raising her glass. "Well then, let's all toast to Theo on the night of her stabbing. Job well done on the completion of your first task."

Cecily, Kaz, and Phineas held up their glasses to her. Theo was surprised at the genuine approval that was coming from Cecily, but couldn't help smiling in return.

"Oh, and let's fix this," she said, motioning to Theo's dress. With a quick flick of her wrist the blood was gone, the hole repaired, and the dress looking like it had at the beginning of the day.

"I do have a question, though. What's a thrip?" Theo asked after a few more sips of wine.

Cecily choked on her wine and laughed harder, Kaz and Phineas joining in.

"Did he call you one?"

Theo nodded.

"We toasted too soon! A thrip is a bug considered to be a pest. For a garden gnome, there's really no higher insult."

"He also called me a spider mite and a cabbage worm," Theo said, making Cecily cackle.

"Also," Theo continued. "If you'll forgive me for asking, did you set the fire in the duke's guest wing?"

Cecily's eyebrows creased in confusion. "Set fire to a castle? Of course not!"

Just as Theo was about to apologize, the fairy's face changed to a smirk. "It was Kaz who lit the match, since it was his idea. Phineas carried the bucket of oil."

When Theo looked to Kaz, he grinned.

"I did write the letter, though," Cecily said.

"Well, thank you," Theo said. And she meant it.

For the first time in a long time, sitting among a fairy and her two familiars drinking and laughing, Theo was having fun.

Cecily conjured fruits and cheeses to accompany the endless wine as Theo, Kaz, and Phineas recounted the day's events to Cecily's great amusement. When Theo came to the part about Locklan's bargain, Cecily seemed pleased and even said she'd make sure to dress Theo for the occasion, telling her that when she got dressed to put a gold leaf in her pocket and her ensemble would transform. To a drunk Theo, it made perfect sense.

———————————•———————————

At some point late in the evening, Theo must have fallen asleep because when she woke she was no longer in Cecily's house, but back in her own bed, morning sunlight streaming through her windows. The green dress was gone, as was any sign that she had been bloodied up at all. Even after touching and prodding the spot where she'd been stabbed, she found no pain, redness, or mark that would suggest she'd been cut open.

Thinking on Dwyn and the stabbing, she had a little fluttering feeling that had been frustrating her since they left the Court of the Woodland Elves. She was supposed to have helped Dwyn, and even though the others assured her that she did, his over-the-top reaction to the conclusion of his case didn't make her feel like she had helped him very much at all.

But the feeling floated away when she got to her dressing table and spied one little gold leaf, as though it had been plucked off the chains of the dress she had been wearing.

She wasn't surprised that neither her sister nor her mother had noticed she'd been missing. But it was a bit disappointing. No questions at breakfast about her whereabouts the evening before meant that neither of them had poked a head into her room to check up on her. As far as they knew, she'd been at the manor alone all day, so they just assumed she'd done nothing, and there wasn't even a polite ask of how she fared by herself.

No, as usual, they spent the following day talking about themselves.

Chapter 13

Where Unlike Some Other Gatherings, at This Party the Harp Is Very Popular

The following day, Theo was preparing for a fairy party. She had some songs memorized but did not want to be embarrassed by losing herself to nerves and forgetting every song she'd ever learned. So she searched through the sheet music collection, selecting her favorites and others that would be appropriate for a party, as well as showcase her abilities.

She tuned her harp for good measure, then got dressed and ready. When it was close to nine, she returned to the music room, triple-checking that the leaf given to her by Cecily was in her pocket before she sat at her harp. Blending in and going unnoticed by the other magical beings at the Court of the Woodland Elves had made her want to look the part at this fairy gathering as well.

She also rechecked the sheet music, making sure it was on the stand exactly where she had put it only this morning. Of course, since no one else ever came into the music room, it was all present and accounted for, waiting and ready to be played.

The clock on the mantel read five minutes to nine and she figured she had better warm up.

She started strumming, loosening up her fingers and trying not to dwell on the fact that she'd be performing in front of people. She had never played in front of a crowd, her mother insisting that a recital for anyone other than guests in a drawing room would be too scandalous and boastful—two traits not worthy of a proper woman for a proper marriage.

But would it even be a crowd? What if she arrived and it was only a small number of fairies in a drawing room staring at her while she played? Or even worse still, what if it was only Locklan? She hadn't thought to ask how many people would be in attendance.

Her anxieties were flowing freely through her fingers, the piece growing faster and faster until, before she realized it, she had blasted through her warm-up and still had two minutes left to stress.

One minute to go. She shook out her hands and let out a deep sigh.

Here goes nothing.

The clock hand ticked its way around, and with ten seconds left she began to play her first piece, just as Locklan had instructed.

A phantom breeze drifted around her, concealing the

evening-dimmed music room and shrouding her in near darkness. The flower-petal feeling from the first task was brushing along her body and she knew without looking that her outfit was changing as well, but she didn't dare look down yet.

She was thankful she had chosen an easy song to start with so she didn't have to focus on it and instead could take in her surroundings.

She, along with her harp and music stand, had been transported to a raised stone landing turned makeshift stage, the doors to a grand manor at her back. She was facing a large courtyard filled with what had to have been nearly one hundred fairies, framed by huge weeping willows. Their dainty leaves and long branches swayed in the breeze, brushing the ground like tassels on curtains, and glowing from the inside out. Tables, chairs, and sofas had been tucked underneath, luminaries casting a warm, speckled light on the people lounging there. The stars shone overhead, the bright pinpoints looking like a black threadbare blanket had been tossed over the sun.

Her plain outfit had transformed into a backless black satin gown decorated with thousands of crystals, making her feel like she was dressed in her own galaxy. She shimmered in the low light with even the slightest of movements. The perfect outfit for a performance.

As she looked around, still playing her harp, pixies in tiny black livery were flying by carrying wine bottles nearly as big as they were, refilling glasses before they were empty and serving food to the party guests under the willows. Theo wondered if they also owed a debt. Was that how Locklan supplied servants for all his gatherings?

Her song ended shortly after and she received a smattering of applause from a few partygoers closest to her, the others not caring about the background music.

It was only then that she caught sight of Locklan.

He was leaning against the trunk of the willow closest to her, easy to miss in his dark green tunic and black pants. When she met his gaze, he smiled and raised his glass of wine. She managed a polite nod in return, her still-shaky nerves not allowing for more.

Three songs later and she had arrived at Beatrice's mother's sheet music. The first one was a somewhat longer song with a merry melody and upbeat tempo. One of her favorites, it was a song she couldn't help but tap her feet to whenever she played it, and even though she had an audience, tonight was no exception.

About a third of the way through the song, it sounded as though her toe-taps were echoing across the courtyard. But when she looked toward the direction of the noise, her mouth dropped open in surprise. A ring of dancers had formed in the center, a group of about thirty fairies whirling and twirling in step with one another. As Theo kept playing, the group grew larger with more and more fairies joining in until it seemed as though half the party was dancing. They were laughing and spinning, clapping and bowing, even more delighted in the song than Theo was.

When the song ended, the dancers turned to her and applauded, shouts of "Another, another, another!" ringing out. Theo flipped through her music until she found one that she thought the crowd would find suitable, and it was after only the first two bars that she discovered she had hit her mark and then some.

The crowd cheered at their shared recognition of the music and launched into another dance, linking arms, jumping and spinning through the courtyard. The joy radiating from the dancers spread from the center like ripples in a pond, and when it had reached Theo she couldn't help but smile as she played.

A male fairy jumped up the stairs to stand next to her. He tossed his head, shaking his wavy burgundy hair out of his golden face, his eyes aglow with merriment. Before she could even guess what he was doing onstage with her, he had conjured his own harp out of thin air. His was just as intricately carved as hers but much smaller, able to be held in his hands. He started to play a harmony, the higher notes leaping to hers, joining together as if in their own dance. The fairy winked at her as she grinned in return.

As they played, the fairy called to some others in the crowd who jumped up to join them, conjuring their instruments out of nowhere. Soon fiddles, chimes, and a lute were all onstage forming an impromptu ensemble and following Theo's melody. When the song ended, the dancers went wild with laughter and applause.

One of the fairy musicians came over to her music stand. "What next?"

Theo shuffled through her selections, choosing another one of her favorites and holding it out for him to inspect. He grinned and shouted the title to the others. Then they were off again. It seemed as though the entire party was now on their feet. Theo even spotted Locklan dancing.

Song after song they played, and Theo didn't know if she'd ever been happier. It reminded her of the fairy tales she had read as a child of music that would trap the listener into dancing forever. Except this time, she was the enchantress. The fairies danced like they were bespelled by her, never tiring, newly revived as each song started.

For Theo at balls and parties, being the center of attention meant someone had played a cruel trick on her, and others would only look at her to laugh. But here among the fairies, the attention that was being poured onto her was in admiration. The entire party seemed glad to have her there; that had never ever happened before. Neither had this new feeling of lightness in her chest where her sarcasm and insults lived.

But by this point, Theo had been playing for hours. She'd never played continuously for this long before and she was starting to feel the effects of the strings on her fingers and the harp's weight on her shoulder. Locklan did say she only had to play for one night, but what if the one night lasted all night? She would collapse before the party was over. Would that void the bargain?

As if summoning him with her thoughts, at the end of the next song Locklan bounded up the steps and onto the stage. The guests and dancers, noticing the music had stopped, turned to face the stage and cheered for their host. He held up his hands to silence the crowd.

"Thank you, thank you," he started, then facing the musicians, he added, "take a bow, my friends!"

All the musicians, including Theo, stood and curtsied or bowed to the audience to wild applause from the party high on both drink and dancing. The harp player walked over to Theo to give her a kiss on the cheek and the other musicians bowed and curtsied to her. She returned the gesture, beaming.

"We will be taking a brief intermission and then our talented, delightful Lady Theodosia will return!" The party lauded the news with whoops and shouts.

Theo sagged in relief.

Locklan came to her side and took her arm in his. "Come, Lady Theodosia. Let's get you some wine. You deserve a break."

She allowed him to lead her down the stairs and into the courtyard, the other musicians following. With a snap of his fingers, four pixies who had been serving food flitted up to the stage and began to play music in the background.

In the short time it had taken Theo and Locklan to walk to the drink table, the party had gone back to laughing, talking, eating, and drinking. Locklan led her through the crowd, guests smiling at him, some raising their glasses and toasting his wonderful party and, to Theo's surprise, toasting her as well.

Locklan released her and took two glasses of wine, handing one to her. After she accepted, he took her arm again and led her to one of the willows. He held aside the branches as she walked under them and then motioned to a chair that she sank down into as he took a seat next to her.

A pixie fluttered in to check on Locklan's and Theo's wine and, after seeing they were still full, flitted back through the branches, hardly moving them as he went in search for more people with emptying glasses.

"Did they make a bargain with you, too?" Theo nodded in the direction the pixie had flown, taking a sip of her honey wine.

He chuckled. "No. I'm paying them. Quite a bit, actually. But they are efficient. You're the only one here who is paying back a bargain."

"Not the other musicians?"

"Now, that was really something. No, those are just guests who got caught up in your magical playing and joined in. Tell me, how do you know those songs?"

Theo shrugged. "They're part of the music collection at my home. I've grown up playing them. How do *you* know those songs?"

His eyebrows lifted. "You were playing some old, very well-known fairy songs. You didn't know?"

"No. I selected them for tonight because they're a delight to play and I thought people might agree."

"Well, you could not have picked better. That was some incredible playing. You are very talented."

"Thank you. You sound surprised."

"For all your talk at court saying that I didn't even know if you could play that well, I wasn't expecting you to enchant my entire party."

She laughed, still riding the high of her performance. "I've been playing harp since I was a child, but I've never done that. Never played with a group of people. And not to a crowd of people dancing along."

"You looked like you were having fun up there."

"It was amazing!"

"Where did you get that harp? Is it yours?"

Theo's mood sank just a bit, taking the corners of her smile with it. She didn't want to talk about Bea, or about Bea's mother. Not now. Not when she had been having such a nice time. Not when people were actually noticing her instead of Beatrice or Flo for once.

"It was my mother's," she lied.

He smiled at her. "Do you know anything about it? Who made it or when it came into her possession?"

"No idea."

He opened his mouth like he wanted to press the issue, but another pixie came zipping in. Locklan held out his glass, but Theo refused.

When he tilted his head at her, she shrugged. "According to you I'm only on an intermission break, and seeing as how I didn't complete your request, I'm here for the full amount of time. Best keep my head clear if I'm to keep playing."

"My request?"

"Between Dwyn stabbing me and then running, I didn't have time to ask him about his banishment. Though after all that, I am now as curious as you are."

"I still can't believe that weasel stabbed you. Are you going to ask Cecily for your revenge?"

She laughed. "I couldn't believe it, either! But, no, I think I'll let it go."

"That's kind of you. Can't say I'd have the same reaction. After you told me what he did, I wanted to stab him on your behalf."

She snorted. "I don't think anyone would describe me as kind."

"Then what would you call it?"

"I don't know. I guess I just understand why he did it. Looking back, I can see how he may have felt tricked. Doesn't mean he should have tried to gut me like a fish, but the frustration I can understand."

"Well then, I'll still go with kind and tack on empathetic. And while I'm disappointed my curiosity isn't sated, I am not upset about getting to spend more time with you, lovely Lady Theodosia."

And there it was. Time for the arrogant insults. She sighed as her mood took a further hit, disappointed that the nice conversation they were having had come to an end.

"Thank you for the wine," she said, about to stand.

His smile vanished. "What did I say?"

"Look, I may be magically bound to play at your party, but if I recall, there was nothing in the bargain that said I needed to sit here while you mock me."

"Mock you? You said something to that effect at court as well. When was I ever mocking you?"

She gave him a withering look and sat back into her chair. Then, in a poor yet exaggerated impression of him, said, "Hello, *gorgeous*, our *lovely* Lady Theodosia, isn't she *beautiful* to look at."

"I'm not allowed to call you beautiful?"

She gave him a look that conveyed how little she cared for his comment. "It's your party, do whatever you want. I'm just saying I won't sit here and take it."

"You won't accept a compliment?"

"First off, I am under no obligation to ever accept a

compliment. You're how old? I shouldn't be the one teaching that to you. Second, I said thank you when you said something genuinely nice about my harp playing, so yes, I am capable of taking a compliment. And third, I have learned my lesson more than once and from plenty of others that comments about my appearance are not compliments, are they?"

"How are they not?"

"Because it is from people who think they're being clever and funny. 'Oh, my, that dress looks *lovely*. Don't listen to the others—you are *stunning* this evening.'" Theo intoned the sarcastic remarks she had heard countless times before. "Or it's the 'compliments' like my mother's backhanded ones. 'That color completely washes you out, but I bet with some blush we can make you look decent enough.' Or 'That necklace looks pretty on you. It will detract from your eyes nicely.' I know what I look like. I know what my eyes look like. I don't appreciate it being brought up as a joke."

"Your eyes? So you think that when I tell you how gorgeous you look tonight I'm being insincere?"

"And facetious, callous, and sarcastic. Yes."

"You know, Lady Theodosia, some would say it's bad form to insult the host at his own party," he said with his predatory half grin, the glow from the lights making him look dashingly suave.

"Guess you should boot me out."

"Can't do that, I'm afraid. My guests would tear me limb from limb if I don't let you play again." His grin grew to a wide smile as he caught her staring.

"Then maybe I should get back." She stood and walked

under the willow branches, ignoring his offer of an arm to escort her, flustered and annoyed with herself that she was starting to find him just a small bit charming.

"I'm sorry you thought all my comments calling you beautiful were insults."

"I don't have any obligation to accept apologies, either."

He frowned in consideration but said nothing more as she walked back toward the stage.

When she climbed the steps and went to her harp, the audience erupted again, the other musicians noticing and coming to join her. Laughing, she gave a small curtsy.

"So, does anyone have any requests?" she asked, her bravery spurred on by the giddiness of the crowd.

Someone shouted the name of a song and her eyes lit up. "I know that one!" She sorted through her music collection until she found what she was looking for.

Once the other musicians were in place and ready, they began again.

Chapter 14

Where Theo Bargains
with Dances and
Compliments

She played for what felt like mere minutes, the joy and laughter sustaining her like they had healing powers, and before she knew it, hours had passed. When she had run out of her own music, her fellow bandmates summoned more, the dancers and the flowing of their wine never ceasing.

Eventually Locklan, seeming to understand once again that she was human, came to take Theo off the stage and whispered to her that she had paid her debt in full and was free of the bargain. The fairies who were still dancing were fortunately so drunk they didn't seem to notice that she had been replaced by pixies once more.

But when she reached the courtyard, it wasn't Locklan who took her by the hand. The musicians, having gathered around her, led the way to a willow, everyone conjuring a chair around a low table. The harp player, who Theo learned was named Beric, pulled up a chair for her as well. The lute player, Torian, a beautiful female with a similarly gilded complexion and orange hair the color of daylilies, sat on her other side.

A deck of cards appeared at the table and so did a round of wine. Beric, having sat down next to her, was kind enough to explain the rules of the drinking game they were playing. Theo could barely follow along before they started, and it only went downhill four drinks in.

But she didn't care. She was fine with losing every single time.

Because while they played, they talked. They asked her questions about herself, even though she didn't have much to share. They told dirty jokes that made her blush hard and laugh harder. No one corrected her, or scolded her, or made some snotty remark at her expense.

She loved every second.

After the musicians were sufficiently drunk, Beric, who seemed to have a knack for finding fun, suggested they should dance and only a moment later the band was on their feet.

They dragged Theo to the floor with them, but she made her way back to the edge of the courtyard when the others started to move with the music.

A smooth-as-melted-chocolate voice behind her made her jump. "And why, my lovely Lady Theodosia, aren't you out there dancing?"

She turned to find Locklan grinning at her.

"I don't know these dances," she said, trying hard to

look like she didn't mind that she was left out, albeit not on purpose.

"Well, I could show you, if you'd like." He had a glint in his eye that made her pause.

"Hmm. I suppose you're not just going to show me out of the overwhelming goodness of your heart, though, right?"

"A fairy never gives something away without gaining something in return." He smirked.

"So what would you want in exchange? I just got free of a fairy bargain. I'm not sure I want to take on another one."

He laughed like he was about to tell her the punch line to a joke.

"I will show you the dances if you let me compliment you one time."

"*What?* That's your offer?"

"Not exactly. You let me compliment you with no scoffing, no eye-rolling, no groaning, no glaring, no snorting, and no storming off."

"Really?"

"Yes. Dancing for a compliment. Is it a deal?"

She watched her bandmates on the dance floor, Beric and Torian catching her eye and waving for her to join them before they disappeared into the vortex of whirling dancers.

"Fine. It's a deal."

His grin turned devilish as he grabbed her by the waist and tucked her in close, putting her hand on his shoulder and holding her other one in his as if they were going to start a waltz. Following his lead, she took two steps to the side, two steps back.

He was holding her so close and watching her with such intensity that for a moment she forgot she was supposed to be learning a new dance.

"Hey, wait a minute," she said. "I've known how to do this dance since I was four. This isn't the dancing they're doing."

"Not yet it's not." He smiled. Then he tightened his grasp on her hip and spun her around and around until they were in the center of the dance floor. With a mischievous grin, he leaned in and kissed her cheek. She froze as he pulled back and winked at her.

Before she could react, an arm linked through hers and she was spinning and twirling away from Locklan.

And then she realized.

She knew the dance. Without even thinking, she was following along with the others, arm in arm. More than once she was swept away by one of the musicians who spun her and lifted her in the air.

She had never danced like this, her puppet strings cut loose from the stuffy, confining pageantry of court etiquette. This dancing was so freeing, so unexpected, that she knew the dancing of her human realm was ruined for her. No ballroom could ever compete with the joy she was having now.

Later—and thanks to the copious amounts of wine she had drank with the musicians, she didn't know how much later—the dancing was winding down and so was she. Locklan found her as she was veering back toward the edge of the dance floor and pulled her close again, leading her away from the crowd and under a willow.

"You seem to be not only enchanting my guests with your music, but with your dancing as well, Lady Theodosia," he said as he led her through the swaying branches.

She laughed, breathless, still coming down from the pure delight of the dancing. "You can just call me Theo."

"Oh? Does this mean we're friends now?"

"No, Kaz is right. I don't have any of those."

"What about the other musicians?"

"I'm not sure fairies have any desire to be friends with a human. It's fine, though. I'm just happy they were nice to me." She didn't want to go into any further detail about the rarity of that admission, surprised at herself that she had even said that much. She hadn't been to an event where no one knew her, and therefore had no preconceived notions about the type of person she was or that she was Beatrice's wicked stepsister. Here, she had been herself and people seemed to like her for it. And for tonight, that was enough.

"I see. Well, I'm still glad to call you Theo, Theo. And you can call me Lock. All my friends do and I consider you among them, so you have at least one fairy friend."

She smiled.

He leaned in close, the warmth of his breath making her shiver in the cool night. *"Now you have to hold up your end of the bargain,"* he whispered, and then pulled away. "And remember, no scoffing, no eye-rolling, no groaning, no glaring, no snorting, and no storming off."

She laughed and blew out a breath. Like this would be any real challenge. "All right, *Lock*. Do your worst."

He cleared his throat and puffed out his chest as if about

to deliver a soliloquy. And with an overdone intonation, he began his compliment.

"Your hair, as lustrous and tempting as chocolate, glows like the smoldering embers of your heart that is always aflame. And your depthless eyes that shine brighter than any diamond pull me under like the riptide beneath the surf. But when I gaze into them, I drown willingly."

At the mention of her hair and eyes, Theo scoffed on instinct. Realizing her mistake she gasped, her eyes wide. Lock laughed.

"I guess I will have to try again," he said with a grin. "Get ready."

He held a dramatic pause, the effect of that alone almost causing Theo to scoff again.

"The beauty of your gaze cuts me like the sharpest blade. The curves of your body intoxicate me like the richest primrose smoke. The sweep of your hips when you walk tempts me like the smoothest caramel. And yet to utterly destroy me, all you need to do is smile."

The mention of her body parts had her wincing, the urge to roll her eyes overtaking her before she could stop herself. She swore, eliciting an even bigger laugh from Lock.

"Careful, careful, Theo. You might run out of chances." His warning was laced with impish glee.

She put her hands on either side of her face, not entirely sure if the blushing was from the wine or woeful embarrassment. "You have no idea how difficult this is for me."

"I'm getting some idea."

She groaned, then swore at herself again.

Lock laughed. "You really can't do it, can you?"

"How red is my face right now? This is the worst! How about I let you stab me instead." She laughed in desperation.

"You'd rather I stab you than take a compliment? Absolutely not. This is way more fun. Last chance, Theo. You ready?"

She nodded and looked back to him, expecting to see his rakish grin, but all amusement had drained from his face.

"From the first moment I saw you, I knew there was something special about you. When you play your harp, when you dance with that look of pure joy, your beauty outshines everyone around you. I know I don't know you well, but I can see that your smiles and laughs are few and far between, so when I get to see them I consider it a gift as rare and precious as the first bloom of spring.

"And it is a tragedy, Theo, that anyone has ever made you feel that you are not beautiful. Because you are. More beautiful than you could possibly know. But your beauty is not soft or quiet. It is not charming or delicate. And the others belittled you and tore you down not because they couldn't see you, but because they were afraid to. Your beauty is fierce and untamed. You are the wilderness at twilight. The peril between the bolt of lightning and the thunder. Between the swing of the whip and the crack. Between the slice of the sword and the sting of the blade. Your beauty exists in the moments where the world stops and anything is possible. And to look at you is to experience it in all its terrifying glory, knowing that the rest of us can only belong in the insignificant moment when the world begins again."

His eyes were locked onto hers, holding her in place without so much as a touch. She turned and walked away, nearly leaving underneath the tree altogether, just so he wouldn't see the flabbergasted look on her face from the words that, for the first time ever, made her feel like someone saw her. She hadn't been ready for that. Especially not from him.

"Uh-oh. You just stormed off."

She whipped back around to face him. "What? No. No, I accepted your compliment."

"And then stormed off."

"Did not!"

"I'm feeling extra benevolent this evening, so I'll try one more time, Theo. But if you can't hold up your end of it this time, then you'll default on your fairy bargain and I'm sure I don't have to tell you what a nuisance that would be. I'd like to get my magic back without incident, thank you."

Theo paused, feeling silly for a whole different reason. Why had she never thought to ask what the penalty was for not holding up her end of the bargain? She had a suspicion that it would be more than a mere nuisance. "What do you mean by 'get my magic back'?"

"When a fairy makes a bargain, the magic required becomes part of that bargain and is only returned once the payment is complete. There's not a huge amount of magic that goes into showing you some fairy dances, but it is still missing nonetheless until you pay me back."

"What happens if you don't get your magic back?"

"It depends on the magic and the bargain. Bigger bargain, bigger magic. But, fairies will always claim what's owed. If you don't hold up your end of the bargain, I will still get my magic back, but again, it would be a real nuisance for both of us. So, it is in your best interest to let me compliment you."

She glared at him. "Give me a second," she said as she readied herself, shaking her head and hands in hopes of bringing back those inhibitions that the wine gave free rein to.

But even with his warning, she wasn't entirely sure she'd be able to do it, his previous attempts still grabbing at her. They felt true, felt honest, and she was only just beginning to realize how much she wanted him to mean them.

And how much of a heartbreak it would be if he didn't and all of it had been another joke at her expense.

She faced him again, bracing for another onslaught of verbal torture. "Ready."

"You sure?"

She clenched her hands into fists and narrowed her eyes, trying to will her face into stoic immobility. "Yes."

"Then here goes." He leaned in close and she shuddered as his lips grazed the shell of her ear. She sucked in a breath.

"I love your dress, but I think I'd love it even more if it vanished."

She reeled back, surprised. He winked.

A burst of laughter escaped her and she slapped a hand over her mouth, but it couldn't stop the fit of giggles that had begun to overtake her nerves. His grin turned into a wide smile, and soon they were both laughing.

"Well then, Lock. How'd I do?" she asked when the laughter had mostly subsided. "Did I hold up my end of the bargain?"

"Yes, gorgeous. You have paid your debt in full."

"Good. So I can roll my eyes again."

"All you want, lovely Theo."

Just for that she did a very over-the-top eye roll, making him laugh again.

She paused for a moment, not sure if she should ask the next question. Even just the thought of asking sobered her. But fairy wine was still swirling around on its own private dance floor in her head, telling her to just do it.

"Did you mean what you said about me?"

"Every word," he said without any speck of hesitation as he lifted a hand to her face. His eyes twinkled. "Especially the part about the dress."

She laughed and leaned into his palm as he pressed it onto her cheek, his thumb touching the corner of her mouth and then across her bottom lip.

He moved to hold the back of her neck, his fingers intertwining in her hair as he leaned forward and pressed his lips on hers. After only a moment, he pulled back. Not in hesitation, but as if extending an invitation. It was her decision to make.

She'd never been kissed before. Not really. The only time she had ever come close was a cruel game unwittingly played on her by Bea's friends at a garden party, the unlucky boy having been dared to kiss her as his punishment for losing. And when Theo found out, she made sure he did feel unlucky for losing when she spiked his drink at the next ball and he threw up all over a visiting dignitary's daughter.

But with Lock, his unwavering emerald eyes staring into

hers, his hand still at her neck and laced in her hair, she wanted to. She closed the distance between them until her lips were on his again. He kissed her gently at first, but as her lips parted so did his. Seizing his moment, Lock's other hand came to her lower back, pulling her tightly against him as her hands went to his face and hair, the close shave at the sides of his head feeling like velvet under her fingers, the taste of honey wine sweet and warm on his tongue.

A scuff of boots and sweeping of branches startled her and she tore away from Lock to find Kaz staring at them. She tried to take a step away from Lock, not questioning herself on why she didn't want Kaz to see this, but he moved his hand to her hip and held her close.

"Good evening, Kasra. I don't recall inviting you. Did Cecily send you to check up on me?" Lock said with a grin that drifted toward teeth baring and would have looked more at home on a guard dog.

Kaz just smiled in return, as though satisfied in knowing he had rankled Lock.

"Theo and I were right in the middle of something. Feel free to grab a snack on your way out. I'm afraid I don't have any dead mice or last night's dinner scraps on offer, though, little fox."

"Kind of you. It is getting late and it seems like the party is ending. I came to see if Theo needed an escort home since it appears that she's held up her end of the bargain." Then he looked straight at Theo. "Did he say the words to release you of your debt?"

Lock snorted. "How thoughtful and altruistic of you. Of

course I did, but just for you I can say them again. Theo, you have paid your debt in full and are released of your bargain owed to me. See? Done again. You are correct, though, Kasra. It is getting quite late. Maybe it would be best if you stayed here tonight, Theo, and I can return you safe and sound tomorrow."

A shudder rippled through her as his fingers brushed from the base of her spine to between her shoulder blades and then back down again. His fingertips scalded her where they touched as though made of embers, stopping only just above the curve of her backside, his hand eventually resting at her hip. She found herself wishing he'd do it again.

"As an engaged woman, Theo wouldn't want to accept the offer, no matter how pure your motives may be."

She tensed at his words. At the even indirect mention of the duke, anything she had been feeling for Lock fell from her grasp like a tray of the finest desserts plummeting to the ground, ruined. And now that those emotions had vacated, embarrassment took full advantage, blood rushing to her heated face.

She stepped away from Lock's hand and looked up at him.

He was furious. "Theo, you don't have to listen to him."

"No, Lock, he's right. I should go. Thank you for the wonderful evening. And... and the compliments."

His face softened and he gave her a small smile. "The pleasure was all mine," he said as he held her hand and planted a kiss on her knuckles.

He stepped closer, brushing a stray tendril of hair off of her neck. "*Every word*," he whispered.

Their moment was gone, and she was unsure if she'd ever get it back, the weight of the tasks almost as heavy as the reminder of her engagement. Now that she was free of both her bargains to Lock, she knew her time with him had come to an end and she doubted if she'd ever see him again anyway.

She walked to Kaz, Lock glaring again as Kaz continued that maddening look of triumph.

"Stop it," she said to Kaz. "Just take me home."

"As you wish." The wind swirled around them, blocking Lock and the willow from view.

———————————— • ————————————

"So you call him Lock now?" Kaz asked as they appeared in her bedroom, a hint of annoyance in his voice.

"Yes. He asked me to."

Kaz rolled his eyes.

"What does it matter to you, Kaz? Why did you bother coming?"

"To see if you were all right. To make sure he wasn't making you play harp until your fingers bled. Fairies have the tendency to forget that humans can feel things like pain and exhaustion much sooner than they can. I wanted to make sure you weren't in trouble."

"He wouldn't have done that."

"Oh, because you know Locklan so well. Quite the gentleman, was he?"

"He was, in fact! The bargain was fine. I even made a second bargain and he taught me how to dance."

Kaz jerked back. "You did what? Did he release you of that one yet or are you still in a bargain with him?"

"He released me. It's fine, see? He's not as bad as you think. Maybe I know him better than you do."

He shook his head. "Fairies don't just do things out of the goodness of their hearts. You might think you're making harmless bargains, but..." Kaz stopped as if struggling to find the words. "Be careful of him, Theo. You don't know what his motives are."

"And you do?" she asked, irritated.

"No. I have no idea what he wants with you beyond tonight's harp playing."

"And why are you acting like my propriety means anything to you? Look around, Kaz. It's because of you that I'm alone in my bedroom with a man. *You.*"

"Well, it clearly means something to you if the mere mention of your fiancé sends you running."

"It wasn't my *propriety* that ruined the moment when you caused me to picture my ancient, gross, mean, horrid fiancé, you mood-bashing party crasher."

Kaz scoffed but then stared at her hard. "Be careful of him, Theo."

"You said that already. Why does it matter to you? It's not like I'm ever going to see him again. What do you care?"

"I don't. Would you have stayed if I hadn't shown up?"

"I'll ask again. What do you care?" She leveled her fiercest glare at him, but he said nothing. In truth she didn't know the answer to Kaz's question, his interruption allowing her to not have to decide. But she wasn't about to admit that to him.

"Good night, Kaz," she said in a firm dismissal.

"Night, Theo. See you soon." Their eyes stayed locked on each other as a swirl of wind like a tiny contained tornado wrapped around him and he vanished.

Even though her wine-filled body wanted her to fall asleep, she lay awake in her bed thinking about the evening. She had laughed more in the last three days than she had in a decade, and more at this one party than she had in all the parties she had been to in her life.

But Kaz's words had wiggled their way into her thoughts, casting doubt on the whole experience. She was used to people playing nice to her face. And that was the best-case scenario. Tonight felt genuine, but what if it wasn't? Beric, Torian, and the others really did like her, didn't they?

Didn't Lock?

Chapter 15
Where Florentia
Gets Married

"Where were you?"

Theo was jolted awake by Flo's shrill voice.

"Huh? What are you talking about?" Theo sat up, rubbing sleep from her eyes and squinting at the clock that told her it was almost noon. "I was here. In bed."

"Liar. Where. Were. You. I checked on you last night because I needed to speak with you about your bridesmaid dress and you were not in your room."

Theo scrambled for any answer that might appease her sister. "The garden? The garden. I was walking in the garden last night and got lost. When I got back it was late."

"The garden," Flo said, thick with suspicion.

"Correct."

Flo squinted at her, but to Theo's relief, she let it go just the same. "Well, I need you to get up now and try on your dress for the final fitting. The seamstress will be here momentarily." Flo flew from the room, slamming the door closed behind her.

Theo stretched and got out of bed, throwing on whatever dress she reached for first and twisting her hair into a low bun at the base of her neck. She splashed her face with some cool water and put on a small bit of blush. The extensive amounts of fairy wine and lack of sleep were not doing her complexion any favors, though, and she was waging a losing battle.

Her mother and Flo were both at the table when Theo came down to eat lunch.

Her mother shot her an accusatory stare. "Florentia tells me you were gardening yesterday evening?"

"Not gardening. Walking in the garden."

"And got lost."

"Yes."

"In a garden you've been playing in since you were a child?" Her mother tilted her head and widened her eyes in a look of mock innocence.

"Well, it is much different than I remembered now that it is no longer being maintained," Theo said.

"And you did not think to call for help?"

"Who would have heard me and come to my aid, Mother?"

Her mother glared. Theo knew this look. Her mother did not believe her excuse for one moment but had no proof as to what Theo might have been otherwise doing. Theo left the table shortly thereafter, not quite eating her fill but deciding the hunger was well worth not having to sit at the table with her mother any longer than necessary.

———————————— • ————————————

With her wedding only a few days away, Flo was becoming more and more bossy and entitled, which, for Flo, was really saying something. Theo spent the next few days either fully entrenched in the wedding preparations or hiding from the wedding preparations.

She didn't know if it was her imagination, but it seemed her mother was being a bit more suspicious and observant than she had otherwise been when it came to Theo, asking her more than usual where she was off to, not always satisfied with the truthful answer of the music room or the garden.

The wedding was to take place at Flo's new home, the Avenshire estate, so three days before the wedding, Theo and her mother helped Flo pack up all her worldly possessions. Where Theo had felt a small bit of trepidation while she had packed, Flo was delighted, barely able to contain her excitement that she was finally going to be a Wife and Mother. And would have access to the earl's entire estate's worth of servants to dote on her.

Thankfully, the journey south to Avenshire was short and Theo, Flo, their mother, and Morris only had to suffer through one night of one another's company at an inn before arriving in the midafternoon.

Upon their arrival, Flo's fiancé, Ambrose, gave them the grand tour of Flo's new home, and so buoyant was she that by the end of it they could have tied a basket to her and taken in the sights by sky. The place was nice enough with its beige stone walls and red and orange decor. It might have been spring outside, but in this home it was perpetually autumn. It wasn't Theo's ideal manor, but she could see that Flo would indeed be happy here.

The rest of the days and evenings were just as boring, only growing more so as out-of-town guests arrived and were hosted for luncheons and dinners at the estate until the wedding arrived.

———————————————— ● ————————————————

The morning of the wedding, Theo felt like she had woken up in an ant nest. Swarms of servants in black were rushing throughout the manor and the grounds carrying trays of food, setting up chairs, and moving with purpose on errands Theo couldn't even guess at. Flo, her mother, and Theo ate a simple breakfast in their rooms, Flo not wanting Ambrose to even glimpse her for a second on her big day.

With a quantity of lady's maids and servants at Flo's disposal, Theo did not need to offer any help whatsoever and mostly sat in Flo's room watching while her mother hovered around like an angry wasp as Flo got ready. Her mother had Morris do her usual hairstyle, only embellishing it slightly with some buds that matched Flo's bouquet of beautiful pink flowers.

When the hour of the ceremony neared, Theo also began to get ready. Her bridesmaid dress was hideous. She was the only bridesmaid, and with Flo not wanting to be upstaged as her overarching wedding theme, Theo debated whether Flo had done it on purpose, if only to make herself look better on her special day. It was as though she had consulted with her mother on which color would look the worst on Theo and they decided on a mustard-yellow silk gown with droopy tiers of chiffon that grew like a threat the farther down the dress they went. The collar went all the way up to her chin, making Theo's head look like it popped out of a vase. A matching floral headpiece sealed the ensemble. Her mother and Flo deemed it perfect.

Flo's gown, on the other hand, was magnificent. The lace gown bloomed into a billowing skirt with flowers embroidered in a soft pink color all along the back. The train and veil swept out behind her in romantic waves as she walked. Theo thought her sister was always quite lovely, but today she looked radiant.

And as Flo walked down the aisle toward Ambrose, her groom seemed to agree. While the two of them together normally shared a sneering, annoyed look, today he was beaming.

Watching her walk over the sprinkled rose petals to the altar, Theo found she actually felt happy for her sister. It was the culmination of everything Flo had wanted for herself, and Theo was truly glad she was getting it.

The ceremony was beautiful, the reception even more so, to the point Theo wondered just how on earth their mother had afforded this. She knew never to ask, but for all the talk of a bankrupt estate, their mother seemed to have spared no expense. Florentia's new in-laws would never have paid for it, nor would her mother have stooped so low as to ask for assistance. Theo would need to check if the west wing furniture was still there when they returned home. Maybe Lady

Isadora had been correct and her mother had been selling off the silverware.

The declaration of marriage was barely out of the minister's mouth before Lady Balfour had her sights set on her youngest daughter. She was now taking "overbearing" as a personal challenge. If a man sneezed too loudly in Theo's general direction, her mother was there making sure he blew his nose somewhere else because *Theodosia is engaged.* For all her previous talk about no one else wanting to marry her, Lady Balfour was ready to defend her daughter's honor with weaponry if necessary, which Theo found to be particularly unusual. Her mother had been correct about people not wanting anything to do with the youngest Balfour, so her insistence now was rather bizarre.

Not seeing anyone worth speaking with, or caring to make small talk, Theo stood to the side for most of the reception while Flo and Ambrose dutifully made the rounds greeting their guests.

As Theo listened to bits and pieces of conversations that floated over to her, one nasally, gossipy voice could be heard above the rest.

"After the princess sought to purchase all that iron for the palace, I've been fortunate to be invited to dine with her quite frequently," came a voice Theo knew all too well—Lady Elspeth Sanderson, only daughter of the baron, Lord Canton Sanderson.

While not high in rank, the baron was well regarded for his massive wealth as the owner of the largest iron mine in the kingdom. Wealth that saw a huge increase in recent years thanks to the princess.

As one of the princess's pet projects, Beatrice decided to update all the fixtures, and almost everything metal in the palace, with iron sourced from within the kingdom. These purchases endeared her not only to the baron but also to every metalworker and artisan guild in existence. The money she spent revitalized the industry now that her devotees were eager to follow in her footsteps, making iron home decor de rigueur. Just one more thing Theo added to her list of grievances against the calculating and phony Beatrice.

And Lady Elspeth was more than happy to use it to her social advantage. "She's given me personal tours of the new installations. You're not the only one with direct access to the prince and princess anymore, Lady Isadora."

At the mention of Isadora, Theo turned to find the source of the conversation. She had known the duke's family had been invited but just assumed no one would show up. But there she was, standing near a floral arrangement, looking as beautiful as ever. Her gorgeous curls were still left free but pulled away from her face with combs accented with diamonds.

Elspeth, meanwhile, had been a gangly and awkward child, the other children picking on her for her slight, pale, almost sickly appearance. To get back at them, Elspeth would loudly declare that her mother told her the story of "The Ugly Duckling" and that one day she would turn into a swan and everyone else would be sorry they were ever mean to her. Unfortunately for her, that had yet to happen and she was now just a gangly and awkward adult reminding Theo not of a swan but more of a blue heron—all limbs and the look of someone who ate amphibians for breakfast.

Today was no exception. Her light brown hair, shiny only from grease, was in a braided updo that further accentuated her beak-like nose. Her dress was elegant and must have cost a fortune—proof of her family's bottomless coffers—but it draped off of her as if she were merely another hanger in her closet.

And as usual she was flanked by her two closest friends, Lady Gertrude and Lady Mabel. So dull were these two that Theo was convinced she could replace one with a straw dummy and the others wouldn't notice. But Theo wouldn't have any problem with them at all had it not been for their aggravating habit of acting as Elspeth's private cheering section, laughing at her pathetic jokes and making it look like she had the encouragement of those around her when she said hurtful things. Theo was also nasty, but at least she could do it without a support group behind her.

And today, she certainly didn't need one. Seizing her chance to cut that miserable little braggart down to size, Theo strode over to the group just as Elspeth threw another barb at Isadora, Gertrude and Mabel smirking behind her. Elspeth hadn't realized how easy she was going to make this for Theo, but she'd find out very soon.

At the sight of Theo, Elspeth's eyes narrowed, but she plastered a grin on her face just the same.

"Oh, look. If it isn't the beautiful Lady Theodosia. I must say, your dress is exquisite. Your—"

Theo waved her hand impatiently. "Yes, yes, Lady Elspeth. Death by a thousand 'you're uglies.' So very original. For everyone's sake, let's all pretend you said something truly cutting, and that your unique and individually compelling lackeys snickered, and we can move on."

Gertrude coughed on a gasp and Mabel's eyes went wide at the outright dismissal of their friend.

"Lady Mabel, Lady Gertrude, I would offer my compliments to you, but you won't believe me anyway so we can just skip that, too."

Elspeth's eyes had darkened, her mood souring like wine to vinegar now that Theo had come to ruin her fun. Gertrude and Mabel were still staring at her, having no idea what to make of the situation since Theo hadn't taken the bait. Precisely what Theo had intended.

"What do you want, Theodosia?" Elspeth snarled.

"Nothing from you. Just saying hello to Lady Isadora. We've met only recently. How wonderful to see you again." The distrust in Isadora's eyes was obvious, but she gave Theo a polite nod. Good. Let her stew a bit as well. "Were you congratulating her on her engagement to Lord Harrington the Fifth, future Duke of Snowbell? Such wonderful news. You should see him look at her. Stars in his eyes. Can't ever seem to stop smiling. It's just like out of a fairy tale. I bet you wish you had someone who looks at you that way, Elspeth. But, alas, wishes don't buy future dukes. And we all know giant dowries don't, either." Theo exaggerated a wink at her.

Elspeth looked ready to drop all pretenses of manners and hit Theo. Gertrude and Mabel were looking uncomfortably at the bottoms of their dresses and Isadora just looked confused.

"Oh, how rude of me, Lady Isadora—I'm sure you don't know." Borrowing a smile worthy of Phineas, Theo continued. "Our mutual friend Elspeth here tried to buy her way to where you are now. Her father kept offering your fiancé's father more and more and *more* money for her dowry, but Lord Harrington kept refusing. His son was too in love with you, I'd guess." Theo turned to Elspeth again. "Not hard to see why, though, is it?" If Elspeth was a candle of beauty, Isadora was a bonfire—and Elspeth knew it.

From the look on her face, Theo was glad Elspeth wasn't armed. She smiled brightly at her anyway. Theo had overheard a while ago at another garden party that Elspeth's father had a dowry refused and refused again, the name Harrington having been dropped in, but it wasn't until very recently that Theo had put it all together. "Shame you're wearing blue. Green with envy is really your color."

Theo again addressed Isadora. "She's somewhat of a legend when it comes to her jealousy. As children we all called her Jelsy Elsie. Clever, isn't it? Elsie has never laid eyes on anything she didn't want for herself. Unfortunately, your dearest Lord Harrington the Fifth was the first thing her father has come across that money couldn't buy for his darling, covetous Elspeth."

Elspeth's cheeks had gone red, her eyelashes becoming wet with tears of anger and embarrassment that were threatening to spill over. Theo was readying herself for another sparring round, but instead, Elspeth stormed off, the smallest of whimpers trailing behind her.

Gertrude and Mabel looked from their friend to Theo, both not knowing what they were supposed to do without their leader. Theo beamed victorious. Why bother with the foot soldiers when she could take out the general.

"That was cruel, Theodosia," said Mabel quietly as she turned to follow Elspeth.

Theo cocked her head to the side at Gertrude, daring her to say something. But Gertrude found something interesting on the ground and walked away to join her friends.

"It's only ever cruel when it's done to them. When it's someone else it's all in good fun, apparently." Theo didn't know if she was saying that to herself or to cut the thick silence that was coming from Isadora.

"What are you doing here?" Isadora clipped, looking venomous.

"Well, I couldn't very well leave my *future step-granddaughter* in the hands of Jelsy Elsie and her shadows. I'd never squander the opportunity to send her scampering."

"And here I thought you had come over to join them," Isadora said in her icy tone reserved exclusively for Theo. "I figured someone as nasty as you would have equally nasty friends, and those ladies certainly fit the bill."

"We have a history, you know. Me and her. When we were children, Elsie used to tell all the foreign boys that I had been cursed by a witch and anyone who came near me would die a horrible death. One mother sent her son over to play with me and he started to cry. The earl just assumed I had done something and I was sent home early with the governess on strict orders for a smacking, which that horrible wench of a woman delighted in. It happened rather frequently. So no, they are no friends of mine. You seem to know them well enough, so I would have thought you'd have known that. Everyone always assumes I'm the one who starts it. I never am. But I will finish it."

"Well, I'm not going to thank you, if that's what you're looking for."

"I'm absolutely not looking for a thanks from you," Theo responded flatly, even though she had to admit, it would have been nice for Isadora to appreciate Theo's successful efforts just a little.

"So, I'm just to believe that after what happened at the duke's estate you're over here helping me? I don't need your help."

"Of course you don't." A statement that Theo sincerely believed. If anyone could hold their own in a fight it was Isadora. "I bet she's been horrible to you since you arrived. Did you know about her and your fiancé or was that new information?"

At first it seemed like Isadora was not going to answer. "Not exactly. He said someone had been vying for him, but not who it was."

"I can assume a lot of your earlier interactions make a whole lot more sense now." Theo knew Elspeth most likely didn't make Isadora's social life easy. "I am curious, though. She was practically loading the gun for you and you still didn't take the shot. Shocking, really, since you don't seem the type to let someone walk all over you considering what you had to say to me."

"They're at court all the time. Unlike you, I can't make enemies out of everyone." Isadora crossed her arms in front of her.

Theo laughed long and dark, another question answered without her even asking. "Ah. I see. You can't put them in their places, but I'm fair game."

Theo expected Isadora to say…something. Another pointed remark about how Theo deserved it. An insult about what an awful person she was. Or to claim that Theo was wrong. But Isadora just looked uncomfortable.

"I was quite mistaken about you," Theo said. "You're not standing up for what you think is right. You're just a coward only going after people smaller than you. You could have easily put their heads on the chopping block, too. Do you wish Bea—oh, excuse me—your best friend, Her Highness Princess Beatrice, told you what awful people Elsie and company are? Without your princess's blessing, you just have to sit and take the abuse. But with her permission . . . why bother trying to decide anything for yourself when she can give you a free pass to be as bloodthirsty as you want to a stranger and think you've done something noble."

"And this is supposed to change my mind about you?" Isadora fumed. "We are all of a sudden going to be friends because we share a common enemy that you made scamper away by being even worse than she was?"

Theo sighed. "I know there is nothing I can do to make you be even something close to a cordial acquaintance, much less a friend. Because if you liked me even the tiniest amount, then the thought of me marrying the duke would make you just a little bit sad. And that wouldn't do at all, would it? Because then what would you do with your anger for the next fifty years? You don't want me as a friend because you need me as a villain."

"Well, you're certainly not the hero! You didn't need to come over here. You didn't do it for me. You came over because you wanted to be mean. You want to make others suffer because you're so awful. That's what a villain does,

Theodosia." Isadora held her stance in a perfect en garde position, finger raised to Theo's face like a sword. If Theo could see Isadora's legs underneath her dress, she was confident she would find her slightly bent at the knees, readying for a lunge-and-stab maneuver, as though a mere verbal barrage wasn't enough to demonstrate just how awful she thought Theo was.

"Did you know," Isadora continued, "Miss James has placed the blame squarely on you as the reason why Margot has become such a terror? It started the day after you left. Being rude to the staff, to her father, to Miss James. Making her brother cry almost daily. Defacing paintings. That sort of thing. The last time she was in the garden, she kicked all the flowers off their stems. Made quite the mess. The gardener was out for blood."

"Well, if she needs more inspired ideas, I'm willing to provide private tutoring."

"You'd love that, wouldn't you? I bet it would make you so happy to show her how to be just as awful as you are."

"You wanted a villain. Here I am." Theo held out her arms, putting herself on display. "Though, I'll tell you what. If you need any sordid tidbits for all your social events, let me know. I'll give you so much gossip ammunition about me you'll be able to invade the next dukedom over."

Isadora stared at her, a frown marring her beautiful face.

"Cheer up, Lady Isadora. You should be glad to get exactly what you wanted. But just one quick question for you to think on. If your idea of a fun time is making me feel worthless, are you really that different from the person you think I am?"

Without so much as a backward glance, Isadora walked away, leaving Theo standing alone again.

Flo and Ambrose departed for their honeymoon not long after. Looking like she had practiced earlier in the mirror, Flo was delicately wiping a few tears from her eyes, Lady Balfour doing the same. Theo hugged her sister and said goodbye, Flo declaring loud enough for everyone to hear that she would miss her and would write—both sisters knowing this was not true. But Theo smiled anyway and promised to write back.

A familiar hot feeling of envy took root in her chest as Theo watched her sister's carriage make its way down the drive, both Flo and Ambrose waving from the windows to the cheering wedding guests. While Theo was happy for her sister, she was jealous of just how easy it was for Flo to get all this. Everything she'd wanted—without having to try.

Meanwhile, Theo was bargaining with fairies, running around with strange men who turned into animals, and getting stabbed, all so she could avoid her impending nuptials. But then what? What if Cecily came through and she didn't marry the duke? Would her mother still disown her? She had told Cecily the truth—she was not waiting for a love match. But would there be a possibility of another marriage opportunity? What if that one was worse?

Maybe this whole thing with Cecily was pointless.

Theo's mood and resolve were sinking lower and lower the farther away Flo's carriage got from the manor, until it disappeared entirely from view.

Chapter 16

Where the Wedding Date Is Set and So Is the Second Task

"Wonderful news, Theodosia!"

Her mother barged into Theo's room first thing in the morning, waking her up.

Never before had her mother ever cared where Theo spent her time, but now that Flo was gone, her mother needed someone to hover over, and though she wasn't thrilled by the idea, her youngest daughter was the only option. Theo knew her mother missed Flo and it became all that much more apparent during their nightly card games in the drawing room when they struggled to talk about anything since Theo had absolutely no opinions on wedding plans and had no good gossip to share. Regardless, her mother had spent the last few days of their return from Flo's wedding keeping closer tabs on Theo's whereabouts, checking in on her throughout the day.

"What?" Theo answered, rubbing her face.

"The date for your wedding is set! Six weeks from now!"

Theo shot up. "Six weeks?"

"I know. I wish it was sooner as well. I was hoping that the duke would send word about the repairs from the fire, but so far I haven't heard anything. No matter. I've arranged for the seamstress to come over soon with some wedding dress options and we can get going quickly. The duke's estate will be handling most of the other details, so we should be fine in terms of flower arrangements and menus." At this point, her mother was mostly talking to herself as she walked out of the room, leaving Theo to fully absorb the news.

Six weeks. Not a whole lot of time considering she'd only done one task so far and it had been five weeks since she had made the bargain with Cecily. If the time frame was one task a month, she wouldn't have enough time to complete the other two tasks.

There was no way she'd be able to go back to sleep after being woken with that horrible news, so she rolled out of bed, put on a simple dress, tied her hair back, and went downstairs for a quick breakfast.

Her mother had found something else to occupy her time, so Theo was left on her own to go to the music room.

She hadn't had much of an opportunity to play since returning from Lock's party. The morning after, she did rush to the room to make sure her harp had been returned safely and found that it was right back where it had started from, no one the wiser that it had moved. Not that anyone would have noticed anyway, but Theo was relieved all the same. Today was the first day since Flo's wedding that she'd actually be able to sit down and play.

But rounding the corner into the music room, she halted. Sitting on one of the wingback chairs in his usual finery was Phineas, and standing at the window in his usual lack thereof was Kaz.

"There you are," Phineas exclaimed.

Kaz was doing his customary impatient finger tapping on the windowsill by way of greeting. "We've been waiting here for a while now."

Theo scowled. "Well, maybe if you told me when you'd be randomly dropping by, I could better manage my time. And it's first thing in the morning. You haven't been waiting all that long unless you once again showed up at the exact wrong time."

Kaz threw himself into the other chair, not bothering to rise to the challenge. "Where are all your staff, by the way? I hadn't even heard footsteps in this wing until yours."

"We don't really have any. Just a cook, scullery maid, stable hand, and my mother's lady's maid. My mother had to let go of the rest because she's run out of money."

"Ah, no wonder everything around here looks the way it does." He made a show of looking her up and down.

She returned it with a sneer. "What are you doing here, Kaz? Trying to be my chaperone again?"

"Why? Has Lock asked you to work at any more parties?"

"If I had been, I certainly wouldn't be telling you about it."

Phineas winked at her. "I heard you were absolutely fabulous at the party. I also heard you were absolutely fabulous after your harp duties were finished."

But before she could come up with a retort, footsteps could be heard down the hall headed straight for the music room.

"Theodosia!" came her mother's voice.

Theo turned to Kaz and Phineas, eyes wide. In one blink, Phineas turned into a mockingbird and flew out the open window.

"*Go away!*" she whispered at Kaz, hoping he would just disappear in a whip of wind like he normally did.

"*I can't! Not enough time. Cecily isn't here to vanish me. Your mother would see the wind and me!*" he whispered frustratedly in return.

"*Fox fox fox fox fox,*" she whispered furiously at Kaz. He changed in a flash and started sprinting around the music room for places to disappear. But there was a tragic dearth of hiding spaces, even for a fox a mere fraction of his human size. The chairs were on dainty curved legs leaving the area underneath exposed, there were no pillows or blankets, and the drapes were too sheer to hide behind. And just as noticeable as a poorly hidden fox would be, a fox dashing to and fro would not exactly be inconspicuous, either.

Her mother was almost to the door.

"*Get over here,*" Theo mouthed, waving him to her.

He understood what she was trying to communicate and in an instant he ran to where she was standing in the center of the room. She lifted her skirts and he ducked under, settling right between her feet. Only a heartbeat after she righted her dress, her mother turned the corner and entered the room.

"Who were you talking to?" she asked, skipping any polite greetings and going straight to accusations.

"What? Talking to? I wasn't talking to anyone. Just me by myself."

Her mother narrowed her eyes.

Faster than Theo thought she could move, her mother darted to the door and slammed it shut as if expecting someone to be behind it.

"What are you doing, Mother?"

"I heard you speaking to someone in here. Who?"

"I was talking to myself! There's no one here but me!" As she said this, Kaz's fur was rubbing up against her calves and it was taking every ounce of willpower she possessed to keep her feet planted on the floor and not reflexively kick out.

"Theodosia, I'll need you to be completely honest with me. Have any men approached you?"

"Men?"

"Yes. Men who maybe seem much more interested in you than they should be? Men who seem like they want to get to know you? Want to know about the estate?"

"No, Mother. No men have shown up here to express interest in me. Why would that be a concern?"

Dismissing her question, Lady Balfour stalked to the curtains, throwing them back and shaking them like the mystery person might be hanging from the rods. Unsatisfied at the lack of a body, she scanned the room almost in the exact same manner Theo and Kaz had done only moments before. And just as they had, she ran out of suspected hiding places.

"Did you need something, Mother?" Theo asked, trying to

sound like a person who didn't have a woodland animal under her skirts rubbing against her bare skin. She wasn't sure she was being successful.

"I didn't know where you'd gone off to."

"Just practicing my harp for a little while," Theo said.

"I don't know why you're bothering with the harp. The duke made it clear his thoughts. I would think you'd be spending your time a bit more wisely." She frowned at her disappointing daughter who was still standing stock-still in the center of the room like she was a piece of furniture.

"Yes. Of course. You're right, Mother. I'll be out shortly." She plastered on her best *Everything is fine* face and hoped her mother would finally leave so she could get Kaz out from under her dress, which was becoming more uncomfortable by the second, both in terms of having a fox between her legs and having a man between her legs.

Her mother took one more suspicious look around the room just in case she had missed some incredibly creative hiding spot and then left, not bothering to close the door behind her on the way out.

Theo stayed still, listening intently for her mother's footsteps to reach the end of the hall, then continue down the stairs.

When she was convinced she was alone, she lifted her dress and kicked Kaz out from under her. He transformed in an instant back into a man, his eyebrows raised and a smile forming.

Phineas flew back into the room and turned human once more. "I bet you enjoyed that hiding spot, didn't you, Kaz?"

Theo scowled, pointing at Kaz. "I swear, Kaz, if you looked up I will skin you and make a stole out of your fur."

Kaz put up his hands as if surrendering. "Wouldn't dream of it."

Phineas continued, his grin growing. "It was quite quick thinking, really. If I didn't know better, I'd think you hide men under your skirts regularly, Theo."

"No, just other small animals I find roaming the halls of my house. You'd be surprised how many confused raccoons I can fit under here."

Kaz let out a surprised laugh as Phineas's grin turned into a chuckle.

"Your mother seems wonderful, by the way," Phineas said once their laughs had died down.

"Now that Flo's gone, she's been strangely concerned with what I've been doing. And that was her on a good day. You should have seen her at Flo's wedding," Theo said.

"No wonder Cecily wanted nothing to do with her," Kaz said, earning a sharp look from Phineas. Theo bunched her brows, but before she could ask anything Phineas spoke up again.

"So, as much fun as hiding from your mother under skirts was, we actually came to bring you back home to prepare for your next task."

"Next task? Thank goodness." Theo sighed.

"That's the spirit!" Phineas said.

"I found out this morning that the wedding date has been set for six weeks from now."

"I see. Time crunch. Well, we'll make sure to let Cecily know. Ready?"

"Wait, we're leaving right now?"

"Yes. Cecily figured it would be easier if you just came to

her this time instead of meeting at the fountain since we're all going together anyway."

"Where are we going?"

"She'll explain in a minute."

"What about my mother? She will notice I'm missing."

"Cecily is taking care of that," Phineas said. Then, with an overdone frown, he continued, "Terrible news, Theo. You've come down with a highly contagious and rather disgusting stomach bug and are confined to your room for the next few days or until your task is done. She should leave you alone to be sick in peace."

"That will probably work just fine." Theo shrugged. As long as Theo's mother thought she knew exactly where her daughter was, she wouldn't care all that much. The last time Theo had been sick, her mother pretty much did the same thing, the maid bringing and taking trays from outside her door.

"Wonderful. Then let's get going."

She took Phineas's arm and her music room disappeared from view.

———————————————— ● ————————————————

The trio landed just outside Cecily's beguiling manor. Phineas held the door open for Theo and ushered her inside. In the daylight, it was much less foreboding. Instead of looking sinister, the snake railings were rather beautiful. She didn't have much time to gawk, however. Kaz and Phineas were walking toward the back of the manor. Theo followed after them and out to a stone veranda.

Lounging on a plush settee under an ivy-coated pergola was Cecily, who sat up and smiled brightly at her familiars. She had been covered with a light blanket, but set it aside as they came closer. This time, there was no mistaking her colorless pallor and the dark circles under her eyes.

With a sweep of her hand, Cecily conjured a tea service on the low table in front of them, Phineas and Kaz both helping themselves then sitting in the chairs near her.

"Have a seat, Theo, dear," Cecily said. "Have some tea."

Theo obliged and poured herself a cup.

"So," Cecily continued. "Second task. I have been invited to the regent's anniversary party at the Palace of the Fae. The regent, Tace of the Oak Fairies, and his partner, Aimon, have been together for nine hundred and ninety-seven years. It's not a round number so it's only a two-day celebration. You should have seen their nine hundred and fiftieth. The party lasted a week and a half. Of course, I'm bringing you three along. If you haven't ever been to a royal fairy party, and I'm assuming you haven't, you're in for a real treat, Theo.

"At this party will be Aimon's sister, the delightful fairy Endlin. She has in her possession a necklace that does not belong to her. It has quite a bit of sentimental and monetary value. Your task is to retrieve the necklace and bring it to me. The tricky part is this: Endlin will most likely be wearing it for the duration of the party. Even though it isn't hers, she's quite attached to it, both literally and figuratively."

Theo stared at her. A heist was her second task? She'd never stolen anything in her life.

Cecily sensed her hesitation. "While I can't help you

reclaim it directly, I will be at the party and can assist you in other ways, should you need it. But this is important—no one at this party knows you are working for me and we will need to keep it that way. It is considered rather poor form to steal from the sister of one of the hosts of a royal ball, after all, and as a human you'd be punished most severely if you are caught. Since pretty much everyone knows Kaz and Phineas are mine, they won't be able to spend much time around you while we're there, but they will also try to help where they can."

"When do the festivities start?" Theo asked.

"Tonight," Cecily said with a grin. "In the meantime, settle in, get ready. Kaz and Phineas can show you around if you'd like the grand tour. I am going to get a bit of rest before tonight, but I'll see you later."

She stood, pinching the bridge of her nose like she had a headache. When she tried to take a step forward, she wobbled, dropping back down to her seat.

Phineas leaped from his chair and rushed to her. Theo nearly did the same. It was the first time she'd seen the fairy anything other than graceful and poised, and the disparity was unsettling.

"I'm fine, I'm fine, my dearest," she said to him, but still let him take her arm in his and help her stand. She gave Theo an apologetic smile as Phineas escorted her back inside.

Phineas returned shortly after and gave Kaz a meaningful look as he sat back down.

"Is...she all right?" Theo ventured cautiously.

Phineas sipped his tea. "She's...no, she's not. She's quite sick actually."

"I didn't realize it was possible for fairies to get sick."

"It is extremely rare, but yes, it is possible," Kaz answered. "For her, it comes and goes. Some days are good, others aren't. Today hasn't been her best."

Theo stared into her teacup.

"Is there a cure?"

"Yes, there is," Phineas said. "We are working on it and are hopeful."

"Anything I can do to help?"

Phineas smiled. "Just keep doing what you're doing, Theo. In the meantime, the tour awaits."

Chapter 17

Where Theo Spends Time Like a Fairy's Familiar

Phineas seemed rather excited to give Theo the tour of their home, if the extra spring in his step and wide smile were any indication. Kaz walked next to her, ushering her into the various rooms as Phineas acted as the guide.

"Cecily's suite is in the west wing," Phineas said, pointing. "But you can maybe see that some other time."

Theo recalled all of his secretive smirks and the earlier concern he had shown Cecily. "Are you two . . . together?"

Kaz and Phineas both barked out a laugh. "No. My tastes lie elsewhere. Namely, men only."

Kaz raised a finger. "Not quite true. Attractive men only. That's the threshold."

"Oh, isn't that the truth," Phineas agreed. "I've met bean salads with more going on than my last lay. But, wow, was he beautiful. Don't need brains when you look like that."

"And you, Kaz?" Theo asked.

Phineas's eyes gleamed. "Are you asking Kaz the man, or Kaz the fox?"

"Wait...have you been with foxes?" Theo asked with a blend of humor and horror.

"Of course not!" Kaz scoffed. "Phineas, what is wrong with you?"

"So much. I could list all of my inferiorities for you, but we have better things to do. Come on, Theo, let's go to the game room while we wait for tonight."

Once in the game room, Kaz strode to the billiards table, racking the balls and passing out cue sticks. Theo had only played a few times, her mother deeming it an inappropriate activity for young ladies that would completely turn off any man, but Kaz and Phineas seemed to have no qualms about her participating.

"So, is this what you do all day when you're not helping me with tasks?" Theo asked as she put her cue stick back on its rack against the wall, the game having concluded.

"It is a lot of this," Phineas said, motioning to the game room. "But we also help Cecily with her other bargains sometimes, too."

"Oh? Are there scores of young ladies who have made bargains with Cecily to get out of marriages?"

Kaz laughed. "No, you're the only one trying to get *out* of a marriage."

"Does she have a lot of bargains going on currently?"

"Not really. Sometimes we have to collect payments and whatnot from older bargains. For instance, Kaz recently had to collect what was owed from a pixie who Cecily helped out. He had some humans encroaching on his territory, so he made a deal with Cecily that she'd remove the problem and he'd pay her in spirits," Phineas explained as he put his stick back on the rack as well.

Theo's eyes went wide. "He pays in spirits? Like souls?"

Phineas and Kaz burst out laughing. Kaz walked behind the bar and pulled out a small glass bottle with a clear pink liquid inside. "Spirits as in liquor. This is Pixie Rose Water. Beware, though—it's very strong alcohol that they make with rose petals and is exceptionally rare outside pixie society. Pixies do not sell it to non-pixies, so it was quite a lucrative deal for Cecily. She serves it up at parties and gives it as gifts to royalty. And occasionally lets us have some as well." He procured three small shot glasses from underneath the bar and poured them each a small amount. Kaz passed her one, clinked it with his own, and downed it in one gulp.

Following his example, Theo did the same. A cool burn similar to peppermint erupted in her mouth, followed by a sweet explosion of roses as she swallowed. She shivered as a sparkling sensation flowed over her skin like she had been dipped in champagne. For a moment, her body felt weightless. Her mind began to feel weightless as well, as though all her problems had vanished. Everything was fine. Everything was better than fine. It was great. Problems? What problems? She closed her eyes and smiled.

But as quickly as the feeling came on, it started to retreat. She opened her eyes to see Kaz and Phineas watching her with expectant grins.

"Yes, I can see why others would want to get their hands on that," she said as she set her glass back down.

"A few more glasses and that feeling sticks around for a while," Phineas said. "But seeing as we have a task to get ready for soon, we will probably cap our dosage at one. We'll have ale instead." He put three tankards on the bar and filled them up.

"Ever play darts, Theo?" Kaz asked.

The earl had enjoyed playing darts and had a few boards set up in the various game rooms and drawing rooms around the manor. He even had a few outside in the gardens. Theo had been throwing darts since she was a little girl, much to the chagrin of her mother. "Why, yes," she said with a sly smile. "I have."

"Great!" Phineas exclaimed.

"Ladies first, I assume?"

"Of course," Kaz said. "Where is one so we can invite her to play?"

She snorted, but smiled as he passed her a dart. Stepping up to the line, she aimed and fired, lodging her dart only a fraction outside the bull's-eye.

"Wait a second, Theo. Are you actually good at darts, or was that a lucky shot?" Phineas asked.

"I guess we will find out, won't we?" she said demurely as she stepped away.

Phineas went next, easily hitting the board and then bowing at his earned applause from the others. The game carried on this way for a while, with laughter and ribbing from Kaz and Phineas. But soon, she was surpassing Kaz in points, becoming neck and neck with Phineas.

Kaz, abandoning any pretense that he had even a slight chance of winning, began cheering on Theo.

"Theo, I'm counting on you. Phineas hasn't lost a game of darts in over seventy-five years," Kaz said as Theo took her turn.

"And I don't plan on losing now," Phineas said after sinking his dart into the upper ring. "Especially not to another human. I can't remember the last time that's happened."

"Over a century ago, I bet," said Kaz.

Theo paused, dart in hand.

"How long have you been here?" she balked.

Phineas chuckled. "Awhile. I'm at over five hundred years now and Kaz is right around three hundred."

"How?! I mean...so that's what she meant by not aging in her service? Did you make bargains for how long you'd be here?"

"No. With fairy familiars, the magic is different," Phineas said.

Kaz elaborated. "When you make a bargain with a fairy, you're getting fairy magic in exchange for something. Once the bargain is done, that's it. A trade. But with familiars, we are not bound by the same magic as bargains. We are in her service until we either get replaced or die."

"But I thought you didn't age in her service. How would you die?" Theo asked.

"When Kaz said 'die,' what he actually meant was 'get killed,'" Phineas said.

Theo's eyes went wide.

Phineas shrugged. "Obviously, Cecily is not the 'murdering familiars' kind of fairy, so we've both been here for centuries."

"So how did you come into being her familiars?" Theo asked, curiosity thoroughly piqued.

"Long stories for another day," Kaz said. "Theo, you're up."

If Theo could make at least twenty points on this turn, it would make her the winner. She let the remaining questions about familiars drift away while she took the dart and stood on the line.

"You can do it, Theo!" Kaz said from behind her.

Concentrating hard, she steadied herself, lined up her shot, and threw the dart exactly where she meant to, hitting the bull's-eye dead in the center.

Kaz and Theo erupted in cheers. He picked her up and spun her around and around as she tipped her head back and laughed, wrapping her arms around his neck.

"You did it, Theo! You've finally unseated Phineas! All hail the new champion!"

He put her back on the ground and slung his arm over her shoulders, pulling her close. Whether it was the ale or the high of the win, she didn't know, but she leaned into Kaz, wrapping her arm around his waist in return, reveling in her victory and the feel of him next to her.

"Well then, Phineas. Say it," Kaz said, near floating with excitement. "I've been waiting *decades* to hear you say it."

"Say what?" Theo asked.

Phineas cleared his throat, then bowed deeply to Theo. "You, dearest Theo, are the superior darts player."

Theo cocked her head at Kaz. "Wait. That's it?"

"Yes! But oh, the joy of hearing him say it! Do you know what it is like to finish every single game of darts by having to say that to Phineas? For hundreds of years? And for it to come out of his mouth... Theo, I'm thrilled you're here."

She knew he probably meant it more in jest, but her heart swelled hearing those words. That someone was excited to have her company. Grateful for it, even.

"Are you all right, Theo? Too much ale?" Kaz asked, looking down at her. She realized her smile had faded.

Before she could say or do anything else, Cecily breezed into the room, looking slightly more refreshed than she had earlier. "Was that Phineas I heard telling Theo she is the superior darts player?"

"I'm not sure how you did it, my fairy queen and mistress," Phineas said, "but you have managed to find the only person in the realms who can best me at darts."

Cecily laughed. "And I can see Kaz is grateful for it too."

Theo's cheeks went red as she stepped out from under Kaz's arm.

"I knew you had a great many hidden talents, sneaky Theo. And those talents shall be put to good use this evening as well." Cecily winked.

Theo stiffened as she mentally scolded herself. It was evening already and she hadn't even thought about the task since this morning. In no way was she prepared to go to the party.

"Phineas, my love, did you want to change, or would you like me to do it for you?" Cecily asked.

"I will head to my room to change, I think. I have a jacket I've been dying to wear and all I needed was an excuse. Tonight's festivities seem like a good one." He nodded at the group and left, his footsteps resounding off the marble foyer and up the stairs. Cecily asked the same question of Kaz, who chose to have Cecily dress him.

With a snap of her fingers, his outfit transformed. His hair was left loose, falling around his face until he pushed it back, completely uninterested in his new ensemble.

Theo tried to look anywhere else but his face or the part of his chest under the deep cut of the tunic's collar.

"Yes, I agree, Theo. He does look quite handsome in those pants," Cecily said as she appraised her own work with her hands on her hips. Kaz rolled his eyes, but when he looked at Theo, he smiled.

"Now for you," Cecily said, turning her attention to Theo. "I'll be honest, after hundreds of years of dressing Phineas and Kaz, I think I'm having too much fun with you." She was tapping her chin. "Aha! Let's try this," she said, snapping her fingers.

Theo looked down at herself and gasped. Wrapping around one shoulder and covering her body were thousands of small pink butterflies. When she touched her shoulder in wonder, a handful flew away and then disappeared, revealing a small spot of bare skin underneath. The hole was filled in by more butterflies like she hadn't touched her dress at all. Her hair was pulled into a low bun, matching blossoms tucked throughout.

"Well? What do you think?" Cecily asked.

"It's...it's gorgeous," Theo said. "But, are you sure this will make me blend in? Shouldn't we go for something a bit simpler?"

Phineas stalked in wearing his new jacket. But he stopped short when he beheld Theo. "Wow, Theo, you look stunning!"

"Well, she thinks we should tone it down," Cecily said.

"Absolutely not," Phineas said, shaking his head. "That dress is too perfect on you."

"What do you think, Kaz?" Cecily asked.

"You look beautiful," he said with no hint of humor. She could feel her face going red once more.

"See? There you have it. My turn." Cecily snapped her fingers again, her outfit changing to a strapless black dress so shiny and dark it looked like she was wearing ink. Theo was certain that if she touched it, her hand would come away wet. Around her neck and head were coils of black diamonds on thin silver chains. For the first time that Theo had seen, Cecily's hair was down, hanging like a sheet of darkness past her waist. The black makeup around her eyes made her look especially terrifying, her ensemble the death to Theo's fluttering life.

"*Wow*," Theo whispered, not being able to help herself.

"I will take that as a compliment," she said. "So, we seem to be all ready to go. And just to reiterate, Theo, we really can't let anyone know that you're working for me. Since I can't very well bring you in through the front door, we will be sneaking you in. I'm going to send you alone to the back of the palace. You need to go to the sixth window from the left."

"Wait. How will I know who Endlin is, though?" Theo asked.

"Excellent question! It makes me so happy to know you're paying close attention and taking this seriously. I will make sure to point her out. Then you do what you need to do to get us that necklace. Sound good?"

"I think so," Theo said.

"Wonderful. Then off you go to the Palace of the Fae! Good luck! And remember, if they catch you, they'll probably want to kill you, so don't get caught. For the greater good!"

Before Theo could respond, she was swept away to her second task.

———————————•———————————

Similar to her first task, she found herself outside a magical palace in the dark. Except this time, she was alone. Even in the low light, it was easy to see she was in a garden. Statues of mythical creatures were positioned on the path ahead like guards looming over her. She spared a glance at a stone minotaur, but it looked so realistic, its angry eyes glinting in the moonlight, she was not entirely confident it wasn't going to come to life and grab her.

She decided not to linger and made a brisk advance toward the palace, hoping Kaz or Phineas would be waiting to let her in. The path was made of stone tiles instead of gravel so at least she was not announcing her arrival with crunching footfalls. When the hedges cleared she went to the grass, now able to move in silence to the palace.

Following Cecily's directions, she counted the sixth window from the left and darted under it.

The window above her slid open, the sash creaking. She froze, doing her best impression of the garden statues.

"Who's the party crasher now?" came an amused whisper above her.

She let out her breath in a whoosh as she looked up to see both Phineas and Kaz smiling. They hauled her through the window like fishermen reeling in the daily catch, and indeed, she landed in the room with all the grace and delicateness of a net full of flopping sea creatures. A cloud of tiny butterflies burst into the air as she hit the floor, fluttering indignantly before returning to their positions, covering her once more.

Kaz hoisted her to her feet. "Did you want to try that again, Theo? I don't think the party heard your entrance."

Theo huffed as her dress settled. "I think you are overestimating my abilities and mistaking meanness for criminality. I have never been hauled through a window before, so I'd like to think that for my first time breaking and entering, I'm doing all right. If anything, I would have thought you'd be better at that, since I'm assuming you two do this kind of thing quite a bit."

"Well, no worries," Phineas said. "We didn't do the breaking part, just the entering, and you're in now."

"Why do I have to do this at a party anyway? Couldn't we just go to her home and steal the necklace?"

Phineas shook his head. "Fairy houses are warded quite securely. She would know if there was someone uninvited inside. And if the necklace went missing while people she knew were in her house, the list of suspects would be small. With so many people in attendance tonight and the palace wards less stringent, it will be harder for her to figure out who took it."

Kaz was standing at the door, peering out a small crack. "We are going to head to the party. Wait here for five minutes, then take a left, follow the hall to the end, up the stairs, then just follow the voices to the atrium. And remember, you don't know us, and you don't know Cecily."

Theo nodded as the two dashed out of the room, leaving her to watch the clock on the mantel.

Chapter 18

Where Another Popular Blond Is Making Theo's Life Difficult

Almost exactly five minutes later, Theo was poking her head out the door just as Kaz had. Neither seeing nor hearing anyone, she left the room and followed the directions she'd been given. Sure enough, as she came up the stairs she could hear the cacophony of voices reaching her like a wall of sound, the occasional shrill laugh or bold guffaw rising above the noise.

Theo had entered on the second-floor balcony of an atrium overlooking a wide court. She walked to the railing, gripping it to steady herself as she marveled at the view before her. The glass roof high above her was black from the night outside, causing the party to be reflected in its surface like a mirror, the effect making her feel like she was encased in the revelry. Fairies were dancing in the center of the room, others milled about on the edges drinking and talking. Even the balcony was filled with fairies. A calmer sort, to be sure, but still filling themselves with plenty of drinks, food, and conversation.

On the far end of the court sat two thrones, intricately carved and inlaid with gems and jewels. Sitting in them were two male fairies reaching across their chairs to hold hands. One, dressed in a gold tunic only a shade lighter than his bronze skin, was wearing a small crown, his short brown hair styled neatly around it.

This must be Tace, the regent.

The other fairy's head was unadorned save for his blond hair that was styled as though he simply ran his hands through it. Given the hand-holding, this fairy had to be Aimon. They faced the party, content to just watch the festivities. Stewards hovered nearby, ready to offer more wine or food.

With her current vantage point high above the court, Theo assumed she'd have no trouble spotting Cecily, Kaz, or Phineas, but it was proving to be quite difficult. Theo had thought Cecily's ensemble was the most magnificent and magical in existence, though now she was having second thoughts. Everyone here looked beyond spectacular. One fairy was wearing a dress that looked like it had been made of water, the skirts ending in a waterfall, but leaving not a drop behind as she moved through the crowd. Another wore a tunic made of purple feathers. Similar to Theo's butterfly dress, the feathers seemed alive. Every once in a while a feather would float off and drift lazily down before disappearing.

Theo began to walk around the balcony, scanning the crowd below. Just as she was becoming frustrated, trying to decide if she'd have to leave the balcony for the party proper, she spied Kaz. He was on the balcony as well, glass in hand, leaning up against a pillar and talking with a small group of other humans, likely other familiars. He only spared her a quick glance, but when he did manage to catch her eye, he turned to look down into the court below. Taking the hint and following his line of sight, Theo finally found Cecily.

Cecily looked up at Theo and winked, then began to walk into the crowd. At first it didn't look like she had a destination in mind as she ambled through the room, pausing every now and then to smile or chat. But Theo watched carefully just the same.

As she greeted one fairy in particular, Theo stiffened. Cecily spoke to the female fairy, reaching her hand out to a large brass pendant necklace the woman was wearing. Theo couldn't hear what was being said, but when Cecily pulled her hand back, the other fairy clutched it and smiled like she was thanking Cecily for a compliment. When Cecily turned away, she glanced up to where Theo was, raising her eyebrows for a split second before greeting someone else. The gesture was so discreet that it would have been impossible for anyone else to notice, but Theo got the message loud and clear: This was Endlin.

Theo could tell as she watched her target that the mission would be harder than she initially suspected, and she'd already assumed it would be quite difficult. That thief was apparently the most popular fairy at the party, given the quantity of other attendees who wanted to be near her. Endlin was so bright and bubbly that if all the lanterns went out, they could just use her shining personality to light the room. Surrounded by a group of at least fifteen others, she was captivating her audience with what must be the most comical story they'd ever heard, if the overdone peals of laughter whenever she paused long enough to take a breath were any indication.

And she was *beautiful*. Just like her effervescent disposition, her dress sparkled like it was made from champagne. Her wheat-blond hair, wrapped into a high chignon on top of her head, shone like the sun. Funnily enough, Endlin's hair was done almost exactly like Lady Balfour's signature style. But Theo knew if her mother ever saw this fairy, she'd try to slit her throat in a jealous rage; Endlin wore it the way Lady Balfour could only hope for. Instead of pulling her skin back from her face, on Endlin the hairstyle lifted her cheekbones so well they reached all the way to her temples. Her neck wasn't elongated, it was elegant. In fact, her every move was so graceful and controlled that she looked like she'd just taken a bow and walked offstage as a prima ballerina before coming to this event.

Theo hated her.

Even from afar, this fairy evoked such a visceral reaction it sent her stomach roiling. There was only one other person who gave Theo that feeling: Beatrice. Of course this would be the fairy who stole from someone and got away with it. Endlin didn't even look sorry. Birds of a feather apparently connived, stole, and were smug about it together.

Laugh it up, fairy. I'm coming for you.

But none of the disgust counted for anything if Theo couldn't figure out how to get that necklace off her. What was a *good person* even supposed to do in this situation? She couldn't very well walk up to the fairy, make a grand speech about morals and ethics, and expect the thief to hand over the necklace with a tearful apology. Theo was many things, but naive was not one of them. People like Endlin didn't care about the effects their behavior had on those they believed to be beneath them. And if this fairy was anything like Beatrice, she wouldn't even bother paying attention to someone who wasn't useful to her upward social trajectory.

However, in this situation, Theo's lack of usefulness to Endlin could be useful for herself. So while no plan was being formulated in her head, at least she could try to get close enough to follow her and figure something out without Endlin noticing. With her beginnings of a strategy and a subtle nod to Kaz, whose eyes had been darting over to her every few minutes, Theo made for the stairs...and froze halfway there as she saw a familiar face watching her from the other side of the balcony.

Standing with a group of fairies and smiling at her was Lock. In another situation, she might have been pleased to see him. But one of her only instructions was to not let anyone here know she was working for Cecily, and here was a fairy who definitely knew exactly whom she was in service to.

Her body was screaming *flee* as she stood stock-still, unsure of what to do next as he walked around the balcony toward her. She looked to the archway she had come in through, trying to figure out how fast she could move without garnering any attention. Or maybe she could try another way to get to the atrium where she could disappear into the crowd and lose him. Then once she did, she could subtly hint to Kaz or Phineas that she was compromised and they could help her think of a new plan.

But before she could get herself to do anything, he had reached her.

"Well, good evening, Theo. Imagine my delight when I saw you from across the balcony. You look absolutely marvelous this evening. Feel free to roll your eyes; I can keep the compliments coming all night." He stood close, grinning down at her. But his smile faltered when the look of shock on Theo's face did not change. "Is everything all right?"

He opened his mouth to say something else, but Theo grabbed his arm and dragged him over to the wall. "I'm here by myself. I came alone."

"Alone?"

"Yes. I'm not here with anyone else."

"All right," he said slowly. "Then how'd you get here?"

"Light breeze."

"Sure. Uh, Theo...what's going on?"

"I'm not working for anyone, all right? It's just me here alone. All by myself. I came by myself. No one brought me here. I just decided to come to this gathering on my own and not in the service of any fairy in particular, understood?"

His brows were creeping up on his forehead as though aspiring to join his hairline.

"Understood?!" she said, gripping so tight her nails were digging into his arm.

"I guess?"

"Good." She sighed, releasing him.

"Can you tell me what is happening now?"

"Nothing is happening. Everything is fine. Now, I should go."

As Theo made to step away, he grabbed her hand. "Did I do something? Is this about how things ended at my party? You left upset and in a hurry. If I made you feel awkward or uncomfortable, I'm sorry."

She shook her head. "No, Lock. It's not that."

But Lock didn't stop. "What Kasra said to you was horribly unfair."

"Lock, it's fine." She smiled sadly, touched and surprised at how much that moment had bothered him.

"I hope you know that you are allowed to do whatever you want, Theo, with whomever you want," he said as he brushed an errant butterfly off her collarbone, his fingertips lingering. "Whenever you want to."

He leaned in and she froze. A huge part of her wanted to kiss him, wanted to find a dark corner and pretend she was one of the fairies at the party. Wanted to be pushed up against the stone wall while she wrapped her arms around him. To be selfish and take what he wanted to give her.

But even though it was only a small part of her telling her to stop, that part was screaming in her ear. Good people weren't selfish. Good people would figure out how to steal a necklace off a thieving fairy to convince other fairies of their goodness.

"*Maybe we shouldn't,*" she whispered when his lips grazed hers.

He stopped but only pulled back a fraction. "Why not? Kasra isn't here to spoil our fun." He winked.

"Oh, he's right over there." Theo tipped her head toward where Kaz was standing. He was still watching them, his expression a mask of boredom, but even from this distance she could see the fire in his eyes.

Lock shook his head. "Of course he is. Why have fun yourself when you can spoil it for others instead?"

"Is that what he's doing?"

Lock snorted. "Watch out for that one, Theo."

"That's funny. He said the same thing about you."

"Oh he did, did he?"

"He said your motivations were unclear."

His gaze darted between her eyes and mouth. "I'd say my motivations are crystal clear. And I'd also say he's just jealous."

"Jealous? Have you met him? Ornery and cranky, yes. But jealous?"

Lock barked a laugh. "Absolutely. I'm having a lovely chat with a lovely lady and he's stuck over there, socializing with probably equally as boring familiars while pretending he doesn't know who you are. If he could come over here right now, he would."

"Because you're just that interesting to be around?"

"Maybe I am." He shrugged. "You certainly are."

"Is that why you're telling me to be careful? Because you think he finds me so interesting? I can tell you right now, that's not the case."

"Maybe. Maybe I just don't like competition. Maybe I want you all to myself."

"Why?" *Why me?*

"You're a breath of fresh air, Theo."

She rolled her eyes. "The more you try to compliment me, the more I realize you don't know me at all."

"Maybe I do."

"If you tell me that my smile lights up a room or I'm your ray of sunshine on a cloudy day, I'll be forced to consider you an absolute stranger."

He tipped his head back and laughed. "And with lines like that, you only keep proving me right."

Theo couldn't help smiling. But then once again that little voice started to nag at her. The corners of her mouth sank as she remembered that she was standing in the Palace of the Fae with a mission.

"You probably should make it a point not to be seen with me."

"Is this about you being here alone? By yourself? Not having come to the party with anyone? Because you're all alone?"

"I get it, I get it. But yes. That is the reason. Thank you for not asking follow-up questions."

He winked. "See you around, then, gorgeous," he said before going down to the main party.

She turned to see if Kaz was still standing at the pillar, but he was gone. Theo walked back to the balcony railing to once again take in the scene below, Endlin now no longer where she had been. Instead, Theo watched Lock as he drifted through the crowd. Her instructions for him didn't seem to be difficult to follow as he paused every few feet to greet, hug, or kiss other partygoers, not ever looking up to where she was.

She sighed as she silenced that familiar hum of jealousy vibrating around her chest, her nails clicking on the wooden railing as she tapped them. This was not her party to participate in. She had a task to complete and she'd better pull herself together and get it done. Replacing the image of handsome, flirty Lock with the decrepit Duke of Snowbell to get her head on straight, she scanned the crowd for Endlin and the necklace.

This time, it didn't take nearly as long to find her target. Endlin was dead center on the dance floor, spinning and laughing with a group of other fairies. Clearly, Endlin was not going to make this easy for her. How would she ever be able to get close enough to steal a necklace from her with no one seeing?

No matter what, she wasn't going to accomplish anything from the balcony. Keeping one eye on her target, Theo went down to the party. Having clung to the edge and sneaking as fast as she could without looking suspicious, she found that Endlin, ever the social butterfly, had once again moved. Theo had only just managed to spot the spritely fairy in her fizzy dress as she walked through a doorway on the far side of the atrium.

The room Endlin disappeared into looked to be some sort of game room. It was rather full, which would allow Theo to slip in unnoticed and watch from a distance. Watching for what, she still had no clue. She was continuing to wing it, hoping something clever would come to her while she did.

She was just about to walk through the archway when a hand held up to her face stopped her in her tracks. Theo looked up to find the owner of this hand and discovered it attached to the most massive fairy she'd ever seen. If his telltale pointy ears weren't poking out of his mess of spiky hair, she would have guessed him to be an ogre instead. His round head teetered on his thick neck like an overfilled balloon with a brow so prominent it could double as a bookshelf. Not that he looked like someone who would use it for that purpose. He didn't seem like the type who would recognize literature even if it was sitting directly over his eyes and offering shade on a sunny day.

"Just where do you think you're going?" the fairy said in a guttural baritone voice.

Theo pointed to the room. "In there."

"No, you're not."

"I need to go in, so if you'll excuse me." She plastered on a polite, demure smile.

He grunted, feet planted, blocking the entrance. "I don't remember ever seeing you here before," he said as he looked her up and down, crossing his arms over his wide barrel chest.

Theo huffed and mimicked his stance. "Do they tell all the fairies to use that line? Is it in some sort of handbook for starting a conversation? No, you haven't seen me here before. But thank you for checking in with me on your great memory. Now, excuse me."

His brows became so furrowed they were trying to hug the bridge of his nose. "Familiars are not allowed in. You have three seconds to scamper off before I call your fairy over and have you both thrown out of the party." He raised a meaty hand and held up a finger. "One."

"Oh, knock it off," she snapped. "I won't be threatened by an oversize doorstop who can't count to four. If I *was* with a fairy, I'd call them over myself, just to see you try. Because doing anything other than standing here showing off your math skills would require you to do actual work, and we both know that's not going to happen."

He dropped his arms and stepped toward her.

She had to crane her neck to look up at him, but she held her ground and raised her chin to show she would not be intimidated. He might spend his evenings bullying other humans, but she was not going to join those ranks.

He growled through his next words. "You're not here with a fairy?"

"No. I'm an unbonded human," she said with an air of authority, hoping that this time, instead of name-dropping a fairy, the absence of a name-drop would secure her entry.

The guard snarled at her like she'd spit in his tea after running over the family dog.

"What are you doing out here? Who said you could leave?"

"Pardon?"

"How did you get out?"

Get out? She had been laboring under the assumption that, like all the other parties she'd ever been to before, the room with a doorman was for the party elite. Which were places people wanted to *get into* and then could also freely leave from. Certainly not anywhere someone would need to *get out* of. Any place that required permission to leave was not a place she wanted to be.

She had a sneaking suspicion she'd made a terrible mistake. One that she would now need to hastily backtrack from.

"Who let me leave? Uh...I did not get the gentleman's name, but I had let him know I needed to use the powder room. Oh, and it looks like I forgot something in there, so I should go back and get it." She retreated a step, but he matched her stride and continued to stand over her.

"Scrawny fairy with red hair?"

Who? "Yes, that is the one," she lied. Maybe that fairy had had the clearance to let her out so she could be on her way. "Lovely, articulate fellow. I'm sure he aced the interview process."

"He wasn't supposed to let you out."

"That sounds like something you should take up with him directly."

But this advice did not seem to make the ogre-fairy hybrid in front of her any happier.

"You're not going anywhere, you nasty little rodent." He grabbed her arm.

"I just told you I need to use the powder room. I do not need an escort. I can get there on my own." She tried to shrug out of his grip, but he held firm.

"I don't think so. Back you go."

"I'd rather not, thank you," she said, planting her feet and leaning away from him.

He raised an eyebrow. "Trying to play nice now? Manners won't help you. Get in."

Without waiting for her reply, he dragged her into the room. He was large enough where it didn't seem to take any more effort to move her than it would a feather, but he released her with enough force to send her stumbling. She collected herself, brushing off her arm like his hand had been dirty.

First order of business: bearings gathering. She moved to the wall, wanting to get a hidden vantage point in order to get the lay of the land. But when she looked around, her instincts told her to run. It was plain to see why the humans were in this room.

They were the entertainment.

Chapter 19
Where Theo
Formulates the Plan

Her initial impression had been correct. She was in a game room. And in almost every area were humans. In the middle of some laughing fairies, a man and a woman were dancing animatedly. Their faces were brick red and pained as they dipped and twirled in unison.

A slightly luckier man was dealing cards at another table, but at every other card he was being accused of cheating by a very tipsy fairy. Two more were acting as pawns in a game of chess between two highly competitive players.

But those humans were not the cause of the stomach-churning dread.

On the wall next to her were five stoic humans, shoulder to shoulder in a neat line, each with an apple on his head. Across from them, about twenty paces away, stood a group of fairies.

"Five coins says he misses!"

"Nah, ten says he gets it!"

A male fairy stepped up in front of the group. In his hand glinted a small silver knife. He positioned his feet and aimed a few slow practice swings before letting the knife fly. It whipped through the air faster than Theo could follow it, embedding right below the sternum of one of the humans. Theo clapped her hands over her mouth to stifle a scream. The fairies cheered as the human dropped to the floor with a cry, the apple falling off his head and rolling to the feet of the fairy who had thrown the knife. He scooped it up and took a bite, grinning at the others as he chewed.

"He missed! You owe me five coins!"

The knife wielder chuckled. "Did I? You never asked what I was aiming for. It wasn't the apple."

Two other humans had grabbed the man's arms and were dragging him away, leaving a smear of blood on the floor as they did. The knife was still lodged in his chest, his head lolled back. Theo thought the other humans in the line would be shocked or scared, but instead, they just moved closer to the center, filling the gap that had been made.

Another fairy had stepped up, knife in hand.

Theo thought she was going to be sick. She'd never seen a man get killed before, and now she was about to witness her second in as many minutes. She needed to leave pronto. But as she looked around, the only exit she could see was the door she came in through, and there was no way she was going to get past that giant doorman.

The next fairy started to lift his arm to aim at a human. Without anywhere else to look, she squeezed her eyes shut.

"Theo, what are you doing in here?"

Her eyes flew open and she saw Lock.

"*They're killing them*," she whispered, ignoring his question.

"No, look."

The man who had been stabbed in the chest was now propped up against the wall, the knife having been pulled out. Other humans were pressing a cloth to the wound as the man blinked.

"See? He's all right."

"You're using 'all right' very loosely here, Lock."

"I know, I know. But they're used to it."

"Used to it?!"

"Yes. They're humans who bargained with the house for favors. They'll be fine. I'm assuming you got in here because they found out you're not here with a fairy?"

She nodded.

"Humans who aren't familiars are brought to parties, usually having made a bargain with the host, to act as entertainment for the other guests. You're either here with a fairy as a familiar or in service to the host. Since you've told them you're not here as a familiar, it only leaves one option. But hang tight. I'll see if I can get you out."

She was about to nod in agreement when she spied Endlin strolling through the room, drink in hand. Theo watched her waft to a nearby table, greeting the few others who were already there, then taking a seat herself. As she set her drink down, her hand reached to her chest where she grabbed the pendant and twirled it between her fingers as though it was a good luck charm.

"I can't leave yet," Theo said to Lock.

He was about to say something else but stopped when he heard his name being called from behind. Both Theo and Lock turned toward a fairy seated at the same table as Endlin.

"Lock, I thought that was you."

"Hello, Koel," Lock said in his usual jovial tone. But when he turned back toward Theo, he leaned down and whispered, *"Stay here, I'll be back as soon as I can."*

Theo was more than happy to stay where she was, but the fairy named Koel wasn't.

"Don't leave your friend standing by the wall," Koel said, watching Theo.

At the snap of his fingers another chair appeared next to him. He patted it, his eyes crinkling with overt amusement. "Join us."

Theo tried to catch Lock's eye so he might be able to give her some sort of context clue about Koel, but he had just sat down and was greeting Endlin with a peck on the cheek.

Koel looked like a peacock personified, both in outfit and character, as he leaned back in his chair. While Kaz's disregard for fashion and appearance was legitimate, this fairy was trying too hard to seem as though he didn't care what he looked like, when it was quite clear he did. So coiffed was his appearance that it looked like he had sat in front of a mirror for hours in order to get his look just right. His tunic was open at the top to expose his gleaming, almond-colored and probably oiled chest, the buttons perfectly undone. His sleeves were rolled up as though he had something important to do that required his hands, but they were way too silky and smooth to show that he did anything other than lotion and maintain them. His shiny brown hair was pulled away from his face with sapphires sprinkled like dewdrops in his braids. He was watching Theo with such light amber eyes they appeared gold.

As soon as Theo sat down, a glass of bloodred wine was placed in front of her.

"I remember you from Lock's party," Koel began after she had taken a sip. "You're quite the harp player." He turned to look at the others sitting at the table. "She had everyone on their feet. We were dancing for hours."

The few other fairies sitting around the table were watching Koel with rapt attention. She already knew she wouldn't like them. As far as Theo could tell, they were the magical male versions of Lady Mabel and Lady Gertrude. They existed not to have any of their own thoughts flowing through their heads, but instead followed around the big dog in the yard, thrilled to trade devotion for any scraps of attention that came their way.

"You were at the party?" Theo asked. For the life of her, she couldn't recall seeing him at all.

"Mm-hmm." He nodded and then tipped his head toward Lock. "Guess you were too enthralled with the host to pay attention to anyone else."

Oh, fine then.

"Not entirely true. I was also too busy mingling with the other musicians to notice you."

He chuckled as he sipped his drink. "So, are you here with Lock again tonight? Did he win you in another bargain and now you get to mingle with fairies again, pretending to be above your station?" The other fairies at the table let out over-done laughs, and Koel winked at them.

"He never won me in a bargain to begin with. I made a bargain and am here on my own this evening. Running into Lock was pure happenstance."

"What did you bargain playing your harp for? Some fairy favor, I assume? Gold? Luck for a day? Getting some poor sap to fall in love with you?"

"You assume wrong. Playing the harp was repayment for taking on the debt of a gnome who was in jail. I had him released by making a bargain with Lock."

Koel laughed in disbelief. "Why would you ever do some-thing like that?" He turned to Lock. "I'm surprised you agreed to it. Isn't this the same gnome who had put a blight on your vineyard for a century? Nasty little fellow, if memory serves. Harp playing was all it took?"

"Only nearly a century. But yes, harp playing from Lady Theodosia was all it took, since she made him remove the blight. I'd say I made out like a bandit. No more blight, no more annoying gnome on my property, and beautiful music from a beautiful woman."

"Well, it was a bargain well-made, then, since it was one of your more entertaining parties in recent memory. Who knew the trick to liven up your get-together was a talented human?"

Endlin had been watching the exchange, her eyes lingering on Koel and fluttering her lashes when he looked her way. Just as Theo had suspected, she wasn't content to sit on the side-lines not being the center of attention for very long.

Endlin sighed. "Shame I had to miss the party. I'm always so busy."

"Well, next time Lady Theodosia deigns to play for us again, I'll make sure you know about it," Lock said.

One of the other fairies spoke up. "How long have you been playing?"

"I've been studying the harp since I was a child," Theo said.

Endlin sighed again. "Oh, how I wish I had the time for such things. It must be wonderful to have that much free time to devote to such simple pursuits. It would be such a treat to take a break from my busy schedule and play an instrument."

Now, this Theo was familiar with. She'd had plenty of conversations like this with Beatrice over the years. It was a real skill to be able to take any compliment that Theo had received, no matter how deserved, and not only twist it to sound like an insult, but also manage to pivot the conversation back to talking about herself. Why let someone else have a few precious moments of glory?

A fairy sauntered over to their table. "Good evening, good evening, lady and gentlemen." He bowed to Endlin and then to the other fairies at the table, acting like he hadn't even seen Theo seated right in front of him. "Anyone else care to play Knives with us? It's winner takes all this round." He raised his brow at each of the fairies at the table.

Lock shook his head, as did Endlin and Koel, but the three other fairies who were sitting at her table decided to take him up on his offer.

As they walked off, Theo turned her attention back to her own table. Koel was staring directly at her, a dark gleam in his eyes. "Not a fan of fairy games, then? Makes sense for you, though. I suppose it wouldn't appeal to a human. Are they friends of yours?" He jerked his chin toward the game.

"No. I just don't find amusement in deliberately harming others who have done nothing to me. Either the fairies are terrible shots or terrible sports. Both of which should have disqualified them from playing, not resulted in them being applauded."

Koel chuckled. "What would you know about sportsmanship? Don't tell me you're a ranked competitive harp player?" His grin turned into a full smile when Endlin laughed at his odd joke.

"Why, yes, I am. Our contests are right next door to the competitive hair-bejeweling league. I'm surprised I've never seen you there."

Lock snorted into his wine and Koel sobered, a snarl crossing his mouth before he turned it into a smirk once more. He pointed to where the humans were recuperating. "Oh, come on. Look at how much fun they're having, though! You're sure you don't want to put your name in to play, Lady Theodosia?"

"I don't think I'd be very good at standing and letting people throw sharp objects at me," she replied.

"How would you know unless you tried? We can enter you into the game and you can report your findings back to us."

She didn't want to bother explaining she knew exactly what it felt like to be stabbed.

What he mistook her silence for, she didn't know, but he spoke as if offended by her lack of reply, his voice dropping low. "We could make you play, you know. You're an unclaimed human. I could put you in the game right now."

An idea struck her. Maybe this was the opening she had been looking for.

She took a swig of her wine and mimicked his expression. "Did you want to play a game, Koel? I'll play with you. But I'm not going to stand in front of a wall just to have knives thrown at me by drunk fairies. If I am to play a game, I want to have a turn throwing, so I suggest a game of darts. And all four of us at this table have to play."

Koel looked at Lock and Endlin. "What do you say, friends? Are you in?"

Lock shrugged and nodded, but Endlin said nothing.

"Oh, come now, Endlin. It will be fun." Lock playfully nudged her shoulder.

Theo knew this ploy, too, having watched Beatrice use it hundreds of times. Here was the part where everyone else was supposed to try to convince Endlin to participate, just so she could hear how much they wanted her to.

"Oh, all right, all right. If you insist." She looked to Koel, giving him the space to also encourage her.

"It wouldn't be fun without you, Endlin," Koel said as he drummed his hands on the table and winked. Endlin beamed.

"Well, if that's all—" Koel started.

"It's not," Theo interrupted. Now that Endlin was officially in the game, Theo had to seal the deal. "I was led to believe the human players were in it for a boon of some kind. If I play, I want one."

"This should be interesting. What do you want? Money? Power? The ability to smite an enemy with more than just your bratty tone?"

Theo stole a glance at Endlin. She knew she couldn't outright ask for the necklace. But was there another way she could barter for it?

"If I win, one of you has to give me something," she finally answered.

"And what is that something?"

"I'm not telling until I win. It is a risk you'll just have to take if you want me to agree. But I will say it isn't very large."

Koel looked toward the other two for approval before he agreed to her terms. When neither Lock nor Endlin objected, Koel turned back to Theo and nodded.

"Sounds reasonable. Do we have a deal?"

"It's a deal."

It was all Theo could do to not hover off the chair in her excitement. She'd done it. She'd lined herself up the perfect cover for scoring the necklace. And she could do it via her own upstanding talents and not by some sneaky, covert method that she wasn't going to be very good at anyway.

She could hardly wait to see the look on Endlin's thieving face when she would be forced to hand over the necklace.

Chapter 20
Where Darts and
the Plan Both
Get Dizzy

Koel jumped to his feet, ushering the others over toward the dartboard.

"So, do the standard rules of darts apply?" Theo asked, relishing her own foresight for checking the rules first when playing games with fairies. She twisted a dart between her thumb and forefinger, eager to get the game going and be finished with task number two.

Koel grinned. "They would if we were playing a standard game of darts. Since you never specified which game, we are playing Dizzy Darts. Heard of it?"

Uh-oh.

"Can't say that I have. What's Dizzy Darts?"

"It's just like regular darts except not at all. First you roll some dice and spin around that many times before throwing. We count up instead of down, and the first player to make it to or past seven hundred wins."

Well, that put a kink in her confidence. But no, she wouldn't let this get her down. The throwing was still the same—mostly—and she could do that no problem. So what if there was a bit of spinning thrown in?

"And just to make it a bit more intriguing," Koel said, eyes shining. "We each take turns standing in front of the board. But don't worry. Unlike the other game, we'll deduct points if you strike someone, so if you're planning on winning, best not to stab anyone with a dart."

Theo braced her spine and mimicked his grin. "Sounds fun."

"Excellent," he purred as he dropped two dice on the small table. Then he went over to a human carrying a tray of drinks.

While he was distracted, Lock stepped closer to Theo.

"Are you going to do this, or do you need me to get you out of here?"

"I made a bargain. I'm doing this. Just don't hit me with a dart while it's my turn up there."

"Likewise," he said as Koel returned.

"As a show of good faith, for the first round, I shall stand at the board," Koel said. "Endlin, why don't you start us off?"

Endlin smiled. "I can't remember the last time I played darts. I'm sure I'll be terrible. I will try my hardest not to hit you!" She paused, giving the others a chance to chime in and compliment her. Koel fell for it, telling her she was most likely an excellent darts player.

He walked to the board, standing with his back straight.

Endlin rolled the dice, picked up a dart, and stepped up to the demarcation line on the floor.

"Here goes!" She started to spin like she was a dancer on a music box, Koel and Lock counting out loud. She launched her dart, only just making it onto the board.

"Theo, I believe you are up next," Lock said as he gestured to the table.

After rolling and taking a dart from the pile, she stepped up and began to turn in circles. While she had taken plenty of dancing lessons over the years, she knew she was nowhere near as graceful as Endlin. But she wasn't going for grace anyway, she was going for the high score. When she stopped spinning, she found the line again, aimed, and embedded her dart into the wall four feet to the left of the dartboard. Koel burst out laughing. Theo scowled at the sound of Endlin's giggle from behind her.

"Sorry if I didn't make the rules clear enough for you, Lady Theodosia," Koel said, still chuckling. "The point of the game is to hit the board."

All she could do was huff, her disappointment in herself forcing out any witty comment she could have lobbed at the board instead of a dart. Koel only laughed some more.

After a few more rounds, it was Theo's turn to stand at the board. She took a deep breath and tried to square her shoulders. Under no circumstances was she going to let Koel or Endlin see her squirm. When she caught Lock's eye, he gave her the smallest of nods and she was at least a little relieved for the moment of encouragement. Lock wasn't going to try to hit her with a dart, and so far, he was doing well hitting the board. Endlin and Koel both had higher scores than she did, so she tried to tell herself that they wouldn't want to risk points by hitting her.

She was still trying to decide whether she wanted her eyes open or closed when Lock fired off the dart. It was too fast for her to see the dart coming at her, but the sound was enough to cause her to flinch. She turned to look at where the dart had landed, finding it in the lower quadrant, a hair's breadth away from missing the board entirely.

Koel had noticed the throw's lack of accuracy as well. "What do you call that?" he asked Lock, chuckling in disbelief.

"Slippery fingers, I guess." Lock made a show of laughing and wiping his hands on his pants, but when he looked at Theo, he winked. She mouthed *"Thanks"* at him before anyone else noticed.

The rest of her time at the board went just as easily, Endlin scoring decent points but pouting enough in Koel's direction for him to shower her with praise. On his turn, Koel raised his eyebrows at her in a taunt but threw with precision.

As the game wound on, Theo started to get a bit more nervous. She was beating Lock for points and only just behind Endlin, but Koel was way ahead of her. He was also spending a good portion of the game watching her, as though studying her every move, every bit of speech.

Soon enough, it was Theo's turn to stand at the board again. Lock patted her back in a show of support as she walked to the board. When she turned around to face the game, Koel was twirling a dart like a teensy baton between his fingers, his gaze on her like he'd just caught her in a trap. The look left her questioning whether he wanted to win more than he wanted to spear her with leisure sports equipment.

He had just stepped up to the line before Lock interceded him.

"I know you're excited to win points and *not* hit Lady Theodosia with a dart, Koel. But I do believe it is my turn."

"Ah, you're right! My mistake!" Koel ushered Lock to the line.

Lock finished his turn and Koel picked up a dart, his smile thick and curling at the corners like wet paper, and just as pleasant.

"Better hold still," he said, lining up his shot.

He set down his glass on the table and started to spin as Endlin and Lock counted along. But Theo could barely hear it over the squeaking of her teeth as she ground them together.

Just breathe.

She took one last gigantic breath and whooshed it out, then pretended her head was glued to the board so she wouldn't move.

Without warning, he whipped the dart straight at her. Just as she heard the dart sink into the board, she felt a searing pain on her earlobe. She cried out and leaped away from the wall, clasping her hand over her ear. When she took her hand away, there was a swipe of blood in her palm.

Endlin's brows furrowed in confusion and shock, while Koel was biting his lip like he was trying hard not to laugh.

Lock was staring at Theo's ear like it had been ripped clean off. He rushed to her, clutching a handkerchief and pressing it to the side of her head. Rage swarmed his face, his jaw flexing as he dabbed at the wound. She reached up to her ear again, just to make sure it really wasn't as bad as Lock was making it out to be, and was relieved to feel that it was perfectly intact.

"What was that, Koel?" Lock growled.

"Slippery fingers, I guess," he said as he held up his hands. "And look, she's already healed. Aren't you, Lady Theodosia?"

She touched where the dart had grazed her only to find that it had, in fact, closed already. She took the now-red-speckled handkerchief from Lock and wiped the remaining blood from her ear and hand. "Quite all right, Koel. Shame you didn't have slightly worse aim. I could always use another spot in my ears to put jewelry."

"Theo," Lock started, his back turned to Koel.

"Lock, it is fine. Really. This is nothing. Promise." She gave him a reassuring smile.

"I can get you out of here if you decide it is too much."

As he spoke, Endlin went to the table to take her turn, brushing the necklace with her fingers.

"No," Theo said. "I'm going to stay in the game."

He sighed, but nodded.

"Oh, I do hope I don't hit you with the dart. I do *not* like the sight of blood. It makes me so lightheaded." Endlin added a little shiver with her shoulders, just to really drive her point home as she stepped up to the line. "Though, if I do faint, you'd make sure to catch me, right, Koel?"

Theo was surprised she couldn't feel the breeze from Endlin's energetic lash batting as Koel told her that of course he would.

Whether it was the length of the game, the sticky-fingered narcissist, or the faint but lingering sting in her ear, Theo was more than ready for her turn to be over.

"Would you just throw the dart already?" she snapped, patience finally exhausted from having to stand at the board while Endlin put all her effort into her self-absorption.

If Endlin was anything like Beatrice, which she clearly was, then it was a rare day that anyone would speak to her in that tone. Sure enough, Endlin stiffened with indignation. Then, with a stony look more suited to the news that her favorite goldfish had died, she twirled in place and launched her dart at the board. She had hardly bothered to see where it had landed before marching off back to her drink and downing the rest of the contents in one wet gulp.

The mood only soured further. Theo wasn't sure she'd ever witnessed a more grim game of darts. Even the earl's overly competitive friends were never this morose. Yet the game continued on, no one wanting to surrender.

Endlin sulked off to the side, only deigning to return to the game when it was her turn.

Lock was trying his hardest to maintain his light tone, but even he was wearing down, his amusement now sounding more like apathy as he tossed darts that sometimes didn't even hit the board.

Theo was mostly just eyeing the scoreboard, watching with dread as Koel's score was creeping closer and closer to seven hundred.

And Koel was staring at Theo like he wanted to throw something larger than a dart her way. Maybe a chair or spear, if his creased brow was anything to go by.

But her desperation to win combined with Endlin's earlier petulance and Koel's look of light sadism gave her an idea.

As her score stood now, there was no way she'd ever make enough points to jump into first place. Not unless she could lower the scores of Endlin and Koel.

And there was only one way to do that.

Koel had already taken a hit to his points. Maybe he'd do it again.

She wished she had thought of her new strategy a little earlier, since now she only had one round to make Koel and Endlin angry enough at her.

She braced herself as the next round began.

Here we go.

Luckily, Endlin returned to begging for flattery, giving Theo the opening that she needed.

Theo scoffed at her latest attempt to coax a compliment from Koel.

Endlin narrowed her eyes. "What?"

"What do you mean, 'what?' I didn't say anything," Theo said in a mockery of innocence.

"Well, you made a noise."

"Am I not allowed to make noises in your presence? All right. Any more fairy edicts I should be aware of?"

Endlin just turned away from her as though she didn't hear her.

Koel was shaking the dice in his fist like he wanted to crack them. He had barely stepped up to the line before throwing, hitting the board with his usual accuracy.

She only had a few precious moments left.

Theo sighed loudly. "Oh, pardon me! That was a noise. Whoops! I hope I didn't distress you too much, Endlin."

"Will you stop it?" Endlin huffed.

"Stop what? Doing what you've asked me to do? I mean, I could. But in return I'd ask that you please make up your mind. Your rapid changes in instructions are going to give me whiplash."

Lock moved away from the board, coming to stand near Theo.

"Theo, stop," he pleaded.

But now would be the worst time to quit. Time was running out before she'd have to march up to the board.

"No, Lock. I don't think I will."

Koel planted his feet and crossed his arms. "Please don't, Lady Theodosia. By all means, if you have something to say, then say it. Tell us what you really think." Great news for Theo's plan, still on his face was his smarmy little smirk, one eyebrow arched.

Theo gave him a wicked grin. "You want to know what I really think about you? All right. I've seen circus ponies less showy than you. But at the end of the day, I guess you don't have to worry too much about it, because you are incredibly handsome. There's no insult there. I'm sure you and your mirror are going to be very happy together, since you are the only one who could stand to be in your presence for any longer than five minutes. Might be a bit chilly and hard, but at least your reflection willingly kisses you back."

She turned to Endlin. "And you. You're beautiful, too. You know it. I bet you hear how gorgeous you are all the time. I bet, after you've said something you thought was cute, or funny, or clever, people respond with 'Wow, you're so beautiful.' But after every party, when you're home by yourself sitting at your vanity and taking off your makeup, do you wonder where all your friends are? I heard people laughing around you before. Were your jokes truly that good? Or are you just that good-looking? What is the last thing you got complimented on? Your wit? Your charm? Or was it your *hair*?

"I know someone exactly like you. Dazzlingly pretty. So dazzling that she was blinded by it, blinded to how her actions affected those around her. And everyone else was just a supporting player in her show, reduced to one character trait. Charming, or wicked, or ugly, depending on how you fit into her narrative. Which is exactly how you see the world, isn't it? Everyone here is supposed to notice you. Supposed to laugh at your witticisms. Supposed to tell you how wonderful you are. And when someone doesn't, well, then you've got all the gunpowder you need to fire yourself out of a victim cannon into a lake of your own tears. And it is why you think you can get away with all your bad behavior. I see through it. Because your personality is as thin as paper."

"And, Lock." She spit his name like poison, tilting her head in consideration as she made a show of sizing him up. He froze, as though bracing himself for whatever gouges Theo was preparing to inflict on his self-esteem. "You throw enjoyable parties."

Conjuring her best impersonation of her mother, she stuck her nose in the air and glided to the board, only taking in their stunned faces when she turned around to press her back to the wall. "So that is what I think about you all. Shall we finish the game now?"

She let her lips curl up, because not only did it goad them further, her plan seemed to be working. Koel was attempting to remain stiff and still, like he wasn't at all bothered by what she had said. However, his absurd hair jewels were twinkling in the light from his tremors of aggravation. Endlin, on the other hand, was swaying on her feet, drooping like garden party decorations after a rainstorm.

Lock, well, she couldn't really tell what Lock was thinking. Mostly he just looked disappointed. Fine. She was not here to make friends with him or anyone. She was here to retrieve stolen property by any means necessary and she chose weaponized sass. If he was going to try to get in her way, she was ready to run right over him as well.

Theo stood at the board with much more determination this time. It was one thing to wish she wouldn't get hit, but now she was about to do all that she could to make sure she was punctured with a dart. Anything to get the necklace off that brazen swindler, even if she had to sacrifice herself to do it. Isn't that what good, selfless people do? She supposed so.

Lock took his turn, hitting the board well away from Theo. But he didn't make eye contact before walking back to the table.

Then Koel stepped up to take his turn. In any other context, Theo would have been laughing hysterically at the angriest fairy she'd ever seen being forced to twirl around and around like a vindictive spinning top. But with all that anger aiming for her, she was bracing for impact and not finding it all that amusing. Koel stopped so fast his feet squeaked on the floor. With the most confident, steely gaze she could muster, she stared directly at him, her thoughts solely on getting that necklace.

Hit me. Come on, hit me. Do it.

She was screaming the words in her head, wondering if she had done enough to inspire violence. With a stare meant to mutilate and nostrils flaring like an enraged bull, he let his dart fly.

It hit the board right next to her temple. She sucked in a sharp breath, waiting for the sting. When it didn't come, she reached a hand up to her head to feel for a mark. Her skin was smooth and her hand came back clean.

Theo looked to Koel only to find him grinning once more. "I win."

Shit. Shit!

Koel turned to Endlin. "Unless you'd like to try for first place?"

His words seemed to snap her out of whatever pouty daze she'd been in. Her wobbly lower lip all of a sudden hardened into a straight line as she marched up to the table, tossed the dice, and grabbed a dart. With her fists clenched, she spun on her heel, graceful as ever. She gave Theo a look of such pure hatred Theo wasn't sure if Endlin was going to use fairy magic on her. But instead, Endlin threw the dart to the floor where it skittered across the marble before resting at Theo's feet. "Guess I lost."

And so had Theo. The only thing she could do was watch as Endlin stormed out of the room, the necklace moving farther and farther away until it was completely out of sight.

With a mix of defeat and exasperation, Lock shook his head at Theo and walked out as well.

What was she going to do now?

Koel moved to stand in front of her. "Well, well, Lady Theodosia. Look at you. All hiss and no teeth. You thought your little insults were going to affect me? Please. Though, I do see why Lock keeps you around. You do have entertainment value."

He placed a finger on his chin as though he was pondering something important. "It seems to me we only bargained for something if you won. Since I am the winner, I should get a prize of some sort, don't you think?"

"That wasn't in our bargain, Koel," Theo said, trying to stand tall and realizing a moment too late she was still pressed up against a wall with nowhere to go.

"You're so right, Lady Theodosia. But guess what? We aren't in a bargain anymore since the game is over. And lucky for me, you're an unclaimed human, aren't you?"

Theo drew in a sharp breath.

"Oh, calm down. As much fun as it would be to really use my imagination, I think I'll keep it simple this evening. After all, I wouldn't want to permanently harm Lock's favorite harp player over a silly game of darts."

Before any retort or exit strategy could come to her, he brushed his hand over the collar of her dress, causing a hundred butterflies to fly up and around them before disappearing into the air.

"That dress is stunning. Too beautiful to be on someone like you."

He touched a finger to her shoulder and they both watched as one more butterfly flitted upward, only to turn brown like a leaf in autumn and plummet to the floor.

Chapter 21
Where Theo Concocts a New Plan in a Dress That Won't Die

Unlike every other time a butterfly left her dress, a new butterfly did not take its place. There was a little hole of exposed skin on her shoulder, the other butterflies acting as though they wanted nothing to do with the spot.

Another butterfly flew off, only to lose its color as well and swirl downward.

Koel smiled. "There. Now your outside will match your horrid inside."

Soon multiple butterflies were taking off at a time, crumbling and dying, leaving even more bits of her skin on display, her dress now looking ironically moth-eaten. Horror wove through her as the situation was being revealed as fast as her body. Nothing was filling the gaps, and nothing was underneath the dress.

Koel laughed at her wide eyes, agape mouth, and hands that hadn't yet decided where they should go to cover her up. The sound of it shattered any remaining scrap of pride she still had and left her dignity hanging on by a spider thread.

She turned and fled, sprinting past the doorman as the butterflies dropped faster and faster. But where was she supposed to go? She ran through the first archway she found and careened down a long hallway, every room she passed already occupied by fairies.

It was only when the world went blurry that she realized she was crying. She stopped at the end of the hall, not knowing which way to turn while watching the butterflies fall to the floor like wisps of torn paper. Her shoulders were now completely bare, as was her side and most of her legs.

A jacket was thrown around her shoulders and she looked back to see Kaz.

"Come on." He grabbed her hand, pulling her down hallway after hallway until they could no longer hear the party. He led her to a tucked-away alcove on what must have been the other end of the palace. As she sat on the little bench, she wrapped his jacket tight around her body, concealing most of her but leaving her legs exposed as the last of the butterflies dropped to the ground.

He sat down next to her.

"Kaz, my dress. He ruined my dress."

"I know, I'm sorry. I'm sorry I couldn't stop it."

"That was humiliating," she said as she wiped her face on the sleeve of his jacket, tears still falling.

"Well, I don't know if this is good news or not, but humans

are often humiliated at these parties. Likely that no one who saw it is even remembering it now, considering how drunk most of them are."

"Did it ever happen to you?"

"Humiliated at a party? No. But I have been made to do other things."

"Like what?"

He shook his head. "It's not important right now."

She paused for a moment, sniffling. "I didn't get the necklace. I tried to win it in a game of Dizzy Darts, but I failed. I have no other plan, Kaz. It's over."

Kaz knelt down in front of her, putting a gentle hand on her shoulder. "No, it's not over. You still have one more night. I'm sure you'll think of something."

"I don't think Endlin is going to let me get anywhere near her. I was losing the game badly, so I thought if I could get them angry enough, they'd hit me with darts and I could win. They certainly got mad at me."

When she looked up at Kaz, a small smile was dancing on his lips. "I'm assuming you rolled out the heavy verbal artillery?"

She snorted. But when she repeated to Kaz everything she said, he burst out laughing, the effect lightening her mood a little.

"Wow, I wish I could have been there to see that. Koel definitely deserves whatever you threw at him."

"You know him?"

"Go to enough parties and you meet pretty much all the well-known fairies."

Footsteps echoed down the hallway and Theo held her breath as Kaz peered around the corner. And then sat next to her again as Lock came into the alcove.

"Out you go, Kasra. I'll take it from here."

Kaz scoffed but gave Theo's hand a squeeze before he started walking away.

"Hey, you can't tell him to leave," Theo said, riled by the indignity of dismissing Kaz that way. "He doesn't work for you."

Kaz turned to her. "It's all right, Theo. I'll see you later."

She nodded.

"Run along now, woodland critter." Lock motioned with his hands to usher him out of the alcove.

She glowered at Lock as Kaz's footsteps faded. "That wasn't very nice. He was the one who helped me get here. Without him, I'd be sobbing naked in the hallway. You left me at the mercy of Koel."

"I would have caught up before you were completely bare. Now, as lovely as this spot is, we should probably find someplace a little bit more private for you to hide out in. Come on."

Theo had to agree. She couldn't sit on this bench forever.

They walked next to each other in silence until Lock finally spoke up. "That was a bold move, trying to get them so upset they'd hit you with a dart. Not the strategy I expected."

"An unsuccessful strategy. Took you long enough to figure out what I was doing."

"I'm glad it didn't work, to be honest. I did not like watching you getting hit with a dart."

"You sound just like Endlin. I was the one bleeding."

He glanced sidelong at her. "You really seem to dislike her."

Theo wondered whether she should even bother explaining. She couldn't very well tell him Endlin was a jewelry thief, so Theo settled for the other truth. "As I said, she reminds me of someone I know."

"Is that the 'dazzling beauty' you were comparing her to in your epic tirade? Your stepsister, I presume?"

She nodded but didn't look at him to gauge his thoughts. Nor did she want to explain any further. Why did Beatrice still have to live in her head and worm her way into every facet of her life? Even in the fairy realm, Beatrice was still around.

Lock didn't ask any follow-up questions. Instead, he stopped at a door and ushered her into a well-appointed bedroom. A gigantic four-poster bed was taking up nearly half the space. The other half was dominated by a fireplace large enough for her to stand in with a sitting area in front of it.

He shut the door and stretched while letting out a long groan. "Well, I think I'm going to go to bed. Are you coming?"

"To bed with you?"

He grinned. "I meant to go to sleep, but yes. I know the gentlemanly thing to do would be to offer you the massive bed to sleep in all by yourself and I would sleep on the floor. I will stay on top of the covers if it makes you feel better. But that bed is gigantic, so I see no reason we shouldn't be able to share it."

"I do. I have no clothes. And while I may not be the most respectable girl in the kingdom, I do have a limit. And that limit is not sleeping naked next to you."

His grin vanished. "Oh! With you wrapped up like that I

forgot you're not wearing anything underneath! Give me a moment. It has been a while since I've conjured any clothing for someone else. What would you like?"

"I'm not bargaining for anything right now, thank you," she said while scanning the room for anything that might substitute for clothing. She supposed the curtains might work, but she'd have to then figure out how to get them off the rod. With the ridiculously high ceilings, it would involve climbing.

"Bargain? Who said anything about a bargain?"

"You told me that a fairy never gives something away without getting something in return. And the last thing I want to do right now is make a bargain with you for clothing."

"Ah, well, I am getting something out of it. You get clothes, and I get to spend time with a slightly happier Theo. Sound good?"

She nodded. "Then it's a deal. Nightgown, please."

"Coming right up."

Theo wasn't sure what he would conjure, only having ever seen Cecily's work. But the familiar flower-petal feeling wrapped around her, and when she looked down, she was wearing a plain, long white nightgown. She shrugged off the jacket and laid it over the back of the chair.

"How'd I do?"

"Perfect," she said. "Thank you."

He smiled as he tossed himself onto the bed. With a snap of his fingers, the lights in the room dimmed.

She hadn't realized how exhausted she was until she saw him settle in. The fluffy bedding was reminding her of a soft cloud. The distance between her and the bed was an epic trek.

Lock was right; the bed was massive. Plus, the only other place to sleep was the chair, and that was far from ideal if she didn't want to wake up with a crick in her neck. So she dragged herself to the bed and slipped underneath the covers, nestling into the pillows.

She felt Lock shifting closer to her.

"*Hey, Theo,*" he whispered.

She rolled over to face him. "Yes?"

"I just wanted to tell you that it was infinitely more enjoyable than I thought it would be to make your acquaintance. I'm glad I did."

"Even though I've spent a good portion of our time together insulting you?"

"Especially because of that."

"I'm glad I made that bargain with you."

"Which one?" His eyes glittered even in the low light.

"Both." She smiled.

"I very much wish this isn't the end of our time together."

"It probably is. I don't know when I'd ever see you again."

"Maybe we can think of something." He grinned, tucking a stray tendril of hair behind her ear and then tracing her cheek with his fingers.

Her breath hitched as he moved even closer, and for a moment she thought he might kiss her again. And he did, sort of, as he kissed her forehead.

"Good night, Theo."

"Good night, Lock."

She turned back over again, pulling the blanket up to her chin.

———————————— • ————————————

When she woke up, she was tucked in close to Lock, his arm draped around her, their legs tangled together.

So much for him staying above the covers.

Impropriety aside, it would have been a lovely way to wake up, had three people not been standing at the foot of the bed. At first she thought she was still dreaming as Phineas, Cecily, and Kaz were smiling down at her. Well, Phineas and Cecily were smiling. Kaz was fixing a stray thread from the bottom of his shirt.

Theo sat up with a little squeal of surprise and tried to push Lock off her. He moved his arm with a bleary *"What?"* and rubbed his face before also realizing they had an audience. But instead of shouting in surprise like Theo, he sat up and stretched, grinning at the trio.

"Good morning, Theo," Cecily said in a singsong voice. "Or should I say good evening? Night two of the celebration has arrived!"

Looking at Cecily, Theo could see the circles under her eyes were even more pronounced.

"Hello, Cecily. Looking incredible, as always." Lock was pushing the sheets off while Theo was attempting to pile more on top of herself so no one would see her nightgown. Especially not Kaz. In fact, she was wishing Kaz wasn't here at all to see her in bed with Lock. By the intensity with which he was examining his buttons, it appeared that he felt the same.

"Hello, Lock. I need to speak with our rested and refreshed Theo in private, so I'm afraid you'll need to vacate."

"This is my room."

Cecily didn't deign to answer. She merely tipped her head to the side and smiled.

"All right, all right. Back to the party!" He got out of the bed and stretched. With a snap of his fingers, he transformed his outfit and slicked back his hair with his hands.

Theo was still watching from the bed.

"Until we meet again, Theo," Lock said with a bow and a wink before walking out.

The door had hardly clicked shut before Theo blurted out, "We didn't do anything. Just slept, I swear."

Cecily followed Theo's sight line to Kaz, who was finding a spot on the wall of particular interest, and then looked back at her.

"No need to explain yourself, my dear. You are not bound by the silly rules of the human realm here and may do whatever you'd like with whomever you'd like with zero justification. Isn't that right, Kaz?"

"Sure." He shrugged, still not bothering to look at her.

Even though Cecily said she didn't need to explain anything, she still felt like she needed to make sure Kaz believed her when she said nothing happened. Him no longer wanting to look her in the eye was making her heart hurt in a way she couldn't describe.

"Now that that's out of the way...Theo. The necklace. Kaz filled me in on how last night went and I do commend you for your efforts, but praise only counts for so much. Do you have another plan?"

The biggest hurdle facing Theo now was that Endlin not

only knew what she looked like, but absolutely hated her. There was no way Theo would get into the same room as her again, much less take a necklace from her throat.

Theo sighed. "Not yet."

"Well, think hard. I'm sure you have a wealth of talents and experiences to draw from."

True. However, none of them ever involved thievery. And most of her exploits were the result of seeking revenge, but… A new idea began to form in her head. Dastardly, to be sure, but did that matter when it was aimed at an already morally deficient fairy? "I will need a disguise. Is that something you can do?"

Cecily scoffed in jest. "Did you forget who you were talking to? Of course I can give you a disguise. I'll do you one better. I'll put a glamour on you."

"A what?"

"A glamour. You'll look like someone else entirely. Does that work?"

Theo nodded. "That would work perfectly."

"Great! Now, here's the thing, my calculating Theo. Glamours don't change you. Rather, they cover you, much like if I threw a blanket over your head. And to carry on with the blanket analogy, you need to hold on to the glamour the whole time you're wearing it. If you let it go, it disappears. Make sense?"

Theo nodded again but wasn't sure she entirely understood. How would one hold on to a magical disguise? That would be a bridge to cross when she got to it, she supposed.

"Wonderful," Cecily said. "If that's everything, then let's get started!"

"It's not," Theo added. "May I have some Pixie Rose Water?"

Cecily scrunched her brow, looking at Theo with confusion. But as understanding dawned on her, a wicked smile bloomed on her face.

"*Oh, Theo.* I knew I could count on you. Phineas and Kaz will make sure you have all the Pixie Rose Water you need. Now, why don't you hop out of bed so I can dress and disguise you?"

Theo crawled out of the warm, fluffy sheets and stood in front of Cecily.

"Let's see," she said as she inspected Theo. "I certainly won't be dressing you in another outfit that can die. That was such a pity. And rather rude. Oh, I know. How about this?"

A new ensemble took shape and Theo looked into the mirror. Her hair was pulled into a high bun, so as to fully display the choker around her neck made of obsidian shards the length of her thumb. She wasn't sure that tilting her head down wouldn't result in a puncture wound in her chin. Her dress was equally as brutal. The shiny gray material looked like it was carved from stone, gleaming as it caught the light. But when she moved, it felt as soft as morning dew against her skin.

"Well? What do you think?" Cecily asked from behind her.

"You look amazing, Theo," Phineas said. "The gray really brings out the murder in your eyes."

Kaz said nothing, but she did see him watching her from the reflection in the mirror.

"Now for the glamour," Cecily said. "We'll do a fairly simple one, since I don't want you to have to worry too much about holding on to it. The slighter they are, the lighter they are. Here we go."

And strangely, it did feel as though Cecily had thrown a silk scarf over her. The magic was hovering around her, and like a scarf in a breeze, she could feel it ripple, like it would fly off if she didn't hold it on top of her. So that's what Cecily meant, then.

Theo looked at herself again. Her hair was still in its high bun, but Cecily had darkened it until it was nearly black. Her nose was longer, her cheekbones sharper, and her eyes syrupy brown.

"Well, that's all for me." Cecily grinned. "Unless you have any other surprise ideas, Theo?"

Theo shook her head.

"Excellent! Then I am going back to the party. Remember, you still don't know me, or them." She pointed to Kaz and Phineas as she breezed out of the room.

Phineas clapped once. "I'll go get you that Pixie Rose Water!" He disappeared into a swirl of wind.

She didn't look at Kaz as she walked to one of the wingback chairs and sat. "How long do you think it will take?"

"Not long," Kaz replied, still standing at the foot of the bed.

They said nothing more. The silence that surrounded them was the auditory equivalent of pudding—thick, heavy, and uncomfortable to sit in. But before Theo could do anything other than watch the logs in the fireplace smolder, the air started twirling and Phineas stepped out of the vortex with a big grin on his face and a satchel held out to Theo like a first-place ribbon.

"There you go! The finest Pixie Rose Water ready for whatever plan you've cooked up. What is the plan, by the way?"

"I'm going to get her drunk." That was it. That was the entire plan as of this moment. She knew it wasn't a great one, but it was all she had. She took the satchel from Phineas, peering inside to see five bottles. Plenty to get Endlin sufficiently scammered.

"All set? Good. Then we had best be going. Wait here for a bit and then head back to the party." Phineas clapped her on the shoulder and walked out. Kaz said nothing as he followed.

Alone with her déjà vu, Theo watched the clock.

Chapter 22
Where Theo Gets Her Hands Dirty for a Righteous Cause

While the glass bottles were clinking in the satchel, questions of ethics were clinking around in her head. As far as Theo knew, *good people* did not intentionally try to get others drunk on rare liquor. Beatrice had never tried to do that, as far as she knew. But then again, Beatrice would probably just have one of her lackeys do it for her to keep her hands clean. And no matter what, Theo was not like her. Beatrice might never have resorted to plying thieving fairies with drinks, but she also never had to retrieve a necklace from the neck of one. Maybe this task did call for a good person who was also capable of getting the job done. And Theo could do that.

With new resolve, Theo began night two of the festivities.

Finding out if Endlin was in the ballroom yet seemed to be

the appropriate first step. Her vantage point from last night had done the trick, so she figured if it worked then, it would work now. She returned to the balcony and scanned the party below. Tace and Aimon were on their thrones, still drinking, still holding hands. Dancers were spinning around the room as though the party had never stopped. For all she knew, it hadn't.

But where was that pilfering, prissy Endlin?

There she was. Standing off to the side, drink in hand, chatting in the middle of a group. Theo moved slowly down the stairs and through the party, just in case there were interested eyes on her, but if a fairy did look at her, they turned away to something else, not bothering to waste any time looking at a human. Perfect. Theo sneaked behind some potted plants, her back to Endlin.

Then she waited. And waited. For what, she wasn't entirely sure.

Theo was about to give up her hiding spot and try to think of something else, not sure if she could stomach any more of Endlin's particularly dull tales of her time at other fairy parties. But one of her squad cut in first.

"Let's go to one of the lounges!"

Endlin's voice petered out midsentence as all the others agreed with the idea. Theo moved out of the plants to follow the group as they made their way down a hall and into a room. As nonchalant as possible, Theo halted outside the door, peering in and listening. Another one of Endlin's disciples was speaking to a group of fairies who had already been in the room.

"You'll need to clear out now," a redheaded fairy said with a haughty grin.

"And why would we do that? We are still using the room," one of the other fairies said, undaunted by the simpering ensemble.

"Do you know who this is?" The fairy pointed to Endlin. But instead of looking smug and enjoying the game with the others, Endlin was smiling rather sheepishly, as though embarrassed by the attention that was now on her.

"No," said the other fairy. "And I'm not sure I care."

That was what the first fairy wanted to hear. Her face went purely predatory, staring at an anchovy foolish enough to pick a fight with a shark.

"This is Aimon's sister." Her words landed exactly as intended. The other fairies shifted uncomfortably, some already getting up from their seats and making for the door. She continued, "So, you can either walk out now and visit this splendid palace again in the future, or she'll have you *thrown* out and you'll never come back. Ever."

Her grin spread into a wide smile as the fairy glared at her. He was trying to act as though he had been planning on leaving anyway but was slinking out like a dog with its tail between its legs.

It only made Theo hate Endlin more. Letting her friends bully other people while staying silent was a page straight out of Beatrice's book. Memories of her own treatment by Beatrice's friends rose in her like the tide. The embarrassment, the helplessness, the unfairness of it all. She had lived it more times than she cared to count.

Theo stopped suffering any ethical dilemma with her plan.

Once the room was cleared, Endlin's group stretched out on the couches and chairs. Now Theo just had to figure out how she was going to get in. She walked back down the hallway and into the party, scanning for ideas. Her eyes settled on another human who was carrying a large tray of drinks. As soon as her tray was empty, Theo approached.

"Excuse me. I need a tray and six glasses. Do you know where I could get them?"

The other human stopped what she was doing and turned to face Theo. "And who are you? I've never seen you here before."

Theo stifled a groan.

What is it with you people?

But instead of saying exactly what was on her mind, she took a breath and smiled politely. "If you cannot help me, can you please point me in the general direction of where I can get what I need?"

The human gave her a skeptical look but pointed behind her toward another hallway.

"Thank you," Theo said sincerely.

Finding where the glasses and trays were proved to be quite simple. Following the lead of the other humans, she went into the kitchens. With all the activity, no one looked twice at her as she grabbed the glasses and a tray. After arranging the bottles of Pixie Rose Water, she chucked the empty satchel in a corner and returned to the lounge.

Glamour held firmly in place, Theo walked into the room and cleared her throat. Conversation stopped as the fairies looked at her, mild revulsion appearing on some of their faces.

"What do you think you're doing here?" the redheaded fairy asked with no shortage of disgust.

"I was sent with a gift for Endlin and her friends."

The redheaded fairy tilted her head. "Oh? And what gift might that be?"

"Pixie Rose Water."

At that, the look of annoyance disappeared, replaced by surprise, which was mirrored by everyone else. Then they all burst into laughter again, a few even clapping.

"Well, come on, then! What are you waiting for?" the redheaded fairy snapped at Theo.

She brought the tray over, the fairies converging on her like chickens at feeding time. It was all she could do to keep the bottles from tipping. The fairies clinked their drinks in a toast to Endlin, who beamed before knocking the glass back, chugging the contents in two big gulps, the rest following suit.

The effects were instantaneous. Faces went slack and dreamy-eyed. Theo recalled the feeling she had experienced when she drank it, knowing just how good it had felt. Each member of the group had just drank four times the amount she did. They all giggled, delighting in the high, paying no mind at all to anyone or anything.

Before they even had a chance to demand more, Theo was there, filling their glasses to the brim, as attentive as any experienced footman. Not bothering with toasts this time, the fairies downed the Pixie Rose Water, laughing as soon as they finished swallowing and settling into the hazy high.

Theo was readying another round when the redheaded fairy held up her hand.

"Wait," she said. "Who sent this?"

They all turned to face Theo. *Shit.* She hadn't thought that far ahead. "Secret admirer" came out of her mouth before she even knew what she was saying. But the taunting *ooohhh* leveled at Endlin left no room for doubt among the group.

"Maybe it's from Koel! Maybe he finally got all of your hints!" One of them shrieked with a laugh that sounded like a cat whose tail got stuck in the door. "Is it? Is it Koel?" she asked Theo.

"I believe that's the *secret* part of *secret admirer.*"

"Did he have braids and sapphires in his hair?"

"Yes," Theo said slowly.

The group laughed. "Maybe he'll date you, after all," one shouted. "See, Endlin? Having Aimon as a brother has its benefits!"

Endlin laughed along with her friends, but the joy wasn't reaching her eyes.

Theo poured another round.

"And because of *him*, being friends with Endlin has its benefits!" Another fairy raised her empty glass at Endlin, her arm swaying like seaweed under the surf.

"Then let's toast to Aimon! Hero of the night!"

The group laughed.

This time, Endlin's smile looked like a stretched line, no curve to be seen.

Theo kept pouring.

With each glass, their high was lasting longer and longer. By the fourth round an hour later, the group was done for. Half were sprawled out on the couches sleeping, the other three, Endlin included, were still drinking, but Theo wasn't entirely sure they even knew their own names anymore.

After two more rounds, even they started to drift off to sleep.

Theo decided it was time to make her move. On silent feet, she approached where Endlin lay in the chair, eyes closed and limbs flopping over the sides like she'd lost all the bones in her body.

When Theo first laid eyes on the necklace from afar, she'd found it to be unattractive. Up close, it was hideous. The thick chain was made of brass so tarnished it seemed to absorb light rather than reflect it. The palm-size pendant hanging in the center was the same dirt-colored metal, but there was a jagged pattern of marks engraved into the surface. Mounted in the center was a shiny brown gemstone that looked like someone had captured the essence of silt from the bottom of a stream. Why anyone would have stolen this was beyond Theo.

But she wasn't here to admire it. She was here to rescue it.

Like she was stealing gold from a sleeping dragon, she slowly, slowly reached her hands behind Endlin's neck. She felt for a clasp, but there was no break in the chain. Great. She'd just have to pull it over Endlin's head. And she'd better do it now because Theo wasn't sure how long the effects of the Pixie Rose Water would last. Could be hours. Could be minutes.

Like she'd been called out of her slumber by Theo's thoughts, Endlin blinked her eyes open. Theo jerked back, throwing her hands behind her.

"What are you doing?" she asked with a yawn. Another fairy stirred but shifted her position and went back to sleep.

"Oh, I was just admiring your necklace."

Endlin gave her a bleary smile as she clutched the pendant, rolling it between her fingers. "Thank you. It's dwarven made. Exceptionally rare."

"Can I see it up close?"

"Sure," Endlin said as she held it out.

"You're still so far away. It looks so beautiful. I would love to really take in the details. Can you take it off so I can hold it?"

Endlin hiccupped. "I'm not supposed to take it off."

"Why not? I won't tell anyone."

"It is for protection. Why are you asking about it?"

"Just curious."

"Well, don't be. You'd never have any use for it. You're a human."

"What does it do?"

Endlin made to sit up a bit straighter, though the effects from the alcohol seemed to make her body too heavy to push up all the way. She gave up and sank back down onto the couch with a very unladylike groan.

"It negates the effects of iron—you must not be very good at your job if you didn't already know iron lessens our magic. If there's enough of it, we can't use our magic at all."

Theo could suddenly see how that would be a valuable token to own, and why a fairy would want to steal it.

Endlin was studying Theo with a childlike look of consideration. "Do I know you?"

"No."

"Are you sure?"

"Yes."

290

"Oh. You remind me of another human. A real nasty one called *Lady Theodosia*." She said the name as though it tasted foul. "You sound like her, anyway. Are you sure you're not her?"

"Positive."

"Because she was so mean, you know."

Theo said nothing as Endlin continued to slur her words.

"But the worst thing was, she was right."

What? That's new.

Endlin tipped her head back, resting it on the chair, and closed her eyes. "I never feel like I say the right things, or make funny jokes." She gestured vaguely at the other passed-out fairies. "But they all laugh anyway and it always makes me wonder if I have any real friends at all, or if they just want to be near me because my brother is the regent's partner."

Endlin had reached the truth-telling portion of being drunk. Theo knew it well—she'd watched plenty of others at various balls imbibe too much and let socially devastating secrets slip.

Endlin sat up, blinking slowly at Theo. "You could be my friend." Endlin snorted and giggled like she had just told Theo the most hilarious joke. "Friends with a human!"

Theo forced a laugh. Another fairy stretched then mumbled a bit before settling again.

The high was wearing off, and the clock was ticking on task number two. If she didn't get the necklace soon, she'd never get the chance again.

"Yes, I am your friend. And friends share! Let me see the necklace, please." Theo tried to sound light and fun, doing her best impersonation of Beatrice.

But Endlin had once again fallen asleep. Just as well.

With slightly more speed and desperation, Theo grabbed the necklace and tried to lift it over Endlin's head. If she had been the tiniest bit more delicate, maybe Endlin would have stayed asleep. Instead, she opened her eyes just as Theo got the necklace over her hair.

"What are you doing?"

"Nothing. Go back to sleep."

But Endlin saw what Theo was holding. She reached out and grabbed the necklace. "Stop that!" She gripped it with both hands, heaving it toward herself. "It's *mine!*"

"It is not yours!" Theo growled. "I'm going to return it to its rightful owner."

"What are you talking about! You can't take it!" she shrieked, her knuckles white as she tightened her hold.

It was time to finish this task. Taking one hand off the chain, Theo balled it into a fist and struck out, hitting Endlin squarely on the nose with a gut-churning crack.

Both women yelled out in pain. Endlin because her nose was now dripping like a gruesome faucet, and Theo because she might have broken a few bones in her hand. But the desired effect was reached, since Endlin had let go of the necklace to clutch her face.

The screaming, however, seemed to rouse the other sleeping fairies, a few of whom were now blinking awake.

With her prize won, Theo sprinted to the door, the sounds of Endlin shouting *"No!"* and *"Give it back!"* plus a few confused questions from the others trailing behind her.

But when she flung open the door and ran out, she crashed

full speed into Koel, his hand in front of him like he was about to turn the handle. Her momentum was enough to send him stumbling back a few paces, but not enough for her to make a hasty getaway. He grabbed her arm and yanked her back as he peered into the room to see Endlin still in her chair, sobbing and bleeding.

"What is going on here?" he asked, whipping his head back and forth between Endlin and Theo.

Before Theo could think of a satisfactory and believable lie, Endlin shouted, "Her...she...amulet...mine!"

Koel turned to Theo and growled as he dragged her back into the room. If Koel kept her here, it would be the first step toward her walk of death. She struggled as best she could against his strong grip, but it did nothing.

Without any warning he released her arm, only to grab her by the shoulders and slam her against the wall. The force knocked the breath from her and she felt with terror the glamour rustle.

"Who are you working for?" His hands pressed on her shoulders like he was going to squeeze the truth out of her.

"No one," she gritted out between clenched teeth.

"You lie. *Who*." He pulled her forward only to slam her against the wall again when she didn't answer. She winced and groaned as her shoulder blades smacked against the stone. The force and pain caused her to lose her hold on the glamour. Before it fell away entirely, she managed to grab it and hold on, snapping it back into place, but it was too late. Koel had seen who was hiding under it.

His eyes went feral.

"*You*," he snarled. He put a hand around her neck, squeezing the obsidian shards into her throat. She clawed at his arm, trying to make him let go, but she might as well have been fighting with a marble statue for all the good it was doing.

He leaned in close. "You will tell me who you work for. You can either tell me now, or I will make you tell me. And I promise, that experience won't be pleasant."

"I don't work for anyone," she croaked, her voice strained by the hand pressing into her neck.

"*Liar!* I saw you heal from that dart wound. Humans do not heal that fast unless they are in service to a fairy. *Who. Is. It.*" With each word he tightened his grip, the obsidian slicing into her skin. She could feel a trickle of blood running down her neck and between her breasts.

Black spots were flickering in her vision.

The necklace she had taken off of Endlin was not designed for self-defense, but it was the only tool at her disposal. She swung it like a chain mace. With an apparent natural affinity for this type of weaponry, she hit her target exactly where she meant to. Metal met skin with a dull thud. Koel cried out as he released her, sputtering and stumbling back while gripping his head. Blood was oozing out from between his fingers and spilling down over his eyes, obstructing his vision like she'd thrown paint at him.

Still not having a straight shot to the door, she rushed farther into the room and reached for the last bottle of Pixie Rose Water. As Koel stalked toward her, she gripped the bottle by the neck and swung it like a club. He put his arm up to block the attack, causing the bottle to shatter on impact. Both glass and Pixie Rose Water showered him, the former cutting his face and forcing him to squeeze his eyes shut, the latter soaking him with the liquor, some of which had gone straight into his open, snarling mouth. He fell to the side, cursing as he hit the floor.

Given the minuscule amount of Pixie Rose Water he had inadvertently ingested, Theo knew the high would last only mere seconds. Wasting none of the precious time, Theo scooped up the bottom of her dress and started sprinting out the door and down the hall. She didn't know if fairies were fast runners, nor did she want to find out. Especially not from the ones she'd just assaulted with jewelry.

Theo had only made it halfway down the hall when she heard Koel yell, "I will *kill* you!"

Looking behind for only a second, she saw him stumbling after her. She couldn't tell if it was his footsteps or her racing pulse that was beating in her ears as she willed her legs to go faster. She rounded the corner, almost crashing into the wall on the turn, and ran as fast as she'd ever run in her life toward the main party area.

If Theo had any extra air, she would have used it to cry with relief as she neared the ballroom and saw Kaz coming her way. With her lungs at capacity and unable to say anything, she held the necklace out in front of her as she ran. His eyes went wide as he sprinted toward her. When he reached her, he grabbed the necklace, then her hand, nearly pulling her arm out of its socket as he ducked into the crowd before Koel had made the turn.

Holding her hand hard enough to hurt, Kaz wove them

through the party. Theo checked to see if Koel had spotted them, but his eyes were darting around the room in a furious panic.

Phineas was leaning against a wall on the far side of the atrium.

"Phineas!" Kaz shouted.

When Phineas turned, Kaz threw the necklace to him. A huge smile burst onto his face as he looked at what he had caught.

"I'm taking her back to her house," Kaz said in a winded rush.

Phineas nodded and then ran off in another direction, cradling the necklace like a precious baby bird.

Kaz pulled her farther along the side of the atrium through an archway and into an empty room. She held on tight as he transported them away from the Palace of the Fae and back to her music room.

Chapter 23
Where Theo Finally Talks About Buckleberry

As soon as the wind died down, Theo fell to her knees, gasping for breath. Kaz walked over to one of the chairs and sank into it, throwing his head back and gulping down air, chest heaving from exertion.

The blood on her neck and chest was as thick and sticky as honey as she tried to wipe at it. The movement only amplified the ache in her shoulders and back.

"What did I just do?" she said as she hauled herself to standing. "Kaz, what did I just do?" She turned to face him. "None of that felt right. None of it. I know I am not an expert on how good people behave, but nothing about that felt good. I spent most of the evening getting a group of fairies wildly drunk. Then I ripped a necklace off a fairy who seemed pretty confused about my reasons. And then I punched her. And then I used the necklace to bash someone else over the head as he was trying to strangle me. *And then* I had to run for my life from him. Which one of those was the good deed?"

Kaz sat in the chair watching.

"Say something! Tell me I did something right! Tell me that is what a good person does! Because right now, I feel *horrible*, Kaz."

Kaz rose out of his seat and went to her.

"Theo." He sighed as he held her face in his hands. "You completed your second task. You got the necklace. You accomplished something on your own. Don't let anything take that away from you."

She nodded and he dropped his hands, a small sense of relief spreading through her as he looked straight into her eyes.

"We should probably get you cleaned up, though," he said.

Theo cringed. She must look truly awful for Kaz of all people to suggest changing.

"Wait here. I'll be right back," she said.

She hoped the enchantment that Cecily had put on her room was still in place and her mother was none the wiser that her daughter was up and about after her supposed terrible illness. But as she crept around the manor to her room, she neither heard nor saw any evidence of her mother anyway and was able to get into her room with no interference. But as she washed herself off and put on a new dress, all she could think of were the events of the past two nights.

Yes, she did get Endlin drunk enough to pass out. But she did it to recover stolen property. And Koel would have not only prevented her from taking the necklace, but definitely turned her over to the guards, where she'd be at the mercy of fairies who really didn't like humans. That "mercy" would be whether or not she'd receive a painless death. So of course she needed to fight back. And Phineas looked beyond pleased when she delivered the necklace. If Cecily was as happy about it as he was, maybe the ends did justify the means. Kaz seemed to think so, at least.

On the way back to the music room, she stopped at the top of the stairs and listened, attempting to figure out where her mother was. Still hearing nothing, it was safe to assume she had probably gone into the village.

Kaz was right where she left him when she returned.

"So, now what do we do?" Theo asked.

"We wait. By now, Phineas has taken the necklace home. I'll stay here with you for a bit just to make sure no one has followed us. I don't want to bring you there until we know for certain that no one has connected you to Cecily. She'll stay at the party to keep an eye on any fallout."

Theo nodded then plunked down in the chair next to him with all the finesse of a dropped doll. "If that was the second task, I can't even begin to imagine what Cecily has in store for me next. Probably help a troll find love only to get shoved off a bridge or something else that sounds innocuous but turns out to be bizarrely life-threatening."

Kaz huffed a laugh.

Theo went on. "For all the stories about Beatrice's magical night, none of them said anything about *her* getting bloodied up. Unless she left out the part about having to run a gauntlet of knife-wielding sprites before she could get into the carriage."

He shook his head with a grin.

"What about only getting her dress by having to remove it from an ogre who had grown rather fond of it?"

"Nope," Kaz said with a chuckle.

She smiled and put a finger on her chin. "Hmm. Then let me think. She only got her hair done after bringing Cecily the left pinkie toenail of an overworked, underpaid dragon."

He laughed. "You should keep quiet lest you give Cecily any more ideas."

At first, she laughed along with him, her earlier panic drifting away. But as she tried to think of more asinine challenges, another thought took hold. Her smile and mood started to fall.

"No, she didn't have to do anything to prove she was worthy, did she? Her biggest injury was pricking her finger. Leave it to Beatrice to be the only one to receive benevolence from a fairy." Theo gritted her teeth and shook her head. "Which isn't even remotely surprising. That's exactly how she operates. Get everyone to feel sad for poor, innocent Bea and then they rush to do her bidding without further questions."

Kaz rolled his eyes. "You just pulled off a completely amazing feat and all you can think about is your stepsister not getting the same treatment. I would say you have a chip on your shoulder, but it's more of a crater, isn't it?"

Theo scoffed. "That little chain of events happened every single day. Everyone took her one-sided stories of injustice at face value. Because who would ever doubt dear, sweet Beatrice? It worked on you, too. You had your mind made up about me before we even met, on Bea's word alone. So to answer your question—yes, I do have a chip on my shoulder. So large I'm surprised there's anything left of me."

"You really do hate her," he said, as though it was some sort of revelation.

"She hates me just the same, you know."

"I didn't get that impression."

"You met her for what, five minutes?" Theo shook her head in resignation. "You wouldn't be saying that if you had grown up with her."

Kaz raised an eyebrow. "Enlighten me."

"When I first moved here, we were actually the very best of friends. Flo and I have never been that close, but Bea and I were two peas in a pod from the moment we met. We would play together all day, every day. But then I learned what a sneaky, disloyal liar she really was. To everyone else, she was the perfect golden child who could do no wrong. Her father doting on her, showering her with love, affection, gifts. She had him and everyone else in this entire estate wrapped around her finger. Everyone felt so bad for poor Beatrice who lost her mother, like I hadn't also lost a parent. I was the only one who saw through it. No one is that perfect."

"She was a child, Theo."

"So was I!" She paused, gripping the armrests. "Do you want to know what I felt when we moved here? Excitement. Little eight-year-old me was just so excited to come here. I was too young to remember my own father loving me. And my mother's affection was finite and only won by competition, and let me tell you, Kaz, I was rarely the victor.

"When my mother became engaged to the earl, people told

me about what an amazing father he was to his little girl, and I remember thinking that would be me, too. That I would have a father who loved me and a sister who wouldn't see me as a competitor. How pathetic for that to be my biggest wish. That someone would find me loveable. But no. He only had room in his heart for one daughter. Flo never really cared because she had the attention of my mother. But I tried. I tried so hard to win his love. To prove myself as worthy of being loved. It was like he never saw me. Like I didn't exist.

"So then I thought that if I became like Beatrice, he'd notice me and love me. I played the harp because Bea played the harp. I wore what she wore. I even ate what she ate. It never worked. He just ignored me. Our governess would tell Bea how adorable she looked with her hair bows, then sneer at me for copying her, like I was a deceitful little brat who was trying to one-up the poor, motherless Beatrice. Through all of it, Bea never said a word to help me. Never corrected them when I would take the blame and punishment for our childhood misadventures. She was happy to let them keep believing that I was bad and she was good. Like she was afraid they'd stop loving her if she admitted to any wrongdoing. She had her perfect image to protect and I was her shield. And then one horrible day, it finally became crystal clear that I was never, ever going to be loved by them."

"What happened?"

Theo sighed, debating whether to tell Kaz the story she had kept to herself since she was a child. But it had been a very long few days and she finally had someone's ear. She wasn't about to squander the opportunity.

"For Bea's twelfth birthday, her father gave her two white stallions. Bea said they were descendants of fairy war mounts. They were beautiful. Truly gorgeous creatures. Their names were Starlight Daydream and Winter's First Frost. And if you thought you could shorten their names to Star or Frost, think again. No, no. Only their full names for Bea's precious horses. Bea always wanted me to ride with her, but on the earl's orders, I was not allowed to ride either of the stallions. And I wasn't a strong enough rider to use any of his other horses in the stable, so she would usually just ride alone.

"For my twelfth birthday eight months later, I got a pony. His name was Buckleberry, but he was just called Buckle. He was this little thing with a squat body and short, stubby legs. And he was gray. Not silver, or dappled, or pewter. Just gray. No matter how much he was brushed, he never shined. He was just like a little storm cloud. Which suited him because that was his temperament, too. He always looked so ridiculous in the stable. Two beautiful white stallions...and Buckle the grumpy gray pony.

"Buckle and I certainly didn't have any sort of relationship like Bea did with her horses. I wasn't out there stroking his nose and giving him sugar cubes. And he wasn't whinnying and running toward me when he saw me out in the pasture. Unless you brought him a dozen apples to bribe him, he wasn't going anywhere near you. He didn't care much for riding, but neither did I, so it was fine. We had an understanding, Buckle and I did. We just sort of made do with what we were given.

"Well, one time, Bea wanted to go on a ride with everyone. A grand adventure all around the estate grounds, complete with a picnic at the end. Which meant all of us, plus a good number of the staff. Except my mother doesn't ride, so she was excused, and so was Flo since she hated riding and whined enough for Bea to not want to include her anyway. But because they had gotten me a pony, I was expected to show my gratitude and participate. The problem was, Buckle didn't like leaving the riding ring. I think being out in the open frightened him. When I tried to explain, the earl called me selfish for not wanting to go on Bea's ride and I was forced to.

"Buckle was the only pony. The rest of the horses took off and Buckle couldn't keep up. He was running so hard, panicking about being left behind, and all I could do was hang on and try to steer him in the direction I thought the others were going. No one had thought to look behind to see if we were there."

She paused, taking a shaky breath and looking into the dark, unlit fireplace instead of at Kaz as the memories surged.

"We didn't see the rabbit hole. He went in and I flew off, landing hard and hitting the back of my head on a rock. I was knocked out, but I don't know for how long.

"It couldn't have been that long, though. I woke up to him screaming in pain. I was so dizzy so all I could do was crawl, but I made it over to where he had fallen. His leg was broken so badly it was nearly severed. I knew what that meant, but I still started screaming for help anyway. I hoped that maybe they'd be able to fix him.

"They either heard us or finally noticed we were missing and came back. The earl got off his horse, took one look at Buckle, and sighed. Just *sighed*. Like Buckle's injury was some sort of inconvenience. Then he pulled out his pistol and shot him in the head. I had been sitting next to Buckle, wholly unprepared for what the earl did. He hadn't even told me to move back. Buckle's blood was all over me." She could still feel the hot, metallic blood hitting her in a spray of gore, smoke burning her nose, ears ringing from the gun blast.

"I did nothing. I stopped screaming. Stopped crying. Like he had shot me dead, too. But Bea...she started wailing. Louder than even Buckle had been. Hysterically crying. The earl and the servants rushed to soothe and comfort her. The earl put her on his horse with him and rode straight back to the manor. A servant brought her horse back to the stables, the others following.

"You know what they did with me? They left me there. Bea had created such a scene that they all forgot me. I wasn't making any noise at all. I was just staring at Buckle's dead, open eyes, blood leaking out of his skull. And blood dripping out of the back of my own. No one had asked if I was all right, by the way. Maybe they couldn't see all the blood because of my hair, but no one even bothered simply asking if I was all right after that fall.

"I was there for a while. A long while. I either passed out again or went to sleep. I'm not sure. When I woke up, I was still alone in the field. A little girl lying next to her dead pony, scared and all alone, not sure how I was going to get back to the manor. My head was killing me and I didn't even know if I could stand. So I waited with Buckle until the flies started landing. Then I slowly walked back to the manor by myself, leaving Buckle where he was. The sun was going down and no one had thought to look for me. I learned afterward that they all just assumed that someone from the group had brought me back and I had been in my room the whole time. No one checked. *My* pony. *My* fall. Not a single person bothered to pop their head into my room to see how I was faring.

"I got back to the manor covered in blood. Buckle's all down the front of me and my own down my back. It had started drying and I remember it being so itchy. Isn't that strange that that is what I remember about the walk home? I had so much blood under my fingernails because I was scratching at it as it dried."

Theo rubbed her thumbs over her nails, remembering. She had spent hours trying to clean her hands and nails, convinced she hadn't gotten all the blood off. It was only after her own blood started leaking out from under her fingernails that she realized she had scrubbed them so hard she made new wounds. Her fingers were so raw she couldn't play the harp for two weeks—the longest she'd ever gone without music since she started her lessons.

"Anyway, Bea was coming down the stairs when I walked through the door. When she saw me, she came running, dissolving into tears again. At first I thought it was because she had been worried for me. I was relieved, you know? That maybe they had been looking for me and someone was glad I had made it home.

"But as she was hugging me and crying, she was telling me how terribly upsetting the events of the day had been *for her*. How sad *she* was. I snapped. I pushed her off me. Then I slapped her. Then I tackled her and kept hitting and hitting her until someone pulled me off. I don't know who.

"I stayed in my room for days. No one visited me then,

either. I was punished for hitting Bea. But at that point, I just didn't care anymore. Bea had somehow managed to make one of the worst things that has ever happened to me all about her. The ride was all about her. Buckle's death was all about her. Even my grief was all about her.

"I don't know where they ended up putting Buckle. If they dragged him out of that field or if they just left him there to rot. I never checked. I never asked.

"I won't ever forget what she did that day. How she behaved. It had been like that with her all the time, but that day…I will always remember what her self-centeredness did.

"And I was done. Done with her. Done with the servants. Done with the earl. If everyone wanted to hate me, then let them hate me. Why try when it was much easier to be who they already thought I was: the nasty stepsister.

"Then the earl died. And perfect Bea was treated just like I was. Ignored and unimportant. For a while, it felt like come-uppance for everything she had done to me. But then here goes perfect Beatrice again making everyone feel sorry for her treatment at the hands of her 'evil stepfamily.' She got a fairy's help to convince the whole kingdom of just how special and perfect she is. And here I am having to risk my life for that same fairy. Bea never had to prove to anyone that she deserved help. But I still have to try…" Theo couldn't help the crack in her voice. "I am still trying so hard to prove that *just maybe* I, too, am deserving of help. That I'm worth helping."

She finally looked over to Kaz, who was staring at her with an unreadable expression.

"You're worth helping, Theo."

She huffed. "Tell that to your boss. Maybe she'll let me out of the bargain." But another thought suddenly sprang to her mind. "Kaz, I've been meaning to ask—what happens if you don't pay back a fairy bargain?"

"You always pay back a fairy bargain."

"How so?"

"Whenever you make a bargain with a fairy, your life is the collateral. If you pay back the bargain, with the payment you agreed to, then that's it; it's done. If you can't or don't, the fairy will claim your life for the payment instead."

She gasped, making Kaz jump. "So *that's* what he meant by 'a nuisance.' I'd say that's a little bit bigger than a nuisance."

"What are you talking about?"

"When I made the bargain with Lock at his party, he said he would teach me the fairy dances if I would accept a compliment. I made the deal, but when he was trying to compliment me, he said that if I didn't hold up my end of the bargain it would be a *nuisance*."

Kaz snorted. "Well, good thing you were able to suffer through him calling you pretty."

Theo cocked her head. "Now, wait just one minute. You need me to tell you all about the chip on my shoulder, but what about you? You seem to have the exact same problem with Lock. So what's your excuse?"

"You don't know him like I do."

"That's not going to work. Not after the hard time you just gave me about Beatrice. If there really is something I should know, then tell me."

"Like you'd believe me anyway."

"What's that supposed to mean?"

He shot her a disparaging look. "Apparently, all he does is call you gorgeous a few times and you're so enamored you're ready to go to battle for him."

"And what's so wrong with that?"

"So, that's really all it takes with you? Just be called beautiful?" he asked with disdain.

"Yes! I've never been called that in my life. Sorry for wanting to feel like someone likes looking at me. No. No, actually I'm not sorry. You don't get to sit there broodier than all the hens in the henhouse because I liked having someone think of me as attractive."

Kaz leaped up and started pacing. "Anyone can call you beautiful! That doesn't make Locklan unique or special."

Theo jumped out of her chair. How dare he lecture her about the merits of being called pretty. She marched up to him, stopping his pacing with a finger shoved into his chest. "You'd never understand what it is like. You with your impossibly angular cheekbones, jawline sharp enough to make knives jealous, and your intolerable honey-molasses eyes. It wasn't about *Lock* being special. It was about someone else making me feel like *I* was unique and special. For *once*."

"That is not what makes you unique or special, Theo."

"Trust me, I know!"

"If all he sees when he looks at you is how pretty you are, then he's practically blind."

She reeled back. "Thanks for that, Kaz. Everyone else has made it abundantly clear. Congratulations on joining the ranks of people who can't stand the sight of me."

He huffed, pinching the bridge of his nose, and resumed his pacing, the carpet in danger of becoming threadbare under his feet. "That's not what I meant."

"No, that seemed pretty clear."

He shook his head. "Do you really not know?"

"Know *what*?"

"About you!"

"I'm not sure why you're yelling at me right now."

"You're...It's..." Kaz let out a frustrated groan. "Yes, you are beautiful. But you are so much more than that. You are incredibly brave, Theo. You managed to scare an elf guard into doing your bidding. In all my hundreds of years I have never seen that happen before. And you're trying so hard. Any other person would have given up by now. But not you. You got stabbed and still managed to get up and finish what you started. The first time I got stabbed, I sulked for a week.

"And your ability to spin insults out of thin air is unparalleled. Truly, it is a gift. Even when it is directed at me, I have to admire it. The confounded faces you leave in your wake are legendary.

"Or how about when you let people see underneath the fire spitting? When you open yourself up to people even a little, you become a magnet. When you played the harp at Locklan's party—fairies are *still* talking about it. You were even invited to drink and dance with the fairy musicians. A human treated as their equal. *That doesn't happen.* How do you not see this about yourself? How rare you are. I've met a lot of people, but I have never met anyone like you."

He ran his hands through his hair, pushing it out of his

face. "And it hurts knowing how much I had misjudged you when we met. I wish I could take it back. But maybe it's a good thing I didn't know you then. Because if I did, I probably wouldn't have been able to speak.

"So if all you want to hear is that someone thinks you're beautiful, then fine. But just know you're selling yourself short."

Theo would have been less stunned if he had hit her in the face with a frying pan.

He was looking straight into her eyes, waiting for her to say something. But it was the genuine earnestness on his face that had her closing the small gap between them. Just as her body pressed up against his, she pulled his face to hers and kissed him.

He didn't hesitate as he wrapped his arms around her, like she'd somehow disappear if he didn't hold her tight. But she wasn't going to move. It was all she could do to even remain standing.

The kiss was not playful or lighthearted. It was fierce and demanding. She couldn't help the little moan that escaped her as he entwined his fingers in her hair to bring her even closer, kiss her deeper.

He pulled back and smiled as he gazed into her eyes, his breath uneven.

"So, just to summarize all that," she said with a grin. "You're saying you also think I'm pretty."

"Very pretty, yes." He laughed, shoulders sagging with relief before leaning in to kiss her again.

When he released her, he held her hands in his. "Theo, after your third task, come with me."

"What do you mean? Come with you where?"

"Anywhere. We could go anywhere we want. After your last task is done, I'm leaving. Come with me."

She looked at him, the sincerity and urgency reflecting back at her. And in it she saw freedom and adventure. A future filled with happiness. Someone she wanted to be with. Someone who wanted to be with her. "Yes. I'll go with you."

He leaned in and touched his forehead to hers. She dropped his hands only to wrap her arms around his neck and kiss him.

But they broke apart sharply as they both heard the unmistakable sound of a gun cocking.

Theo spun toward the doorway to see her mother pointing the earl's flintlock pistol at Kaz.

"Get away from her."

Chapter 24

Where Lady Balfour
Loses It

They jumped apart, hands shooting up in surrender.

Theo could see the small tremor as Lady Balfour trained the gun on Kaz, as though she were seeing a grizzly bear standing in the room and not a man.

"*Kaz, you should go,*" Theo whispered.

"I'm not leaving you alone with her."

"I'll be fine." But as Theo said it, she wasn't sure if that was the case. Her mother was falling apart at the seams. Her hair was barely holding together, her bun now so tangled with knots it was as though someone had set off a firecracker on her head. Her grinding teeth were squeaking like a loose floorboard, and the bags the size of change purses under her eyes suggested she hadn't slept in days. She was so void of color it was only the slight sweep of blush that signaled she hadn't just been stolen from a tomb and reanimated.

"Theo, come over here right now," Lady Balfour said with that familiar menacing calm that had Theo's hairs standing on end.

"Mother," Theo began.

"Right now!"

"Go," Kaz said out of the corner of his mouth.

With her arms still raised, Theo moved slowly to stand near her mother.

"Who sent you?" Lady Balfour snarled at Kaz. "Who are you working for?"

Kaz creased his brow in confusion, as did Theo.

"Mother, who do you think sent him?" Theo said in a voice that would have been better suited for the nursery. She hoped the soothing tone might encourage her mother to calm down and tell them how she knew about any of this.

"Our *enemies*, Theodosia! People who do not want you to marry the duke. People who are out to destroy us!" She shook the gun at Kaz. "I won't let you!"

"No one is out to destroy us. No one sent him. Put down the gun."

"Of course someone sent him! Did you actually think he was here for you? What sort of treacle did he pour in your ears to make you think he was interested in you? Use your head, Theodosia! Look at him! Convenient that an attractive man showed up out of nowhere, isn't it? Someone is trying to tarnish your reputation so that the duke won't marry you!"

"You've lost your mind," Kaz said under his breath, then he looked at Theo. "Come on. We're leaving." He held out his hand as the smallest wisps of wind gathered around his feet.

"Don't even think about it," Lady Balfour growled. "How are you even going to get out? Jump through the window? You are not going anywhere, you charlatan. Whoever you're working for is going to regret sending you here."

But Theo had had enough. Her mother had completely snapped and Theo was not going to stay here a moment longer. She took a step forward, just as Kaz started to walk toward her, his hand ready to grab hers.

As her outstretched fingers brushed his, Lady Balfour pulled the trigger.

Theo shrieked at the sound, the blast ringing in her ears. And then shrieked again when she saw Kaz. The force of the bullet had knocked him off his feet and he was lying face down on the carpet, not moving.

Lady Balfour was gaping at the gun.

Kaz groaned, rolling to his back and clutching his chest, blood coating the entire front of him. Theo started to run to him, but before she even made it a half step, she was wrenched back by her hair. Her eyes watered at the sting in her scalp as her mother dragged her from the music room.

For the first few moments, Theo thought it might be worth it to fight. Her mother must have had similar suspicions because when Theo brought her hands toward her head, Lady Balfour cocked the gun again.

"You would kill me, Mother?" Theo rasped as she felt strands of her hair being ripped out under her mother's fingers.

"Kill you? No. But you can still be pushed down the aisle in a wheelchair if you sustain a bullet wound to your leg. So if you'd like to avoid that, I'd suggest coming along quietly."

Somewhere in the back of her mind, Theo knew that if she was shot, she'd heal relatively quickly. But that thought was just as overpowered as she was, the threat of her own mother shooting her shocking her into compliance.

When they reached Theo's room, her mother shoved her in with such force that Theo fell to the floor, kneecaps wailing from the impact. Before she could even get to her feet, the door slammed shut behind her, the lock clicking into place. She flew to the door anyway, banging her fists and screaming for her mother to let her out. But unlike when Beatrice was trapped in her room, there'd be no help coming for Theo. Even if the servants of the house did like her, no one was around to hear her.

She walked to her bed with her head in her hands, wondering how long she'd be confined.

The answer turned out to be mere minutes.

The door blasted open like her mother had used a battering ram. And if Theo thought she looked crazed before, she was wrong.

Her eyes were darting around the room like she was expecting people to jump out from under the bed and behind the chairs, and she was brandishing the pistol in case anybody did. "He's gone! I went back to the music room and he's gone! He's going to go straight to his employer and tell them what you did! We will be ruined if that happens, Theodosia! Ruined!"

Theo almost collapsed with relief that Kaz had enough strength left to get himself out. "Mother, this is preposterous. You aren't making any sense. How would we be ruined if I don't marry the duke?"

Fists clenching and unclenching, Lady Balfour looked at Theo with violent condescension. "*Money*, Theodosia! We are out of money!"

"What does that have to do with my marriage?"

"You don't get it!" she shouted as she stomped her foot. "The duke settled our outstanding debts in exchange for your hand in marriage. If you don't marry him, we have to pay that money back. *And we don't have it.* If you don't marry him, we will default on everything. We will lose everything! Creditors have been sniffing around. They were either sent by the duke to make sure you're chaste enough to marry, or sent by someone who doesn't want you to marry the duke. Either way, if they find out that there is nothing but a couple of moths flying around our vaults, we are done for! And you fell for it!"

Her mother might as well have stripped Theo's skin with sandpaper. It would have felt the same. "The duke...paid you to marry me?"

"Yes! Do you think anyone else was lining up to wed him? He's decrepit and disgusting. But he wanted a wife, and we needed the money. And now you're promiscuously kissing whatever spy they send your way. I am trying to save you from a life of poverty, and you are so close to destroying everything! You selfish, selfish girl."

Theo jerked back. "Selfish? You sold me like a fourth-place cow! How am I supposed to feel about that?"

"It is selfish! Like it or not, the fate of you, me, and the entire Earldom of Merrifall rests on this marriage. And you're ready to cast that all aside for what? For who? Some love match you think is out there waiting for you?"

"What? No—"

"You are not a princess. There is no fairy-tale ending for you. And sometimes people like us need to accept the hand we've been dealt and do what we have to for the good of our family. Oh, stop crying. You act like you're all alone in your suffering. That I couldn't possibly understand what it is like for you. I do, Theodosia. But unlike you, I did what needed to be done."

Theo looked at her mother in teary disbelief. On her mother's small list of positive traits, empathy was not one of them.

"I was happy as the wife of a merchant," her mother said, anger roiling. "So happy to be married to your father. You were too little to remember him, but we were all so happy, Theodosia. Then the love of my life died, leaving me alone with two children who I was then supposed to provide for. There was no way for me to do that as an unwed woman. So to keep you and your sister out of the streets, I married the earl. And got you titles that would secure your future. If you were under the impression we married with even a modicum of love, you're sorely mistaken. I needed a husband for your future, and he needed a wife for appearances. I spent my marriage to the earl being constantly compared to his perfect dead wife and perfect child, all so I could give my daughters the best life I could.

"You've been surrounded by wealth without ever thinking about what I had to do to get that for you. *Everything* I have done was for you! Now you sit in front of me acting like becoming a duchess is not good enough. Like you are suffering more than anyone has ever suffered. *Selfish.* The world owes you nothing, Theodosia. *Nothing.* Grow up."

Theo would have preferred her mother to have slapped her. The sting of that would have been far less painful.

Lady Balfour continued. "So to save what you are close to wrecking, we are leaving right now. We can make it to Wainwright before that man tells his employers. Maybe the duke will marry you the day we arrive. Once it's official, there's nothing anyone can do about it. So dry your face and let's go." She grabbed Theo by the arm and dragged her out of the manor with a surprising amount of strength.

"The gun is cocked and loaded," Lady Balfour growled as she shoved her daughter into the waiting carriage. She climbed in after her, making sure Theo was well aware of the consequences of trying to make a final stand.

Theo had run out of time. No one was coming to help her. No one was going to save her from this marriage.

And Cecily's tasks had been for nothing.

She wiped her eyes, but the tears continued to fall.

For a wonderful little while, she had thought that maybe she actually was nice, and helpful, and fun. A friend to others with friends of her own who was putting a little bit of goodness back into the world.

That was over.

Maybe, deep down, she had known this was how it was going to end. After all, she was Theodosia Balfour. Good things did not happen to her.

They never would.

Maybe she should stop fighting it. Stop pretending she was anything other than what she really was: selfish, petty, nasty, ugly, and wicked.

Theo looked out the carriage window. Dawn was just breaking over Merrifall, the sun casting its colors onto the clouds, turning them into soft puffs of orange against a lilac sky. But the still-dark manor where she'd had the worst years of her life so far loomed over her, blocking any morning light from reaching the carriage and enshrouding her in shadow. And in these last few moments while she waited to be whisked away to an even more miserable existence, she mourned the life she could have had if this impossible scheme had worked.

While Theo mourned, her mother stuck her head out the other carriage window, swiveling it back and forth before declaring the area free from henchmen who doubled as accountants. She checked her pocket watch, then congratulated herself out loud for acting so quickly and getting ahead of whoever was following them.

But ... the carriage hadn't moved.

Lady Balfour smacked her hand on the roof, demanding in a shrill and panicky voice to know what the holdup was. When the driver didn't answer, she leaned out the window again.

"Excuse me," came a voice from outside. "But I'll need you to release my despairing Theo."

Lady Balfour leaped from the carriage as Theo's heart leaped from her chest. She wasted no time scrambling out of the carriage after her mother, overwhelmed with both relief and gratitude for who she knew she'd find.

Standing in front of the carriage were Cecily and Phineas.

"Who are you? Who sent you? What credit agency do you work for?" Lady Balfour screamed, fumbling for the pistol as Cecily sauntered toward them.

Theo only made one step toward the fairy before her mother grabbed her. "Don't even think about it!"

"First," Cecily said. "My name is Cecily. Second: Kasra, the gentleman you shot in the chest, sent me. Well, he didn't send me. After landing in a bloody pile on my doorstep, he quickly explained what happened and I came to get Theo. Third: I do not work for a credit agency." She turned to Phineas. "Dearest, do I look like a creditor to you? I can't decide if I should be insulted. Oh well."

Lady Balfour finally freed the pistol from her pocket and held it out in front of her, inches away from Cecily's chest. Cecily looked at it, then smiled at Lady Balfour like she was nothing more than a feisty chipmunk.

She reached out and tapped the barrel. "No."

The pistol disappeared so quickly that Lady Balfour's arm was still outstretched, her finger curled like it was still on the trigger. She jerked back in surprise.

"Theo, time to go." Cecily turned back to Phineas and motioned for Theo to follow.

"*THEODOSIA!*"

Theo stopped and turned to face her outraged mother.

"You will get away from them *right now* and come with me," Lady Balfour snarled. "I don't know what you think your plan is, but if I have to tie you up and drag you down that aisle, I will."

"I don't doubt that for a second. But I am leaving, Mother. And your threats will not stop me."

"You wicked, spoiled, selfish child! What will become of Merrifall? What of *your own mother?*"

Theo felt like she was staring down a starving wolf as her mother stalked toward her, teeth bared and desperate enough to still put up a fight.

But Theo was not prey. So she stood her ground. "I cannot be a life raft for your bad decisions when all you've ever done was put holes in your own boat. I know you well. Even with your own ship sunk, you will just drill new holes in mine and row us farther out to sea."

Lady Balfour was shaking with rage as Theo trotted to Cecily and Phineas.

"I can't save you," Theo continued. "I don't think I'm capable of that. Goodbye, Mother."

Chapter 25

Where Theo Learns
the Third Task

The three of them landed on Cecily's doorstep and Theo, still shaking, was led into the drawing room.

Cecily stretched out on her chaise longue and conjured a glass of wine. "What a whirlwind adventure you've had! Your mother shoots our Kaz and then tries to kidnap you. I'm glad we got to you before she put any bullet holes in your body, or a ring on your finger."

"I'm glad, too," Theo said, sniffling.

Phineas pulled out a handkerchief from his pocket and passed it to her.

"Thank you." Theo dabbed her eyes and sat down.

"My pleasure." He pointed to the handkerchief. "You can keep that."

She laughed. "I meant for coming to get me."

Phineas sank into a chair with his own glass of wine. "You

didn't think we'd leave our dear friend Theo at the mercy of her armed and dangerous mother, did you?"

Cecily added, "And besides, Theo, I have every intention of holding up my end of the bargain. I want to make sure you have the opportunity to finish the third task. Which meant rescuing you before your mother forcibly turned you into the Duchess of Snowbell."

"Where is Kaz?" Theo asked, looking around the room in case she somehow missed him.

"Convalescing." Cecily waved her hand dismissively, as if Theo had asked about the state of his hangnail, not bullet wound. "I need him to heal as quickly as possible, so he's sleeping it off. Should be right as rain soon." She took a gulp of wine. "Oh, and given the events of the past few hours, I did not have the opportunity to congratulate you on your successful second task. You have no idea how relieved I am to have the necklace in my possession. I heard Koel was trying to blame the theft on a human harp player named Lady Theodosia, but unfortunately for him, no one could verify his story. Not even Endlin, who not only insists she would have recognized Lady Theodosia, but was also unreliable as a witness anyway given just how out-of-her-mind drunk she was. Well done all around, Theo."

"Aren't you going to return it to its owner?" Theo asked, figuring something that important would have been delivered upon receipt.

"Yes. As soon as I am able." She clapped her hands together. "So, now you've made it to your final task!"

"Wait, already? But I just finished the second task." And hadn't had a chance to sleep, or eat.

"Why not? I'd think you would be just as excited as I am to wrap this up."

"But—"

Cecily's eyes flashed and she sat up. "We are finishing this *now*."

Phineas was also staring at Theo, no light in his eyes, no amusement on any line of his face. Only cold anger coating his rigid posture.

Theo blinked. "All right. Now."

Phineas's shoulders relaxed and Cecily smiled. "Wonderful. As I was saying...final task."

Theo braced for what she could only assume would be a nightmare of an assignment. It would have to be something monstrous to compete with the first two tasks.

"You need to give Beatrice a gift."

"*What? That's* my last good-person task?" That was, indeed, a nightmare of a task.

"It's time to put the past behind you so you can start your new, unmarried life with a clean slate. Mend fences, maybe forgive. We'll see." Cecily leaned back on the chaise longue.

Theo was fighting a losing battle with her face to not contort into a scowl. Beatrice had haunted her every step of the way during this outrageous bargain, and now she had to give her a gift in order to prove to Cecily that she could be just as good as her. Of course Theo did all the hard work and Beatrice was the one who got *a gift* at the end of it. Sounded about right.

"What better way to show you can put your personal grudges aside and be the better person, my raging Theo? You can find out if it is possible to let go of those nasty, hateful feelings you have for her."

Doubt it.

"Fine. Just give her a gift, then? That's it?"

"Well, there are caveats. First, the gift can't just be any old thing. It has to be a thoughtful gift of your choosing. Something that would matter to her, make her pause. Second, you have to give it to her directly, when she is alone. You can't give it to a courier, or hurl it at her head from across the room. Third, you have to do this on your own. Neither I, nor Phineas, nor Kaz will be able to help you." Cecily held up a finger at Theo's wide eyes. "But since I truly want you to be successful in your last task, I will give you a leg up. I will not only help you get into the palace, but I'll give you explicit directions as to where Beatrice's suite is and how you can get there using the servants' hallways."

"How will I use the servants' hallways? Won't someone notice me?"

"Not if you're dressed to look like one of the servants."

Phineas laughed. "Ah, the sneak-in-as-the-help trick. It's classic for a reason."

"Then do I just report back when it is done? How will you know when I've finished the final task?"

"Theo, you never fail to impress me with your thoroughness." Cecily held out her hand, and a small white candle appeared in her palm. "After you give her the gift, put this in her window and light it. I'll be able to see the moment your task is done."

Theo took the candle from her, as well as a pack of matches from Cecily's other hand.

"And, Theo, I am counting on you to finish this task. You've done so well. I know you can do this. Any ideas as to what you want to give her?"

What on earth would be a thoughtful gift for a princess she despised? Beatrice probably had everything she wanted already.

Beatrice's room at Merrifall swam back into her mind to when Theo had found the instructions to summon Cecily. And to what else she had found then.

"Yes," Theo said. "But it's back at Merrifall." She wondered if it was worth risking the wrath of her mother again.

But Cecily must have had the same thoughts. "Wonderful. Phineas can get you there. The good news is that it seems your mother is hightailing it to Wainwright to most likely attempt damage control now that she has no idea where you are. So if there's nothing else, I'd suggest you get going. I will meet you two outside the palace as soon as you're ready."

"We're off," Phineas said. Together they walked out to the veranda and, as he linked Theo's arm with his, were wrapped up in a swirl of wind.

When it cleared, they were standing in Beatrice's old room.

She made a beeline straight to the closet and knelt down in front of the chest of drawers. It had remained untouched since Theo had last been there. The portrait of Bea's mother was exactly where she had left it tucked in its shroud behind the blankets. She pulled out the bundle and unwrapped it.

"How did you even know that was in there?" Phineas asked, perusing the closet.

"Some good old-fashioned snooping. I was looking for

accessories for my first visit to Wainwright and came across this." Theo rewrapped the painting, then put it inside one of Beatrice's old canvas workbags, adding the candle and matches.

"Are you ready to do this, Theo?" Phineas asked when she had slung the bag over her shoulder.

"As ready as I'll ever be, I suppose."

"You can do this. Cecily believes in you. So do Kaz and I."

He took her hand and when the swirl of wind died down, they were standing on a hill overlooking the royal palace, where Cecily was indeed waiting for them.

———————————————•———————————————

The palace had always been exceptionally beautiful, but in the midday light, it glinted like a multifaceted jewel, the many spires and turrets sparkling. Even from their distant vantage point, Theo could see the iron detailing that now decorated not only the front gates, but around the outside walls as well, making the palace look like it was sitting in a giant crown. No wonder the iron guilds loved Beatrice. Theo didn't even know there was that much iron available in the kingdom.

And surrounding the palace was the famed botanical garden. Instead of palace lawns, the same flowers from Beatrice's wedding had been planted in swirling, mazelike patterns, with paths that doubled back on one another, or went nowhere. Other flowers and plants sprouted up here and there throughout like the floral equivalent of freckles.

"So, do I just walk through the front gates, then?" Theo

asked, eyeing the sentries positioned at the gates and along the walls.

"Oh, no, my dear. You'll go in through the servants' entrance."

"But even if I'm dressed like a servant, won't they be checking to see who is coming and going at that entrance as well?"

"So thorough!" Cecily shook her head in awe. "Don't fret about that part, my cunning Theo. First, we'll make you look convincing." Cecily transformed Theo's ensemble into a plain black dress that came all the way up to her neck, and all the way down to her simple, practical shoes. Her hair was coiled neatly into an unadorned crocheted hairnet.

Compared to every other outfit Cecily had dressed her in, this one was rather lackluster.

Cecily apparently thought the same. Frowning at her handiwork, she said, "Well, it's not my favorite, but you'll certainly blend in. Now for the directions." She reached out and touched Theo's nose. "There you go!"

Just like when Lock had given her dancing instructions, Theo knew exactly where to go once she got into the palace, the memory of the internal layout so strong it was as though she'd lived there her whole life.

"And this is for you." She handed Theo a gold coin almost identical to the one given to Dwyn.

"What's this for?" Theo asked.

"Pass that to the sentry."

"I'm supposed to bribe the guard?"

"Something like that. When you give it to him, make sure to let him know that you are employed at the palace and you belong there."

329

Theo slipped the coin into her pocket.

Cecily held Theo's shoulders and stared into her eyes. "This is an important final task, so I expect you to put as much effort into this one as you have the previous tasks."

Theo nodded.

"Good. Now, off you go."

Theo walked down the cobblestone lane to the home of goodness incarnate and her third task.

At the start of the lane that would lead her to the servants' entrance, a sentry halted her. But before he could say anything to her, she held out her hand to him, fist closed so he couldn't see what she was holding. "For you."

He tilted his head in confusion but held out his hand. The moment the coin touched his palm, a dreamy look washed over him.

"I am employed at the palace," she said, remembering the words Cecily had told her to use. "I belong here."

He gave her a kind smile, stood back, and motioned for her to keep walking. She wondered how long that dazed look would last.

The sweet but earthy fragrance of the botanical gardens wafted over her as she walked toward the palace walls. Looking at these little yellow flowers reminded Theo of the evening primrose in the meadow all those weeks ago. Beatrice must've really had a thing for them since they also lined the lane, and were even growing on a wide trellis that Theo had to walk under before going through the gates and into a small courtyard.

Walking through the servants' door was like entering a

beehive. With the morning meal approaching, servants were darting to and fro with enough precision and coordination to impress any army general. But Theo only remained unnoticed for less than a minute before a man in black livery approached.

"You there! Take this upstairs to the footmen immediately." He thrust a covered tray into her hands and strode back into the fray of rushing servants.

With as good of an excuse as any to get farther into the palace, she joined the line of other servants carrying trays. Dressed all in black and moving silently like an efficient, helpful funeral procession, they walked up the stairs and toward the dining room. She passed her tray to the waiting footman and followed the others back to the stairwell. But instead of going down to the kitchens again, Theo followed the directions given to her by Cecily and went up, farther into the palace.

Chapter 26
Where Everyone Just Loves the Princess

The hallways she walked down were mostly deserted, with only a few other servants passing her. Busy with their own tasks, they hardly noticed her. Before she knew it, she was standing in front of the peephole to Beatrice's suite.

Looking through it, Theo could see a large sitting room with a table in the center, the door to the bedroom visible beyond. However, it appeared to be empty. She stayed for another moment, hoping that maybe Beatrice was inside, but the room was silent.

Theo could have sat and waited, but it could be hours before Beatrice returned. And if anyone noticed her camping out right outside the princess's room, she'd have a real hard time explaining why. So instead, she started roaming the servants' corridors using the information that Cecily had planted in her head.

After what felt like hours of wandering aimlessly through the palace, she heard the din of voices coming from a side room. Peering in, she could see a small sitting room with women around a table taking their noon tea.

And there among them was the princess. For the first time in nearly two years, Theo was looking at Beatrice. She looked just as glowy and happy as she did at her wedding, if not more so, as she laughed and chatted with her friends, head held high and not a care in the world.

"Oh, Your Highness," started one of the women. "I must say your charitable donation of flowers to the hospital was so wonderful. You truly are such a gift to the kingdom."

Beatrice gave the preening sycophant a bashful smile and put her hand to her chest. "That is so kind of you to say. I just want to make sure that our kingdom's generosity is provided to everyone, especially those without a voice. We cannot judge the prosperity of our kingdom by the success of those most fortunate, but instead by those of us who are the least fortunate."

The other women at the table were nodding their heads, each joining the chorus with their own versions of "Hear! Hear!" and "Well said, Hightness."

It was lucky their singing of praises was so loud, otherwise they might have heard Theo's groan.

"Good, you're here," a voice snapped behind Theo. She jumped in surprise, turning to see an older woman wearing a black servant's dress pushing a cart filled with various serving trays of finger sandwiches and pastries. While she might have said she was relieved to have found Theo, her overall manner indicated she was not. The stern lines around her eyes and mouth suggested that she even slept with a frown. "Take that in and put them on the table."

The woman did not wait to see if Theo obeyed the order before spinning on her heel and striding with purpose back the way she came.

Theo waited until she could no longer hear her footsteps, then grabbed a platter of iced scones, leaving the cart for someone who cared to bring it in. Treasure in hand, she went back toward Beatrice's suite.

———————————————•———————————————

Theo woke up with a stiff neck and sore butt. After devouring the entire pile of scones, she had fallen asleep curled up behind a curtain in a little alcove near Beatrice's suite, and she had no idea for how long. She scolded herself not only for potentially missing an opportunity to get Beatrice alone, but also for wasting time that Cecily didn't seem to have. Stifling a groan and shaking out her achy limbs, she went back to the peephole and peered in.

Sitting at the table, sorting through a mess of maps and deep in thought, was Beatrice. Alone. Just as Theo was about to turn the handle on the servants' door, the door on the other side of the room opened and Prince Duncan strode into the room.

Beatrice was so invested in her work that she didn't even look up.

"Hello, my love," he said as he stood behind her, planting a kiss on her hair. He took a seat next to her at the table. "How was your talk with the landowners? Any success?"

"No." She sighed. "I still haven't found anywhere suitable for the school. Since I can't go and look myself, I'm just having to take their word for it."

"What about your tea with the ladies?"

"That, at least, is some good news. The flower benefaction went over well, and they're each offering to donate funds toward building a new maternity wing at the hospital."

Duncan smiled. "Well done, dear. Promise to name it after whoever gives you the most money."

Beatrice huffed a laugh.

Theo wondered if her gift-giving task would count if she did it with a sneer and an eye roll. Cecily said she couldn't hurl the portrait at Beatrice from across the room, but what about from across the table?

All Beatrice had to do was pass out some flowers and the whole kingdom went wild. Now she was upping the ante with this business about a school. *Princess Beatrice's School for Perfect and Perfectly Insufferable Children.* Classes would include learning how to blame others and smile innocently.

All Theo was learning from the final task was that she still hated her stepsister. And it was frustrating to know that she was the only one in the entire kingdom who felt that way. That saw her for who she really was under all the righteous causes that occupied her time.

Even Cecily fell for Beatrice's facade. Then again, Cecily did send her to help Dwyn, who must have also tricked her into believing in the goodness of his character, so maybe she was just as easily fooled as the rest of them.

Beatrice sighed and looked back at the papers on the table.

"Take a break and join me for dinner," Duncan said. "You won't be able to find any locations if you're passed out on top of those maps."

"Oh, darling. Maybe I should just get dinner delivered to me here."

Duncan was undeterred. "How about this, my love. You join me for dinner downstairs, and I'll have extra desserts sent up here for you to enjoy over your piles of maps while I have drinks with some of those insufferable barons."

She smiled brightly at him as he held out his arm to escort her. "It's a deal."

Theo watched as they walked out of the suite, closing the door securely behind them.

She slid down the wall again to sit and wait.

The last words Beatrice had said were clanging around in her head. *It's a deal. It's a deal. It's a deal.* How many times had Theo said those words over the course of this bargain? She made deal after deal to finish these tasks. A fairy never gave something away without getting something in return. How many times had she heard that from fairies and familiars? Lock delighted in telling that to Theo on multiple occasions. Theo never heard any mention of a "perfect person" clause, where fairies would give something away based on moral character. Why would Cecily want to? Why Beatrice?

Although, Cecily wasn't getting anything out of her deal with Theo, either, was she? Once Theo completed the tasks, Cecily would help her. There weren't strings attached to that when she made the bargain. Only that she had to prove she could be a good person.

But she still had to make the bargain.

Theo couldn't help the feeling that something was off. Theo knew Beatrice. Beatrice spent her whole life spinning narratives that she was better than everyone else around her, and everyone ate up the lies. Why did Theo believe that this one thing was any different? It wasn't adding up. Which would make more sense: Beatrice was the only person ever to get a fairy to help her without having to make a bargain because she's *that wonderful*, or Beatrice was just like everyone else?

That lying, deceitful Bea.

She didn't get anything based on the goodness of her character.

She made a bargain.

Chapter 27

Where Theo Learns
the Truth About
the Ball

Theo was fuming as she waited for Beatrice and watched the empty room.

Liar liar liar liar liar.

The door to the suite opened, and Beatrice came into the room, taking up her place at the table and getting back to work. And since Prince Duncan was drinking with the barons, she would be alone for a while.

Theo pushed open the servants' door and stepped into the suite, her eyes burning into the back of Beatrice's head like she could make it explode if she concentrated hard enough. The door shut behind her with the smallest click and blended back into the wall.

Beatrice did not look up from the table. "If you could add

a couple more logs to the fire, that'd be wonderful. Thank you."

"I'm not here to do the fire, Bea. If I recall correctly, that was your job."

Beatrice spun around in her chair.

"Hello, Bea."

"*Theo*," she gasped. "What are you doing here? You're not supposed to be here."

"I'm well aware I'm not supposed to be here. Why do you think I'm dressed as a servant instead of strolling through the front gates shouting 'I'm the princess's stepsister!'?" Theo walked to the other chair and took a seat. "You and I have some things to discuss."

Theo took the portrait out of the satchel.

"First, I have something to give you." She began to unwrap it. But she could tell by Beatrice's wide, wet eyes she knew exactly what was under the cloth. She reached out a hand toward it, but Theo shook her head.

"No, no," Theo said as she took the matches and candle out of the satchel. While Beatrice looked on in confusion, Theo lit the candle and picked up the portrait, holding it just out of range of the flame.

Beatrice was shaking. "Don't. Please, Theo. Don't."

"You are going to sit there and answer my questions. If you don't, I will light the very last portrait of your mother on fire. Am I understood?" Theo's anger felt like another person in the room, like Lady Balfour was standing behind her pulling the puppet strings.

Beatrice nodded.

"I want the truth of what happened the night of the ball."

Beatrice swallowed, her gaze fixed on her mother. "I...I found that dress in storage. And the carriage—"

Theo held up a hand. "Sorry, I should have mentioned I know about how you summoned the fairy at the frog fountain, so you can cut the rubbish. Try again or this goes into the flame."

"How do you know about that?" Beatrice asked, her voice low.

"Your instructions for summoning a fairy were next to this painting. Found one, found the other. So I know where the dress, the shoes, the carriage, and everything else came from. I want to know about what really happened."

Beatrice's eyes narrowed. "Then why are you asking? You apparently know everything already."

"No. The only story I'm familiar with is the horseshit you sold to the rest of the kingdom. I want the true story."

"What is there to tell? My father died, your mother turned me into a servant, you treated me like a slave, and I got out."

"Where did you find the instructions?"

"I had found the book stuffed behind a false shelf wall in the library when I was cleaning. I looked through it and saw instructions on summoning a fairy. So I tore out the pages, put the book back, and brought them to my room. The evening primrose page came from a botany book."

"And then?"

"What do you mean *and then*? And then I summoned her and went to the ball."

"When did you summon her?"

"The night of the ball. Your mother locked me in my room before you left. She had been trying to change the will to cut me out of it. Disown me completely. She wanted to keep me there so she could change it with zero interference."

"Who let you out of your room?"

"Me. I saw you leave for the ball, and then used my bedsheets to sneak out the window. I had the coin in my pocket. Once I was down, I went back into the kitchen to get the wine, and then to the field to get the primrose flowers at sunset. Then I summoned her. And it worked. I told her all about how awful your mother had been to me, and she wanted to help."

"What did you ask for?"

"Her help to get into the ball."

"Why the ball?"

"I needed to get to Duncan."

"But why? You were just hoping you'd look pretty enough for him to notice you and then marry you?"

She scoffed. "We'd been friends since we were children. We didn't get to see each other all that often, so we would write letters. Then our friendship turned into more. Duncan was convinced we'd be married. But after my father's death, your mother found our correspondence. She didn't want me to marry him. Didn't want me overshadowing you and Flo. So she wrote a letter to him explaining that I was sent away to a boarding school and that he should not bother trying to contact me. She destroyed all the old letters.

"I needed to see him before my title was stripped away and I wouldn't be allowed anywhere near the palace. Turns out, he was devastated when I went away. He thought he'd never see me again. He knew who I was the moment he saw me. When we went out to the garden, I explained everything. How I wasn't in some faraway school but had been in my house the whole time, stuck being a servant. How she was going to change the will and disown me.

"But then the guards came asking me who I really was. They wouldn't listen to Duncan. So he went to get the king while the guards kept me in the garden. One went to find your mother. I knew she was devious, but I never thought she'd stoop so low as to lie to the royal guards. So after that, there was no way that anyone would believe me, and the guards were going to take me to the dungeons."

"But why go back home?"

"I was never intending to return to Merrifall. I went back as a last-ditch effort to try to find the will. I thought maybe I could hide it—or destroy it to buy a bit more time. I don't know where your mother put it, but it wasn't in my father's desk. I didn't have time to keep searching because you arrived. I ran to my room to pull the sheets out of the window in case she locked me back in there, and that's when she found me.

"When Duncan found out I'd been chased from the palace, he was furious. He told his father about me and then came to get me. He said that if we announced our engagement before your mother could rewrite the will, it would be impossible to disown me. So that's what we did. He loved me but said if I didn't still love him we could just stay engaged until we figured everything out. But I loved him, too, so we got married."

"And then sold the kingdom that ridiculous story."

"Duncan said that if we could drum up enough public

support, I'd be untouchable and then it wouldn't matter what your mother did with the will. But we didn't even need to make up a story. We just told them all the truth. Even if they didn't believe the fairy helped me, it was just one more example of how I was a good person, deserving of her help. Deserving of the prince. So there, Theo. There's the true story."

"I believe everything you said." Theo leaned back in her chair. "Except for the part about the fairy. Here's what else I know about fairies. They never do anything without getting something in return. 'Good and deserving'? You're a *liar*. You decided to tell a cute little story about you being just so perfect instead of saying anything about a bargain."

Beatrice's eyes flashed at the last word.

"That's right! I know you made a bargain, Beatrice! You're held up as some paragon of morality. You are so perfect that a fairy abandoned her principles and helped you, wanting nothing in exchange. All my life, I was constantly compared to you. I was constantly comparing *myself* to you. From the moment I arrived at Merrifall, you used me to make yourself look better. I knew who you were since we were children. And even when you won—when you became a princess— you couldn't pass up another opportunity to drag my name through the dirt and use me as your shield."

"And you somehow think you don't deserve that? You treated me terribly the moment my father died."

"Because you treated me that way the entire time he was alive! You never helped me, never stood up for me. You earned that treatment."

"You were a menace long before that."

"Because of you!"

"You think I'm to blame for your behavior?"

"Yes! I got blamed for everything that you did. And you let them punish me for it." Theo stopped. "You know what? I've had enough. I have finished this task. I am done. Take the portrait." She shoved it across the table, scattering the papers. Beatrice snatched it up and held it to her chest.

"Have a great life, princess," Theo said. Then she took the candle and marched over to the window.

Why did she think Beatrice would finally say sorry? Would finally own up to how she treated Theo? Would finally admit to anything she did wrong? Cecily was mistaken. This task was not going to make Theo a better person, was not going to inspire forgiveness for that lying, conniving princess who still thought she was justified.

When she put the candle down, she could barely contain her sneer. Even the windowsills were made of iron here. In fact, the entire window was framed in iron. Outside, the iron fence was glinting in the moonlight. A monument to her disingenuous altruism for everyone else in the kingdom to think she was the greatest princess who ever existed.

Theo looked at the yellow flowers that were open to the night. Of course Beatrice wouldn't just plant flowers for their beauty. No, even the flowers were tools to convince the kingdom of her ultimate goodness.

She froze, staring at them. Earlier, she had thought they were evening primrose. Except when she went past the gardens on her way into the palace during the day, the buds were open. Evening primrose flowers would have been closed.

These were not evening primrose. These were look-alikes. Saint-John's-wort.

She wouldn't have otherwise been able to recognize Saint-John's-wort, or even cared to, except that it was referenced in the summoning spell. The instructions specifically warned the summoner to be careful of this look-alike because it was toxic to fairies.

The spell said something similar about iron. Using iron would void the spell and repel the fairy. And Endlin had told her that iron lessened fairy magic. If there was too much, it voided their powers entirely.

Molten rage churned in her gut as she turned to face Beatrice. She had been stabbed, had made more bargains, had been speared with a dart, had been debased and humiliated, and had been strangled within an inch of her life. All to pay her side of the bargain. All to prove she was good enough. To prove that she could be like Beatrice.

"And here I was, Bea, thinking you were only a conniving liar. But that's not quite the full story, is it? What's the real reason for the Saint-John's-wort and iron? Don't you dare look me in the eye and tell me it was to help your kingdom. We are standing in a fortress warded against fairies."

Beatrice went pale.

"You not only made a bargain. You haven't paid it back." Theo stalked to the table. "What did you bargain with, Beatrice?"

But before she could answer, the servants' door opened. Theo and Beatrice both turned to see Kaz walk into the room.

"I'm not ready to go home yet, Kaz," Theo said, assuming he had shown up now that the task was complete.

"I'm not here to take you home."

"Then what are you doing here?"

He pointed to Beatrice. "Making sure she doesn't leave."

"Kasra?" Beatrice was staring at him in horror. "*Theo*," she whispered. "*What have you done?*"

Theo saw red, and every other thought she had was tossed out, including Kaz's answer. "See, Kaz? This is what I was talking about! Straight to blaming me. Always *my* fault! Something is going wrong? Must have been something Theo did! Let's blame her first and ask questions later." She turned back to Beatrice. "To answer your question, princess, I summoned a fairy godmother. Your fairy godmother. Because I needed help, too. Here's the fun part. Unlike your story, she didn't show up wanting to help me. No. First, I needed to prove that I could be a good person *like you*. But we both know that's not the truth. There is no such thing as a fairy godmother, is there? So, the question is not what I've done. It's what you've done. What did you bargain with, Beatrice? What have you not paid back?"

Beatrice was taking big, rasping breaths.

"Answer me! What did you bargain with?"

But instead of answering, she let out a distressed sound at something behind Theo.

"Oh, my marvelous, persevering Theo. It's not *what* she bargained with. It's *who*. And that *who* is *you*."

Chapter 28
Where Theo Gets
Another Accurate Look
at Her Future

Theo turned to find Cecily, smiling from ear to ear and wearing Endlin's necklace. Phineas was next to her, matching Cecily for excitement and staring at Beatrice with glee. And standing next to them, of all people, was Dwyn, who was not smiling. No, he was covered in dirt and looking mutinous.

"Well, you or your sister," Cecily said, waving a casual hand. Then she turned that smile to the princess. "Hello, Beatrice."

"Dwyn?" Theo was having difficulty wrapping her mind around what she was seeing and hearing. "What is going on?"

Theo was relieved that Dwyn wasn't wearing his tools, given the hateful look he was throwing her way. "Yes, you traitorous human thrip! I hope you're proud of yourself. It's your fault I just shredded a perfectly good garden!"

"Enough, Dwyn," Cecily groaned. She turned back to Theo. "First, Theo, let me say congratulations on your final task. I can't even begin to tell you how pleased I am. Now, I can see you're very confused. And for good reason, I know. I'm more than happy to explain everything. Believe me when I say you've earned it. Now, I—"

"Hey!" Dwyn interrupted.

Cecily's shoulders fell and she growled to the ceiling. *What?*

"I've done my part, you fairy aphid. I've paid my debt. Let me out!"

"*Gladly*, you nasty little cretin. Dwyn of Shady Hollow, or wherever it is you're allowed to live now, you have paid your bargain in full and are released from my service. Go away."

Dwyn made a crude gesture at her. "I will, you cutworm! You flea beetle! I hope tomato hornworms eat all your tomato plants! I hope a—" He vanished as Cecily snapped her fingers.

"He is the *worst*. If I hadn't needed him, I would have been more than happy to let him rot in Elf Prison." Cecily conjured a third chair at the table and sat down, motioning for Theo to do the same. "As I was saying, we have a lot to discuss."

Tears were streaming down Beatrice's face as Cecily made herself comfortable, eyes gleaming with satisfaction.

"So, Beatrice. Before you get any silly ideas about leaving, you should know that this lovely necklace makes me immune to iron, so I can use magic. I've sealed the room. I'm just letting you know so that none of us waste any time. Right, that's out of the way. So, should we explain to Theo what is going on here?"

"Are you two working together?" Theo asked, appalled.

"What? No. As you guessed, Beatrice and I had a bargain.

And then she double-crossed me, holding hostage a large chunk of my magic, and then hid in this palace."

"You said I was the bargain," Theo said.

Cecily nodded. "Yes. Or your sister. But maybe we should start from the beginning? Beatrice, feel free to jump in at any time with your perspective." Beatrice just let out another sob as Cecily continued. "Right, here we go. A little under two years ago, I was summoned to the frog fountain by Beatrice. Did she tell you any of that?" Theo nodded. "Good, we can skip that part. Let's just go straight to the bargain. So Beatrice was at the fountain, crying about her awful life, her awful stepmother. She said that she needed to get to the royal ball. When I asked what she had to bargain with, she looked at me with a straight face and told me I could take her stepmother. The one she just told me was a horrible woman. Why would I want her?"

"How could she even bargain with her?" Theo asked.

"You can bargain with pretty much anything when making a deal with a fairy. It is up to the fairy whether it is an acceptable trade. Fairies are best known for accepting firstborns when they take humans, but really we can take anybody. Like I said, though, I did not accept that trade from Beatrice because I really didn't want your mother as a familiar. Could you imagine that woman living forever? No. When I asked if she had anything else, she said, *Take one of my stepsisters.* She hadn't mentioned sisters when she told me her story, but now said she had two. I asked which one she was going to give me. Now, Theo, remember when I said Beatrice was clever. Well, hold on to your petticoat. She said, *Take the one who loves me the most.* Doesn't that sound lovely?"

"Loves her the most?"

"Hold your questions, my percipient Theo. We'll get there. So, let me tell you why I was so interested in taking this bargain and gaining another familiar. You see, Kaz would like to leave my service. Which he can't do until he either dies—and I am not interested in that route—or we find a replacement. Replacement found, then, courtesy of this sad girl over here! This was all going great."

Kaz was looking at Theo with anguish.

Cecily continued, not paying any attention to the hurt on Theo's face. "Right before I accepted the bargain, Beatrice said she would need a full five days to get done what she needed to get done. Fine. I accepted the bargain. And because it was such a good one for me, I put a lot of effort into Beatrice's royal escapade."

Cecily clicked her nails on the arms of her chair. "And here's where it started to fall apart. So, those five days end and I turned up at Merrifall to collect one of the charming stepsisters who loved Beatrice so much she'd give up herself for Beatrice's chance at happiness. And then I saw you and your sister. Yikes. There was certainly no love there. Hell, I would have even taken whichever one of you was the most apathetic toward Beatrice. But you and your sister *hated* her."

Theo turned to the still-sobbing princess. "After everything you did to me, you tried to sell me to a fairy?"

"I needed to get out of that house, Theo! I thought it would help all of us if your mother was gone. I didn't want her to take you or Flo, but I didn't have anything else. I—"

Cecily clicked her tongue. "No, no, no. Don't try to make

it sound like you did Theo any favors. You are not the victim here. Although, that story was a creative one. The magical curfew? Hilarious! Why would I care what time she got back from the party? I brought you to a party, Theo. And as you'll recall, I didn't care what you were doing, or when. Beatrice had five days to mess around at the palace."

Beatrice covered her face with her hands as she wept harder.

Cecily picked up the story again. "Since Beatrice bargained with something that didn't exist, she now had to pay with her life. Which was fine because I was still going to claim a familiar. Except when I got here, she had taken every piece of iron in the castle and spread it around this suite. Not enough to entirely keep me out, but enough so that my powers would be severely diminished and the odds of me leaving with her would have been slim. Plus, she had brought in more Saint-John's-wort than I had ever seen in my life. And I realized that she had purposely played me. I couldn't get anywhere near her. I'll admit I was a little annoyed. I did not appreciate being taken advantage of." She held up a finger. "Now, I know what you're thinking. 'Cecily, you have human familiars! Just send them!' Smart idea on the surface, Theo, except their magic is fairy magic, too. Saint-John's-wort may not be toxic to them, but their magic wouldn't work with all that iron. And if my dear ones were captured, I'd have no way of rescuing them. I couldn't risk it. My hands were tied.

"And then you appeared, Theo. One of the stepsisters right there in front of me. You needed me; I needed you. At first, I was hoping that maybe you did have a shred of love for Beatrice. Then I could just take you and be done with

351

this. But there was still no love there, so you couldn't fulfill the bargain. My option with you, then, was to have you assist me in getting what I needed to bypass Beatrice's clever fortifications.

"I wasn't sure what to expect, so I'll admit my hopes weren't high, but you returned triumphant from the first task. Because of you, I had a gnome in my service who could tear up the absurd amount of flowers with ease. And then—the amulet. I couldn't steal it from a fairy, but you could and did! With the amulet and the gnome, I could get into the palace. With your candle, I knew that your third task was complete and I'd find Beatrice all by her lonesome without having to traipse around this colossal castle."

The truths crashed into Theo like a wave, knocking her over and tumbling her so thoroughly she could barely tell which way was up. "You lied to me," Theo said, her breath turning ragged. "They were not selfless acts at all. It was fake."

Cecily tilted her head, an infuriating look of pity on her face. "No, it was not fake. Honestly, please don't think that. You completed selfless acts that benefited someone else. That someone else was me." She turned her attention back to Beatrice. "And *now* we need to figure out what to do with you. Your life is now mine to do what I want with. I could kill you right now. But I don't really want to deal with that. Murder makes Kaz cranky, Phineas would throw up, and Theo is a good person now, thank you very much. So, you'll be coming with me. I hope you enjoyed being a princess, Beatrice. Because that is over."

Beatrice collapsed onto the floor. She huddled over her knees, her back moving like a bellows as she tried to gulp down air between sobs. Her head was shaking back and forth as she managed to cry out, "*No, no, no, no.*"

Cecily snorted, completely unmoved by the scene in front of her. "You could have stopped this at any time, Beatrice."

"Please," Beatrice wept. "Please, Cecily."

"You're begging me? You stole from me and now you want leniency? Do you know what stealing magic *does* to a fairy? You could have killed me!"

Her illness, Theo realized.

Not an illness at all—the missing magic was weakening her.

Cecily was still berating Beatrice. "You're not sorry that you swindled me. You're upset because you got caught. Because the path you made has finally led back to you."

Theo wasn't even sure Beatrice could hear her over her cries. Her hands were splayed out in front of her, tears falling like rain between them.

And all of a sudden, Theo was in the courtyard at Merrifall, watching her mother burn the portraits. Then she was in the tower, watching as her mother and sister tore apart Beatrice's dress. And then she was in the earl's study, watching as her mother promised to take everything away.

A lifetime of hatred, of bitterness, of anguish.

Of Theo watching.

Beatrice had made the bargain as a desperate, last-ditch effort to save herself, to stop the abuse at the hands of her stepmother and stepsisters. It was the only option left for her fight for survival.

Which was exactly the same reason Theo made a deal with Cecily.

She was in the eye of the tornado, watching as everything around her was caught up in the destructive vortex, as everything Theo knew was being reduced to rubble.

Beatrice's deception was slowly killing Cecily. If Cecily took Beatrice for the payment, Cecily would be whole again. All her magic would be returned and she'd be healthy.

And the kingdom would lose its beloved princess.

Even though Beatrice had used the iron and flowers for her benefit, she was still bringing prosperity to scores of people. That would end. Merrifall would turn to ruin. Theo would be powerless to stop it. Unable to stop her mother from wrecking it, unable to stop the duke from taking all that the estate had left.

She could just hold still. If she didn't move, if she didn't reach out, she would walk away unharmed.

Only to return to the life she was living.

Theo had spent her entire life being set up to continue the hateful spiral of her mother's making. Maybe her mother had been set up, too, and had spent her life tumbling down, down, down. And just like her mother, Theo would take the next generation with her. Because standing next in line, about to be pulled in, was the duke's daughter, Margot.

Theo remembered what Isadora had told her about that little girl Margot at Flo's wedding, remembered what she had said to a child simply looking for affection. Remembered her teary face, the stories of the terror she was becoming. She had treated Margot the same way everyone had treated her as a child: with dismissal and disdain.

With only one visit, she had set Margot on the path she

had been on. A little girl so convinced that she was unlovable, lashing out at everyone because it was easier to hurt other people than it was to be hurt. Who would grow up to be angry, nasty, lonely. The cycle would continue on and on.

Unless she decided to end it.

"*Stop*," Theo whispered.

But Cecily couldn't hear her. "I don't care if you cry for the next five hundred years, Beatrice. I will not feel sorry about any of it."

"Stop," Theo said, louder.

Cecily turned to Theo, confusion scrunching her brow.

"That's enough." Theo stared back, her gaze hard. "Take me."

For a heartbeat it was as though sound ceased to exist. Even Beatrice stopped crying.

"I'll fulfill the bargain. Take me instead."

Cecily held up a hand.

"Do you realize what you're saying, Theo?" Cecily asked.

Kaz looked horrified. "Theo, no! Don't do it!"

Theo gave Kaz a small, sad smile. "It's all right, Kaz." She turned back to Cecily. "I know what I'm saying. Take me. Leave Beatrice alone."

"*Theo, don't!*" Kaz pleaded, eyes wide with panic. "You paid your debt. You don't owe her anything. You don't have to do this!"

"Kaz, I'm so sorry."

"Theo, please. We can leave. You and I. Right now. We can just go. It is done. It is *over*. Come with me." There was such frantic desperation in his voice as he tried to throw as many ropes out as he could, hoping she'd grab on to one.

She shook her head. "That's the problem. It isn't over. Not yet. Not if I don't do this."

Her heart was ripping in two. Standing in front of her was a man on the precipice of a whole new life about to start, and he had his hand extended toward her. It would be so easy to take. So easy to finally get what she wanted, for once.

But it was an unequal tear. And she didn't reach out her hand to him in return.

"If Beatrice pays the bargain, nothing will change. If anything, it will get worse. And there will be no way for me to fix it."

Kaz's eyes were rimmed with tears. "That's what I'm trying to tell you, Theo. This is not your responsibility to fix."

"Well, not *fix*. I've never been good at fixing things. I'm more known for breaking things. So I'm going to break this—this pattern, this spiral. I can clear the way for Beatrice to put some goodness into the world. And maybe that's the goodness I can put into the world."

Beatrice let out a sobbing, shaky breath. "Theo—" she started.

Theo couldn't help her own tears that started to fall. "Bea, I don't think we'll ever love each other the way sisters should. There's just too much history there. But we can forgive each other. We can make it right, and I think that's plenty. So, let's be done with this. Cecily, I know what I'm saying. I'll pay what she owes."

Beatrice came over to Theo, kneeling in front of her and taking her hand. "Thank you," she sobbed over and over again. Theo slid down off the chair and wrapped her arms around Beatrice. Theo held her and cried with her as she trembled in her arms.

"But, Bea, can I ask you for a favor?"

"Anything, anything," Beatrice wept into her shoulder.

"Take Merrifall. Send my mother to go live with Flo in Avenshire. Please just give her a dignified out. I know she doesn't deserve it, but consider it yet another one of your good deeds."

"*Anything, anything, anything,*" Beatrice whispered over and over.

Theo released Beatrice and rose to face Cecily, whose own tears were very close to falling.

"Theo," Cecily began, "I release you from our bargain, settled in full. You have completed the tasks I have given you; I have halted and otherwise prevented your marriage to the Duke of Snowbell. And you, Beatrice, are released from your bargain with me, paid in full by Theo."

As soon as Cecily finished the words, she staggered, holding a hand to her heart. It seemed almost impossible for her to be any more beautiful than she had been, but as her magic returned to her, she was filled with a radiance that had her skin glowing. The deep circles under her eyes vanished and color bloomed on her cheeks. She let out a breath and smiled. Phineas's eyes were rimmed with tears as he looked on.

"There. Now, let's be done with this." Cecily turned to Kaz.

But he was still watching Theo, the tears now overflowing, his panic replaced by pain. Theo went to him, not knowing what to say to make this right.

Before she could say anything, he pulled her into a tight embrace.

"*What am I supposed to do now?*" he whispered into her hair.

"Anything you want."

"I don't know what I want." He made a noise somewhere between a laugh and a sob. "I wasn't supposed to fall for you. I didn't even think that was something I was capable of after everything. But then there you were, bursting into my life, and suddenly you were in every single one of my plans."

"If I remember correctly, you did the bursting, actually," she said, her voice muffled by his shirt. He did laugh then, and she was grateful for the sound. "I'm sorry I can't come with you on your next adventure. But thank you for inviting me, for caring about me, for making me feel like I mattered. For...being my friend. You deserve happiness, and I hope you find it. You need to go live, Kaz."

He kissed the top of her head. "I'm sorry, too. Thank you for being the most interesting person I've come across in hundreds of years. I am so thankful to have met you."

Theo looked up at him. He gently held her face, wiping the tears from her eyes, even as the ones in his kept falling. "I'm going to miss you, Theo."

"I'll miss you, too."

He released her, giving her hand a squeeze right before he let her go. Then he nodded at Cecily.

"Ready, my dear?" Cecily asked, wiping her eyes with another one of Phineas's handkerchiefs. "I will see you at home," she said to Phineas as she took Kaz by the hand.

But before she could leave, Theo spoke. "Can I make a quick stop somewhere first?"

"For you, Theo, of course. Phineas?" She nodded at him. Then in a blink, Cecily and Kaz disappeared. Even though her heart was breaking, she was glad that the last image she had of Kaz was of him smiling at her.

Theo stood next to Phineas and looked at Bea, tears still streaming down her face, and realized that Bea had won. The bane of most of Theo's life, the person she blamed for her misfortune, was still a princess in her palace, getting everything she'd ever desired yet again at Theo's expense.

But for the first time in a very long time, Theo also realized she didn't hate her for it. In fact, she didn't feel anything but relief. It was over, and Theo could finally leave it all behind her.

As she turned to go, she could only think of one thing left to say.

"Goodbye, Bea."

———————————•———————————

Fortunately, Margot was alone when Theo found her in what appeared to be a small study. She was curled up in a window nook, staring out at her brother and Miss James, who were playing in the garden below.

"Hello, Margot."

Margot turned to the greeting, a scowl on her little face. Her eyes went wide for only a moment as she saw who had come in.

"Oh, it's you," she said, before looking out the window once more.

"Yes. Me. May I have a moment of your time?"

Margot shrugged. Theo took it to mean that she was at least a little bit receptive to company, so she walked closer and sat in a nearby chair.

"Why aren't you out there playing with Miss James?"

"Because I'm in a time-out. I'm supposed to be thinking about how my actions affect other people."

"And are you?"

"No."

"I figured. I had heard from Lady Isadora that you've been having a bit of trouble lately."

"What does it matter to you?" she huffed.

"Well, because I think I might be mostly to blame for it." Theo paused. "I want you to know that I'm sorry. I'm sorry for how I treated you the last time I was here. I'm sorry for the things I said. You showed me tremendous kindness and I returned it with nastiness. I was upset and afraid and I took it out on you. You did not deserve that. And I know how you're feeling."

Margot snorted. "No, you don't."

"Unfortunately, I do. Because I was once in your shoes. And right now, I'm seeing a lot of myself in you. Which I think we can both agree is rather unappealing.

"When I was about your age, I was angry, too. Angry with everyone around me. I was hurting, and the only way I knew how to cope was to bring others down with me, to show them just how deep the hurt went. But they didn't see a little girl who was reaching out for help. They only saw someone mean, nasty, vindictive, cruel. Eventually, that's what I started to believe, too, so that's what I became. I built a fortress around myself thinking that if I did, nothing could hurt me anymore. I tried to convince myself that I didn't need anyone. But it didn't work. Trapped inside was still the sadness, still the loneliness."

Margot fidgeted and started picking pills off the cushion.

"But you have something that I didn't," Theo continued. "You are surrounded by people who love you. An entire castle full, actually. And they do see a little girl who is hurting. A little girl who needs help. So I want to tell you something that I wish someone had told me. You are worth loving, Margot. You deserve all the love that they want to give you and then some. And tearing down those walls that you're building isn't going to let more hurt in, because waiting on the other side are people who love you for who you are. The good, bad, and in-between."

Margot still didn't turn to look at her, but the scowl was gone, replaced by a tiny, wobbling lower lip.

Theo stood and walked toward the door. "I also wanted to tell you I'm leaving. You'll never have to see me again. I wish you all the best. I'll let you tell Miss James that bit of good news. Maybe write it on a cake or something like that." Theo stopped in the doorway. "Oh, and if you do feel like getting one last trick out of your system, swapping the salt and sugar was always my go-to."

Margot did turn to look at Theo then, surprise flashing across her face, followed by the faintest, flickering smile. Theo winked and walked out to Phineas, who had been waiting in the hall.

"Ready?" he asked, wind already swirling at his feet.

She took his arm.

Chapter 29
Where Theo
Discovers One More
Truth

When they arrived at the manor, Cecily had still not returned from wherever she and Kaz had gone.

"What will happen to Kaz?" Theo asked.

Phineas shrugged. "He'll live his life as a regular human. No powers. He'll age normally again."

"Do you know where he went?"

"I don't. Maybe he'll go back to where he originally came from. Though, I'm sure it has changed a lot in the time since he's been there."

Theo took in his uncharacteristically solemn expression. "You miss him already, don't you?"

He gave Theo a sad smile. "I do. He's been like a brother to me for three hundred years. But he's wanted this for a long time, so as much as it hurts, I'm glad he is finally able to get it." He motioned to the stairs. "Anyway, while we wait for Cecily to return, why don't I show you your room?"

He walked with her upstairs and through the manor, ushering her into a wide suite with soft lilac walls the color of a summer sunset. Gold leaf coated the trim, crown molding, accents, and fixtures. Standing against the wall was a large four-poster bed, the organza canopy falling like a silk waterfall off the sides, swaying in the light breeze coming in from the open balcony door. On the opposite wall surrounded by soft white sofas and chairs was a marble fireplace. The two other doors in her suite led to the dressing room and bathroom.

Phineas then excused himself so she could take in her surroundings on her own. He told her she could get some sleep if she wanted and he'd check on her in a bit. He also told her that when Cecily returned, she would help her with whatever necessities she might need, including clothing.

Theo wandered around for only a brief moment, exhaustion finally hitting her in full. It had been less than a day since completing both the second and third tasks, yet she felt like a lifetime had passed. She took off the servant's dress and crawled into bed.

When she woke, the sun was beginning to set. Cecily must have returned, because Theo's bathing chamber and closet had been stocked. She took a quick bath, then put on a simple but elegant yellow gown. She had just finished pulling her hair into a low bun when Phineas knocked on her door to escort her to the dining room.

"I don't know if this will make you feel better or worse," he started as they walked to the dining room. "But I'm glad it is you here instead of Beatrice."

"I don't know if that makes me feel better or worse, either."

They found Cecily sitting at the head of a large, dark table, the legs carved to look like clawed feet. Phineas sat down next to her after giving her a kiss on the cheek. Theo sat on her other side. Cecily snapped her fingers and conjured a simple meal of a hearty soup and bread.

"Are you settling in all right, Theo?" Cecily asked when they began to eat.

"Yes, thank you," Theo said, not looking up from her bowl.

"I know this was not what you had planned for yourself. It may take time, but I do hope you can be happy here."

Theo nodded.

She was about to say more, but at the sound of the front door opening and closing, Cecily straightened.

"Hey, sis!" came an amused voice from the foyer. "I'm here to pick up the amulet and give it back to Aunt Ursula. Endlin is still pretty upset, just so you know. Not that I feel bad for her. That's what you get for not sharing: a punch to the face by a mystery human."

Theo's head snapped up. Cecily and Phineas put down their silverware and were both cringing as they watched her.

The smooth, alluring voice continued. "I also wanted to see how it went last night. Honestly, I am a bit sad that it's all over and Theo is no longer working for you. You need to tell me where I can find her. Even if she doesn't want to play the harp at another party, maybe I can convince her to come just so she can insult more people. You should have heard what she said to Koel. I'll fill you in." He laughed. "I doubt your new familiar will be nearly as fun as—*Theo?*"

Lock halted in the doorway to the dining room, his mouth open as he saw her sitting at the table.

Cecily, who had dropped her head in her hands, looked up. "Theo," she said slowly. "This is my baby brother, Locklan. Lock, this is my new familiar, Theo."

"That's...that's your brother?" Theo asked. "And Endlin is your cousin?"

Cecily nodded, still cringing.

"She...she didn't steal that amulet, did she?"

Cecily shook her head. "In my defense, I never said she stole it. I said it didn't belong to her. It is her mother's necklace."

Theo couldn't help her trembling lip as she looked at Phineas. "You knew. Kaz knew."

Phineas was frowning at her.

Lock remained standing in the doorway like a surprised statue.

Theo looked down, wiping away the traitorous tears that slipped out, unable to stomach the looks from any of them, the pity. She took the napkin from her lap and put it on the table. "*If you'll excuse me,*" she whispered.

No one said anything as she walked away from the table and past Lock into the foyer, desperate to make it to her room before she completely fell apart.

But before she even made it to the stairs, a hand on her arm stopped her.

"Theo, wait." She turned to face Lock, who remembered he had functioning legs and managed to extract himself from the doorway. But he had traded the look of shock for devastation. "I . . . I don't know what to say. You were never supposed to find out."

"All right," she said as she made to turn back to the stairs.

He stopped her again. "Please talk to me."

"Why?"

"I want to know what you're thinking."

Theo shook her head, wiping her face with the back of her hand. "I am thinking that I am a fool. When I asked how you knew who I was after you approached me, Phineas said it was because you 'run in similar circles' to Cecily. But you knew who I was the moment you saw me."

"No, Theo—"

"What an astonishing coincidence that you needed someone to play music at a party you were having. How did I not see that? You knew I played the harp before the trial, didn't you? And at the Palace of the Fae, you knew Kaz wasn't supposed to come near me. And when I told you about the person Endlin reminded me of, you guessed my stepsister. But I had never told you about her. I was too busy reveling in your false compliments and charms to bother questioning any of it."

"It wasn't like that—"

"I worked so hard to prove that I could do those tasks. You were laughing through all of it. It was all a joke to you. I was so proud of myself. I thought that Cecily was proud of me, too. No one, including me, has ever been proud or impressed at anything I've done. But it wasn't real."

The tears she had wanted to hide were falling faster than she could wipe them away. "Kaz tried to warn me about you.

He probably wasn't allowed to tell me, was he? But I wouldn't listen. I was convinced you liked me."

Lock was shaking his head. "No, that isn't what happened. Before court, Cecily told me she'd be sending a mortal to help because she needed Dwyn. She couldn't tell you about me on the first task, because if you knew what the plan was, the court wouldn't have accepted it. You needed to come to it on your own as a representative of Dwyn's, not in collusion with his accuser. I thought I'd help her and then that'd be it." He ran his hands through his hair. "But it was you. I wasn't expecting you. And then you made that bargain and came to my party. I hadn't had that much fun in ages, and it was because of you. Not just your playing, but spending time with you. I . . . I meant everything I said that night, Theo.

"Then Cecily asked me to keep an eye on you at the palace, but I was happy to do it. I wanted to be around you. None of that was fake. And I was sad about you leaving. About your bargain with her being over. I was going to find you. To see you again."

"Please stop." She tried to turn away again, but Lock held her arm.

"I am so sorry, Theo."

"*Don't*. What do you want from me? What do you want me to say?"

"I don't know. I thought you'd be angry. This is worse."

"You want me to scream at you? Say something cutting so you can tell yourself I'm fine? That you didn't break me apart? Or is it even worse? You want me to hurt you so you can feel punished? Then you can just apologize and pretend this never happened. I'll do neither. I am angry with you. But to give you anything would mean that I cared, even a little, about what you thought of me. And I can't care about you or what you think anymore. I let myself believe that I mattered to you and look what happened. I wish this was goodbye, but I live here now and you're related to the fairy I'm eternally bound to, so see you later, I guess."

She shrugged him off and walked away. This time, he let her go. To add to her embarrassment, she only made it half-way up the stairs before the sobs hit her in full.

Chapter 30

Where Theo Is Now

Two Months Later

Theo sat on her balcony watching as the guests arrived. It wasn't a grand procession like the parties and galas she had known in her other life. Fairies and other magical beings just appeared near the threshold of Cecily's manor and walked in through the open front doors.

Cecily had enough of these parties that watching arrivals and drunken departures had become Theo's primary evening activity. Phineas said that she was invited and welcome at any time, but Theo had never bothered to attend.

He had been coming to her room every other day to check in on her and bring her books and playing cards. Sometimes he would stay with her for a bit. Cecily had mostly left her alone, leaving her trays of food outside her door. Theo came out of her room only occasionally, and usually not for anything else other than a midnight snack if she was sure no one else was awake.

Phineas had told her that Lock stopped by once to try to see her, but Cecily wouldn't let him upstairs, for which she was grateful. She had nothing to say to him.

A knock came from her door and Phineas poked his head in. "Theo?"

"Out here," she said.

He joined her on the balcony, taking the other seat.

"Seems like a big party tonight," she said.

"Yeah, turning out to be a good one." He sighed. "How long are you going to stay up here, you think?" It was a question he had been asking with a bit more frequency as of late.

"I don't age, so I could conceivably stay up here forever, couldn't I?"

"You could. Seems pretty boring."

"I don't know what I'm supposed to do with myself now anyway."

"Who says you need to decide? Like you said, we've got plenty of time to figure it out." He paused for a moment as they watched a few more guests meander into the manor. "Are you still angry with Cecily?"

"I don't know that, either. I'm not sure how I feel about her right now, to be honest. I get why she did it, but I wish I hadn't been the one she tricked. It just all feels so pointless now."

"Except it wasn't pointless. She was very sick, Theo. We didn't know what to do, how to help her, or how to get her magic back. But then you came."

Theo huffed a humorless laugh.

Phineas continued. "I can't even begin to tell you how

happy Cecily was. You gave her hope, and she hadn't had that for a long time. Are you still angry with Lock?"

"Yes."

"That's fair." He paused. "Do you think you'll ever forgive him?"

Theo thought about it. "If I can forgive a stabby gnome, then I can probably forgive him. Not today or tomorrow, but eventually."

Phineas nodded. "I stopped by Merrifall the other day. Your mother wasn't there. Beatrice kept her word and she's now at Avenshire with your sister. According to Beatrice, your mother graciously donated Merrifall to the crown so Beatrice could turn it into a boarding school for orphans."

Theo snorted. "Of course she did."

"There was a grand opening celebration, so I decided to take a look. There are about forty children there, with more coming soon. Beatrice was there. She finally left the palace. I stopped by your old music room, just to see if anything had changed. She left everything almost exactly the same. Except, there was a plaque above the door. It said THE THEODOSIA BALFOUR MUSIC ROOM."

Theo turned to look at him, shocked.

"You did a good thing, Theo. You're just as responsible for that school as she is, for the lives of those children. If it wasn't for you, it never would have opened. Also, she and Prince Duncan made an announcement shortly after the grand opening. The whole kingdom is celebrating. She's due in about four months." He faced her. "She understands what you did. What you sacrificed. What you gave to her. You saved her

371

child's life. Protected that baby when she couldn't. As long as she lives, she will never forget it."

Theo wiped her eyes on the sleeve of her sweater.

"Anyway," Phineas said lightly. "That's not actually what I came to say. I came to ask you to come to the party."

"Not tonight."

"Well, I'm not the only one who would like you to make an appearance. There is a fairy by the name of Beric who found out you were here and has been pestering me about it. Something about playing the harp with him again. He is very persistent."

The corners of her mouth twitched up, but she shook her head. "I don't think Cecily would want me at the party."

"She's the one who sent me up here. And Lock is not here, if that sways your decision at all. So what do you say? Why don't you put on one of your new dresses, run a brush through your hair, and come downstairs."

She thought for a moment as a group of fairies laughed from the landing.

She nodded.

"Excellent! See you down there in a few!" He jumped out of his chair and left her room.

She took a quick bath—something she hadn't been doing with as much frequency as she probably should have been. And it took her longer than she cared to admit to get a brush through her tangled hair and pin it out of her face. Then, riffling through the nearly one hundred dresses that Cecily had put in her closet, she selected a simple purple dress the color of violets in spring.

The party was taking up the entire downstairs, filling the foyer, dining room, drawing room, and even spilling out onto the veranda. She wondered how she was going to find Phineas in this sea of magical beings when her name was shouted from across the room.

"Theo! Over here!"

When she turned to look, a burgundy-haired fairy was winding through the crowd.

"I'm so glad you're here!" Beric said as he planted a kiss on her cheek. "Come on! The others are going to be so excited to see you!" He grabbed her hand and pulled her into the drawing room. "Look who I found!" he shouted to a group of fairies, some of whom she recognized as the other musicians. They greeted her with cheers and raised glasses.

Torian came rushing up, linking her arm through Theo's and leading her toward one side of the room. "You're going to play with us, right?"

Beric cleared a small area, then looked to Theo. "I suppose you'll need an instrument." He snapped his fingers and a harp appeared in the center, then he conjured his own as the other musicians gathered theirs.

Theo sat at the harp as a small crowd formed around them, one of the musicians having made the announcement that they were going to play. When she looked over the crowd, she saw Cecily watching with a soft smile. She lifted her glass to Theo in a small toast.

"Ready, Theo?" Beric asked.

She nodded, plucking a few strings while the rest of the band tuned and strummed their own instruments. Torian gave her a wink when she caught her eye. Theo smiled in return and it was then she realized what she was doing: playing music with friends.

Both her smile and her heart lifted as she turned to look at the eager crowd.

"So, does anyone have any requests?"

The story continues in...

HOW TO SURVIVE A FAIRY BARGAIN

Book 2 of the Fairies and Familiars series

ACKNOWLEDGMENTS

First and always, thank you to my husband, Will. There will never be enough words to tell you how much I love you. Your support for me in this and all things has meant everything.

Thank you to my beautiful children, Isla and Malcolm. Thank you for being the first people to ever read this story and encouraging me to put it out into the world. Thank you for your unwavering belief in me and Theo. I am honored to be a part of your lives. I love you both more than you'll ever know.

Thank you to Stephanie Clark for pretty much everything. Thank you for your guidance, support, editing, and being so fun to work with. But mostly, thank you for making this dream of mine come true. I am forever grateful to you.

Thank you to Emily Stone, Crystal Shelley, Eric Arroyo, Six Red Marbles & Jouve India, Tim Holman, Brit Hvide, Bryn A. McDonald, Lauren Panepinto, Alex Lencicki, Ellen Wright, Maggie Curley, Natassja Haught, Angela Man, and everyone at Orbit US. I am so happy to have had the opportunity to work with you and to be on this new adventure with all of you. Thank you to Alexia E. Pereira for your amazing cover design and Zoë van Dijk for the beautiful cover. Thank

Acknowledgments

you to Nathan Lincoln and the team at Hachette Audio, as
well as Josie Charles for your tremendous work.

Thank you to Bethany Weaver for your belief in me. I'm
so thrilled to be a part of the Weaver Literary Agency family.

Thank you to Hannah Gramson, Aisha, and Kevin Craw-
ford, the first grown-ups to ever read this book. Your thoughtful encouragement and feedback made all the difference.

Thank you to my family, including Linda and Mike Mayo,
Eileen and Paul Frangione, Lindsey and Mike Mayo, Aimee
Mayo, Elizabeth and Jeremy DuClos, Kristin and Matt
Ruggiero.

Thank you to Birch for joining me on our thinking walks
in the woods, and Smoky for keeping me company on late
nights.

And thank you to anyone who has read this book. Truly,
and from the bottom of my heart, you have my eternal
gratitude.

MEET THE AUTHOR

Anna Solo Photography

LAURA J. MAYO is a fantasy writer who lives in New Hampshire with her husband, their two children, a dog named Birch, and a ball python named Smoky. Unsurprisingly, many of Laura's other interests are solitary, including reading, sewing, cooking, baking, admiring her air plants, and getting figuratively lost in deep, dark woods. *How to Summon a Fairy Godmother* is her debut novel.

Find out more about Laura and other Orbit authors by registering for the free monthly newsletter at orbitbooks.net.

9 780316 581158